ESCAPE *from* BERLIN

ESCAPE from BERLIN

IRENE N. WATTS

Tundra Books

Good-bye Marianne was first published by Tundra Books, 1998
Remember Me was first published by Tundra Books, 2000
Finding Sophie was first published by Tundra Books, 2002
First published in this edition by Tundra Books, 2013

Published in Canada by Tundra Books, a division of Random House of Canada Limited,
One Toronto Street, Suite 300, Toronto, Ontario M5C 2V6

Published in the United States by Tundra Books of Northern New York,
P.O. Box 1030, Plattsburgh, New York 12901

Library of Congress Control Number: 2012954604

Library and Archives Canada Cataloguing in Publication

Watts, Irene N., 1931-
Escape from Berlin / Irene N. Watts.

Good-bye Marianne — Remember me — Finding Sophie.

ISBN 978-1-77049-611-8. — ISBN 978-1-77049-612-5 (EPUB)

1. World War, 1939-1945—Refugees—Juvenile fiction.
2. Kindertransports (Rescue operations)—Juvenile fiction.
I. Title. II. Title: Remember me. III. Title: Good-bye
Marianne. IV. Title: Finding Sophie.

PS8595.A873E73 2013   JC813'.54   C2012-908007-1

We acknowledge the financial support of the Government of Canada through
the Canada Book Fund and that of the Government of Ontario through the
Ontario Media Development Corporation's Ontario Book Initiative.
We further acknowledge the support of the Canada Council for the Arts and the
Ontario Arts Council for our publishing program.   ONTARIO ARTS COUNCIL
CONSEIL DES ARTS DE L'ONTARIO

Heidenröslein. Words by Johann Wolfgang von Goethe, 1771. (1749-1831).
Music by Franz Schubert, 1815. (1797-1828).

Designed by Kelly Hill
This book is set in Goudy

www.tundrabooks.com

Printed and bound in the United States of America

1 2 3 4 5 6   18 17 16 15 14 13

For those who do not look away

Acknowledgments

I am grateful to Kathy Lowinger for her encouragement, insight, and in-depth editing; and to Sue Tate, for her meticulous copy-editing in "three" languages. Special thanks to Sylvia Chan for her thoughtful attention in bringing together the stories in this new format and to designer Kelly Hill.

Many thanks to Stephen Walton, Archivist, the Department of Documents, The Imperial War Museum of London, England; to Dorothy Sheridan and Joy Eldridge, Archivists, the Mass Observation Archive, University of Sussex Library, Brighton, England, for their invaluable assistance in my research; to Julia Everett, Geoff Shaw, and to the staff of the White Rock Library, White Rock, British Columbia.

Particular thanks to the following individuals who have shared their stories and remembrances of the time: the late Hilda Farr, the late Inge Gard, Margot Howell, Judith Keshet, the late

Joseph Selo, Renate Selo, and A.J. Watts. Thanks to Kit Pearson for her early encouragement.

Thanks to Noel Gay Music Company Ltd. for permission to quote the lines of the chorus of "The Lambeth Walk"; to Random House UK Limited for permission to quote the text of the telegram from *Swallows and Amazons* by Arthur Ransome (Jonathan Cape, publisher); and to the Literary Trustees of Walter de la Mare, and the Society of Authors as their representative, for permission to quote from the poem "Five Eyes."

Preface to Omnibus Edition

In the early morning of December 1st, 1938 in Berlin, Germany, the railway station platform was crowded with children. Relatives embraced them for a last good-bye as SS guards and their dogs kept a watchful eye. The train hissed steam, as though in a hurry to depart.

This was no ordinary morning, no ordinary train. This was the first *Kindertransport*, a train bound for freedom. It would not be an ordinary journey.

The SS guards held the adults back as the children boarded, clutching their small possessions. Only unaccompanied children under the age of sixteen were permitted to travel out of Germany. No one knew what would happen. Would the Nazis change their minds at the last moment and forbid the children to cross the border and escape? The longed-for, but dreaded and heartbreaking time had come.

On December 2nd, over two hundred children arrived safely in England. The exodus had begun. The *Kindertransport* continued its lifesaving mission. In the nine months preceding the outbreak of World War II in September 1939, almost ten thousand children made that difficult journey to a new and safer life. They were supported by the British government—the first to answer their plight—by the Refugee Children's Movement, by many dedicated groups, and by ordinary people. The children at risk—most of whom were Jewish—were of many different religious and economic backgrounds.

Marianne in *Good-bye Marianne* says, "Mothers don't send their children away." But they did. There was no better alternative. It must have taken great courage for parents to let their sons and daughters go. They did not know when, or if, they would ever see them again. Those who escaped were the lucky ones. One million and a half Jewish children under the age of fifteen did not survive the war.

I was the same age as Sophie when I left for England. I am not Sophie or Marianne. They, their friends, and their neighbors are imaginary, though their experiences are similar to those of many young refugees of that time.

This omnibus is historical fiction, set against the backdrop of world events between 1938 and 1945. December 1, 2013, marks the 75th Anniversary of the first *Kindertransport*.

Good-bye

MARIANNE

I

One, two, let me through
Three, four, police at the door
Five, six, fix the witch
Seven, eight, it's getting late
Nine, ten, begin again.

Marianne had made a pact with herself that if she could go on repeating the skipping rhyme without stopping, even to cross the street, and all the way till she reached the school gate, she'd pass the math test. Math had always been Marianne's worst subject. She'd been dreading this day all week, but she was as prepared as she could be. Today she'd arrive at school on time, in fact, with time to spare. The rhyme was just an extra precaution.

The school clock said 8:20 A.M. *Good,* she had ten minutes.

Why was the school yard deserted? Where was everyone? The front doors were shut. Marianne tried the handle—locked. She knocked, waited, and knocked again. Someone must be playing a joke on her. At last the doors opened and Miss Friedrich, the school secretary, stood in the doorway looking at her.

"Yes?" she said at last.

For some reason Marianne felt guilty, though she'd been so careful lately, being extra polite and not drawing attention to herself.

"Good morning, Miss Friedrich. I'm sorry to disturb you. I couldn't get in," she said.

"What are you doing here? I suppose you've come for your records?"

Marianne thought she was having a bad dream. "Don't you remember me? I'm Marianne, Marianne Kohn, in the fifth grade. Please let me in; I'll be late for math," she said.

"Wait here," said Miss Friedrich, and shut the door in Marianne's face. Marianne heard her heels clicking away. It seemed a long time before the clicking heels returned. The door opened and Miss Friedrich stood there holding some papers. Marianne could make out a list of names on the top sheet.

"You are to go home at once, Marianne. Here are your records."

"Why? What have I done? This math test—it's really important. I'm already late. There's choir practice today, and I haven't handed in my library book."

"You may give your library book to me." Miss Friedrich took the book and handed Marianne a brown envelope. She avoided looking at the girl. "Now go home. Just go home—I have work to do."

Miss Friedrich went back inside and the door shut. Marianne looked at her name on the envelope. People only got their records when they changed schools. There was something going on that she didn't understand.

A cold splash hit her cheek. She wiped it away, and saw that her palm was streaked with ink. The sound of giggling made her look up to the open first-floor window. Faces grinned at her. A second pellet, blotting paper soaked in ink, hit the sleeve of her school coat. The giggling turned to laughter.

Marianne relaxed—it was a joke after all. But what kind of joke? This wasn't April Fools' Day; it was the third Tuesday in November, and she was freezing out here. The school clock struck the half hour: 8:30 A.M. She heard the sound of a teacher's voice thundering, "That's enough, settle down." The window above her slammed shut. The school yard was perfectly quiet.

Marianne reached up to knock at the door again. It was then that she saw the notice. She read the typed words nailed up for everyone to see, and felt colder and more alone than she had ever felt in her whole life.

She ran out of the yard, afraid to look back; crossed the street without looking; and went into the park. The words of the notice resounded in her head, and she knew that she would hear them for the rest of her life.

2

Marianne needed time to think. The words she had read on the door were as clear as though they had appeared on a billboard in front of her:

AS OF TODAY, NOVEMBER 15, 1938, JEWISH STUDENTS
ARE PROHIBITED FROM ATTENDING GERMAN SCHOOLS.

Expelled because she was Jewish!

The sun came out, warming the gray winter morning, but not Marianne's icy fingers which were cramped from holding the envelope so tightly. She sat down on a bench near the deserted band shell, loosened the flap of the hateful envelope, and pulled out her records:

NAME OF PUPIL:	Marianne Sarah Kohn
SEX:	Female
DATE OF BIRTH:	May 3, 1927
ADDRESS:	Apartment 2, Richard Wagnerstrasse, 3 Berlin, Charlottenburg
RELIGION:	Jewish
FATHER:	David Israel Kohn
OCCUPATION:	Bookseller
MOTHER:	Esther Sarah Kohn (nee Goldman)
COMMENTS:	Marianne has been a diligent pupil. A. Stein, class teacher

Diligent? Much good that did her. What was she supposed to do now, be diligent by herself all day?

There was hardly anyone about, just a few nursemaids with babies and toddlers. Even if there had been crowds, today she was going to do as she pleased. She'd sit down like a normal person; that would show them. She might even ignore the KEEP OFF THE GRASS sign and walk on it! Better not, that might get her arrested— Mutti would have a fit!

Suddenly Marianne remembered that she was not supposed to sit on a public bench, or even be in the park. She jumped up guiltily and saw that she'd been leaning against the now-familiar words: ARYANS ONLY.

Marianne sat down again very deliberately, her back against the hateful words. She unbuckled her navy schoolbag and rearranged the contents to her liking. She pulled out her lunch, and put the wooden-handled skipping rope beside her on the bench.

Marianne unwrapped the neat, greaseproof paper parcel that contained the cream cheese sandwich her mother had made for her that morning. Only a few hours ago Mutti's hands had held the bread. It was a comfort. She put the envelope back in her bag, next to her apple. She'd save the apple till later.

This was a horrible day. Marianne knew her mother would say something comforting like, "Things will get better—it'll probably just be for awhile—what fun it will be to study at home."

Well, it won't. This was one of the worst days she could ever remember, much worse than any math test, even worse than Mr. Vogel's sarcasm. She could just hear him in her history class:

"Now, Miss Kohn, as we are privileged to have a member of your race in our class, I am sure you could enlighten us by describing Bismarck's Child Labor Laws. No? I assure you the laws prohibiting child labor under the age of twelve were not designed for the sole purpose of permitting *your kind* to sit at your desk daydreaming! You will write an essay on child labor in Europe before 1853. Hand it in to me on Friday."

At least she'd be spared any more of Mr. Vogel's sneering remarks, and the sniggers at his mockery of Jews.

There were some nice people in the school though. It was really decent of Miss Stein to write that comment on her records. She didn't have to do that. She'd miss Beate and her jokes—like that time she'd put a fake ink blot on Miss Brown's chair before English class! Gertrude was really nice too. Last year she'd been invited over to her house for a birthday party. There'd been a magician who had made her laugh, even though he'd pulled a paper flag with a swastika out of her sleeve, and everyone had stared at her! Then this year, Gertrude had apologized for not inviting her again, because her parents had said it wouldn't be possible to ask everyone in the class. Marianne knew it was because some of the parents would complain if she came, but at least Gertrude had been brave enough to say something. Most kids didn't.

Marianne wished her father would come home. He'd been away since that awful night a week ago when Jewish synagogues, homes and stores had been looted and set on fire. He'd gone to check on the bookstore, phoned and said everything seemed fine, but next morning Mutti told her that Vati had been called out of town on business. So why hadn't he sent her a postcard for her collection as he usually did?

Could her parents be getting a divorce? She didn't think so, although they seemed to be arguing a lot lately, after she'd gone to bed. There was a girl in her class whose parents got divorced. She lived with her mother and hardly ever saw her father. Marianne couldn't imagine being without one of her parents for so long.

She noticed a tall thin girl, with yellow braids wound around her head, staring at her. The girl sat down on the bench beside her and asked, "Why are you looking so worried?"

"I'm not. I was just thinking about my father."

"I'd rather not think about mine," said the girl. "He yells at me all the time. He's a platoon sergeant in the army and thinks I'm one of his recruits! Hey, why aren't you in school? Don't tell me, I can guess . . . you forgot to do your homework, so you're not feeling well."

She seemed good at answering her own questions, so Marianne mumbled something about a math test. She didn't want to lie, or explain to this strange girl that she no longer had any need to make excuses to miss school, that the *Führer* had made the decision for her.

"I knew it. I'm taking the day off too. They won't notice. The whole school is practising for tomorrow's concert in honor of some important Nazi officials from Munich. My music teacher always says, 'Now Inge,'—I'm Inge Bauer, by the way—'just mouth the words, dear, like this.'"

Inge contorted her lips in an exaggerated imitation of her teacher. "I've got a voice like an old crow, the worst in the sixth grade. I'm never allowed to sing. What's your name?"

"Marianne." Marianne picked up her skipping rope quickly, avoiding any more questions. The rope flew under her polished shoes and sailed smoothly over her short, straight brown hair.

> *One, two, let me through*
> *Three, four, police at the door*
> *Five, six, fix the witch*
> *Seven, eight, it's getting late*
> *Nine, ten, begin again.*

Inge joined in effortlessly. They skipped together until they were out of breath, chanting the familiar rhyme, faster and faster in unison. They collapsed on the bench, at last, laughing. Inge said, "Phew, I'm starved. I left my lunch in the cloakroom when I sneaked out. Have you got anything?"

Marianne rewound the rope. "I've got an apple in my bag. Help yourself."

Inge opened the schoolbag eagerly, drew out the apple, and took a huge bite. The brown envelope slid from the bag to the ground.

"Oh, sorry," said Inge and bent to pick it up. She read the name out loud, "Marianne Kohn." Inge jumped to her feet and stood in silence for about three seconds, then spat out the apple so that Marianne had to jump aside to avoid the spittle. "Kohn, that's a Jewish name—you're a Jew. Can't you read?" She pointed to the sign. "The yellow benches are for your kind."

She wiped her mouth on her sleeve, and her hands on her skirt. Then she grabbed Marianne's bag, and threw it onto the path as hard as she could. She wiped her hands again. Marianne picked up her things and moved toward the bench. Inge screamed.

"Keep away from me, you hook-nosed witch. I hate you."

Then she pulled the rope out of Marianne's hand and threw it at her. The wooden handles just missed her face, but Marianne felt them strike her chin.

Marianne longed to slap Inge, to wipe that ugly look from her face the way Inge had wiped her hands. Instead, she picked up the rope and put it into her bag. She fastened the straps with trembling fingers. Marianne smoothed the scratched leather, then looked up at Inge. The blonde girl was still standing there like one of the park statues, her face carved in hatred.

Marianne knew that nothing she could say or do would make any difference. She wanted to say, "I had fun—you made me laugh. We were almost friends for a little while, and now you hate me. How did that happen? Because of my name? Because I'm a Jew? My father fought on the Russian front in the 1914 war. He fought for Germany. He's got a medal to prove it. I'm as German as you are."

Instead she walked away. She could feel her shame like the aching bruise under her chin. Her shame felt worse than the words Inge had hurled at her.

A park keeper looked at her sternly as she walked toward the gates. "Shouldn't you be in school, young lady? Everything alright?"

"Yes, sir. Thank you, sir."

Marianne walked on, her head lowered. She just needed to get home.

3

Marianne reached the corner of her street and breathed in the familiar smell of Otto's shop. Her father always bought his newspaper there on the way home, and sometimes a cigar to smoke after supper.

She'd walked all the way home without ever looking up, once ignoring a cyclist's bell as she crossed in front of him. Mutti was always warning her to be careful at the Wilhemstrasse's busy intersection.

Home at last. Now she had only to avoid Mrs. Schwartz's curiosity. Mrs. Schwartz was the caretaker for their building. She lived in the ground-floor apartment facing the street. It seemed her life depended on knowing everyone's business! The slightest detail was of utmost importance to her, and she knew almost everything that was going on in the building, on their street, and even what was said behind closed doors. The mailman often paused on his rounds to have coffee with her.

Luckily, today she was not scrubbing the front steps, skirt tucked into her apron waistband. Nor was she peering from behind the spotless white muslin curtains on her gleaming windows.

Marianne opened the front door and tiptoed past Number One. She crept up the stairs, careful not to step on the polished wood surround of the new, green, stair carpet that was Mrs. Schwartz's pride. Marianne's apartment was on the first floor. She rang the bell. No reply. Oh well, she had her key. Mutti was probably out shopping. "Oh, please, come home quickly. I have to tell you now," whispered Marianne.

Marianne had tied a piece of blue ribbon to her key, so that she could find it quickly. She unstrapped her schoolbag, but couldn't see the key. She shook the bag's contents onto the linoleum, so highly polished by Mrs. Schwartz that the Misses Schmidt upstairs complained that it was more dangerous to walk along the hallway than to cross the Kurfürstendamm: skipping rope, math textbook, notebooks, pen, pencil, eraser, compass and ruler, sandwich paper for her mother to wrap up her lunch the next day. Of course, she wouldn't be needing one tomorrow; she'd forgotten for a moment. Marianne checked her pockets— just her handkerchief and emergency subway fare. The key must have fallen out in the park. Marianne didn't even want to think about going back there to look for it.

She felt the day would never end. She heard a clock chiming twelve noon. Was it really only four hours since she'd left home that morning? Marianne slumped on the floor, leaned her head against the apartment door and closed her eyes.

There might be a letter from her cousin Ruth today. She'd promised to write and tell her about the new school. How long would a letter take to reach Berlin from Holland?

It must be at least two weeks since they had the good-bye supper for the Fischers, just after the High Holidays. Auntie Grethe was Mutti's older sister. Her daughter, Ruth, was thirteen and, unlike Marianne, went to Hebrew school, so the cousins didn't see each other that often. Uncle Frank was much more orthodox than Vati. Marianne and her parents attended the liberal synagogue, but she and Ruth would miss each other all the same.

Uncle Frank had lost his job months ago, so this was a lucky break for the Fischers—for him to find a position as a furrier in Amsterdam. At that last visit they'd eaten roast chicken and apple cake, and Mutti had made good strong coffee. Then the grown-ups played cards and she and Ruth had done the dishes, being extra careful of Mutti's Rosenthal china that had been a wedding present.

The china was beautiful: thin white plates with gold bands around the rim, and a different design of fruit painted on each one. There were little side plates to match. Marianne's favorite was the sprig of cherries; Ruth liked the grapes best. Vati always used to pretend the grapes were real, and then acted disappointed when they wouldn't come off the plate. Of course, that had been when she was little.

Ruth and Marianne listened to Marianne's records in her room with the door shut, so they could talk in peace after they'd finished in the kitchen. Ruth said she couldn't wait to get away from Germany. Her friend Lilian's family had been picked up by the Gestapo. Her father's name had been on a list. The apartment had been given to someone else. Lilian never came back to school.

Everyone knew that the Gestapo came without warning, usually at dawn. Ruth told her that she had nightmares about being picked up. That's why she was pleased to go to Holland, even though she couldn't speak Dutch.

Surely Vati couldn't be on a list too? Was that why he was away? That couldn't be the reason. All he did was buy and sell books, and make jokes—usually the same ones, over and over. The shop never seemed to make much money. Mutti was just wonderful at making do. She and Marianne would look through the fashion magazines together and laugh as if they were the same age, and then Mutti would say, "Don't you think, Marianne, if I changed the buttons, and put a new collar and some pockets on my navy dress, it would look just like that model? I'll try it."

And then she'd get to work and have her mouth full of pins for days, and they'd have cold suppers, but there would be the dress, or the new winter coat for Marianne.

But Mutti didn't laugh so much anymore, in fact, hardly ever.

The other day when he hadn't made a single sale all day, Vati had said, "Books aren't so popular in the Third *Reich*!" He was smiling when he said it. Mutti had told him to be quiet.

"You never know who's listening, David."

Her father laughed, but he got up and closed the window all the same, and drew the heavy blue curtains.

Marianne dozed. It was quite comfortable on the floor, warmed by the midday sun shining through the hall window. A blaring noise sounded, uncomfortably close.

"Hands up, you're under arrest, stand against the wall."

Marianne jumped up, pressed her back against the wall, and slowly raised her hands.

"I'd say that worked pretty well, didn't it?"

In front of her, dressed in a tweed suit, the trousers ending just below the knee, a peaked cap of the same material perched on his red hair, stood a boy holding a motor-horn, and smiling the friendliest smile she'd seen in a long time.

4

"**S**orry to wake you up," said the boy, and laughed.

Marianne couldn't help joining in, though her palms were still sticky from fright. "You really scared me. I thought you were the police."

"Ah, guilty conscience I see," said the boy in an exaggeratedly deep voice.

Marianne changed the subject. "That's a terrific motor-horn. It sounds exactly as though a car were parked right beside me. Wherever did you get it?"

"From a kid in my class. We traded. I did his math homework for a week for it. He got it from his grandfather's old car. Here, try it if you want. Just press the black rubber bulb and the noise comes out from the horn. Can't you imagine driving along and having to hold the horn in one hand when you want someone to get out of the way?"

Marianne took the horn and gave one gentle squeeze to try it out, then three great blasts, before handing it back. She'd have Mrs. Schwartz up here if she weren't careful!

"Thanks a lot. It's wonderful—just like Gustav's in *Emil and the Detectives*. That's my favorite book. Is that where you got the idea?" said Marianne.

"Good deduction. Exactly right. I hope to be a detective one day. I'd better introduce myself—I'm Ernest Bock. Tourist from Freiburg, at your service." He gave Marianne a small bow.

"Hi, I'm Marianne. I live here. I mean not in the hall, but in there." Marianne pointed to her front door. "I lost my key."

Ernest said, laughing again, "I guessed that. I'm pretty smart at picking up clues too. You are lucky living in Berlin. This is my first visit. I've never seen so many shops and lights blazing, and cars, and flags waving. Fantastic! My dad gave me this trip as a birthday present. He works on the railway, so he gets cheap tickets. Yesterday when we were on the train from Freiburg, I was thinking of the part in the book where Emil falls asleep, and the man in the bowler hat steals all his money. I can tell you, I kept my hand on the motor-horn the whole time, and didn't close my eyes once."

"Did you travel all that way on your own?" said Marianne.

"Oh, no, my mother's here with me. We're staying with Mrs. Schwartz, an old friend of hers. They went to school together."

Marianne asked as casually as she could, "You mean Mrs. Schwartz in Number One?"

"Yes, I've hardly spoken to her yet. As soon as we arrived, she and my mother rushed off to some big department store for bargains. They won't be home for hours."

"Wertheim's, I should think," said Marianne. "All the mothers like shopping there."

"That's the one. They said I should keep an eye on things till they come back. That won't be till the stores close, I bet. I'm exploring; hope you don't mind."

"Of course not," said Marianne. "How long are you staying in Berlin?"

"I wish it was forever, but it's just for two weeks. My dad and my brother know how to cook only one kind of food—sausages— boiled, fried, or grilled. Anyway, can't miss school for too long. You know how it is. Have you got the afternoon off?"

"Yes. I'm off school for awhile." Marianne bent down to pick up her things, stuffing them into her bag. Ernest helped her.

"You are lucky. Tell you what—while you're waiting for someone to come home, we'll pretend I'm Emil. I'll sit here on the top step, and close my eyes. You have to reach into my pocket and steal this ten-pfennig coin without my hearing you. I'll sound the horn if I catch you."

Marianne said, "Alright, but let's start with just snatching the cap. You put it beside you, and I have to take it away without you hearing me. We can advance to more sophisticated crimes later."

"Excellent. You have first go," said Ernest, and removed his cap. He leaned against the banisters, and closed his eyes.

Marianne removed her shoes, then began to creep up behind

him. Unfortunately, the glossy floor squeaked even under her light step, and Ernest blared the horn triumphantly.

They changed places. Ernest picked up Marianne's skipping rope and formed it into a lasso. He slid forward on his stomach, and gently curled the rope over the cap.

Marianne heard the sound of a button scraping on the floor, opened her eyes, saw the rope miss her ear by inches and capture the cap. She shrieked, "Stop, thief," squeezed the horn, and both children shouted with laughter. At that moment Mrs. Kohn opened the front door and, hearing loud voices, one of which was Marianne's, ran across the hallway and up the stairs.

"What are you doing on the floor, Marianne? What's happened to you? Are you hurt?" Mrs. Kohn was deathly pale, and she was gasping for breath.

"Mutti, calm down—we were just playing. I lost my key and couldn't get in."

Meanwhile Ernest had picked up the rest of Marianne's things, put them in the schoolbag, and handed the satchel to her. He raised his cap, clicked his heels together, and gave the same little bow.

"Mother, this is Ernest Bock—he's here from Freibourg on holiday. He kept me company," said Marianne. She did not look at Ernest, knowing she'd giggle if she did.

"I'm very pleased to meet you," said Ernest politely.

Mrs. Kohn smiled a stiff little smile—she still hadn't got over her fright. "Good day, Ernest."

"I'd better be going. I haven't had lunch yet. Good-bye Ma'am, 'bye Marianne. See you again."

"'Bye, Ernest. Thanks."

Ernest ran down the stairs, two steps at a time. He gave her a final motor-horn salute before disappearing into Number One.

5

As soon as they were inside the apartment, Marianne and her mother burst out talking at the same moment.

"Where were you?"

"I've been so worried about you."

Mrs. Kohn fastened the safety chain on the door, then turned and gave Marianne a hug. "I've been sick with worry, darling. I heard the announcement on the radio, and rushed out to meet you, but of course you'd left. Was it dreadful for you?"

"Yes." She wasn't going to pretend. The morning settled like cold rice pudding in her stomach. "At least I missed the test."

Mrs. Kohn hung up her coat on the hall stand and followed her daughter into the kitchen. She picked up the brown envelope Marianne had taken from her schoolbag.

Marianne sat at the kitchen table, one elbow leaning on the blue and white checked oilcloth. She brushed her arm, in its clean white-sleeved blouse, across her eyes. "I'm getting a cold."

Her mother sat down facing her. She studied the records. "Oh Marianne, this was so brave of Miss Stein. She could be in a lot of trouble for writing such a nice comment about you." She replaced the papers and put them in the kitchen dresser drawer. She arranged two honey cakes on a plate and poured Marianne a glass of milk. "Now tell me, how in the world did you lose your key?"

Marianne said, with her mouth full of cake, "In the park."

"The park! Marianne, you know better than that. Anything could have happened. It's bad enough just coming straight home from school. I'm sorry, darling, but you know it's not safe for us to be in public places."

Marianne chewed her thumbnail. She shivered, remembering Inge.

"I still don't understand how a key can fall out of a closed schoolbag," said her mother.

"It must have fallen out when I got my skipping rope. Sorry."

Mrs. Kohn was about to say more when she noticed Marianne's flushed cheeks. "I think you really are catching a cold. Just as well you're home for a few days."

"A few days! Don't you mean forever? Why can't we go to Holland? Then I could go to school with Ruth." Marianne knew she sounded spoiled and childish—she couldn't seem to help it.

"We can try. Don't forget it took Uncle Frank a long time to get sponsored by his new employer. It's very hard to obtain a visa these days. We have to wait our turn. Now, as for going to school—of course you're not going to miss school forever. Do you think we would let that happen? The Rabbi has called a meeting for this afternoon so that all the parents can discuss the situation. There are lots of things we can do—set up classes in our homes even—for those students for whom room can't be found in Jewish schools."

Marianne began to chew her thumb again, something she hadn't done since she was a toddler. She didn't want to go to Jewish school and have bricks thrown through windows, and stones hurled into the school yard. It wasn't that she was more of a coward than anyone else, but she just wanted to *be* like everybody else, that is, like the kids in her old school—some of them, at least. "I'm not going to sneak around and join some homemade class!"

"Marianne, that's quite enough. Whatever's got into you today? Now tell me—and please, darling, I'd rather you ate your cake instead of your thumb—who was that boy? When I heard you scream, I thought you were being attacked."

"Is that why you were so unfriendly to Ernest? I told you, Mutti, he's nice—we had fun while I was waiting for you to come home."

"Did he ask you anything? What was he doing in our hallway? He doesn't live here. For all we know, he might be from the Hitler Youth, checking out the building." Mrs. Kohn brushed cake crumbs fiercely from the tablecloth, then poured more milk for Marianne.

"I can't drink all this milk; it makes me feel sick."

"You can. Drink it. It's good for you. And this is no time to be talking to strangers. We know absolutely nothing about him."

"But, Mutti, he's staying with Mrs. Schwartz."

"Mrs. Schwartz! Marianne, think! He could be spying on us, reporting everything we say and do. You know Mrs. Schwartz doesn't like us living here, you *know* that. She's a Nazi party member."

"Mutti, please listen. I know kids. Ernest's not spying. He's alright. He's just here for a couple of weeks with his mother. We like the same book. He's from Freiburg. He's perfectly safe."

"Marianne, you have to understand, we aren't safe. No Jew is safe anywhere in Germany. Do you think there are no Nazis in Freiburg? The Nazis are everywhere. The *Führer* has said we are enemies of the people. We are no longer considered citizens. If we are attacked in the street, or in our homes, no one will help us. There are countries who will take us in, but only a few people at a time, and an exit visa costs a lot of money. So Marianne, until we can go, we must be very very . . ."

"I know, careful," interrupted Marianne. The caution was becoming a family joke.

Mrs. Kohn began to clear the dishes. "Hand me my apron, please." Marianne took the blue apron that hung over the back of her mother's chair, and tied it round her waist for her. She gave her mother's waist a little squeeze to show she understood. Marianne sat at one corner of the kitchen table and said as casually as she could, "Mutti, when is Vati coming home?"

Her mother turned on the cold tap to rinse the glass, and said without turning around, "I don't know."

"Why won't you tell me where he is? I'm not a baby."

"Marianne, I don't know. I mean it. But even if I did, I wouldn't tell you."

"Wonderful. You don't even trust your own daughter."

"It's not that. It's just if you know something, and mentioned it, or were overheard, and reported . . ."

"Mutti, I don't have anyone to play with, or to tell stuff to. Who would I talk to? I don't have any friends anymore."

"You were talking and laughing with Ernest just now, weren't you?"

"I didn't even tell him my full name! I've a right to know where my father is. He's not in prison, is he?"

Her mother took off her apron and folded it. "No, he's not. All I know is what I told you—he's away on business. Now, I *must* go, or I'll be late for my meeting. I'm supposed to be there at 2:30 P.M. We're all arriving at different times, so it won't look like a protest. I told you, didn't I, the government has forbidden more than three Jews to meet at one time, but this is an emergency."

Mrs. Kohn sighed, put on her coat and hat, and picked up her string shopping bag. She kissed Marianne's cheek. "I'll be home for supper. I'll make potato pancakes. Vati's favorite."

"What's the point when he's not even home?" Marianne said.

"Because it's important to remember. Have a nice afternoon, darling."

She left. Marianne fastened the chain behind her. The apartment still felt safe and warm and quiet. She sang the refrain of the skipping rhyme:

One, two, let me through
Three, four, police at the door
Five, six, fix the witch
Seven, eight, it's getting late
Nine, ten, begin again.

As long as she was inside her own home, who could hurt her?

6

Marianne looked through the living-room window. The first snow of winter was coming down in great blobs, and settling on the square yard that all the tenants shared. The neatly dug flower beds, the two chestnut trees, and the narrow bench were already covered with a thin white layer.

Marianne hoped last year's skates would fit her, though the way things were going, she probably wouldn't be allowed to skate on the river Spree this year. The list of forbidden activities was piling up like the compost heap by the back fence.

An apron hung stiffly on the line. One of the Misses Schmidt (Marianne always found it difficult to tell the old ladies apart) hurried out with a shawl over her head, to bring in the washing. The scrawny cat, Sweetie, who wasn't in the least "sweet," picked her way daintily after her mistress, wanting to be let in out of the cold.

Marianne heard the back door slam twice. You had to give it a good tug in damp weather to make it close. The Schmidt sisters were elderly, their hands were gnarled with arthritis, and they never managed to shut the door properly the first time. Sometimes her father carried groceries up the stairs for them. When Mrs. Schwartz wasn't around, they'd be really friendly and stop to chat with her.

"Dear child, how was school today?"

Marianne would bob a curtsy—she knew the old ladies appreciated a well brought-up child.

The afternoon loomed endlessly. She turned away from the window and switched on the radio. Didn't the network ever broadcast anything but marching tunes?

Marianne sprawled on the deep couch. The room was getting dark and it was only half past two. She hoped her mother hadn't had any trouble getting to the meeting. The Rabbi's house was right next to the synagogue, which had been burned in last week's anti-Jewish demonstrations.

The Menorah gleamed on the mantelpiece. Hanukkah in four weeks, her favorite time of the year. She'd never forget that time two years ago in the synagogue when the Rabbi reminded the congregation that the festival was about more than gift giving, was more than a children's holiday. "Thousands of years ago, at another time of persecution, a small group of Jews fought against overwhelming odds, for religious freedom. The Menorah tells the world our spirit will never die," he had said. "Let Hanukkah be as important for us as Passover and Purim."

Marianne hoped her grandparents would come from Düsseldorf

as usual. They'd all miss Uncle Frank and Aunt Grethe though, and without Ruth she'd be the only child at the table. Nothing stayed the same.

What was she going to do this afternoon without school to go to? There'd be lots of afternoons like this now. Would she always feel this restless? Maybe she'd read—work her way through every book in the room. Just last month her father had finished putting up another shelf to hold all the books he kept bringing home. Mutti complained she couldn't reach the top ones to dust. Soon they'd run out of wall space.

Marianne helped herself to a peppermint from the cut glass dish on the coffee table beside her. This wasn't too bad. Right this minute her class was cleaning up after gym, the final class of the day. She could imagine Beate and Gertrude planning the first winter snowball fight and, of course, looking very innocent when a teacher walked by.

"I hope Miss Friedrich walks right into a snowball!" Marianne spoke aloud. When she was younger, she and her father had built a snowman in the yard with bits of coal for eyes and a long carrot nose. She'd wound a muffler round his neck, and cried when the snow melted.

Marianne's first school photograph stood on the coffee table. She was holding a big paper cone packed with treats. The cone was almost as big as she was. Every child in the first class had one. Marianne remembered the feel of the shiny blue and silver paper, the stiff paper frill around the top, and the taste of the first chocolate. It did sweeten school, and she had loved it from that first day.

Five years ago, 1933. It seemed so long ago. The same year the Nazis came to power. Her parents talked of a time before the Brown Shirts, before the red flags with their black swastikas were hung from every building, before the anti-Jewish slogans were scrawled on every wall—JEWS NOT WANTED HERE.

She even remembered when school was different. Now kids refused to sit next to her, and she was hardly ever allowed to play with the others at recess. She felt humiliated having to ask permission to join them.

Every day there seemed to be another regulation that made life a bit harder for her. Instead of saying, "Good Morning" to the teachers, the class had to say *"Heil Hitler,"* and raise their right arms to salute the *Führer*. She never knew what to do about it. She hated to join in, but she'd be in trouble if she didn't. Well, that was one problem she didn't have to worry about anymore.

Her grandmother always said, "Look on the bright side."

Marianne looked at the photograph of herself when she was six—hair cut in bangs straight across her forehead, a big bow stuck on top of her head. Why couldn't she have naturally curly hair like her mother? No, she looked like her father—skinny, with straight brown hair. She wouldn't mind having glasses like him—they'd make her look older!

The radio blared out the shrill voice, familiar to every man, woman and child in Germany: "One people, one country, one *Führer*."

Thank goodness there's only one of him. Marianne began goose-stepping around the room, her legs raised high in imitation of the military. She liked the way her navy blue skirt billowed out, and then fell back into tidy pleats.

Marianne switched off the radio and ran into her bedroom, the one place that had always calmed her. She loved her little room, especially since she and her mother had redecorated it for her last birthday. It held all the things she loved most: her teddy bear, skinny from so much hugging; the scratched oak desk that used to belong to Grandfather; and the bookshelf her father had made specially for her, along which marched a parade of glass animals that only she was allowed to dust.

The wallpaper was a very pale yellow, cream almost. It was covered with sprigs of tiny rosebuds, each one with a dark green leaf. Her mother had found a green silky material that exactly matched, and made a new cover for her eiderdown to replace the babyish pink one she'd had for years.

Marianne looked out of the window; it was still snowing. The people who lived in the house on the other side of the lane had their kitchen lights on. When she went on errands, they never said hello anymore—lots of their neighbors looked away when they passed by now.

Marianne drew her muslin curtains, and then opened her sock drawer. That's where she kept her money box. Today was a perfect time to buy her mother's birthday present. Mutti's birthday was only three weeks away and Marianne longed to give her something really special.

She kept her allowance (when she didn't spend it) in an empty cigar box that she'd wheedled out of her grandfather. Opa and Vati loved their Sunday Coronas. She lifted the lid and breathed in the rich "party" smell of the tobacco that still lingered in the box. Her mother and grandmother always made a big fuss of opening windows to get rid of the blue haze of the cigar smoke.

Marianne counted her money. She had seven marks. She'd been saving for a bike to ride to school, so she had much more than last year.

Marianne buttoned her new winter coat, put on a scarf and beret, and remembered the spare front-door key hanging on the hook behind the kitchen door. She locked the door and ran downstairs.

7

Marianne stood on the front steps and stuck out her warm tongue to capture the snowflakes. The sensation of melting snow was almost as good as eating ice cream. Marianne turned around slowly, her face up to the wintry skies. She stopped when she noticed the curtains of Number One twitch, and became aware of a face partly hidden by the muslin folds. Staring. Eyes. Berlin was full of eyes. Everyone was watching everyone else.

The street was quiet at this time in the afternoon. She was debating whether to take a streetcar to save time, when she saw a group of young men in Hitler Youth uniform handing out pamphlets. One grabbed her arm.

"*Heil Hitler*. Here, sweetheart, take this home to your parents." He pushed the pamphlet into her gloved hand. She didn't dare throw it away, but walked on. A voice shouted after her, "Say

'*Heil Hitler*' next time." Marianne heard them laughing, and the same voice said, "No respect, these kids."

What would they have done if they'd known she was a Jew? Marianne shuddered, remembering Inge Bauer. She still had a bruise under her chin. She pulled her scarf up around her face.

Marianne turned down a side street. "I won't run, I won't."

Her mother always said, "If I had a magic wand, I'd use it to make you invisible. Meanwhile, whatever happens, don't draw attention to yourself."

Marianne forced herself to continue her walk. She passed *Fraülein* Marks's ladies' and children's wear. The door was boarded up and a big sign on the glass said, KEEP OUR STREETS JEW FREE.

Marianne, hurrying past, slipped on the icy cobblestones. Trying to break her fall, she landed on her right knee. There was a hole in her woolen stocking, and she'd skinned her knee. It hurt.

The pamphlet she'd been holding lay face up in the snow. The headline glared at her:

THE JEWS LIE. BEWARE THE ENEMY.

Underneath was a cartoon of an old man wearing a yarmulke— the skullcap that orthodox Jewish men wore. The cartoon showed a face with a huge hooked nose and sidelocks.

Marianne was used to propaganda, to the ugly slogans she'd seen ever since she had learned to read, but she felt sick for a moment. It was a feeling she was getting used to. Was this what

Hitler wanted, to make kids feel they were hated and not wanted by anyone?

Marianne walked on. When she reached Taubenstrasse she heard footsteps behind her. Was she imagining that she was being followed, or were the Hitler Youth out to teach her a lesson? She knew they needed no excuse to twist an arm, or worse if you weren't one of them, and they were everywhere.

Marianne walked on for a few paces, listening. Then she stopped abruptly and looked into the window of a small leather-goods store. The footsteps stopped. Marianne walked more quickly. Her knee was bleeding; she could feel the drops trickling down her leg. There was a marketplace at the end of the street. There'd be lots of people there.

She felt a hand on her shoulder, and a voice said, "Don't be scared, it's only me." The sound of the motor-horn echoed in the quiet afternoon. Marianne whirled round. Ernest grinned at her. "I followed your tracks in the snow—watched you out of the window too. You're a fast walker. Did you hurt yourself just now?"

"I grazed my knee. It's bleeding a bit. You are cheeky follow-ing me. Why didn't you say something?" Marianne wasn't going to let this country boy do as he liked in *her* city.

"Don't be mad. I've got to practice tracking suspects if I'm going to be a detective. Now, hold out your leg. Go on—I've got my first-aid badge."

Ernest took a handkerchief out of his pocket and folded it into a narrow bandage. Marianne held onto the wall for support, and raised her knee. Ernest knelt in the snow and bound up her leg most professionally. He finished by tying the bandage with a reef knot.

"Thanks, that feels better. I knew I was being followed. I never guessed it was you, though. I have to buy a birthday present for my mother—you can come if you like," said Marianne.

"Shopping!" Ernest groaned. "That's all you women ever do. But I can smell something cooking, and I'm starved. Let's go."

Taubenstrasse led into a small square. Market stalls were set up, and a mixture of the most delicious smells filled the snowy air: hot chestnuts, gingerbread, fresh-baked rolls, oranges and vats of sauerkraut.

Ernest went straight to a sausage stall. A woman wearing a shawl over a man's overcoat topped by a huge white apron turned fat sausages on an open grill. They sizzled over the fire. The woman stamped her feet in her heavy work boots.

"Who's next?"

"We are. Two *weisswurst*, please," said Ernest. "Is that what you'd like, with mustard?" Ernest looked at Marianne. She hesitated for just a minute. She'd never eaten one before. She felt as if *she* were the tourist in Berlin, not Ernest.

"Please," she nodded.

The woman speared two sausages, spread them thickly with mustard, and put one in each of two crisp, white rolls. She gave Marianne the first one. "Good appetite," she said.

Ernest had grandly refused to let Marianne pay. She took a bite. Juice dribbled down her chin; mustard dripped from Ernest's.

They ignored the mess, looked at each other and laughed. No one took any notice.

Afternoon shoppers hurried to finish making their purchases before dark.

"What we need now . . ." said Marianne.

". . . is gingerbread," finished Ernest, eyeing a stall piled high with honey cakes, chocolate pretzels, gingerbread mice with sugar whiskers, and gingerbread houses, dolls and animals.

"My treat, but don't take all afternoon," said Marianne. "I still have to get my mother's present."

Ernest chose a gingerbread soldier with a chocolate sword, and Marianne said, "I'll have a tree, please." She handed over twenty pfennigs for their purchases, and began to nibble her way round the outline of the triangles edged with white icing.

One year she had passed Mrs. Schwartz's door, and had been allowed to peek at her Christmas tree. She'd never forgotten the fresh smell of the pine, and the bright ornaments hanging from every bough. The warmth of the candle flames, flickering in their holders on the branches, was the most magical thing she'd ever seen. Somehow, eating gingerbread in this peaceful square had reminded her of that.

Ernest, his mouth full, said, "This is absolutely the best gingerbread in the world, and I'm an expert, because my grandmother works in a bakery in Freibourg."

They walked round till they came to a stall selling carved walking sticks, wooden whistles, ornaments and toys. Marianne looked for something that would appeal to her mother.

"My sister, Anna, wants a doll from Berlin. Your advice will be gratefully accepted," said Ernest, trying out a walking stick whose handle was carved in the shape of an eagle. Marianne realized that Ernest was embarrassed to be seen looking at toys. She thought it was really nice of him to think of his sister.

"How old is Anna?"

"Nearly six. She's the baby in the family, so of course she's spoiled. She might like this." He pulled the strings of a ferocious-looking jumping jack.

Marianne picked up a small jointed doll with real braided hair, the golden ends tied in red bows to match the doll's skirt and the braiding on the black bodice. Her blue eyes and spiky eyelashes were carefully painted; her wooden face had a sprinkling of freckles, rosy cheeks and a mouth that looked surprised.

"Your little sister would like this. Look at the embroidery on the sleeves—it's perfect," said Marianne.

"You're right," said Ernest.

The doll cost three marks. While it was being wrapped, Marianne noticed a careful arrangement of music boxes. She particularly admired one which had a delicate carving of flowers on each corner of the polished wooden lid. The stall owner turned the key, and Marianne hummed along with the familiar tune. It was a lullaby her mother used to sing to Marianne when she was little, to comfort her when she awoke in the dark:

Sleep my baby sleep,
Your Daddy guards the sheep.
Mother shakes the gentle tree
The petals fall with dreams for thee
Sleep my baby sleep.

The man asked Marianne, "Do you like Brahm's 'Cradle Song,' Miss?"

"Yes. My mother taught it to me. She would love this music box," said Marianne. "Is it very expensive?"

"It costs four marks, young lady. It is my own carving."

Marianne gave him a five-mark note and said, "Thank you very much. It's a beautiful box—all your things are beautiful." The man wrapped the box, handed Marianne the change and said, "I'm glad my work will find a good home. Come back again."

The street lamps came on. A man trundled a wooden cart over the cobblestones. On it was a gramophone. The man turned the handle. A Wagner march filled the air. Ernest went over to him, and put a coin in a tin cup standing on the trolley.

"He says he's a war veteran—he's only got one leg," he said to Marianne.

The snow started to gently fall again.

"Let's go home," said Marianne, and they turned to leave. As they reached the edge of the square where the row of apartment houses stood, a scream of tires disturbed the winter afternoon.

8

A truck roared into the square. It skidded to a halt in front of a gray house, one of a row overlooking the market. Storm troopers carrying rifles jumped out, their glossy boots shining in the lamplight. One kicked over a basket piled high with apples, which was standing by the fruit stall. Apples rolled in all directions. The troopers hurried up the steps. A voice shouted, "Open up. *Juden raus.*"

Marianne was unable to move. She wanted to run, but she seemed to be trapped in one of those dreams where she could not make her feet obey her. Ernest gripped her arm, "There's going to be an arrest; this is my lucky day."

The sounds of breaking glass and splintering wood rang out over the square. A few people watched, like Ernest, wanting to know what was going to happen next. Mothers took their small children by the hand and hurried away. The fruit seller picked up his apples, and polished them one by one on his striped apron.

Marianne whispered to herself as much as to Ernest, "I have to go now. I'm going." She crossed the square. Away from the truck, away from the storm troopers, away from the sounds in the house, which the gramophone could not muffle.

"Wait, I just want to see what's going on," said Ernest.

Marianne wasn't listening, except to a voice in her head which was saying, *Go home.* She turned her head, forced to do so by the sounds of glass breaking, a cry, the thud of a body landing on cobblestones.

The soldiers clattered down the steps and picked up the body of a man lying facedown in the snow. They dragged him to the truck and hauled him over the side. The truck pulled away, its tires spinning.

The square was quiet again. Drops of blood glistened, scarlet as winterberries, under the street lamp where the man had fallen. His black cap lay forgotten in the snow. People moved on.

Marianne began to run. Ernest sounded the motor-horn behind her. "Wait for me." He caught up with her. "I don't think he was dead," said Ernest, to comfort her.

A cold wind blew little flurries of snow against their faces. Ernest turned up the collar of his jacket, and Marianne pulled her scarf over her mouth. It gave her an excuse not to speak. There was nothing to say.

When they got home, Ernest said, "You look like a bandit with your face all muffled up. Good disguise. It was fun today. Thanks. See you." He disappeared into Number One.

As soon as Marianne was back inside her own apartment, she took off Ernest's bandage. Her knee had bled. She ran cold water and washed the handkerchief in the kitchen sink. The stain came out easily.

Marianne went into her bedroom and dropped her clothes on the floor. She put on her nightdress and lay down on her bed. Then she unwrapped the music box and turned the key. She sang the words of the melody:

> Sleep my baby sleep,
> Your Daddy guards the sheep.
> Mother shakes the gentle tree
> The petals fall with dreams for thee
> Sleep my baby sleep.

When the tune was finished, she put the box under her pillow, curled up under the covers, and slept immediately. She did not stir when her mother came in, folded her clothes, and quietly closed her bedroom door.

9

I t snowed all week.

Marianne opened her eyes. She stretched, sat up, and smiled at her mother, who stood beside her bed holding a tray.

"Breakfast is served, Your Highness."

"I'm not ill, am I?" asked Marianne.

"Just a treat," said her mother. "I *am* sorry I got home so late again last night. I'll make up for it with the best potato pancakes ever, for supper. Now, please eat your breakfast before it gets cold."

"I'm starved," said Marianne, tapping the top of her boiled egg. "Sit on my bed and tell me about the latest meeting. Will there be school classes for me to go to?"

Mrs. Kohn sat at the end of Marianne's bed. "First I have a surprise."

"Vati's coming home?"

"Not quite yet. But . . ." Mrs. Kohn put a thin blue envelope beside Marianne's cup of hot chocolate. "This is nice, too, don't you think?"

Marianne opened the letter, slitting the envelope with her knife in exactly the same way her father always opened his mail. "It's from Ruth! Listen . . ."

> 107, Leidsegracht, Apartment 5
> Amsterdam, Holland
>
> November 14, 1938

"Dear Marianne,

"I'm writing my first letter to you in our 'new' apartment on the fifth floor of this skinny old building, which is at least two hundred years old. The house overlooks the canal. It's almost as good as living on a boat. I can watch everything that's going on—kids playing, people meeting, quarreling, flirting. Here is a sketch of our building; it looks foreign, doesn't it? There are furniture hooks on the outside of the house because the stairs are too narrow to bring up big furniture. It has to be pulled up by rope. Luckily my piano doesn't have to go through that treatment. I had to leave it behind, as you know. I hate to think whose sausage fingers will touch the keys.

"I do miss my music and lots of things about Berlin, but *not* . . . well, you know what. Papa is still worried that we are not far enough away. He listens to the BBC (the British radio station) all the time, and thinks there may be a war soon. Then what will happen to the Jewish people?

"Papa bought me a secondhand bicycle so I can ride to school and save money by not taking the street-car. The school I go to is on Jodenbreestraat, the Jewish quarter, near the Rembrandthuis. I have lots of home-work to do because, of course, I'm behind, not knowing Dutch yet. The kids are really friendly and don't laugh too much at my efforts to speak. I'm glad we took French and English at school, at least I can keep up in those classes.

"Marianne, it's so much better here. I feel free, almost like everyone else. The markets are wonderful. There must be at least a hundred different kinds of cheese. I'd love to send you some. Can't you just imagine Mrs. Schwartz poking the parcel and telling the mail-man, 'There's something very funny in here. Sniff, sniff.'?

"I'm getting writer's cramp. I want a letter from you very soon, with news about everything you're doing. Love to Auntie Esther and Uncle David. Mutti is writing to them. A kiss for my little cousin.

From Ruth

"What a lovely letter. I must answer right away," said Marianne.

"Yes, she does sound happy. But Marianne, please don't leave the letter lying around. Put it out of sight. Ruth writes too freely. She's forgotten so quickly how things are here."

"Mutti, no one but us is going to see it—no one ever comes here anymore." Marianne looked up and saw her mother's worried expression. She remembered the man in the market last week. "Of course I'll put the letter away, as soon as I've answered it. Thank you for my delicious breakfast. Now, tell me about the meeting—I can't wait one more minute."

Mrs. Kohn said, smiling, "Even ladies of leisure must get dressed. As soon as you're ready, I'll tell you. I'm just going to start clearing up the kitchen. Don't forget it's my day for volunteering at the orphanage." She left the room.

Marianne washed quickly, longing to hear her mother's news. She put on her favorite red and white wool sweater over a gray pleated skirt.

"I'm ready."

"How nice you look, darling." Mrs. Kohn put down her coffee cup and said, "It was a long meeting. People are worried and upset. It was mostly mothers there. So many men are in hiding, or . . ."

"Mutti, you can say it."

"Alright I will—or are in concentration camps. I'm sure they'll be released soon; it's just a question of time. Now, about school. The Jewish community is short of teachers, books, and space for all the children who can't go to German schools anymore. Some of the mothers prefer their children to be taught at home. They feel that's safer than allowing them to walk to the classes we'll set up. The Rabbi says room will be found for the rest of you somehow. It will all be sorted out in a couple of weeks. Meanwhile, darling, you have your books here. You must try to carry on by yourself for awhile.

"Now, I must hurry to the orphanage. Wonderful news. The orphans are to join a group of more than two hundred children who will be allowed to leave Germany. They are being sent to England. Good homes will be found for them there. They're leaving in a few days, and each child must be packed and ready. Think of all those suitcases! It's like a miracle that they'll be sent to safety. The Rabbi hopes many more Jewish children will be taken in by countries wanting to rescue our children."

"But, Mutti, having to go so far away, how awful!" said Marianne.

"I explained to you before, we don't always know what will happen. The most important thing is for them to be safe."

Marianne flung her arms round her mother's neck. "Thank goodness I'm not an orphan. I'd never leave you and Vati to go so far away. You wouldn't send me away by myself, would you, Mutti? Promise me you'd never do that."

Mrs. Kohn kissed the top of Marianne's head and said, "When you've finished your letter to Ruth, why don't you come and pick me up at the orphanage, say about one o'clock? I like to walk home with you."

"I'd love to. You go now, Mutti, or you'll be late. I'll put the dishes away. And be careful."

"You're beginning to sound just like me. Thanks, darling. I'll see you later." Mrs. Kohn patted her daughter's cheek, put on her hat and coat, and closed the front door softly behind her.

England! Marianne had begun English lessons two years ago. She liked learning languages. She tried to remember what to say when asked, "How do you do?" Was it "very well" or "werry vel"? She could never remember. She tried saying it both ways, speaking aloud to her reflection in the kitchen mirror, "Tank you werry much."

The sound of a horn blaring sent her rushing to the front door. "Ernest, are you crazy? We're going to be in big trouble."

"I knocked on the door. Were you asleep?"

One of the Schmidt sisters leaned over the banisters and called out, "What's happening? Is something wrong?"

Ernest stuffed his fist in his mouth to stop himself from laughing. Marianne called out politely, "Good morning, Miss Schmidt. It's nothing. I'm sorry we disturbed you. Someone was showing me how his alarm system works." Miss Schmidt clucked disapprovingly. A moment later her door shut.

"Lucky Mum and Aunt Helga are out," said Ernest.

"Aunt Helga!" Marianne howled with laughter.

"What's so funny?" asked Ernest.

"I didn't know Mrs. Schwartz's name was Helga," said Marianne, and went on laughing. "I never even thought of her having a first name!"

"You've gone mad. Please excuse my friend, ladies and gentlemen." Ernest spoke to an imaginary audience.

"Do you want to come in for a moment?" asked Marianne.

"Thanks." Ernest followed Marianne into the kitchen. "I have to do this school project on the Brandenburg Gate. Like to go with me? Then, this afternoon, I'm meeting my mother. She says I need new winter shoes. She's taking me out for ice cream and pastries afterward, as a reward for good behavior."

"I have to pick up my mother as well, but I've got a couple of hours. Just wait a minute—I'll put on my coat. I'll get your handkerchief too."

When Marianne came back into the kitchen, Ernest was holding Ruth's envelope. "Here's your handkerchief; it's quite clean now," said Marianne. For a moment she remembered her mother's warning.

"Thanks. Could I have this Dutch stamp? I've already got it, but I could use it for a swap."

"Of course. Have the whole envelope. I'll just take out the letter." Marianne put Ruth's letter in a drawer.

"Thanks a lot. Let's go."

10

Walking along to the streetcar, Marianne felt completely happy. Ernest had said, "My friend is mad." *My friend.* Perhaps everything would turn out alright after all. Vati would come home; she'd start school again. Things would get better. Everyone kept saying that.

"What are you smiling about?" asked Ernest.

"I'm mad, remember? So of course I smile at nothing at all. I'm really smiling, though, because I get to watch someone *else* do a school project."

"You Berliners have got it good."

Ernest made a face at her and they ran for the streetcar.

"Not in school?" the conductor commented cheerfully.

"I'm doing a project on the Brandenburg Gate," said Ernest.

"Nice-looking helper." The conductor winked at Ernest, and

Marianne blushed. The conductor rang the bell and they got off just before the gate.

Ernest stood absolutely still. People moved around him. He stared first at the wide sweep of Unter den Linden, the avenue of parades and victory marches, that stretched through the center of the city. Marianne knew he was imagining great armies coming through the Brandenburg Gate. She had never really looked before at the twelve huge stone pillars supporting the gate, or at the Goddess of Victory above, driving her chariot drawn by four stone horses. A sea of red flags hung from the surrounding buildings.

"It's sixty-five feet tall," said Ernest.

"You tourists know everything." All at once it was fun seeing Berlin through a visitor's eyes.

The sounds of drumming and marching feet drew near. Led by a drum corps of boys wearing khaki shirts and black shorts and the armbands of the Hitler Youth, a troop of young men in uniform stepped in perfect unison toward Pariser Square. Behind them marched the girls' corps, in white blouses, blue pleated skirts and brown jackets. They stood at attention facing the small crowd.

Ernest grabbed Marianne's hand and pulled her right to the front of the crowd. His arm flew out in salute, and his voice rang out with those of the watching people and of the Hitler Youth, "*Sieg Heil. Sieg Heil. Sieg Heil.*" Ernest seemed to grow taller. He was a stranger. It was as if she had never seen him before.

Marianne stooped to tie her shoelaces. She stayed down, hoping not to be noticed. She'd do anything to get out of hailing the *Führer*.

"What's the matter?" said Ernest. "You'll miss everything."

Marianne stood up. The words of the "Horst Wessel" song echoed over the square:

> *We raise our flag, our ranks in tight formation*
> *Our troopers march, with firm and even tread*
> *The spirit of our fallen comrades . . .*

Marianne did not hear another word because at that moment, she looked straight into the shining eyes of the girl she had met in the park. It was Inge. She wasn't imagining it. She'd never forget Inge Bauer. Inge's eyes glittered. She seemed under a spell.

"I feel a bit dizzy," Marianne whispered to Ernest. She excused herself politely till she got through the rows of people, and then walked back toward her tram stop.

Ernest caught up with her. "What a shame to miss the concert. My mother doesn't like crowds either. Shall we find a bench and sit down a minute?"

"No, I'm fine, really. I have to meet my mother soon anyway. Please go back. You still have to do your project. There's my streetcar now."

"Good-bye then. See you later." Ernest raised his hand in a half wave and hurried back into the throng of Nazi worshippers.

That was really nice of him, leaving the parade to make sure I'm alright.

On the way home, Marianne sat hunched and small in her

seat, trying not to be noticed, thinking about the way her life had changed so abruptly.

Every single day since she'd been forbidden to attend school, Marianne had forced herself to go for a brisk walk round the neighborhood. She was afraid that if she missed even once, she'd never leave the safety of her apartment again. She walked with her head up, but avoided the eyes of anyone in uniform. It wasn't easy because there were so many soldiers and police everywhere— marching, saluting, often dragging passersby into trucks and cars.

One afternoon, she joined a small group of people who were good-naturedly watching two boys fighting. Their local police- man, whom everyone knew, separated them. He was in a good mood, smiling and greeting some of the women by name.

The younger boy said to the policeman, "Please, sir, I left my bicycle leaning against this lamppost, and I was gone only for a minute to post a letter for my mother. Then when I came back, he'd taken my bicycle and he won't give it back."

The other boy, who was bigger, said, mimicking the younger one's voice, "Please, sir, this boy is a Jew. That's not stealing, is it?"

The policeman's mood changed abruptly. He cuffed the Jewish boy so hard, he hit his head against the lamppost. "You're getting off lightly," he said. "Next time you make a complaint against a citizen of the *Reich*, I'll take you into custody." The boy ran off, holding the side of his head.

As Marianne turned to go home, she heard the policeman chuckle and say, "You've got yourself a fine bicycle there. You tell your mother I gave it to you—confiscated goods from Jewish vermin."

The red and white flags with their ominous black swastikas, which hung from every building, waved in the wind with more menace than usual that day. They signalled a very clear message to Marianne—YOU AND YOUR KIND ARE THE ENEMY IN THIS LAND.

One dreadful morning a few days later, a woman whom Marianne knew slightly because she worked part-time in Otto's Cigar Store, saw her in the street and said, "Turn around and go the other way; go by the back lane. There's been a bad accident. A woman got killed when the Gestapo came and took her son away. Her body is still on the street." She'd taken Marianne gently by the shoulders and pushed her in the opposite direction because Marianne had been too shocked to move. That day, Marianne ran all the way home. She had quite forgotten she was not supposed to draw attention to herself.

How could the grown-ups say, "Things will get better"?

11

L ate one morning, Marianne came back to the apartment. As usual, Mrs. Schwartz was on her knees polishing the entrance hall. It seemed to be her favorite place to keep an eye on the house's inhabitants. Marianne was sure she reported everything to her husband, who had recently been made block warden.

"Excuse me, please," said Marianne politely.

"Up and down, back and forth—you should be in school. How am I supposed to get my work finished? Don't put your fingers on the banisters; I've just waxed them." Mrs. Schwartz reluctantly made room for Marianne to get by.

Marianne managed to get inside her door with just a few dramatic sighs from Mrs. Schwartz. The telephone rang. Marianne hung up her coat. The telephone went on ringing.

"Yes?"

"Marianne, I've been trying to reach you all morning. Is something wrong?"

"Sorry, I went out for my morning exercise. Sound like a dog, don't I?"

Her mother seemed in a hurry, and did not give Marianne her usual warning about not going too far away from home. "It's better if you don't meet me at the orphanage today. We're all behind. I may be later than usual. Would you start getting supper, darling? Thank you. See you as soon as I can get away."

Marianne replaced the receiver. It was a relief not to have to go out again. Facing hostile streets more than once a day was becoming very hard, even though she loved meeting her mother who was now working almost daily at the orphanage.

Marianne made herself a cheese sandwich, and that reminded her that she hadn't replied to Ruth's letter. She got paper and an envelope from her father's rosewood desk, and settled down in the armchair to write to Ruth. There was lots to tell her . . .

> Apartment 2,
> Richard Wagnerstrasse 3
> Berlin, Charlottenburg

> November 28th, 1938

Dear Ruth,

It was lovely to get your letter. Thank you. Sorry I haven't answered before this.

Your new home sounds so quaint, (I've been dying

to use that word). I expect you'll all be skating along the canals. Wish I could join you. Did you get new skates?

I'm happy you've got your bicycle at last. I've decided not to save up for one just now.

I have to change schools too. But I don't know where I'm going yet. I expect you heard what happened. Meanwhile, I'm not bored at all. There's lots to do.

I met a very nice boy from Freibourg. Unfortunately, he's only here for a couple of weeks, but we're becoming good friends. His name is Ernest and he's thirteen. He and his mother are staying downstairs with Mrs. Schwartz (that's how we met). I found out old Schwartz's name is Helga.

Marianne smiled. The doorbell rang. She put down her pen and went to answer it.

"Who is it?"

"Me, Ernest."

Marianne opened the door. "Come i . . ." She did not finish the sentence. She felt sick and cold at the sight of Ernest in the full uniform of the *Jung Volk*—the boys' branch of the Hitler Youth—shirt with epaulets, black tie, brown leather belt and shining brass buckle embossed with victory wands. He wore the Nazi party armband.

"This is from Aunt Helga," said Ernest, handing Marianne an envelope addressed to Apartment 2. Marianne took it without saying anything.

"What's the matter? Are you in a trance or something? It's me, Ernest Bock, your friendly house detective."

"I didn't expect to see anyone in uniform," said Marianne in a voice not even she recognized.

"My mother's taking me out to tea. I *told* you before, remember? She likes me to look smart when we go out. I brought my uniform to Berlin especially. Next year I'll be promoted from the young people's group to the proper Hitler Youth. I can hardly wait."

Marianne spoke slowly and clearly so there could be no mistake. She did not lower her voice at all. "I'm Jewish," she said. She drew out her gold Star of David which she generally wore hidden under her sweater. The Star, on its delicate chain, shimmered as brightly under the hall light as did Ernest's belt buckle.

"I'm tired of hiding this."

Ernest said, "I've never met a Jew before. I mean, I never spoke to one before. I didn't know. Wait till I tell my brother . . . maybe I'd better not . . . he'd have to tell his group leader. Martin's sixteen; he's in the Hitler Youth."

"So!"

"Martin went to a rally in Munich last September. He shook hands with the *Führer*. Can you imagine? Shaking hands with the country's leader?"

"I suppose he's never going to wash that hand again," said Marianne bitterly.

"What's the matter with you? Of course Martin's proud of that. It was a great honor. Why are you so mad?"

Marianne said, "Why am I so mad? What's the matter with *me*? You come in here, dressed in uniform, showing off about your precious brother and your precious *Führer*. Don't you know what Hitler's done? He's stopped me going to school."

Ernest said, "Lucky you, that's nothing to complain about!"

Marianne said, "You don't understand. You don't understand anything. This isn't just missing a few days—it's never, ever going back. I'm eleven years old. I haven't finished learning everything. I'll be a person who left school after five years. When people ask me, 'And what are you going to be when you leave school?', what'll I say? That I've left already?"

Marianne looked at Ernest a moment, taking in his neatly brushed hair and polished shoes. "And another thing, look at you, cleaned up to go out somewhere special with your mother. I'm not allowed to do that. The restaurant wouldn't let us in, DOGS AND JEWS NOT ADMITTED." Ernest stood silent.

A voice shouted from the bottom of the stairs, "Ernest, I'm nearly ready. I want you down here in five minutes."

Ernest said, "That's my mother calling me. I know her idea of five minutes—ten more likely."

Marianne said more quietly, "My mother wouldn't dare call out like that; she's afraid to talk above a whisper in case she draws attention to herself. She walks in the gutter so no one can say she's taking up too much room on the pavement.

"I have no idea where my father is. The Nazis took away his business. For all I know, he might be in a concentration camp being punished and starved because he's a Jew. The Nazis smash

Jewish shops, burn our synagogues, and the police don't do anything about it. Just stand and watch."

Marianne stopped. She was out of breath with an anger that she did not know she had inside her. Ernest's face was red, his fists clenched by his side.

"Now you wait a minute," he said. "I didn't start this fight, you did. My father was out of work for three years, but now he's working thanks to Hitler. Our *Führer* is making this country great again. If he says Jews are troublemakers, then he's right."

"Troublemakers?" said Marianne. "We don't make trouble. We spend our lives trying not to get into trouble. You don't know what it's like not daring to answer back, even if you're in the right; trying to make yourself small and invisible so you won't get hurt; being scared all the time; not wanting to tell you my name— Kohn—in case you found out I was Jewish."

Ernest stood motionless, listening.

"And how would you like it if one day you were told you had to change your name?"

"Great," said Ernest, "I'd call myself Gustav," and he sounded his motor-horn.

"Not choose," said Marianne, "ordered. One morning you wake up and your name is Sara."

"Sara's a girl's name," said Ernest.

"Oh, Ernest, you're being stupid," said Marianne. "Not you— you'd be called Israel. Your leader ordered all Jewish boys to be called Israel, and all Jewish girls to be called Sara. It was even on my school records."

"Sara's a nice name," said Ernest.

"But it's not what my parents chose for me. And another thing—no one ever helps us when we get pushed around, beat up. Just like that man at the market the other day. Did anyone help him?" said Marianne.

"Why should they? I expect he was a criminal," said Ernest.

"You mean a Jew, don't you?" said Marianne. "Your leader hates us; he said so and he wasn't even born here. We're just as German as he is—more."

Ernest's mother called angrily from below, "Ernest, I'm waiting. Come down this instant—I'm ready to leave."

Ernest stood up very straight. "You're a troublemaker—the *Führer* is always right. You're an ignorant Jewish troublemaking girl." He clicked his heels together, saluted, and said, "*Heil Hitler*." He walked away stiffly.

When he was halfway down the stairs, Ernest pressed the motor-horn. It sounded like an insult to Marianne. She shouted after him, "You're just like all the others. You're all the same." Then she ran inside, slammed the door and fastened the safety chain. She stuffed the envelope into her skirt pocket and went back into the living room.

Marianne picked up the letter she'd started earlier and, without re-reading it, tore it up into very small pieces and threw them into the wastepaper basket. Tears ran down her face.

"To think that I told Ruth we're becoming good friends. I *never* want to see him again. I hate him. I hate them all," she whispered.

12

It was almost six o'clock before Mrs. Kohn arrived home. Marianne had finished grating raw potatoes, and was just starting to chop onions. She'd set out flour, salt, eggs, and milk, and had put the heavy frying pan on the stove.

"You get my award for daughter of the year," said Mrs. Kohn, and kissed Marianne. "I honestly don't know how I'd manage without you. Can you believe we were four suitcases short, so someone had to go and buy them? That was just one of the problems. Each child needs changes of warm clothes. They can take only what they can carry themselves, so that means the little ones have to leave behind favorite blankets or toys. Well, the socks are all darned, the shoes polished, the children's hair washed. Sixty orphans will leave from Friedrichstrasse Station on December 1st. It *must* go smoothly."

Mrs. Kohn beat the eggs before folding potatoes and onions

into the flour. Marianne wiped her streaming eyes. "Onions always make me cry," she said.

"Vati's favorite supper," said Mrs. Kohn.

The telephone rang. Mrs. Kohn wiped her hands on her overall. "What is it this time—surely not another crisis?" She went into the hall to answer the telephone.

Marianne set the table. Mrs. Kohn came back into the kitchen. Her cheeks were pink.

"Put the water on for coffee, then stand in the hall. Don't turn on the light. Take the safety chain off. When you hear a tap on the door, open it, and fasten the chain again."

Marianne looked at her mother's face and did exactly as she was told. Three minutes later she stood in the dark hallway, listening for the knock. She could smell the onions frying, and hear the crackle of hot oil.

There it was. She opened the door. A tall, thin figure came in, closed the door, and held her so tightly she couldn't have screamed even if she'd wanted to.

"Vati!"

"Marianne, I've missed you so much."

"Don't ever go away again."

Marianne took her father's hand and held on to it, even while she secured the front-door chain with her other hand. "Mutti, he's home. Vati's back."

By the time her father was seated in his usual chair, sipping coffee from the blue cup that only he was allowed to drink from, her mother was serving up the perfectly browned pancakes.

"I could smell those latkes right across Berlin," said Mr. Kohn, helping himself to applesauce.

"I had to bring you home somehow," said his wife, smiling. No one spoke for a few minutes, but Marianne was too excited to eat much.

"Are you home for good now, Vati?"

Her father said, "You are old enough to understand what's happening in Germany, and old enough to be told the truth. I know Mutti agrees with me. I've had to go underground."

"You mean like in subway stations?"

Her father didn't laugh. "Sometimes," he said. "It means I must keep moving, never staying in one place very long. Many people have managed to escape the Gestapo by just walking the streets. Berlin is a big city. I've not come close to being picked up again."

Marianne said, "I don't understand. What do you mean *again?*" She stared at her father's hands—usually so cared-for, hands which loved to hold books. The knuckles were swollen and misshapen—the skin cracked and split.

"After the terrible night of the fires and looting on November 9th, I was picked up with thousands of other Jewish men. Boys, grandfathers—young and old—marched to Sachsenhausen concentration camp on the outskirts of Berlin. They struck us with whips as we went through the gates."

Marianne held her breath. She didn't want to miss a word of her father's story and yet, she was afraid to hear what had happened next. Her mother said, "David, must you speak of this now?"

Her father continued, "We stood in the yard naked. It was freezing cold. It began to snow. Not everyone survived the night. Next morning, some of us were released. By a miracle, I was one of the lucky ones. I think, perhaps, by mistake. Things were very confused that day. For the moment, until things change in this country, I have to rely on friends and kind people to hide me."

"I still don't understand why you can't stay here," said Marianne.

Her mother said, "The Nazis have lists. They know the name and address of every Jew in Germany."

"My name is on another list as well—I'm especially wanted, you see—popular man, I suppose, charming, intelligent . . . "

Marianne could see her father was trying hard to make one of his jokes. "Please go on," Marianne said. "I need to know."

Her father continued, "When Hitler forbade Jews to own a business, I sold the bookshop. After the new owner took over, he found some books written by banned authors. It was very careless of me. The man reported me. So now, the Gestapo would very much like to re-educate me in one of their concentration camps. That's why even Mutti doesn't know where I am at any time. There, I've told you everything. Don't look so sad, both of you. I have good friends, and I feel sure that any day now, permission will come through for all of us to travel to another country. Who knows, next year we might be in Holland or England or Jerusalem or, perhaps, Canada or the United States."

Mrs. Kohn put the last pancake on her husband's plate, poured more coffee for him and a glass of milk for Marianne.

Mr. Kohn ate quickly. "I must go. I'm just going to change into warmer clothes and dry shoes. Back in a moment." Her parents left the kitchen together.

Marianne cleared the table, and ran hot water into the washing-up bowl. She needed time to think over what her father had told her. What if he was caught again and sent back to a concentration camp? Why hadn't her mother told her all this?

"I'm not a baby," she muttered into the sink. "Why wasn't I told before?"

Her parents came back.

"Be brave, both of you. I love you very much. We'll be together again, even if, for now, it's only in our thoughts. Remember, not even Hitler can prevent that." Mr. Kohn hugged Marianne.

"See you soon. I love you, Vati."

Her parents went into the hall. She heard the front door close and the chain being replaced. "I'll finish in here," said her mother. "No more chores for you today. We'll have a cosy evening. You get into your nightdress, and I'll light the fire in the living room."

"Let's have a game of dominoes—we haven't played that in ages," said Marianne. She would be just as brave as her mother!

Marianne went into her room and changed. Then she opened the bedroom curtains. The sky was black and clear with a few stars shining over the city streets. The yard was white and clean with snow. So peaceful.

Mrs. Kohn had the fire going. A few pinecones gave off a woody smell. "If I close my eyes, I'm back in the forest with my mother. When I was a little girl, we'd pick blueberries and mush-rooms and walk for miles through the trees."

Marianne got the box of dominoes down from the bookshelf. Her grandfather had made the brown wooden box. It was very plain, but the pieces inside were of real ivory, black-and-white. Her father had played with them when he was a boy. They played three games and Marianne won two. She yawned.

"Time for bed. Goodnight, my darling, sleep well. Everything will come out right in the end. I'll just sit by the fire a little longer."

Marianne went to bed. After awhile, she heard her mother's door close. She couldn't sleep. She went over everything that had happened that day. She closed her eyes. There was a Ferris wheel going round and round in her head, and she was on it. When she reached the top she was happy, but the wheel never stayed still long enough before turning again, so the happiness didn't last. She could see it, but she couldn't hold on to it.

Marianne slid into sleep.

13

"Open up. Gestapo."

Marianne and her mother collided in the entrance hall. Mrs. Kohn whispered, "Ruth's letter." Marianne disappeared.

"Open up."

The sound of a rifle butt against the door.

"I'm coming."

Marianne heard her mother open the door. The slap of leather on skin. A stifled gasp. Marianne stood in the doorway of her room. She watched the Gestapo officers, their uniforms as black as the night sky, invade their rooms.

Mrs. Kohn put her finger on her lips. Her face was very white. She waited. Marianne stood without moving, watching her mother. Cupboard doors slammed. Drawers crashed. They heard glass shatter. Something ripped. Gleaming black boots walked toward Marianne. She edged back into her room, picked up her teddy bear, held him tightly.

The officer patted Marianne's head. Turned away.

"Let's go."

They left. Their boots rang out through the building. A car door shut, the roaring engine disturbing the dawn.

Marianne and her mother did not stir until the only sound they could hear was their own breathing. Mrs. Kohn closed the front door, fastened the chain. She and Marianne held each other for a long time.

"My hair—he touched my hair. I feel sick."

"We'll wash it. It's all over now."

"What did they want? Were they looking for Vati?"

"Who knows . . ."

"I hid Ruth's letter."

"Where?"

Marianne kicked off her slipper. The folded letter clung to the sole of her foot.

"You were very brave, Marianne. Now we'll burn it. Come."

Hand in hand, Marianne and her mother walked into the living room. The room looked as if a tornado had hit. Every single book had been dragged off the shelves, and lay on the floor. All her father's beautiful books were scattered, bent, facedown, the pages ripped. His desk was gashed, his chair snapped in two. The Menorah was in the fireplace, buried in cold gray ash. The box that held the dominoes was broken, the pieces strewn on the carpet. Slashed curtains hung like untied hair ribbons. Marianne reached for the Menorah, wiped it on her nightdress. Then she picked up the dominoes.

Mrs. Kohn went into the kitchen. Marianne followed her. It was better to look at the damage together. The glass doors of the dresser and most of the crockery were smashed. The Rosenthal dinner plates were in shards. The plants on the window ledge were overturned, the soil trodden into the floor.

Mrs. Kohn picked up a box of matches and a soft cloth. She took Marianne's icy hand, and they went back into the living room.

"I'm going to get the fire going." She pushed the duster into Marianne's hands. The ashes clung to the decorative crevices and ornamental curves of the Menorah's silver base. The feel of the cloth restoring the shine calmed Marianne.

Mrs. Kohn twisted some papers tightly, lit a match and burned Ruth's letter. She added pieces of splintered wood from the broken desk chair. Next she began to sort the books, smoothing the crumpled pages lovingly. Daylight crept into the room.

"It's nearly seven," said Marianne. The mantel clock went on ticking in spite of a crack across the glass.

"I'm going to make us some coffee. You'd like that, wouldn't you Marianne, with lots of hot milk?" Marianne nodded and her mother left the room.

What could she do for her mother? What would make them both feel safe again?

Marianne remembered the gift she'd bought at the market. It was still hidden at the back of her underwear drawer. She ran to get it. Then she waited by the fire for her mother.

Mrs. Kohn came into the living room carrying a tray. She sat on the floor beside her daughter, and handed Marianne a cup of delicious, sweet, milky coffee. The cups did not match, and one had a handle missing.

"Mutti," said Marianne, "we're going to pretend that today is your birthday."

"I can't think of one reason why I'd want to be thirty-seven even one day sooner than necessary."

"Well I can," said Marianne. "I think you need a present." She put the parcel in her mother's lap.

"What pretty paper; it's much too nice to throw out."

Whenever Mrs. Kohn received anything wrapped in gift paper, she always said exactly the same thing. It used to drive Marianne and her father crazy, because they liked to tear the paper off quickly and get to the present. Today Marianne didn't mind at all.

At last Mrs. Kohn finished. She drew out the box. Her fingers traced the carved flower design gently. She turned the key. Brahm's "Cradle Song" filled the room. Marianne sang the words softly:

Sleep my baby sleep,
Your Daddy guards the sheep.
Mother shakes the gentle tree
The petals fall with dreams for thee
Sleep my baby sleep.

Mrs. Kohn said, "I will never part with this. It's the most beautiful gift anyone has ever given me. Thank you, Marianne."

They finished their coffee, and set to work to clear up. By ten o'clock all the broken china and glass had been swept up, books were neatly stacked, and those that could be repaired put in a box. Marianne had washed her hair and sat down to a late breakfast with her mother.

"I'm glad they didn't find your homemade black cherry jam," said Marianne, spooning some more onto her bread.

"I was thinking we could cut up the bedspread from the spare bed. That would do for curtains, don't you think?"

"Yes," said Marianne, with her mouth full. "What else do we have to do?"

"Would you mind going to the bakery for our breakfast rolls? Mr. Altmann will wonder why we haven't picked up our order. I'm going to scrub this floor, and then wash all the clothes in my room. They're still on the bedroom carpet. The Gestapo threw everything out of my wardrobe."

"I'm finished eating. I'll go right away." Marianne put on her coat. Something rustled. The envelope that Ernest had delivered the day before was still in her skirt pocket. She must have put it there after their quarrel.

"Mutti, I'm dreadfully sorry, I forgot to give you this note from Mrs. Schwartz."

"It doesn't matter. Hurry back, darling. Oh, and take fifty pfennig from my purse for shopping."

"Good-bye. I'll come home as fast as I can."

14

It was good to be out in the fresh air, away from the terrors of the night. Out here, things seemed to be normal. Marianne passed a few morning shoppers with their string bags on their arms.

She loved going to the bakery; it had always been one of her favorite chores. It was the first errand she'd ever been entrusted to go on alone. She had only been seven then and her mother had waited at the corner for her the whole time she was gone. Mr. Altmann never let any child leave his bakery without a taste of something warm and delicious, fresh from the oven.

At the corner of the Schillerstrasse, a familiar name was gone. FAMILY SAMUELS, FAMILY SHOE REPAIRS, had been replaced with a new name—BAUM, SHOE AND BOOT REPAIRS. NEW OWNER. ARYANS ONLY.

Who would mend their shoes now?

Marianne reached the bakery and saw her face reflected in the window, splintered like the broken glass in the door. The heavy, wooden door frame was badly gashed, and the sign on the door said, CLOSED. A pile of shattered glass had been neatly swept up beside the step, which had dark stains on it. The display case was bare.

Marianne saw Mr. Altmann washing down the counter, and knocked on what was left of the door. Mr. Altmann looked up, smiled and walked toward her. For the first time since she'd known him—all her life, really—he looked old. His forehead had been clumsily bandaged; a little trickle of blood had seeped through the material and dried.

Mr. Altmann unlocked the door, and then quickly bolted it again.

"I don't know why I do that; habit I suppose. Don't look so worried, Marianne, it's nothing."

"Did they close you down?" Marianne asked.

"Temporarily. It's not so easy to close me down, even if they do break the glass. Close me down? No. Your mother, is she well? And your father, he is away on business, I hear."

"The Gestapo came last night, looking for something, but we are all fine now, thank you. What happened to you, Mr. Altmann?" Marianne said.

The baker began to sweep the floor.

"The usual things. This time a little more boisterous, perhaps. So they break a little glass, smash an old man's head. Mostly, the police look the other way. This morning they joined in."

Marianne said, "Some people leave."

"Not me. My grandfather built this shop. I use the same oven he did. I was born here, and here I stay. I can wait out a little madness, wait for things to get better. Don't look so sad. I'm going to fetch your breakfast rolls right now. The Gestapo didn't spoil everything."

When Mr. Altmann came out of the back room, he held a brown bag in one hand, and a triangular-shaped pastry in the other. "A little taste—warm from the oven."

"That's a hamantasch," said Marianne, "Purim's three months away. Why are you baking those now?"

"Because from now on the festival of Purim will be celebrated in my shop all year round. I want my customers to remember the brave Queen Esther and her cousin, Mordecai. I want them to remember how a tyrant, who tried to kill the Jewish people, was defied."

Marianne interrupted, her mouth full of the pastry Mr. Altmann had given her. "I love Purim. It's such fun to shout and clap in the synagogue, and wave noisemakers when Haman's name is mentioned. What a wonderful idea," said Marianne, licking the last of the jelly from her fingers.

"Exactly," said Mr. Altmann. "After the cruel Haman's death, the Bible says, 'The Jews had light and gladness, and joy and honor.' I wait for that time to return."

Marianne said, "I know a boy who has a motor-horn. It would make a wonderful noisemaker, but he'd never let me borrow it. He can't wait to join the Hitler Youth. I thought he was nice at first—kind, and fun—but they're all the same."

Mr. Altmann smiled at Marianne, and his eyes looked very bright, even through the cracked lenses of his spectacles. "It's hard to speak out, to be one voice against so many, but there are always some if you listen hard enough. Not everyone is a hoodlum.

"Keep well, child. My regards to your mother. And Marianne, remember what happened to Haman? We know another tyrant whose name begins with the same letter, don't we?"

Mr. Altmann made the sign of the letter H on the damp counter, and then quickly erased it with his cloth. He winked at Marianne. Marianne winked back, and stood on tiptoe to kiss Mr. Altmann's lined cheek.

"Good-bye, be careful," she said.

Marianne walked out of the shop, her head held high, and Mr. Altmann watched her until she was out of sight. Then he turned the CLOSED sign to OPEN, and waited behind the counter for his customers.

15

When Marianne came back with the breakfast rolls, her mother was still sitting at the kitchen table. Her eyes were red. She pushed Mrs. Schwartz's note across to Marianne. It read

AS OF DECEMBER 10, 1938

JEWS ARE PROHIBITED FROM LIVING IN THIS BUILDING.

PLEASE VACATE APARTMENT TWO BY DECEMBER 9TH.

AT TWO O'CLOCK.

HEIL HITLER

    HELGA SCHWARTZ

Marianne said, "She can't do that. That's just a few days away."

Mrs. Kohn blew her nose. "Sorry, darling. She can. It solves some problems, really. I've been thinking we should visit

Düsseldorf—spend some time with Oma and Opa. They'd feel safer having us there. You can share my old room. It will be good to be together in these dreadful times."

"What about Vati—how will he know where we are? What will happen to our things? Will I go to school there?"

"I'll get word to Vati somehow. Things can be replaced. They really aren't so important right now. Perhaps the Schmidt sisters would store some of our furniture. They've always been friendly to us.

"As for school, I'm sure the Düsseldorf community will arrange classes for Jewish children. Opa will find out for us. Think what fun it will be to live in the house where I grew up. I'll fetch our suitcases."

Marianne hugged herself joyfully. How wonderful to go on a trip with her mother. Of course she'd miss her room, but Oma always let her sleep in the little attic, "the ship's cabin" Opa called it. You could see the whole garden from there. All the fruit trees. Oma would have finished bottling the apples and plums, and would make plum tart, Marianne's favorite, sprinkled with golden-brown sugary pastry crumbs. Absolutely no one in the whole world made plum tart as delicious as Oma's.

Marianne loved taking Wolf, Opa's German shepherd, for walks. He was nearly as old as she was. He growled if anyone even looked at her!

She'd take her favorite books, her new green bedspread, her collection of glass animals—there were ten now. Her postcards, and of course all her clothes, especially her new green velvet "best dress" with the lace collar. Oma loved to see her granddaughters dressed up.

Marianne heard the telephone ring, and her mother's voice. A few minutes later, Mrs. Kohn came running into the bedroom. She took Marianne's hands and whirled her around the room before collapsing, breathless, onto the bed.

"A miracle. Listen, Marianne, that was Mrs. Rabinovitch on the telephone. You know, the supervisor at the orphanage. Two of the children have measles."

"Mutti, you call *that* a miracle? Are you feeling alright?"

"Don't you understand? This means the girls can't travel. They will have to wait for the next transport. You've been offered one of their places. It's all happened so quickly, I can't believe it. I have to give Mrs. Rabinovitch our answer in ten minutes."

"Mutti, what about you? Are you coming too? And Vati? How can we leave him behind? What will we tell Oma and Opa? Ten minutes? I'd need ten years to decide something like that. Mutti, how can we leave everyone and everything behind?" Marianne was walking up and down her room, her thumbnail in her mouth.

"Marianne, listen to me. No, don't turn away." Mrs. Kohn took her daughter's hands in hers. "Look at me, darling. We don't have weeks or days to decide. We don't even have hours. This transport is a rescue operation just for children. A *Kindertransport*. The grown-ups must wait their turn. There are bound to be other opportunities for us to leave."

Marianne pulled her hands free. She was almost incoherent.

"You mean, I have to go by myself? No! Absolutely no. I'd have to be crazy to agree to something like that. I won't leave you all. How can you even *think* of asking me that? Mothers don't send their children away. Why did you say you don't know how you'd manage without me if you didn't mean it? Well, I mean it. I can't manage by myself. Who would I tell things to, some stranger? Who'd wake me up to go to school? Who'd nag me, and tell me to be careful when I go out? Anyway, I refuse to be an orphan. I refuse to go. I'd miss you too much." Marianne slumped down on the bed beside her mother, biting her nails.

Mrs. Kohn took Marianne's hand and held it tight. "We all have to learn to say good-bye to people we love, and there never seems enough time to prepare. But I am prepared to live without you, if it means giving you a future."

Marianne said, "I don't believe you. I won't say good-bye to you, and that's final."

Mrs. Kohn said, "Marianne, I think you have to. You see, I can't keep you safe anymore. I don't know how. Not here in Berlin, not in Düsseldorf, or anyplace else the Nazis are. You need to live a normal life, to go to school, to have friends over. To play and walk anywhere you want. How can I let you stay in a country where you dread a knock on the door; where we are afraid to light our Sabbath candles; where our houses of prayer are destroyed? I don't want you to grow up afraid because you are Jewish. Germany is a bad place to grow up in right now. One day it may be safe to live here again. For now, we must take this chance for you to escape to a free country.

"Vati asked us to be brave. Marianne, help us both to be brave enough. Agree to leave."

"Vati said we should look after each other, remember? I can't do that if I'm away from you," said Marianne.

"Can't you see how hard this is for me?" Mrs. Kohn tried to smile. "If you go to England first, it will be easier for Vati and I to follow you. It will mean we'll already have a foothold in a new country. It could make it easier for us to get an exit visa."

Marianne said, "On one condition. You must swear to come."

Her mother said, "How can I do that? But I solemnly swear to try. Marianne, there is no time left. What is your answer?"

"Alright, I'll go." Marianne put her pillow over her head so as not to hear her mother leave the room to telephone Mrs. Rabinovitch.

16

The rest of the day passed much too quickly. Marianne began by piling all her "must-take-this" belongings on her bed.

Mrs. Kohn said, "Two steamer trunks wouldn't be big enough for all of this. Look, I've made a list. The glass animals would really be safer at Oma's, don't you think?"

The pile on the bed swayed.

"The Tower of Pisa's falling," said Marianne. She started to laugh and then looked at her mother. They spoke at exactly the same time.

"I don't want to choose, I love my things. I don't want to go."

"I never want to finish packing, or see you shut this suitcase," said Mrs. Kohn. And then they hugged each other tightly.

Marianne thought, *I'm really saying good-bye. This is good-bye, and I don't understand how it all happened so quickly. It's a horrible dream, and I want to wake up.*

"Why don't we pretend you're going away to a holiday camp? It's true in a way. Campers can only carry one suitcase because it's a long way to the campsite, and there's no one to help."

"Is that what the Nazis said? I don't mean the part about camp, more likely to be a concentration camp." Marianne immediately wished she hadn't made the flippant remark. She was always doing that lately, but it helped her to bear things more easily. Her mother's ashen face made her realize this wasn't the right time, but Mrs. Kohn answered Marianne as if she hadn't noticed the cruel reference.

"Yes. Each child is entirely responsible for his own belongings, even the smallest children. No valuables allowed, nothing that might be sold, or you could have your things confiscated, and be turned back."

"Terrific, you'd hear a knock on the door and it'd be me." Marianne ran to the bedroom door and rapped on it sharply. She turned round dramatically, saw her mother's stricken face and said, "I don't know why I'm behaving like this. I can't seem to help it. Sorry."

"I know, my darling," said Mrs. Kohn. "Let's start again."

Finally they decided on: hairbrush, comb, toothbrush and toothpaste. Dressing gown and slippers. Three pairs of socks. Three pairs of underwear—vests and underpants. Two sweaters— one red and one navy. Two blouses, two skirts. One pair of shoes, three handkerchiefs, paper and envelopes, and a German / English dictionary.

"You'll wear your brown lace-up boots and your Star of David like you always do, under your blouse. And, of course, your winter overcoat. England is very cold and damp, I'm told."

"What about my new dress—surely there'll be special occasions in England?" Marianne stroked the velvet skirt of her party frock.

"I could make room, but you'd have to wear more underwear on the journey. That would leave us enough space."

"Mutti, do you want me to die of heatstroke before I get there?" said Marianne, and this time she was only half joking.

"In December? You exaggerate so, Marianne."

Marianne said, "Are we going to have a fight?"

"Of course," said her mother, "isn't this a normal day? Come here, wicked daughter, and give me a hug. I forgot something. Fold your dress in tissue paper. We'll manage."

As soon as her mother left the room, Marianne squashed her teddy bear down the side of the case. He was quite thin after years of hugging. She couldn't go to sleep without him.

Marianne shut the case, then walked round the room with it, testing its weight. She smiled at her mother as she came back into the room. "I can manage this really easily; it's not heavy at all," she fibbed.

"Here are ten marks. The Nazis won't allow you to take more than that out of the country. It's very little, but as soon as you are settled, I'll try to send you more. Now put five marks in your purse and I'll pin the other five inside your coat pocket. Just to be on the safe side."

"You sound just like Emil's mother," said Marianne, and stopped. She remembered Ernest. She hoped she'd never see *him* again.

"Here is your passport. You'll need to show it when you cross the Dutch frontier. The ss will come aboard, or perhaps the Gestapo. Don't be afraid. Your papers are in order—you are on the list of children permitted to travel. Marianne, you know what I'm going to say."

"Be careful, don't draw attention to myself, be polite. I know," said Marianne.

"No smart remarks. You always make jokes—they could be misunderstood," said her mother.

Marianne looked at her passport. She clutched her stomach. "Oh, the pain, it's awful." She bent over in agony.

"Oh, my darling, what is it? Appendicitis?" Mrs. Kohn helped Marianne to the bed. "Sit down and tell me where it hurts."

"It's just the picture—I look so awful. It's even worse than my school one. And look at that dreadful red J. Do they think I'll forget I'm Jewish?"

"Marianne, you see what I mean, you *have* to stop this play-acting, at least till you get out of Germany. Once you're over the border, you'll be safe. Promise me to be sensible."

"Of course I promise. I'm just nervous. My lips will be sealed. I could even put a handkerchief over my mouth and pretend I've just come from the dentist and can't talk. Alright, I'll stop. Just teasing."

Mrs. Kohn shook her head in mock despair. "You won't like this either, I'm afraid, Marianne." Mrs. Kohn put a cardboard label tied to a piece of string around Marianne's neck. "We have been told all children have to wear this as identification. See, I've printed your name, destination, and your number—206."

"I feel like a piece of luggage. Let's hope I don't get lost."

Mrs. Kohn said, "We'll put all your things in the hall. We must leave at six in the morning. It's a long way to the railway station."

Marianne said, "If I have to listen to one more thing about tomorrow, I'll scream."

"But I haven't even told you about the boat that's waiting at the Hook to take you to England."

Marianne continued quite seriously, "Please, let's not talk about tomorrow anymore. Do you know what I'd like to do? Bake a chocolate cake for your birthday and eat it tonight."

"Before we do that, I have to give you one more thing. Don't groan, it's an early Hanukkah gift. It's from Vati too, and we want you to open it now."

Marianne undid the daintily wrapped parcel. Her mother had glued paper candles on the tissue paper. For once Marianne took her time. She threw her arms round her mother's neck.

"I've so longed to have a copy of *Emil and the Detectives* of my own. I won't even peek at it until I'm in England. I'll save it, something from home to look forward to. Thank you a thousand times."

Mother and daughter went into the kitchen with their arms around each other.

17

Next morning at ten minutes to six, Marianne stood in the hall, dressed and ready to go, with the luggage label fastened around her neck. Her mother was in the kitchen, making a big lunch for Marianne to take on the train.

There was a knock on the door. Marianne opened it.

Ernest, dressed in the outfit he had worn on that first day when he arrived in Berlin from Freiburg, stood there. He was holding a small package. "I'm going back today," said Ernest hesitantly. "Home to Freiburg."

"I'm leaving too, in a few minutes," said Marianne. "I'm going to England."

"I bet it's a long way on the train," said Ernest. "Watch out for men in bowler hats."

They both started laughing, remembering their first meeting.

Ernest said, "Well, I just came to say good-bye. I brought you something." He handed Marianne an oddly-shaped package, wrapped in brown paper and tied with string. "You can open it when I'm gone."

A harsh voice called from downstairs, "Ernest, I forbade you to go upstairs again. Come down this minute." Ernest straightened up, his arm flew out and, for a dreadful moment, Marianne thought he was going to say, "*Heil Hitler.*"

Ernest stuck out his hand; Marianne took it. They shook hands.

"Good luck, Marianne. Perhaps you'll come back to Berlin someday."

"Good-bye. Thanks Ernest," said Marianne.

Ernest ran downstairs, two steps at a time. The door of Number One closed behind him. Marianne went back inside her apartment and shut the door. She ripped open the parcel. Inside was Ernest's most precious possession—the motor-horn. On the back of a postcard with a view of Unter den Linden, Ernest had written

Berlin, December 1, 1938
We are not all the same.
Good-bye Marianne
From your friend
Ernest.

Marianne put the motor-horn in her coat pocket, and the postcard in her purse. Mr. Altmann had been right. Ernest was one of the brave voices.

"Who was that?" asked her mother.

"A friend," said Marianne. "He came to say good-bye."

18

In the subway all the way to the railway station, standing wedged tightly against her mother, Marianne was aware of Ernest's present in her coat pocket. She repeated the words on the card silently to herself:

"We are not all the same."

They comforted her a little.

Now and again, Mrs. Kohn smiled gently at Marianne. It was wiser not to speak in the compartment crowded with early-morning workers. Someone might be listening and cause problems.

It was a relief to get out at last into the frosty December air. Marianne looked at her watch: 7:15 A.M. precisely. There was still almost three-quarters of an hour left. She needn't say goodbye yet.

"Please let me carry my suitcase, Mutti. I have to get used to being on my own." Mrs. Kohn didn't argue, she just squeezed Marianne's fingers and then handed her the case. They walked through the vast pillared doorway of the Berlin railway station. Immediately they were assaulted by sights and sounds of such confusion, noise, and terror that Marianne's questions were left unspoken.

The glass and steel roof of the huge terminal was high and cavernous. The daylight, which entered through the tall windows, seemed pale in comparison to the blaze of electric light that lit up every sad face. There were seemingly endless railway tracks, which Marianne knew sent trains all over Europe. ss guards stood every few paces. Some had powerfully muscled watchdogs beside them. Marianne was afraid to look at the dogs. She thought, 'If one jumps up at me, it could tear out my throat.' Their leather collars gleamed as brightly as their masters' glossy boots.

Once they'd passed through the barrier, Marianne and her mother found the platform crammed with children of all ages. Some in brand-new clothes, others wearing hand-me-downs, or so many layers that their faces were red and sweating.

Parents, grandparents, aunts, uncles, older and younger brothers and sisters stood in mournful clumps, trying to create a small, last-minute zone of comfort to make their grief at being parted more private.

Marianne and her mother walked along the platform, jostling for a place to be alone for a minute.

"The journey won't be easy, Marianne," said her mother. "Have you got your lunch?"

"Right here, Mutti. I won't starve," said Marianne. Mrs. Kohn straightened Marianne's label.

"How will you all manage with only three supervisors amongst so many children? And they have to come back to Berlin as soon as you reach the Dutch border. They promised the authorities, and if they don't keep their word, the Nazis won't allow any more children to leave. Oh, Marianne!" She suppressed a sob.

"Mutti, please stop worrying. I'm almost twelve years old. I can look after myself. There are children much younger than me going by themselves." Marianne looked at the faces behind the barrier. "I thought perhaps, I hoped, you know, that Vati might come to see me off too. I know he can't. I understand," said Marianne. "Tell him . . ." The rest of her words were lost in a hiss of steam as the big green and black and chrome train pulled into the station.

"I'll tell him, darling. I'll tell him good-bye for you."

A voice over the loudspeaker announced, "All Aboard." Pandemonium, as people pushed and scrambled to get their children on board and settled.

"The adults have to wait behind the gate, Marianne. Be quick," said Mrs. Kohn.

The station clock pointed to four minutes to 8:00 A.M. Trains always left punctually in the Third *Reich*. Marianne grabbed her case and hurled it onto a wooden seat by the window to reserve her place, then jumped down the high train steps to spend her last precious two minutes with her mother.

The train filled with children. Last-minute advice was shouted and whispered. Marianne saw a little boy jump into his mother's arms, saw her carry him away through the gate and out of the station.

"I love you, Mutti, I'll write as soon as I get to England. I'll be alright, I promise I'll be alright. I'll remember everything you told me."

"I have to go. We are not allowed to remain on the platform. I'll wave from behind the barrier till you're out of sight. Never forget how much we love you." Mrs. Kohn put her hand to her daughter's face. She kissed her cheek and hurried to stand with the other relatives.

Marianne's eyes were so full of tears she had to feel her way back onto the train. She lifted her suitcase onto the rack. The station guard slammed the compartment doors one by one. The noise echoed along the train.

Just before the guard reached their compartment door, a woman threw in a rucksack, then lifted a little girl and stood her beside Marianne. "Please look after her. Thank you." She kissed the child's hand and moved away without looking back.

I'm not going to talk about today, Marianne promised herself, *not even when I'm old and have children of my own. No one is going to believe this happened to us.*

The train whistled shrilly, and Marianne and the other children crowded round the window again to wave, until the station was left far behind. They took off their coats and scarves. It was a relief to be away from the tension of the station. One of the boys put the little girl's case on the rack for her.

"Thank you," she said. "I'm Sophie Mandel. I'm seven." They

all introduced themselves. Werner was the tallest of the three boys; Heinz was the one who had helped Sophie.

"I'm Liselotte Blum," said a pretty girl of about fourteen.

"And I'm Brigitte Levy." A plump, dimpled face smiled in a friendly way at all of them.

"I'm Josef Stein," said a curly-haired boy who looked about the same age as Ernest.

For the first time Marianne looked at the small girl with short, fair hair and dark eyes, sitting on the edge of the seat. She held a doll. Her legs, in wrinkled brown stockings and tightly laced brown ankle boots, swung far above the floor. Marianne smiled at the child who had been put in her charge. "I'm Marianne Kohn," she said.

They all stared at each other, not feeling a bit shy, and there was almost a holiday feeling in the air.

Brigitte said, "What an adventure."

Heinz said, "I'm starved. I was too nervous to eat breakfast. I'm going to eat my lunch now." They all opened their lunch bags. Everyone had a thick sandwich and a piece of fruit. Marianne had cake as well. They cut up their sandwiches and shared. Marianne sliced her chocolate cake into seven pieces with Josef's penknife, and Sophie contributed an orange from the pocket of her blue and white striped dress.

After lunch they practiced English phrases, and taught Sophie to say, "The sun is shining." The compartment smelled of orange peel and chocolate. They were hot and thirsty, and dozed off after awhile. Sophie slept soundly, her head on Marianne's shoulder.

The train sped on toward the border.

19

They woke up when the train stopped. Werner said, "We must be close to the Dutch frontier." He looked out of the window. "Gestapo coming on board. Sit up straight. Don't say or do anything."

The children sat motionless, waiting.

The Gestapo entered the carriages, one officer to each compartment. "Passports."

The children held out the precious documents. Marianne put her hand in Sophie's coat pocket and, thank goodness, the passport was there. She held it out with her own. The officer barely glanced at the pictures. He pointed to the luggage racks.

"Open up," he ordered.

They put their suitcases on the seat for inspection.

The Gestapo officer, with a quick movement, overturned

each case and ran his black-gloved hand through the contents. He pulled out Werner's stamp album and flicked carelessly through the pages, then put the album under his arm. When he opened Marianne's suitcase, he pushed the party dress aside, reached down inside the suitcase, found Marianne's bear, and hit the cherished toy sharply across his knee.

What was he looking for?

Marianne looked down on the dusty compartment floor, where her dress had slipped out of its tissue-paper wrapping. Under the green velvet sleeve, a small white envelope, with her name written in her mother's neat lettering, protruded.

Silently, without seeming to move, Marianne stepped forward. Her foot covered the paper. Marianne tried to steady her breathing; willed herself not to tremble.

The officer opened the back of Liselotte's framed picture of her parents, stepping deliberately on Brigitte's clean white blouse, which had fallen to the floor. Josef's prayer shawl was thrown aside. Sophie's doll was grabbed, its head twisted off. Then the officer turned the doll upside down and shook it.

Sophie cried quietly.

Marianne saw Josef clench his fist and open his mouth. She knew he was about to say something that would anger the officer. In desperation, she curled her fingers around the motor-horn in her pocket and squeezed. In the small space, the sound was as deafening as an explosion.

The children watched. No one moved. Josef's eyes met Marianne's for a moment. She looked down.

A second pair of black boots appeared at the door of the compartment.

"Enough," said a voice. Marianne looked up. The Gestapo were leaving the train.

Josef smiled his thanks. Marianne's knees were trembling so hard she had to sit down. The train whistle blew, and the locomotive began to pick up speed.

Brigitte said, "Sophie, we're in charge of the doll hospital. *Fraülein*, please hand your doll over for repairs."

Sophie smiled.

With careful fingers, Brigitte twisted the doll's head back onto the neck and said, "Good as new," and returned the doll to Sophie.

Only then was Marianne sufficiently under control to pick up the envelope and take out the letter it contained. It read

My dearest daughter,

You will be far away from me when you read this letter. It is so hard to let you go. I watched you sleeping last night as though you were still a small baby. I wished I could change my mind and keep you here, but that would be too selfish.

You are going to a better, safer life. Here, there might be no life at all. One day you will understand why I had to let you go. If only we had more time together. Someone else will lengthen your clothes, buy you new shoes, tie your hair. Did it grow into curls as you always hoped it would? I miss you already. I will miss having to nag you for coming in late. I will miss complaining about your messy room, or you not doing your homework. I will miss your first grown-up party. Will you still love to dance?

Please try to understand, Marianne, why I must miss all your growing up, all these special things. Because I love you, I want to give you the very best life there is, and that means a chance to grow up in a free country. Here there is only fear.

I pray that you, and all the children whose parents send them away, will find loving families. I will think of you every day, and wish for your happiness, and that you will grow up into a good and honorable person.

Wherever you are, wherever I am, at night we will be looking at the same sky.

Always, your loving Mutti.

Marianne was crying. This time she did not attempt to hold back her tears. "It was a letter from my mother," she said.

Werner blew his nose noisily. Josef turned his back and started throwing all his stuff back into his suitcase. Marianne watched him spend a long time folding his prayer shawl before clicking the lid of his suitcase shut. Liselotte and Brigitte had their arms around each other.

"I need to go to the bathroom," said Sophie, and held out her hand to Marianne.

When they got back, the others had repacked Sophie's and Marianne's things as well as their own.

The train steamed into a station—a Dutch station! The children on the train went wild. Windows were pulled down, hats and handkerchiefs waved, voices shouted greetings, strangers shook hands.

Women, wearing clogs, handed drinks and bags of food through the open windows.

Werner took in a huge basket full of white rolls, butter and cheese. There were even bars of chocolate for each of them. A note with GOOD LUCK was pinned to a clean, white napkin which covered the food. The compartment which minutes before had been tense, angry and tearful, hummed with laughter and thanks.

"Good-bye."

"Safe journey."

"Thank you."

The train passed through the neat Dutch countryside, and the sound of children's voices floated out of the windows, over the dikes and windmills, into the December skies. A train of sadness had been transformed into a holiday train.

Josef began the song, sung at the end of the Passover meal— the festival that celebrates the flight of the Jews from Egypt and the journey to the Promised Land. What did it matter that it was the wrong time of year? Weren't they an exodus of children?

Just as they began to sing the verse about the Holy One, "Blessed is He," the train stopped.

20

The train emptied its load of children. Eager hands helped them down the steps, patted cheeks, found luggage, tucked chocolate bars into pockets, and pointed them towards the quay. Tiredly, they filed out of the small, clean, train station and into the cold December darkness of the cobbled square.

"My face stings from the wind," said Sophie, running to keep up with Marianne. "Where is the sea? Why isn't it here?"

"I can smell it, mmm, like herrings. We'll be there very soon." The long line of children followed the path down to the water.

"My case feels as though there are rocks in it," Marianne said to Sophie. "Can you still manage your rucksack?"

A ripple of sound, like seagulls calling each other, shivered through the weary procession. "The ship, the ship." Everyone took up the cry.

There, looming up out of the darkness like a great white bird against the gloomy December sky, was the boat. They could see it clearly, shifting impatiently on the waves, eager to be free of its moorings.

Marianne said, "It's called De Praag. Look, the name's painted on the side."

Some men in uniform waved and came running toward the straggling line. The small travelers stopped moving. Sophie grasped her doll more tightly. Marianne took her free hand.

Could it be a hoax? The Hoek of Holland. That reminded Marianne of the hooks of the swastika. Were the Gestapo going to drown them?

A whisper filtered through from the front of the line. "They're friends, pass it on. Sailors from the ship. The uniforms are British."

A cheer went up from the ship as the first children reached the wooden gangway and climbed excitedly on board. Marianne stood leaning over the ship's railing, looking out into the darkness. So many children still to come. How had the train held them all? So many parents sitting tonight with empty places at the table.

Ruth out there in that friendly country. Would they meet again one day?

Other children joined her at the railing, wanting one last look at land before they sailed, at all they were leaving behind.

"What are you thinking about, Marianne?" asked Sophie beside her.

"My father said to me once, 'We can be together in our

thoughts, even if we don't live together.' I'm remembering, storing up so I won't forget."

The ship's engines began to hum steadily. The last child was on board. Sailors removed the gangway. The ship started to move.

"At last. We're going. Tomorrow we'll be in England," said Marianne.

"What a long journey," said Sophie.

"Yes, but we're almost there."

The ship sailed on, into the darkness, into safety, into the future.

REMEMBER
Me

I

The guard pushed his way through the corridor. "Next stop— Liverpool Street Station. All change," he called.

The train slowed to a shuddering halt, expelling two hundred apprehensive, weary children. Steam from the engine misted behind them like morning fog. The children climbed down onto the platform. Not knowing what to do next, they formed an untidy line. Eleven-year-old Marianne took Sophie's hand. "Come on, we have to wait with the others. Stay close beside me," she said.

Passersby stared at them curiously. Porters pushing trolleys shouted: "Mind your backs." A few photographers began taking pictures—"Smile," they said. A light flashed, or was it winter sunshine coming through the glass domed roof of the station?

"Like animals at the zoo," Marianne said to the boy standing next to her.

"We'd better smile all the same, make a good impression," he said.

"Wipe your face, Sophie; it's got smuts on it from the train," Marianne told her.

"Are we going to our new families now?" Sophie asked, spitting on her grubby handkerchief and handing it to Marianne, who scrubbed at Sophie's cheeks.

"Soon."

Marianne wasn't ready to think that far ahead. It was only twenty-four hours ago that she'd said good-bye to her mother in Berlin. Today was December 2, 1938, and she was in London— the whole English Channel between her and her parents. The station overwhelmed her with its incomprehensible words and signs.

"A friend of my father's supposed to be meeting me. I don't even know what he looks like. Do you know who's taking you in?" the boy next to her said.

"I don't know anything. I can't even remember how I got here. Don't you feel like we've been traveling for a thousand years?" said Marianne.

"A thousand years, the thousand-year Reich, what's the difference? We're here, away from all that," the boy said. "They can't get us now."

An identification label spiraled down onto the tracks. A woman wearing a red hat climbed onto a luggage trolley facing them. She tucked a strand of hair behind her ear, and spoke to the children in English, slowly, and in a loud voice, adding to the confusion of sounds around them. "I am Miss Baxter. I am here to help you. Welcome to London. Follow me, please."

She climbed down. Nobody moved. Miss Baxter walked slowly along the length of the line, smiling and shaking hands with some of the children. Then she headed up the platform to the front of the line, took a child's hand, and began to walk. She stopped every few moments, turned and beckoned, to make sure the others were following.

"Come on, Sophie, keep up," said Marianne. She could hear some women talking about them and shaking their heads, the way mothers do when you've been out in the rain without a coat.

"See them poor little refugees."

"What a shame."

"Look at that little one. Sweet, isn't she?"

"More German refugees, I suppose. Surely they could go somewhere else?"

Marianne understood the tone, if not the words. Except for "refugee."

"We'll have to try to speak English all the time," Marianne told Sophie.

"But I don't know how. I want to go home," Sophie said.

Marianne was too tired to answer.

A girl dragging her suitcase along the platform said, "This is the worst part, isn't it? Do hurry up, Bernard, we'll be last. Vati said, 'Stay together.'" She called to the small boy trailing behind them, then turned to Marianne and said, "That's my little brother. Why do boys always dawdle?" They waited for the small boy to catch up.

"Look! A man gave me a penny." Bernard held out a large round copper coin. "He said, 'Here you are, son.'"

"How do you *know* what he said? You don't speak English. You're not supposed to speak to strangers," his sister scolded.

"I suppose they're all strangers here and we are too," said Marianne. "I mean, we don't know anyone, do we?"

"No," said the girl and her lip trembled.

"Sorry," said Marianne. "I only meant . . ." She didn't say any more, and they hurried to catch up to the other children.

The ticket collector must have known they were coming. He smiled and waved them through.

Miss Baxter stopped at last.

"It's clever of her to wear a red hat with that little feather. Like a bird showing us the way," Marianne told Sophie.

"Like Hansel and Gretel," Sophie said, giving a little skip. She'd cheered up again. "Will everyone be nice in England?" she asked.

"Well, it's bound to be better than Germany. Can you imagine the Nazis smiling and holding our hands?" said Marianne.

They followed the red hat into a big room at the end of the station. As soon as they were inside, a woman handed each of them a paper bag with an orange, some chocolate, and a sandwich.

Miss Baxter pointed to rows of slatted wooden chairs lined up on one side of the gloomy room, ready for the new arrivals. The children sat. Across from them, on the other side of the room waiting in a separate section, were the adults. Although it was daylight outside, all the electric lightbulbs were on. The two groups gazed at each other. Some adults stood up, craning their necks to look the newcomers over. A few of them held photographs and were trying to compare the reality in front of them with the posed pictures in their hands.

Miss Baxter announced what was happening in English, and a woman next to her translated her words for the children. "Every sponsor will be paired with a child on my list. We must make sure the names and numbers match. Please wait patiently until you hear your name called."

The woman who spoke German sat at a table in the center of the room and smiled nervously at no one in particular. She was dressed in blue. There was a pile of papers in front of her. Miss Baxter began calling out names, and children and sponsors met for the first time. It went on and on—the names called, the walk under staring eyes, the signing of forms. The endless terrifying anticipation.

Marianne noticed how, sometimes, two children went together. There were nods and smiles and handshakes. Occasionally the adults looked as if they'd expected someone different. The new arrivals followed behind their grown-ups, mostly not turning back to look at the others, who were still waiting to be collected. A few children fidgeted, or whispered. Most sat quiet and watchful.

Marianne held her bag of food so tightly that she could feel the sandwich squish between her fingers. "Do you want my orange?" she asked Sophie. "I can't bear the smell anymore." She knew the bright fruit had been a gesture of kindness— meant to comfort. At this moment, nothing could console Marianne.

Sophie did not answer; she was asleep. She'd pushed her chair very close to Marianne's and was half leaning against her.

The girl sitting on Marianne's other side said, "I'll take your orange if you don't want it."

Marianne gave it to her.

The girl asked, "Is that your little sister?"

"No," Marianne said. "The only thing I know about her is her name and her age. Her mother pushed her onto the train just as we were leaving and asked me to take care of her till we got here. I think it was because I was standing closest to the door. It's worked out alright. She's very good for a seven year old. I won't know anyone when she goes."

"Waiting's horrible, isn't it?" said the girl.

"Sophie Mandel," Miss Baxter called.

"That's you, Sophie. Come on, you've got to wake up." Marianne pulled Sophie to her feet.

A pleasant-looking woman in a gray coat and hat said to her in German: "*Nicht stören*—don't wake her. I can carry her."

Sophie woke up anyway.

"Hello, Sophie. I am Aunt Margaret, a friend of your mother's. I've come to take you to your new home."

Sophie put her arms around Marianne's neck and hugged her, as if she didn't want to leave her behind.

"Good-bye, Sophie. She looks very nice," Marianne whispered, and kissed her cheek.

Sophie went off bravely, carrying her doll and her rucksack. Marianne saw the lady smile at the little girl and heard her answer a question. Sophie turned at the exit and waved to Marianne. It was all Marianne could do, not to cry. She blew her nose, pretending she'd caught a cold.

Why do I mind Sophie leaving? It's not as if we're even related. Everyone's being separated. The boy she'd talked to in the line had been one of the first to go, and Bernard's sister had left too, with an elderly man and woman. She'd tried to explain to Miss Baxter about staying with her brother, but the couple were anxious to leave and didn't let her finish talking. Marianne saw the girl turn round to look at Bernard. He hung his head and refused to look up. He sat slumped like that for ages, even when the lady in blue came over to him and put a note in his hand. "Your sister's address," she told him.

Miss Baxter called his name. A cheerful young woman collected him. She had a small boy with her who looked about Bernard's age. The boys began making faces at each other almost immediately. He'd be alright.

The girl she'd given her orange to had left with a woman in a fur jacket. The room was almost empty. *Suppose no one comes for me? Is there a special room for unclaimed children?* Marianne wished she'd never let her mother talk her into coming here. She planned her first letter home:

Dear Mutti,

I'm still in Liverpool Street Station. Please write to me here.

Perhaps Miss Baxter would give her a stamp.

Marianne tried to push this moment out of her thoughts. She closed her eyes, hoping the sick feeling in her stomach would go away.

2

"**A**re you Leah Stein?"

Marianne opened her eyes and saw Miss Baxter stooping beside her.

"I must have fallen asleep. Sorry." She spoke in German, then remembered where she was. "My name is Marianne Kohn."

Miss Baxter checked the number on Marianne's identification label, and scrutinized the remaining names on her list. Marianne saw that most of them had already been crossed off.

"I'm afraid there isn't a Marianne Kohn listed. Nothing to worry about," she said reassuringly. "I'm sure we can sort it out. Miss Martin speaks German and you can explain to her. Follow me."

Marianne carried her suitcase to the table where the lady in blue was sitting. Speaking in German, the woman asked, "Is there a reason why there isn't a record of your name here, my dear?"

"I came with the group from the Berlin orphanage. It was all sort of last minute because two of the girls got measles." It was a relief to speak in German. But before Marianne could continue, the ladies began to confer.

"The orphans are supposed to stay together in the hostel at Dovercourt in Harwich, till homes can be found for them. I don't know how this child got separated from the group. We'll have to make arrangements to send her back to them."

"Send back? *Zurück schicken?*" Those were the only words Marianne understood. "Please, no. *Ich bin Jüdisch*—I am Jewish. No send back." *Don't these ladies understand? But how can they? They don't know about the Gestapo; they haven't been on the train out of Germany.* Marianne sat on her suitcase, and hid her face on her arm.

Miss Baxter said, "No one is going to send you back to Germany."

Miss Martin continued, "You misunderstood. Now, tell us slowly, calmly, all about the measles and why you are not with the other orphans. Please don't worry; I promise you are quite safe."

Marianne looked up at their kind faces and said, "My mother helped out at the orphanage. Two of the girls got measles and couldn't travel, so the supervisor said I could come instead. I'm sorry I took someone's place."

"Now I understand, but I'm sure they'll come when they're better. Don't worry about that," said Miss Martin.

Miss Baxter wrote Marianne's name on the list and showed it to her. "There, you're quite official now."

A tall thin woman wearing a coat with an elegant fur collar approached. In a voice that matched her sharp features she announced, "I am Mrs. Abercrombie Jones. Is this girl Leah Stein?"

Miss Martin turned to Marianne and said quietly in German, "Just wait, dear."

Marianne sat very still, watching, trying to understand what was happening.

"I know you've been waiting some time, Mrs. Abercrombie Jones. I'm afraid Leah has not arrived. She may have changed her mind, or been detained in Holland. This is Marianne Kohn."

The lady ignored the introduction and looked round the room as if Leah might be hiding somewhere. Marianne noticed that she was the last girl. All the rows were empty except for four boys sitting together in the back.

"Marianne does not have a sponsor," Miss Baxter said. "It seems quite providential in a way. You did specify a girl, didn't you?"

The woman's mouth set in a straight line. "This is all rather haphazard, isn't it? The girl's aunt wrote me that Leah is a responsible domesticated fourteen year old—the school leaving age. My husband and I agreed to take in a refugee to help around the house. Why wasn't I notified?"

Miss Baxter said, "I'm sure you're aware, Mrs. Abercrombie Jones, that this is the first *Kindertransport* that has been allowed to leave Germany. We must be grateful that so many refugee children at risk have arrived safely." Somewhere a station clock struck 3:00 P.M. It echoed in the cavernous room. "It's getting late. I'm sure Marianne will fit in splendidly. Won't you, Marianne?"

"Please," said Marianne, totally confused, but sensing this woman did not seem to want her. *She reminds me of that horrible Miss Friedrich at school.*

"How old are you?" the lady asked.

Marianne stood up and curtsied. "I am eleven and one-half years old." She'd practiced this sentence. She could also talk about the weather, and she knew how to say "good morning," "good-bye," "how do you do," "please," and "thank you." She knew lots of words. She'd been taking lessons for two years—the English Miss had been a good teacher, and English had been one of her favorite subjects at school before the Nazis had expelled Jewish students. *Was it really such a short time ago?*

Marianne took her father's German/English dictionary out of her bag. She'd found it lying facedown under his desk the night after the Gestapo had left their apartment. The leather binding was scratched, but the pages were fine after she'd smoothed them out. Her father's name was written inside the cover—"David Kohn." The publisher's name was Hugo. Vati used to say, "Bring my little Hugo and we'll look it up," when he helped her with her English homework. It was a small pocket dictionary, which fitted into her palm, and feeling it was as though she were holding Vati's hand.

I won't cry; please God, don't let me cry now.

Miss Baxter said firmly, "I'm sure Marianne will suit you beautifully, Mrs. Abercrombie Jones." She patted Marianne's arm.

The lady asked Marianne, "Do you speak English?"

Marianne nodded. "Yes, please. I speak a little."

Mrs. Abercrombie Jones smoothed the fingers of the leather

gloves she was wearing. "She looks young for her age. Our house is not suitable for children; however, as I've told everyone we are sponsoring a refugee girl, I shall keep my word."

"Thank you so much. Good-bye, Mrs. Abercrombie Jones."

Miss Baxter turned to the last boys waiting to be called.

"Come along, Mary Anne," said the lady, not even attempting to pronounce Marianne's name correctly.

Marianne followed Mrs. Abercrombie Jones. *She doesn't look very motherly. I hope we get to like each other.*

3

Outside Liverpool Street Station, the city of London soared out of the fog. "Here I am in the biggest, most wonderful city in the whole world." Marianne wrote a letter in her head to her mother. "A big red double-decker bus just passed by, and guess what, Mutti? It says BUCKINGHAM PALACE on the front. Imagine, I could just climb onboard and go right to the palace and see the king and queen and the two little princesses—Elizabeth and Margaret Rose."

Marianne remembered how she and her cousin Ruth used to read every bit of news they could about the royal family. The winter coat Marianne was wearing today was in the same double-breasted style that she and Ruth had so admired when they saw the princesses wearing it in the photograph in the *Berliner Illustrierte*. Her mother had cut down an old coat of her father's to make the coat fit her, and had finished it just before *Kristallnacht*—the Night of Broken Glass. It felt strange wearing Vati's coat and having no idea where he was hiding.

"Watch where you're going, ducks." A uniformed sleeve steadied her. Marianne looked up into the smiling face of a helmeted London policeman.

"I'm so sorry, officer. She's just arrived from Germany." Mrs. Abercrombie Jones sounded as if she were apologizing for a badly behaved puppy.

"No harm done. Good day, Ma'am. Welcome to London, Miss."

"Taxi," called Mrs. Abercrombie Jones. A shiny black automobile halted at the curb.

My first taxi ride, Mutti.

"Twelve Circus Road, St. John's Wood, please." Mrs. Abercrombie Jones settled herself in the center of the leather cushions and pointed for Marianne to sit on the pull-down seat under the driver's window.

Marianne sat down. *Circus? Does the lady live in a circus? She doesn't look like anyone who has anything to do with animals. Perhaps I could help hand out tickets. She definitely said "circus."* Opa loved attending the circus—long ago, when Jews were still allowed to go. One day he'd told her all about the elephants, how they held flags in their trunks and waved them in time to the band. Then Opa had laughed and whispered, "I hear they're training the seals to bark 'Heil Hitler.'" He'd put his finger to his lips in warning. "Walls have ears."

Marianne looked at Mrs. Abercrombie Jones, and was sure she wouldn't make jokes. The lady noticed Marianne staring.

Their eyes met. Marianne smoothed her coat over her knees, and pulled up her kneesocks. She had to make a good impression. *I'll be good and polite. It'll be easy to behave perfectly. My English isn't good enough to answer back yet.* She smiled at Mrs. Abercrombie Jones.

Mrs. Abercrombie Jones cleared her throat. Marianne looked up apprehensively. *Suppose I can't understand what she says to me?*

"I'm dying for my tea, aren't you?"

"Yes," said Marianne, hoping this was the correct reply.

"Where did you learn to speak English, Mary Anne?"

"I learn in school."

"In school? Oh yes, of course, school." She paused, frowning a little. "You will have to go to school, I suppose. Monday, if possible." She sighed.

"I like so much go to school," said Marianne.

"Good," said Mrs. Abercrombie Jones. She took a small gold compact out of her handbag, and powdered her nose.

Marianne could smell her perfume, like lilies of the valley. Mrs. Abercrombie Jones undid the fur collar of her brown coat, and Marianne saw that she wore a strand of pearls and a pale blue cardigan over her cream-colored silk blouse. Her skirt was of brown tweed.

She'd write Mutti everything, tell her about the smart clothes, and the fine shops, and the statues and parks. But the harder Marianne looked at the passing scene through the taxi window, the more blurred the city appeared. Mutti's anxious face kept coming between Marianne and the view. Her mother looked the way Marianne remembered her in those last precious few minutes in their apartment in Berlin. Marianne could still hear her voice, "Everything will be different, Marianne—the language, the customs, the food. You're bound to be homesick at first. You must try to fit in, to adapt. Be grateful, darling. How kind people are to give a home to a child they don't know. It may take a while for us to get a visa to come to England. Who knows? You might be the one to find someone to sponsor us; you're certain to meet lots of English people. All we need is an offer of work, and an address. We must have an address you see, darling, to get a permit. Why don't you try and see what you can do?"

She'd said it with a little smile, and patted Marianne's cheek, so that Marianne needn't take the request too seriously. But Marianne knew she'd been very serious.

Marianne had said, "Of course I will, Mutti." Now she repeated the promise silently.

The taxi stopped. "'Ere you are, Ma'am, 12 Circus Road."

Marianne was startled; her thoughts had been so far away.

Mrs. Abercrombie Jones paid the driver, counted her change, and gave him a coin. He touched his cap, smiled at Marianne, and drove off.

Marianne looked around for signs of animals. It was just a street. Not a circus at all. She couldn't even see a dog.

Mrs. Abercrombie Jones pushed open a black wrought-iron gate, and Marianne followed her along a short path of paving stones to the door. There was a neat hedge around the square front garden and two flower beds.

Marianne had never lived in a house before, except on holiday when she'd stayed with her grandparents in their house. In Berlin, the people she knew lived in apartments.

It was very cold. A maid in a black dress and white apron and cap answered the door. She said, "Good afternoon, Madam," and helped the lady off with her coat.

"This is Mary Anne." Mrs. Abercrombie Jones pronounced it like two words, the English way. "And this is Gladys. Gladys has been with us since she was fourteen—isn't that right, Gladys?"

"Yes, Madam. Welcome," Gladys said. She had a freckled face and a snub nose. Her smile was real, not just polite.

"Tea in ten minutes, Gladys. Come along, Mary Anne. I'll show you to your room and you can wash and unpack before tea."

Marianne couldn't work out if all these words needed a yes or no, please or thank you. So she said nothing at all, and followed Mrs. Abercrombie Jones.

"This is the drawing room; it looks over the front garden. It gets the sun in summer." Mrs. Abercrombie Jones spoke loudly to Marianne, as though she were deaf. Marianne understood one or two words, and guessed the rest.

Mrs. Abercrombie Jones opened the first door in the wood paneled hallway, and Marianne just had time to notice a dark pink couch with matching armchairs, several occasional chairs, and a pink and green rug centered on the polished wood floor.

"This is the dining room. The kitchen is at the end of the corridor. Tomorrow you will eat your meals there with Gladys."

She went up the stairs, her feet silent on the brown wool

carpet. Marianne followed. When they reached the landing, Mrs. Abercrombie Jones showed her the bathroom.

"Do you have running water at home?"

This seemed a strange question. Marianne thought it was safe to say yes.

The lady seemed surprised at her response. They passed closed doors. Then more stairs—this time uncarpeted. Marianne's suitcase felt as heavy as if it were full of bricks. The linoleum squeaked under their feet.

Mrs. Abercrombie Jones switched on the light. "Gladys sleeps next door. Come down when you're ready." She ran her fingertips lightly along the window ledge, checking for dust, and went out.

Marianne said "sank you" to her retreating back. Mrs. Abercrombie Jones did not reply.

4

Everything was green—light green. Marianne felt as if she were underwater. The bed stuck out from a green painted wall. The heavy cotton counterpane was green and white. A wooden chair stood at the bottom of the bed. Marianne put her suitcase on it, carefully, so as not to dirty the towel that hung over the back of the chair.

Under the window was a small wooden chest of drawers, also painted green, and there was a narrow wardrobe for hanging her clothes. There was no bookshelf, but that was alright. There'd only been room to pack one book—her parents' early Hanukkah gift to her—and, of course, her precious dictionary.

There was no bedside table or lamp. A green fringed lamp shade covered the electric lightbulb, which hung from the center of the ceiling. A picture on the wall was of a smiling lady in a white dress, sitting under a tree and reading to a small blonde girl.

Marianne drew the thin curtains. It was dark outside, but the light from the kitchen window below gave a glimpse of the shadowy garden. She could just make out one small tree, bare of leaves, and a shed. Marianne shivered and drew the curtains again, to hide the night.

"This is the loneliest place in the world." Marianne spoke out loud to break the silence. *If I run away, who'd come to look for me? Who'd care enough to find me?* Marianne breathed deeply, forcing herself to be sensible. *Mutti will come soon and get me. I can bear it till then.*

Marianne unpacked quickly. She placed the picture of her parents, which she'd put in her shoulder bag at the last minute, in the center of the chest of drawers.

It didn't take long to put her socks, underwear, and sweaters away and hook her dressing gown on the back of the door. She hung her two skirts, two blouses, and best velvet dress in the wardrobe. There was a mirror inside the door. She looked just the same as she had in Berlin. Somehow she'd expected to look more English. Finally, she picked up her worn teddy bear and held him against her cheek for a moment, before stuffing him under the sheets with her pajamas.

Marianne gave her hair a quick brush, and checked herself again in the mirror. Was it her imagination, or did her face reflect the green of the walls? Marianne closed her bedroom door softly and went to wash her hands and face in the bathroom. Anything to delay the moment of going downstairs.

Voices came from the dining room. The door was ajar. *Am I supposed to knock or just go in?* Marianne stood in the doorway and waited to be noticed.

A dining table and four chairs with carved backs stood in the center of the room. There was also a sideboard, with a radio on one end and a cut-glass decanter and matching tumblers on the other. Two more chairs stood against the wall, which was patterned with wallpaper of green leaves and little bunches of grapes.

Green must be the family's favorite color.

The other wall, the one facing the window, was dominated by a tall cupboard with glass doors. The shelves were full of china. Marianne tried not to think of the mess there'd be if the Gestapo came in the night and smashed it. Her fingertips tingled as she remembered the feel of the sharp edges of broken plates. She heard again her mother's urgent whisper: "Careful, you'll hurt yourself." Deliberately, Marianne willed herself to return to the present.

I wonder why we don't have tea at the table. I hope I don't make crumbs. The fire looks so nice and warm I'd like to curl up in front of it and go to sleep.

Mrs. Abercrombie Jones looked up and saw her. "Come in and say 'how do you do,' Mary Anne."

A man dressed in black, with a stiff round white collar, stood by the mantelpiece, his back to the fire. He was talking to another man, who was smaller and thinner, wearing a business suit. They both stopped talking and looked at Marianne.

Mrs. Abercrombie Jones sat in an upholstered chair in front of a coal fire. Beside her was a tea trolley on which were delicate china teacups, with a rose pattern to match the large teapot. There was a plate of thin bread and butter, and another of finger sandwiches. A dish of raisin scones and a layered jam sponge were arranged on a tiered silver cake stand.

Nodding towards the small thin man, Mrs. Abercrombie Jones said, "This is my husband, Mr. Abercrombie Jones, and this is Reverend James, who has dropped in for tea especially to meet you, Mary Anne."

Marianne curtsied and said, "How do you do." Just the way she and Vati had rehearsed.

The man in black said to Marianne in German, "I like to walk in your beautiful country. I love the Black Forest." And then he turned to Mrs. Abercrombie Jones and said something Marianne didn't understand.

Marianne had never been to that part of the country. It was full of Nazis; she'd heard ugly stories. *Who is this man . . . is he a party member?* He spoke with a heavy accent.

"*Wie war die Reise?* How was the journey?" he asked.

Why is he asking about the journey? Have the Gestapo recruited him as a spy?

She thanked him cautiously, "*Gut danke.*"

Again the man turned to Mrs. Abercrombie Jones and spoke in English.

Marianne wondered if she should make a run for it, try and find Miss Baxter, but how?

Mrs. Abercrombie Jones smiled at the man and said, "Oh, well done, Vicar. Now do sit down everyone please, and let's have tea."

Marianne sat on a small narrow chair and took a sip of the pale brown liquid that Mrs. Abercrombie Jones handed her. This was not the kind of tea they had at home. She was used to drinking it black, with a slice of lemon. She'd never tried it mixed with milk and sugar.

The man who might be a spy spoke to her in German again. In spite of his English accent, she could understand him quite well. *If he asks me about my parents, I won't say one word. Hitler has spies everywhere. Why did Mrs. Abercrombie Jones take me? She was expecting someone else.*

The man said, "Mrs. Abercrombie Jones does a lot of charitable work in our little community. Does your mother work, my dear?"

She'd been right—the interrogation was continuing. Marianne determined to give nothing away.

"Mrs. Abercrombie Jones is the first one in our congregation to offer sanctuary to a refugee. You are a lucky girl."

What is this word "congregation"? He'd said it in English. *Is it some kind of political party? He looks very kind, but that doesn't mean much. It would be like the Gestapo to send a kind-looking spy to fool me.*

Mr. Abercrombie Jones said, "May we *please* speak English?" He offered the bread and butter to Marianne.

The grown-ups talked to each other between mouthfuls of cake and sandwiches. Marianne managed to swallow one small triangle of bread, and then was offered cake by the "spy." She didn't dare refuse. It was very good cake, but Marianne couldn't swallow. This was worse even than the day she'd lost her front door key. She didn't know whether she wanted to cry, or be sick.

Her stomach hurt, the way it always did when she was upset. It hurt a lot. *I want Mutti.*

Gladys came in with a plate of jam tarts. A piece of coal fell from the fire onto the brown tiled hearth. Everyone turned to look, and while Gladys dealt with it, Marianne slid the cake off her plate onto her lap and covered it with her handkerchief.

At last tea was over. The adults made good-bye noises and went into the hall.

"Good-bye, Mary Anne. *Auf Wiedersehen.*"

"Good-bye," said Marianne and stood up.

The moment they left the room, she threw the cake into the fire and watched it flare up for a moment. The voices in the hall continued loud and bright. Gladys came in to clear the tea things.

"Mary Anne," said Mrs. Abercrombie Jones loudly, "go into the kitchen with Gladys and help her with the dishes, then come in and say goodnight."

Gladys gestured at Marianne to follow.

In the kitchen, Gladys put a tea towel in her hand. She made signs and gestures as she spoke. "I'll wash, you dry. Put the things on the table. I'll put them away." She pointed to the table and repeated "table."

Marianne already knew that word. She liked the simple way Gladys communicated. Gladys had strong, very red hands. She worked quickly. "All done. Off you go—say goodnight to Mrs. Abercrombie Jones. Go on, then."

Marianne would have much preferred to go straight up to her room, but it was only polite to say goodnight, and she had an important question to ask.

Marianne knocked on the dining room door.

"Come in." Mr. Abercrombie Jones put down his paper.

"I must write my mother. Where this house, please?"

Mrs. Abercrombie Jones stared at her. Her husband looked over the top of his paper, said "London, England," and laughed as if he'd said something funny. "Here, I'll write down the address for you," he said.

Even English handwriting looked different.

"Also, please, your name?"

The lady said, "Mr. and Mrs. Abercrombie Jones."

He wrote some more. "Bit of a mouthful, isn't it? Tell you what? You call me Uncle Geoffrey; and my wife, Aunt Vera. Go on, try it. I'll write it down for you."

His wife said something to him, and did not look pleased.

Marianne said, "Onkel Geoffrey," sounding a soft J as in the German Ja. Then, "Aunt Wera."

The newspaper went up over the Onkel's face, and Marianne could see the paper shaking. *He's laughing at me. What's so funny?* Vati always said she had a good English accent.

Aunt Vera said, "Mary Anne, in English we say V; it is a hard sound, and Uncle Geoffrey's name is pronounced with a G. Do you understand?"

Marianne nodded. She was so tired. "Please, Aunt Wera, I need stamp," and she held out one of the big round pennies that had been given to her for the ten marks each child had managed to exchange in Harwich.

Uncle Geoffrey waved the penny away, took out his wallet, and gave her a stamp.

"A present."

"Sank you. Goodnight."

"Goodnight, Mary Anne," Aunt Vera said with a sigh.

The Onkel grunted something behind his paper.

Marianne closed the door and went upstairs. Back in her room, she undressed quickly and tried to get under the bedclothes. The blanket and sheet were tucked in so tightly under the mattress that she could hardly pull them free. *How do people get into bed in this country?* The sheets were so cold they felt damp. She longed for her cosy feather bed.

Marianne got up again, put on her dressing gown and socks, and took her writing paper from her suitcase. Then she sat up on the bed and began her first letter home, carefully copying out her new address.

She wrote: "Dear Mutti and Vati," and stopped. Even writing a letter presented problems. *Should I write to both my parents? What about my grandparents?* If the Nazis got hold of her letter, they'd find Mutti and shout: "Where is your husband?" She knew Opa would shout back: "Leave us alone," and they'd all be dragged off to prison.

Marianne crossed out "Vati." Now that Mutti was moving to Düsseldorf to live with Oma and Opa, they could share her letter and get in touch with her father when it was safe to do so. *If only*

I'd had a chance to say good-bye to them all. Marianne wondered how her father felt when he found out she'd left for England. *How could our lives have changed so fast? One minute we were all together and the next, I'm here, in this cold green room, in a house where people talk loudly at me and laugh at things I can't understand.* The linoleum creaked outside her door. *Is someone coming in to say goodnight, to tuck me in?* No one did. Doors shut. The house was silent.

I'll write my letter tomorrow. Marianne got into bed, pulled the covers over her head, and held her poor skinny teddy bear tightly. She talked to him the way she used to when she was a little girl. "We're on holiday abroad, that's all. The reason you feel strange is because it's only the second night away from home. You'll soon get used to it."

If she kept her eyes closed and concentrated on teddy's familiar old fur smell, home didn't seem so far away.

Marianne half whispered, half sang the words of the lullaby her mother used to sing to her:

> *Sleep my baby sleep,*
> *Your Daddy guards the sheep.*
> *Mother shakes the gentle tree*
> *The petals fall with dreams for thee*
> *Sleep my baby sleep.*

Teddy's thinning fur was wet with tears before the song was over. They slept.

5

Marianne woke up on her first Saturday in England and stared at the overhead lightbulb. It was on. She must have fallen asleep before she'd switched it off.

She was starving. When she went down to the kitchen, it was lovely and warm. A place had been set for Marianne at one end of the scrubbed table.

"Porridge," said Gladys, as she placed a bowl of some kind of gray pudding in front of Marianne. "Here, I'll show you." She sprinkled sugar over the top and poured milk from a glass bottle, then swiftly cut triangles of toast and arranged them in a silver toast rack on a tray and left the room.

Marianne eagerly spooned up the porridge. It was lucky that Gladys wasn't there just then because the first mouthful almost made Marianne gag. Quickly she scraped the food into the sink and turned on the tap, so that by the time Gladys came back,

Marianne was sitting down again, the empty bowl in front of her. She could almost smell the warm crusty rolls her mother always served for breakfast, with homemade black cherry jam. She wanted to be with her so much that she had to dig her nails into her palms to stop from crying.

Marianne tried to imagine what her mother was doing. She might be in Düsseldorf by now. After they'd got the notice from Mrs. Schwartz saying she wouldn't allow Jewish tenants in the building anymore, Mutti had said she'd leave as soon as she'd packed up.

"I don't think I can bear it," Marianne said, and only Gladys' stare of surprise and her "what did you say?" made her realize she'd spoken aloud, and in German. *I mustn't do that again. Do the other kids from the transport feel this mixed up?*

Mrs. Abercrombie Jones walked into the kitchen, her coat over her arm.

"Good morning, Mary Anne."

"Good morning, Aunt. . . ." Marianne had forgotten how to pronounce the "aunt's" name.

"Aunt Vera," prompted her sponsor. "Gladys, we are leaving now."

Leaving? Who is leaving? Leaving means going away. Am I being returned to Liverpool Street Station?

Marianne heard her name—she was supposed to do something. *What is it?* Marianne knew she had to pay more attention. She'd missed most of their conversation. She didn't know why her thoughts kept drifting.

Mrs. Abercrombie Jones left the kitchen.

Gladys put a duster in Marianne's hand. "You dust downstairs. Come on, I'll show you."

Marianne was afraid she might break something, or put things back in the wrong place, and only dusted around objects, not daring to move anything. At last she was done and could go upstairs, make her bed, and settle down to write home.

' Marianne didn't want to upset her mother. She was determined to hide her homesickness and how much she wished she'd never come. Instead, she tried to write cheerfully.

12 Circus Road,
St. John's Wood,
London, NW8
England

December 3, 1938

Dear Mutti,

I arrived safely. I liked the boat. I have my own room at the top of the house. There is a garden. I have plenty to eat and can understand a lot of English words. Mrs. Abercrombie Jones, the lady who took me in, says I can start school on Monday.

I was so happy when I found your letter. I'll remember what you wrote about looking at the same sky even though we are living in different countries.

The scene in the train compartment, when the Gestapo emptied the contents of the suitcases on the floor, flashed in front of Marianne. She'd never forget the greedy eyes of the man who'd stolen Werner's stamp album. Funny how she could remember the names of every one of the children she'd traveled with, yet found it so hard to recall Aunt Vera's.

Marianne tried not to think about the way the Gestapo officer had hit her bear across his knee, the way he'd wrenched off the head of Sophie's doll. She relived the moment when she'd edged her foot forward to cover the letter from her mother that had slipped out of its hiding place in the sleeve of Marianne's party dress.

Marianne got out of bed and ran across the cold floor to get her mother's letter from its hiding place in the lining in her suitcase. She smoothed the page carefully and read her mother's words:

My dearest daughter,

You will be far away from me when you read this letter. It is so hard to let you go. I watched you sleeping last night as though you were still a small baby. I wished I could change my mind and keep you here, but that would be too selfish.

You are going to a better, safer life. Here, there might be no life at all. One day you will understand why I had to let you go. If only we had more time together. Someone else will lengthen your clothes, buy you new shoes, tie your hair. Did it grow into curls as you always hoped it would? I miss you already. I will miss having to nag you for coming in late. I will miss complaining about your messy room, or you not doing your homework. I will miss your first grown-up party. Will you still love to dance?

Please try to understand, Marianne, why I must miss all your growing up, all these special things. Because, I love you. I want to give you the very best life there is, and that means a chance to grow up in a free country. Here there is only fear.

I pray that you, and all the children whose parents send them away, will find loving families. I will think of you every day, and wish for your happiness, and that you will grow up into a good honorable person.

Wherever you are, wherever I am, at night we will be looking at the same sky.

Always, your loving Mutti

She folded up the letter carefully and put it back in her suit-case. She knew she would never own anything more precious than this. Marianne had to wipe her eyes before she could continue writing her own letter.

"I'm fine." *Will Mutti know this is a lie? I'm not fine. I'm afraid.* Not afraid of being beaten up in the streets by gangs of Hitler Youth, nor the kind of fear she'd felt when she saw the body of the man tumbling down from the window of his house in the square. This was a kind of fear she'd never experienced before—wanting to cry all the time because she didn't know what to do, or what was expected of her; not knowing how long it would be before Mutti could come for her; afraid because she did not belong anywhere and was trying not to show how strange she felt in this English house.

"Please give my love to <u>everyone</u>." Marianne underlined the word twice. "Don't worry about me. I know you'll try to come here soon.

> Much love and many kisses,
> From Marianne"

When Marianne asked Gladys where to post her letter, Gladys said, "Turn right at the end of the street. The pillar-box is around the corner; it's red." Marianne found the way easily.

She'd be brave, walk on and explore a bit. There was nothing else for her to do. She hadn't seen any books or games when she was dusting.

Marianne walked along the High Street. The shops were crowded, and so were the pavements. Some windows already had Christmas decorations in them. Marianne looked for a bookshop, and found one. It was much bigger than the one her father used to work in. She looked eagerly at the display. At the top of a pyramid of books was a familiar red cover—*Mein Kampf* by Adolf Hitler. The black swastika looked huge. It stared at her.

Suddenly Marianne began to run, pushing through the shoppers as if Hitler himself were after her. She did not stop until she had a pain in her side, and her lungs hurt. She leaned against some park railings to catch her breath. She must stop being so silly. Her father always talked about "freedom to choose." This was a free country, so bookshops could sell anything they wanted to. But why choose that book?

Marianne went inside the park. It didn't look like a place to be afraid of. A river wound in curves through the green lawns. Fat ducks swam among reeds, or sheltered under overhanging trees. Unexpected fountains, small ornate bridges, and paving stones in intricate patterns surprised her. A small girl bowling a red hoop just avoided crashing into her. "Be careful," called the girl's mother. Marianne knew what the words meant from the woman's gesture. She thought longingly of the times she'd groaned when Mutti told her to be careful. She'd give anything to hear it now.

An old lady was feeding pigeons. She made room on the bench for Marianne to sit down, then carefully poured some bird seed from a paper bag into Marianne's hand. A pigeon alighted on Marianne's wrist. A small boy with a red kite ran around making bird noises and the pigeons scattered. The old lady said, "Good-bye, dear," and left.

It was getting cold; other people were leaving. This was the first time Marianne could remember sitting on a bench that wasn't marked FOR ARYANS ONLY—the first time she'd been in a park where Jews could sit anywhere they liked, not only on yellow benches. It was late; the afternoon was over.

When she found her way out of the gates, she didn't know which way to go. She must have come out through a different entrance. It was almost dark. *I'm lost.* An English policeman walked past her. *Is it safe to speak to him?*

"Please," Marianne sobbed.

He turned and walked back and looked at her. "Now then," he said, "no need to cry. Did someone hurt you?"

Marianne hadn't realized she was crying. She shook her head, wiped her eyes, and fumbled for the piece of paper with her address on it. The policeman took it. He spoke too fast for Marianne to understand more than a few "lefts" and "rights."

"Please, I don't understand," she said.

"Follow me," said the policeman, and walked her all the way home to her gate.

Aunt Vera's horrified face, when Gladys opened the front door and said, "Here she is, Madam," told Marianne that she must have seen the policeman. "Where have you been? What will the neighbors think?" She sounded very angry. Not worried— angry—embarrassed angry.

"Sorry," said Marianne. "I lose the way."

Aunt Vera talked loudly at her for a long time before sending her into the kitchen for tea. Marianne was in disgrace.

6

Aunt Vera came into the kitchen, where Marianne faced an unfamiliar Sunday breakfast of fried bread, bacon, and eggs. "Good morning. Finish your breakfast quickly, Mary Anne. Church begins at 10:00 A.M. Gladys, dinner at the usual time, so you can finish early. Mary Anne may eat with us in the dining room today." Mrs. Abercrombie Jones left the kitchen and shut the door.

Marianne carried her plate to the sink. "I wash dishes?" she asked.

"No, thanks. Better get ready for church," said Gladys.

"Please, what is 'church'?"

Gladys turned to her with a look of shock.

Now what have I done? This was the trouble in a new country—you never knew when you said or did the wrong thing.

Aunt Vera called out impatiently, "Mary Anne, put your hat on. We'll be late."

Marianne walked behind Aunt Vera and Uncle Geoffrey along the High Street to a beautiful old gray stone building, with a tall spire. Organ music greeted them. Marianne knew immediately why Gladys had looked so horrified when she'd asked what "church" was. "Church" meant *Kirche*. She'd forgotten the word, that's all. She used to pass *Neuekirche*—New Church—on the way to visit her father's bookshop, and the French Church was near *Unter den Linden* on the *Französichstrasse*. This was the first time she'd been inside one.

They sat down in one of the long shiny pews. Men and women together. Black leather prayer books were on a ledge in front of them, and a cloth-covered footstool was on the floor at each person's place. Marianne was so busy looking at the stained glass window of Jesus wearing long white robes, surrounded by sheep, that she was late standing up. Aunt Vera gave her a small push. Everyone sang, even Aunt Vera and Uncle Geoffrey. Then they all sat down again.

A man who looked strangely familiar, dressed in black robes covered by a sort of white overshirt, began to speak. He went on for a long time and Marianne dozed. She opened her eyes when he stopped, and there was a great shuffle while everyone knelt on the little footstools.

Suddenly Marianne remembered where she'd seen the speaker before. It was the "spy in black," the one who'd come to greet her on Friday for tea.

Marianne tugged at Aunt Vera's sleeve. "Please, Aunt Wera . . ."

"Not now, Mary Anne," Aunt Vera hissed. "The vicar is speaking."

Marianne tried to stifle nervous laughter, but couldn't quite manage it. How could she have thought this man was a spy!

Aunt Vera gripped Marianne's arm and said, "*Sh.*" She bent her pink face over her book.

Marianne imagined what she'd write to her mother about her first visit to church. It was beautiful and seemed like a nice quiet place to be, even if it wasn't a synagogue. She was sure God wouldn't mind her being here!

On the way out her "spy" shook hands with everyone. "I am glad to welcome you to our church, my dear," he said to Marianne in his accented German.

Marianne nearly giggled again. She bit her lip and looked down.

On the way home Aunt Vera said, "You disgraced me, Mary Anne. Everyone was looking at us. You are old enough to know better. Well? Say something."

Marianne was lost in the jumble of words.

Uncle Geoffrey looked at Marianne. "Tell Aunt Vera you're sorry," he said sternly. "Say sorry." He raised his voice.

"I'm wery sorry, Aunt Wera."

"Ver, Vera—speak properly, Mary Anne. You're not trying! Thank goodness you start school tomorrow."

They walked back in silence.

Gladys had set Marianne a place in the dining room, but reset Marianne's place in the kitchen after Aunt Vera spoke to her.

7

That Sunday night Marianne was too excited and nervous to sleep. She'd been in England only three days, and tomorrow was the first day of school.

She got out of bed and checked her clothes again. The linoleum felt as cold to her bare feet as if she were outdoors. Marianne set herself a test to ensure a smooth day at school. She opened the window, ignoring the sharp December wind that blew in. Slowly, she counted backwards from one hundred. She had to do it without shivering, or start again. She did it the first time. *Everything will be alright now.* She closed the window gratefully.

When Marianne finally went to sleep, she dreamed of her math teacher in Berlin. He was dressed all in black; his high boots shone. There was menace in each threatening step that marched towards her. His mouth was twisted in hatred, and opened and closed angrily, but she could not hear his words. His hand reached out for her teddy bear, and raised it to show the class before hurling the bear through the window with a force that shattered the glass pane.

"No!"

Marianne woke up. *Did I scream?* The house was still. "Only a bad dream." She could hear her mother's voice in her head, imagine her forehead being stroked.

Next morning Marianne walked beside Aunt Vera, who had been giving her instructions ever since they left the house. She couldn't get the nightmare out of her mind.

"Mary Anne, are you listening? Answer me, please."

"Pardon, Aunt Wera?" Marianne said.

"I said, oh, never mind. Here we are. I'll come to the office with you."

They crossed the playground, which was full of laughing, skipping girls. Some boys kicked a football; one almost ran into Mrs. Abercrombie Jones. She gave him her iciest look.

Aunt Vera handed Marianne over to the secretary along with a note, said good-bye, and left.

Marianne spelt out her name, and managed to remember her new address.

"Did you bring your records?" the secretary asked.

Marianne looked at her. *Records?* Thank goodness she'd brought her dictionary. She looked up the word. Marianne shook her head.

The secretary said, "Please ask your mother to send them."

A door opened and an imposing-looking lady, with white hair, entered briskly. She read Aunt Vera's note. "You must be Mary Anne Kohn." She shook hands firmly with Marianne. "I am Miss Barton, the headmistress. I am going to take you to your new class. Come along," she said matter-of-factly.

The morning was strange, not a bit like school in Berlin. The teacher gave her a desk in the second row and a curly-haired girl called Bridget was assigned to stay with her for the day and show her what to do.

Assembly was in the big hall. The teachers sat on the stage, and the headmistress stood in front, at a lectern. "Good morning, school," she said.

All the students stood and answered, "Good morning, Miss Barton."

Then they sang a song about Jerusalem being built in a green land. Marianne thought of her father raising his glass and saying, "Next year in Jerusalem." Perhaps they'd all be together in London soon.

Miss Barton said, "We are delighted to welcome a new student to Prince Albert Elementary School. Mary Anne is a refugee from Germany, and we hope she will be happy here."

Every head swiveled to look at her.

Bridget nudged her and whispered, "Don't worry."

Marianne concentrated on pretending to be somewhere else, but felt her cheeks going red all the same.

The morning passed easily. It was good to get back to a routine. Marianne was so busy she didn't have time to miss her mother. Did that make her a bad person? Shouldn't she feel miserable all the time?

Bridget said, "Must be awful to start school so late in the term—poor you." She shared her milk with Marianne at milk time because she hadn't brought any money.

Even math was alright, nothing like the nightmare. The teacher wrote problems on the board that seemed to involve a greengrocer, a customer, and many questions about carrots, potatoes, and onions, and how much they all cost if one added more, or took some away. The teacher saw Marianne desperately looking up words in her dictionary, and called her up to his desk. A boy in the back row snickered and whispered something about Huns. He was given extra homework. Mr. Neame sent Bridget down to the "infants" to get a box of English play money, and he wrote on a card what all the money represented, and told Marianne to learn it:

ONE FARTHING = 1/4d OF ONE PENNY.
ONE HALFPENNY = 1/2d OF ONE PENNY.
TWELVE PENNIES = ONE SHILLING.
TWENTY SHILLINGS = ONE POUND.

(Tomorrow, she would buy two bottles of milk—one for Bridget. Milk was 1/2d a bottle.) There was also a threepenny piece and a sixpence, two of those making one shilling. There was a big silver coin and that was called half a crown, eight of those making a pound. It was very complicated. Marianne wondered if she'd ever understand it all.

In the afternoon there was drawing, and music. The first thing Marianne noticed when she entered the music room was the writing on the blackboard—it was in English and German:

O Christmas tree, O Christmas tree, With faithful
    leaves unchanging;
O *Tannenbaum*, O *Tannenbaum, Wie treu sind deine Blätter!*
Not only green in summer's heat, But also winter's snow
    and sleet,
Du grünst nicht nur zur Sommerzeit, Nein, auch im Winter
    wenn es schneit,
O Christmas tree, O Christmas tree, With faithful
    leaves unchanging.
O *Tannenbaum*, O *Tannenbaum, Wie treu sind deine Blätter!*

The teacher said, "Today we are going to learn the words of 'O Christmas Tree' in the original German. Mary Anne can help us with the pronunciation. Would you read the German text please, Mary Anne."

Everyone waited. Marianne wasn't quite sure what she had to do, so she didn't do anything. The teacher picked up the wooden pointer from her desk and raised it. Marianne bit her thumbnail. *Is the pointer for me?* She hid her hand; her cuticle was bleeding a bit. The pointer rested on "O *Tannenbaum.*"

"Begin please, Mary Anne," said the teacher and smiled at her.

By the time she'd read to the end of the first line, Marianne was transported back to a Berlin winter. She remembered standing on tiptoe in the street as a very little girl so that she could look through the windows at the Christmas trees, with their white candles of flame making halos around each green branch. Her mother had made her hurry away long before she'd gazed her fill at the brightness. "It's not polite to stare into someone's home," she'd said.

Great soft flakes of snow clinging to coats, resting on the cobbles, on the streetlights. Flags hung from every building. Flags, red as blood, their centers snow-white circles and, in the middle, swastikas black as ebony. Red and white and black, like the story of "Snow White" by the Brothers Grimm.

Marianne's heart pounded so loudly she was sure everyone else could hear it. Her voice shook. She just managed to finish reading the last line.

"Thank you, Mary Anne. Now all together, class," the teacher said, and raised her pointer again.

At the end of the day they were given homework—some spelling—a whole list of words connected with winter: Arctic, blizzard, chilling, freeze, glacial, icicle, numb, shepherd, snowdrift, snowstorm. They were told to write a sentence to show the meaning of each word.

That night Marianne looked up the words in her dictionary and wrote: "Aunt Vera's face is glacial when she looks at me. I feel numb with sorrow without my mother."

It took her hours to finish the homework, and her head ached.

8

"Tomorrow when you come home from school," Aunt Vera said one afternoon in late January, "you may help me serve tea to my friends. Change your blouse and brush your hair before you come in."

"Yes, Aunt Vera. Many ladies are coming?" asked Marianne.

"Mrs. Brewster, Mrs. Stephens, and Mrs. Courtland—my bridge group."

Tomorrow. Marianne hurried upstairs. She had lots to prepare: write down her mother's address in Düsseldorf, check out words in her dictionary, and practice her pronunciation. One of those ladies might have work for her parents!

Next day, after scrubbing the ink off her fingers with pumice stone, she handed round plates of thin bread and butter, scones, and sandwiches. Gladys had given her an encouraging wink before she entered the dining room.

Marianne waited for her opportunity to speak.

"Your frock is darling, Phoebe," Mrs. Stephens said.

"Oh, do you like it? I'm so glad. I've found the most wonderful dressmaker. A little Jewess who's set up shop in the Cromwell Road. She works out of two rooms, my dear, only arrived last year from Vienna. Had her own salon there, I believe. Lost everything to the Nazis. She uses a borrowed sewing machine. Her prices are quite reasonable and she'll copy any design." Mrs. Courtland paused and sipped her tea.

"Please," said Marianne, "my mother can sew also, and she is most wonderful cook, and my father is very clever and speaks good English. They want to work in England." Marianne held out the paper on which she'd printed her mother's address. "Here is the place for you to write."

Aunt Vera took it, crumpled the paper into a ball, and dropped it onto the tea trolley.

Then everyone began to speak at once, as if Marianne had done something awful, like spilling the tea.

"Are your parents in Vienna too, my dear?" asked Mrs. Brewster.

"Rather sweet and brave of her to ask. Don't be cross, Vera," said Mrs. Stephens.

"Of course, Dora's been with us for years. I don't think she'd approve if I brought a *foreigner* into her kitchen. No one bakes like your Gladys, Vera, my dear. You are so fortunate. Do let me try one of those little scones now," said Mrs. Courtland.

Aunt Vera found her voice at last. The lines of her mouth looked pinched. Marianne sensed her anger. "We can manage now, Mary Anne. Please ask Gladys to bring in more hot water."

After the guests had left, and Marianne had finished helping Gladys with the drying up, Gladys said, "Don't know what you did, but you're to go and see Mrs. Abercrombie Jones."

Marianne hesitated outside the dining room. She rubbed the sore place on her thumb, where she'd bitten the skin. Then she walked in and stood in front of Aunt Vera.

"I am very displeased with you, Mary Anne. I understand that you miss your mother, but I cannot allow you to make a nuisance of yourself. You embarrassed me, *and* my friends. What you did is like begging."

"It is wrong to try save my parents?" Marianne asked softly.

"Don't exaggerate, Mary Anne. They must wait their turn like other refugees. It is not a question of saving, but of good manners. Now, I am waiting for an apology, and a promise not to behave like this again in my house."

"Sorry," said Marianne.

"And, I've been meaning to speak to you about your hands."

"They are quite clean, Aunt Vera. I brush them."

"You must stop biting your nails, and the cuticles. It is an ugly habit. Try harder in everything, Mary Anne. Now go and finish your homework. Goodnight."

Instead of doing her homework, Marianne began a long delayed letter to her cousin Ruth. She'd emigrated to Amsterdam with her parents last November. Uncle Frank was a furrier and had a job to go to in Holland. That's why they'd got a visa and been allowed to leave Germany.

12 Circus Road,
St. John's Wood,
London, NW8
England

January 25, 1939

Dear Ruth,

I memorized your address, didn't want to risk anyone finding it on the train. Now that I'm in England fears like that seem far-fetched, but we know they aren't, don't we?

I bet you thought I'd forgotten you—of course I haven't. But you can imagine the panic when we had less than twenty-four hours notice that I was coming to England. Settling down here and learning different rules and being *nagged* in two languages from both sides of the Channel isn't my idea of paradise. Mutti writes constantly that I must be grateful and obedient. In England they expect you to be quiet and invisible, but for different reasons than in Berlin. Not to be safe, but to be polite.

I've been here seven weeks now and I've learnt more English than I did in two years in Germany.

The first couple of weeks I thought I'd die of home-sickness, and it's still hard sometimes, specially when I'm bursting with news and no one's there to listen.

School is mostly alright. Some of the kids tease me and imitate my accent, but it's normal teasing, you know, not the throwing stones kind. I haven't found any other Jewish students. If they're there, they are keeping very quiet about it. I can't very well stand up in Assembly and say, "Excuse me, is there anyone here who's Jewish?" I don't expect there were enough Jewish homes to go around for all the *Kindertransport* children. It was a bit of a muddle, especially as no one was expecting me. Did I tell you, I was on the very first one ever?

Bridget, a new friend, helps me with English. Her father is a doctor who left Ireland at eighteen. In Ireland the different religions are always quarreling and the English and the Irish—at least some of them—don't like each other. Bridget's been called names, even though she was born here. We have a lot in common. I'll miss her when she goes to another school—a grammar school for girls. They have beautiful school uniforms, and always have to wear a black velour hat with the school badge when they go out. The motto is in Latin and means 'Trust in God.' I do trust Him, but I wish He'd hurry up and bring my parents over. Aunt Vera (Mrs. Abercrombie Jones, who took me in) is not a great substitute for a mother, even if I was looking for one, which I'm not!

Write soon and tell me all your news. Love to you all from your loving cousin,

Marianne

Marianne had just sealed the envelope, when she heard the door-bell. Footsteps came running up the stairs. A moment later, Bridget knocked at her door. "Ready for your English lesson? I brought Pa's *Times*—you can practice reading from it."

"Bridget, I have a great idea," said Marianne.

"What?" asked Bridget.

"Promise no word to Aunt Wera," Marianne said.

Bridget groaned. "Vera, *V* like vampire, *W* is like in water. Yes, I promise."

"I have to find work for my mother. I will knock on doors and ask. Aunt Vera must not find out. Will you help me write what to say?" Marianne asked her friend.

"It's a brilliant idea—of course I will," said Bridget.

"Sank you," said Marianne.

"*Th*, put your tongue between your teeth like this, thank you," said Bridget.

"Thank you," said Marianne. "Is better?"

"Much," said Bridget. "We can put the advertisements under doors, even if no one's home."

"Hurry, Bridget, I can't wait longer," said Marianne.

"Let's look what they say in the *Times* under DOMESTIC SITUATIONS REQUIRED. You read it, Mary Anne. It's good prac-tice for you."

Marianne said, "This one's from a girl in Berlin! From *Turinerstrasse*. Listen: 'I am a girl of eighteen who likes dressmak-ing and is fond of children.' We can write like this for my mother?" She almost shouted.

"Easy. Just change the words a bit. I'll write it down for now, and type it up on Pa's typewriter later. I'm a bit slow, but I'm accurate. We'll go together. Two's much better than one, and if there are watch dogs, I have a great affinity with animals," Bridget declared.

Marianne and Bridget jumped up and down in excitement.

Gladys came hurrying up the stairs. "Mrs. Abercrombie Jones wants to know if you are deliberately trying to give her a headache?"

"I'm very sorry, Gladys, please tell Aunt Wera."

Gladys closed the door behind her.

"Listen," said Bridget. "Gifted Jewish dressmaker . . ." she started to write.

"Say good cook, no, wery good cook," said Marianne. "Love the children."

Bridget interpreted this as: "Gifted Jewish dressmaker, excellent cook, fond of children, wishes to come to England as a domestic."

"Now, what about your father—what can he do in the house?" asked Bridget.

"Nothing. Vati cannot boil water for coffee. He only likes to read." Marianne smiled, thinking of her father.

"No problem," said Bridget. "We'll say 'Husband works as a gardener / handyman.' That means he cleans shoes, and cuts grass, rakes leaves, that kind of thing. . . . Now give me the address, and I'll say 'Please write immediately to. . . .'"

Marianne printed her mother's name and address. "Thank you, Bridget."

"I'll start right away. How many do we need?" Bridget asked.

"More than one hundred?" Marianne asked hopefully.

"Tell you what—I'll begin with twenty-five, and we'll see how many replies we get."

They ran downstairs.

"Good-bye, Mrs. Abercrombie Jones. I've finished Mary Anne's English lesson. I have to go now," said Bridget.

"Thank you, Bridget. Please give my regards to your parents."

"I will," said Bridget. "And Mother sends her regards to you, too."

"You would never know that child comes from Irish stock. She has beautiful manners. You may go and help Gladys bring in the tea things."

"Yes, Aunt Wera . . . Vera."

Marianne heard Mrs. Abercrombie Jones say, "Do you think she does it on purpose, Geoffrey?"

9

On Saturday after lunch, Marianne and Bridget set off to deliver the first batch of DOMESTIC SITUATIONS REQUIRED.

"We'll start at the top of Avenue Road—those big houses looking over the park. We'd better go to the back, where it says TRADESMEN'S ENTRANCE," Bridget said.

"You think we look like tradesmen?" Marianne giggled to cover up her nerves.

"Mary Anne, we're not doing anything wrong. It's not like we're asking for money."

Bridget had this knack of knowing what Marianne was really thinking. "I'll do the first one," she said.

"No, I must do it. Look, this house is number five, my lucky number," said Marianne. "Even when I was small, I used to make bargains with myself. I would make a kind of promise. Walk to the corner, keep head up. If men in uniform come, if I keep walking, if I'm brave, something good will happen."

"I do that all the time too. Alright, you ring this bell; I'll do the next one."

There was no reply, though they heard the wireless playing though the kitchen window. Marianne pushed the note under the door. The next two houses were closed up, the milk crates sitting empty on the back step.

Then they got three answers one after the other. In one house a very grand butler wearing a striped green waistcoat said, "I will make sure this gets delivered, young ladies."

"Let's do one more," said Bridget, and then walk over to Gloucester Place. "We don't want to put all our eggs in one basket."

"Sometimes," Marianne said, "English drives me mad. Where is the basket with the eggs?"

Bridget's face went red and she laughed so hard the tears streamed down her face. "It means we'll have a better chance of success if we don't concentrate on only one street," Bridget said, when she could speak again! "It's a figure of speech—understand?"

Marianne groaned. "Thank you," she said, exaggerating the *th* sound.

She took the last note for Avenue Road, rang the bell, waited a moment, then pushed her paper under the door. It opened suddenly and she almost fell over the threshold.

"Little girls, vot you doink here?"

Marianne straightened up to face a plump young woman with dark hair tucked under a maid's cap. She wore a pinafore over her striped uniform. Their advertisement was in her hand.

"Come inside, it is cold. My name is Miriam Levy. I vork here."

Bridget hesitated, but Marianne pulled her arm. "It's alright. Trust me." To the woman in uniform, she said, "I'm Marianne Kohn from Charlottenburg, Berlin. I'm trying to bring my parents to England. Do you speak German?" Then she put out her hand and the woman shook it, nodding her head. Marianne saw that she was only a few years older than they were.

Miriam replied in German, "I'm so glad to meet you. I came to England at the end of last October. I'm trying to bring my mother over too. My father was arrested after I left. My brother is in Sachsenhausen Concentration Camp. He is only seventeen." She pressed her hand against her lips to stop their trembling.

"My father was there for a while. I don't know where he is now," Marianne said.

Bridget coughed several times to remind them of her presence.

"Oh, Bridget, I'm so sorry. It was rude of us not to speak English, but Miriam's a refugee too. Miriam, this is my best friend, Bridget O'Malley. She's helping me."

"I am wery pleased to meet you. Come sit. I just now was making the coffee. Madam is shopping. I pour you a cup, or you like better tea?"

"Tea, thank you, Miriam," Bridget replied.

"Coffee, please," Marianne said gratefully. The smell instantly brought back memories of home: poppy seed rolls on the blue and white plate; Mutti and she drinking coffee (hers mostly milk); Mutti's look of mixed horror and amusement as Marianne confessed to walking down *Kurfürstendamm*, watching the elegant ladies perched outside on little gold painted chairs at the pavement *Konditorei* tables; imitating the waiter's voice as he offered them whipped cream on huge portions of apple cake—"*Mit Schlag Gnädige, Frau?*"; the chestnut trees in blossom in spring, rows and rows of them; the lights that never went out in the city; the words of the language she was born with that she didn't have to struggle with every minute. Marianne looked at Miriam. *Does she feel this kind of homesickness, too? For what we've lost, for what we've never had because we aren't Aryans?*

Miriam offered them biscuits from a tin.

"You go ahead, speak German. I don't mind," said Bridget.

Miriam said, "No, I never vant, but perhaps some words—if I don't know how to say."

Marianne asked her, "How did you manage to come over?"

Unconsciously, Miriam replied in her native tongue, "I met Mrs. Smedley in Berlin in 1936. She was on holiday with her husband, for the Olympic Games. I was eighteen. She asked me for directions to her hotel. I walked with her, then she invited me in. I explained it was not allowed because I was Jewish. She took my arm and said, 'I am an English tourist; no one will stop me.' So brave! We had coffee in her suite. She told me if I ever wanted to go to England, if things got worse, to write to her. When my father's business was taken away, and I lost my job as his bookkeeper, my mother told me I should write to Mrs. Smedley. It was an opportunity. I did, and she sponsored me. She is very kind. I make mistakes, but she makes allowances for me. My friend Hannah lives in London too, but she lives in one little room. When she wants a bath, she must pay sixpence for the hot water." Miriam poured more coffee. "She works in a household where they are mean to her. I think she is often hungry."

"Why don't the Jews in England do more to help?" Marianne burst out in German. "Sorry, Bridget, just this one question."

Miriam said, "They help all they can, but there are so many of us trying to get out of Europe. Mrs. Smedley says in England less than one percent of the population is Jewish. A few are rich, but most are like us—poor, or immigrants, trying to bring their relatives to England. I'll keep this paper, Marianne. I might hear of a place for your mother."

The front doorbell rang.

"That will be Mrs. Smedley. I must go." This time she spoke English.

"Good-bye. Thank you," the girls said, and went out the back way.

On the way home, Bridget said, "You looked funny in there."

"That's not very polite." Marianne was offended.

"I didn't mean funny 'funny,' only different. I haven't heard your name said like that before. Marianne, it sounds nice. Look at the time—Pa has fits if I'm home after dark."

"Thanks for coming with me, Bridget."

"Think nothing of it," said Bridget grandly.

They went all the way back without stepping on the cracks of the pavement even once. It couldn't hurt, and it might help bring Marianne's parents over to England more quickly.

10

Two weeks later, Marianne heard from Ruth.

107 Leidsegracht, Apt. 5,
Amsterdam,
Holland

February 6, 1939

Dear Marianne,

It was wonderful to hear from you at last. I'm quite jealous. It must be so much more romantic emigrating across water, instead of to a country where you can just walk across the border. Not that anyone can do that anymore.

When we found out that your train had actually stopped for a couple of hours in Holland, Mother got in a state, and cried. She went on and on about her little niece and no one to meet you, and if she'd known, she could have brought you food parcels. Why is it that mothers think we're going to die of starvation the moment we leave home? Incidentally, the rumor is that English cooking is terrible. I hope that's not true—you're quite skinny enough.

Seriously, Marianne, I think you are very brave to go so far away by yourself, away from us all. Papa says the farther the better. He doesn't think we can ever be far enough away from Hitler. But parents are difficult. When I talk about my plans, I'm told I don't know anything. Poor you being told off by everyone.

I joined a Youth *Aliyah*. The idea is to train us to go to Palestine one day. We *should* have a country of our own, then no one could hurt us anymore. I know it would be a hard life, living communally on a kibbutz and sharing everything, and working on the land, but it's worthwhile, don't you think? At our meetings we learn songs and dances and have a lot of fun. In September we are going on a three-day camping expedition. Mother says I'll "grow out of it," that I'm too spoilt for such a hard life. Papa wants me to be apprenticed to a furrier. He says, "Coats you always need." Not my idea of a fulfilling life. I'm determined to get to Palestine somehow.

I like the sound of your new friend. Perhaps we'll all meet one day. Meanwhile, Mother says you are all in our prayers. We talk about you often.

> Keep in touch, please.
> Your loving cousin,
> Ruth

One week later Marianne received a postcard from Czechoslovakia. The pictures were of the gleaming spires, medieval roofs and turrets of Prague—Vati had always told her it was one of the most beautiful capitals in Europe. She didn't know anyone there. The card was printed, and undated. It said:

Hello Marianne,

    This traveler has found a beautiful city, and hopes to stay awhile. There are cafés, galleries, and bookshops. Some still sell our favorite books. I often think of that fine supper I shared with you and your dear mother.

> Love and greetings to you both,
> D.

D for David. It's from Vati. He's safe! Why has he disguised his identity? Isn't Prague free? She was glad, though, that he was being so cautious. There were spies everywhere. Now, he'd surely come to England. How clever of him to give the Nazis the slip.

Marianne wished she could ask him how he crossed the frontier. It was like a miracle. She twirled around the room in stocking feet. Linoleum was wonderful for sliding. And she had to keep warm somehow. No heat reached the bedroom at all.

Marianne huddled back down on her bed and read Vati's card again. She thought of the last time she'd seen him. She could smell the onions frying, see her mother's flushed cheeks, feel her own cheek pressed against the rough texture of Vati's jacket as he hugged her good-bye after supper.

The last time she'd seen him was when he was on the run from the Gestapo. The pit of her stomach felt as empty as it had then, that awful moment after he left again to go into the cold night to hide goodness-knows-where. *Oh, Vati, I hope you're warm and happy now. I hope you know how much I love you.*

"Mary Anne, where are you? Gladys needs help with the silver," Aunt Vera called.

Marianne went down into the kitchen and attacked each piece of cutlery as if she could make all the bad people in the world disappear by polishing them away.

Gladys said, "If all refugees work like you, there won't be any jobs left for us." She smiled, but Marianne was hurt. It seemed if you were a refugee, whatever you did was wrong.

That evening Aunt Vera said, "I see someone sent you a card from Prague. Do you have friends there?"

"My father."

"Oh, I see. Is he on holiday?"

"Beautiful place," said Uncle Geoffrey. "Medieval city, cobbled streets, and all that. That glass decanter set was made in Czechoslovakia."

Marianne looked at them. *Holiday? Don't they realize what is happening?*

"Mary Anne, are you listening? Answer the question."

"Sorry," said Marianne. "No, not holiday. He's running from Hitler, like me."

"Well, that's hardly the same thing. Have you finished your homework?"

"I have ten more words to learn for the spell test."

"Spelling. Run along then, goodnight."

Three weeks later the newspaper headlines declared: NAZI TROOPS MARCH INTO PRAGUE.

Uncle Geoffrey said, "They just let them walk in. What do you expect? Foreigners—no backbone." He made the word "foreigners" sound like a disease.

Marianne borrowed books about Czechoslovakia from the library. There was one with a street map of Prague. She wanted to imagine the places where her father might hide. There were castles and cottages in the countryside. Someone might help him. *First Austria, now Czechoslovakia—where will the Nazis go next?*

That night Marianne woke up and found herself at the top of the stairs. She didn't know how she got there. The next night Gladys found her wandering again, and helped her back to bed.

Afterward, she didn't remember anything about it. Gladys told Mrs. Abercrombie Jones next morning.

"What's all this nonsense I hear about you walking about the house in the middle of the night, Mary Anne? Are you ill?"

"No, Aunt Vera, I'm quite fine," said Marianne, realizing that for once Aunt Vera was not angry.

"Too much tea, Gladys. From now on, Mary Anne is to drink nothing at all after six o'clock."

That night Marianne put books in front of her bed, so that she'd fall and wake herself up. But it didn't work. She told Bridget about walking in her sleep.

"We'll just have to try harder to get a visa for your mother. Look, I've typed up ten more copies of our advertisement," she said.

Marianne replied, "Thanks, Bridget, but you see it's no good looking for a job for a couple anymore. The Nazis have taken over in Czechoslovakia; it'd be hard to escape."

"If he can get out of Berlin, he can do anything," Bridget said comfortingly, but the next day she changed the words on the advertisement, so that there was no longer any mention of "gardener / handyman."

11

Every evening after tea, Marianne spread a double sheet of newspaper on the scullery floor and cleaned the household's shoes. Sometimes yesterday's paper was so interesting that she'd still be there an hour later. Last week there was a story about a famous film star, and Aunt Vera had come in and stopped her reading "such rubbish."

"No wonder you walk in your sleep. I forbid you to read the paper from now on. Finish the shoes and go to bed."

Shoes were a constant problem for Marianne. She wore her Wellingtons most of the time. In school she changed into brown plimsolls, like the other girls.

The Wellingtons were made of black rubber and came to her knees. The boots reminded her of the Gestapo. All the children wore them. In spite of wearing two pairs of socks, her feet were still always freezing.

Marianne rubbed her feet together to stop them itching. She had developed big red bumps on her heels and toes. Chilblains, Gladys called them. They were a fact of life in England, like porridge for breakfast. When her feet warmed up, they got hot and itchy and swollen. Her fingers were red and cracked, too. Gladys told her to leave the dishes for a few days to give her hands a chance to heal.

If Marianne complained to Aunt Vera, she knew she'd be told not to fuss, so she said nothing. She discovered that if she slid under her icy sheets at night and went to sleep before she got warm, her feet didn't keep her awake.

The shoes she'd brought from Berlin were getting awfully tight. They hurt her toes and she couldn't straighten them.

Last Sunday on the way to church, Uncle Geoffrey, who hardly ever noticed her or made personal remarks, said, "Mary Anne, you're hobbling about like an old lady. Put your head up, shoulders back." Before she had a chance to explain that her shoes pinched, the vicar was greeting them. Aunt Vera didn't refer to the incident and Marianne didn't like to ask for new shoes.

Tomorrow there was a jumble sale. Marianne decided she'd donate her outgrown shoes. The sale was for a really good cause— for the Spanish villagers who'd been bombed by the Fascists.

Next day she put her shoes in the box marked JUMBLE. On Friday, school finished an hour early, so they could all go to the gym. Marianne had sixpence to spend. Perhaps she'd be lucky and find a pair of shoes to fit her.

The gymnasium was crammed full—students, teachers, parents, and relatives. One table was doing a huge trade serving tea poured from a big metal urn, at a penny a cup. Marianne made her way to the used-clothes stall. Next to it was a table with second-hand books. She'd just take a quick look. Bridget's birthday was next month. Arthur Ransome's *Swallows and Amazons* was lying at the back of the table, half covered by a Latin dictionary. Marianne picked it up. It was in really nice condition, and only cost twopence. She leafed through it quickly, and came to the part where the children got a telegram from their father: BETTER DROWNED THAN DUFFERS, IF NOT DUFFERS WON'T DROWN.

The first time she'd read that, she couldn't find a translation for "duffers." Now she knew it meant 'someone useless.' It was the kind of thing her father might have said to her in his joking way. Wasn't she like Roger and Kitty and the others? All alone, and she was making decisions as best she could. She *had* to buy the book for Bridget's birthday. They'd both read the library copy, and Bridget had said, "I'd love to have my own." Bridget had become such a good friend, always doing things for her. This could be something Marianne could do to please her. Sometimes Marianne worried that when Bridget went to grammar school, she'd find another best friend, that things wouldn't stay the same between them.

"Are you going to read the whole book before you buy it?" Her math teacher was smiling at her.

"Sorry, Sir," said Marianne and gave him a threepenny bit.

"How much change would you like, Mary Anne?"

"One penny, please," she replied.

Teachers could never resist a chance to teach, even after school.

Mr. Neame said, "Well done," and handed her the book and the change. That left fourpence. It didn't seem much to buy a pair of shoes. Even the worn-out ballet slippers were sevenpence.

"What are you looking for?" the woman helper at the shoe stall asked her.

"Walking shoes, size, um . . . three (that was the size of her Wellingtons) . . . or three and a half. Thank you," Marianne said.

"There's a big box of shoes under the table; I haven't had time to price them yet. Have a look and see if you can find what you want."

Marianne rummaged through them, finding nothing in her size.

"How about this pair? They should do you, nice leather, and only a bit scuffed. They'd soon brush up. They're hardly worn. Let you have them for ninepence."

"Thank you, but I've only got fourpence left."

"Sorry, dear. I don't think I can let them go for that. Tell you what, if I haven't sold them by the time we close at 7:00 P.M., I'll let them go for a bit less. Come back then."

Marianne did some quick calculations: she had fivepence at home, but she needed stamps and toothpaste. She stood there undecided.

Mr. Neame called her over. "Mary Anne, is there a mathematical difficulty I can help you with?"

Suddenly Marianne felt the whole gymnasium go quiet as if, at that moment, everyone was listening. *How can I explain that I have no shoes, that there's no one to tell what any mother would know?* She could feel herself blushing.

"It's . . . that I did not bring enough money to spend, Mr. Neame. It doesn't matter, thank you. I must go now." Marianne started to edge away.

Mr. Neame said, "Do you know what a short-term loan is, Mary Anne?"

She shook her head.

"Suppose you want to buy a shop, but don't have quite enough money to pay for it. You could borrow the money from a bank, and sign a paper to promise to pay the debt by a certain date. Now, how much do you need for your purchase?"

Marianne thought, *He's a kind man. He does not use the word "shoes," and he is pretending that we are having a math lesson.* She said carefully, "I have fourpence here, and I have fivepence at home, but I'm saving it."

"If you want to buy something, as it is for a good cause, I am prepared to make you an indefinite loan. I am sure you will repay me as soon as you can. Do you think your parents would approve?"

"I think so. One day they'll come to England," said Marianne.

"I'll be happy to meet them," said Mr. Neame. "Here is sixpence."

"Thank you very much, Sir," said Marianne, and gave him one penny change. She handed over her money to the woman behind the shoe table. Marianne put her purchases in her schoolbag, and walked out of the gymnasium. She told herself she had nothing to feel ashamed of. Marianne ran all the way back to the house. The shoes might have sold if she'd waited till seven, and she did need them.

Gladys opened the door. "You're to wash your hands and brush your hair and go into the sitting room. There's someone to see you," she said.

Marianne knocked at the door.

"Come in, dear," said Aunt Vera.

Dear? She never calls me that. This must be someone pretty important.

"Mary Anne, this is Miss Morland. She has come from the Children's Refugee Committee to see how you've settled in with us."

Marianne said, "How do you do." She knew that no reply was expected.

Miss Morland said, "Well, Mary Anne, you *are* a lucky little girl to have found such a beautiful home. Mrs. Abercrombie Jones tells me your English is greatly improved. Is there anything you would like to ask me? No? Well, then, I really must go. I have one more visit to make today. The *Kindertransports* are arriving almost weekly now, Mrs. Abercrombie Jones. It's hard to place so many children. We are so grateful to people like you." Miss Morland stood up.

Marianne asked, "May I walk Miss Morland to the gate, Aunt Vera?"

Mrs. Abercrombie Jones hesitated, and then said too brightly, "Of course you may."

Marianne opened the front door. Perhaps she could talk to Miss Morland properly now.

Miss Morland said, "You were one of the early arrivals, weren't you? That must have been exciting."

Marianne said, "Yes. I am wondering about the orphans in Harwich and . . . and did the other children go to Jewish homes, or—"

Miss Morland interrupted her, "You all seem to be settling down nicely. That's what it's all about. Fitting in, and learning to be English girls and boys. Now I really have to go. Good-bye, dear."

Miss Morland shut the garden gate behind her, and walked briskly down the street.

Aunt Vera stood in the doorway.

"What were you and Miss Morland talking about, Mary Anne?"

"I asked her about something. It's not important."

Her chilblains started to itch. She'd changed into her almost-new shoes before going into the sitting room.

"Where did you get those shoes?" Aunt Vera uttered each word precisely.

"I bought them at the jumble sale," said Marianne.

"You did *what?*" Aunt Vera's voice went a notch higher. "Where did you get the money?"

"I had some left, and Mr. Neame lent me the rest. Aunt Vera, my shoes were too small."

"Do you realize what you've done, Mary Anne? You have made a spectacle of yourself. *Again.* Shamed me in front of everyone. People will say I am not taking proper care of you. You are an ungrateful, thoughtless girl. Why didn't you tell me? I will not tolerate this underhand behavior. Go to your room."

"I am sorry, Aunt Wera . . . Vera. I did not mean to be ungrateful. Are you going to send me away?" asked Marianne. She picked at her thumb.

"That possibility has crossed my mind. However, I accept your apology. You people do not behave in the same way as we do, I suppose," Aunt Vera said a little more calmly.

Marianne said again, "I am sorry to offend," and went upstairs.

Back in her room, Marianne hugged her bear, and looked out at the sky for a long time. Here, in this room at night, all the loneliness that she pushed away during the day settled around her like the fog that was so much a part of London.

12

Marianne usually passed the postman on her way to school. Today he had a letter for her. "Good news from foreign parts I hope, Miss," he said.

Marianne tore off the corner of the envelope with the stamp on it and gave it to him for his little boy's stamp collection.

She read the letter in the playground and was almost late for registration. She got a bad mark for dictation, which she was usually good at, because she'd missed out two sentences.

After school she and Bridget walked to Bridget's house in silence. The girls sat in the kitchen, as they often did. Finally, Bridget spoke. "Why are you so upset?"

"What kind of mother sends letters like this?" Marianne said, spots of anger on her cheeks.

"Like what? Why don't you translate it?" Bridget asked.

Marianne read:

> Hafenstrasse 26,
> Düsseldorf, Deutschland

> March 22, 1939

Dear Marianne,

Whenever one of your letters arrive, Opa, Oma, and I sit at the kitchen table, and I read it aloud several times. It's wonderful to hear of your good progress.

(Bridget rolled her eyes.)

"Well, I can't help it, you asked me to translate," said Marianne.

Oma and I are still struggling with the *th* sound. We pretend that we are English ladies in a tea shop and practice saying "the tea, the cake," but I don't think we're improving very much.

"That's nothing to get angry about," Bridget interrupted.

"Wait—you'll see," Marianne said.

Yesterday, when I came back from the consulate, I found a letter from England. Did you give someone my name, darling? A lady is looking for a cook / housekeeper. She asks if I am interested in the position.

Bridget jumped up and began singing and dancing "The Lambeth Walk," the dance that was sweeping England. She put her hand through Marianne's arm and they twirled round the kitchen.

> *Any time you're Lambeth way*
> *Any evening, any day*
> *You'll find us all doin' the Lambeth walk.*

> *Everything's free and easy.*
> *Do as you darn well pleasey.*

"If we could 'do as we darn well pleasey,' everything'd be alright. Stop it, Bridget. I haven't finished yet."

"Sorry." Bridget sat down and nibbled a biscuit.

Marianne continued:

> I asked Opa's friend to translate for me to make sure that I understood properly. The lady writes that her mother lives in a country village outside Farnham. She is elderly and needs someone to take charge of the household. Naturally I wrote back at once and told her this sounded a perfect situation for me and I would let her know as soon as possible. I'm trying to contact David to ask his advice.
>
> Since you left, restrictions have been tightened. Jews may no longer use the town library, drive cars, own radios, telephones, or pets, and may shop for only one

hour a day. How will Oma and Opa manage without me? If I come, I may bring only one suitcase. I'd arrive with nothing, like a beggar. Yes, you did it too, but you are a child. How will I be able to send for Oma and Opa? It's too big a decision to make overnight. Try to understand, darling, and be patient a little longer.

"Why must *I* be the one to understand?" said Marianne. "It's about time someone remembered me. What's she waiting for—a written invitation from the king?" Marianne stopped, too angry and upset to continue.

Bridget looked down at her plate. She crumbled her biscuit.

"I don't believe she's saying these things. She promised. And now she's making all these excuses." Marianne's voice trembled.

Bridget looked up. "She can't just pack a bag and hop on a train."

"Why not? If she says yes, then she'll get her visa, and come, and I'll have a mother again, like everyone else." Marianne was close to tears.

"Not everyone. There's a girl in my class at school whose mother died last year," said Bridget.

"Of natural causes, not on purpose. There's going to be a war. Don't you ever look at the news headlines? Even Uncle Geoffrey mumbles, 'Bound to be a war.' Everyone will be killed. My father in Prague, my mother and grandparents in Germany, my aunt and uncle and cousin in Holland. They'll all die and I'll be left alone."

"You're being melodramatic, Mary Anne. You know you're exaggerating," said Bridget.

"And you know *nothing*!" Marianne was almost shouting.

Dr. O'Malley came into the kitchen. "I've got ten minutes before my next patient. I was looking for your mother to make me a cup of tea."

"Ma's shopping. I'll make it," said Bridget.

"That's my good girl," said her father.

Marianne burst into tears. *It's not fair—why don't I have a father to make tea for?* "I'm sorry, I have to go," said Marianne, pushing back her chair.

"Sit down, Mary Anne," said Dr. O'Malley, "you'll ruin my reputation. People will say, 'That Dr. O'Malley must be an awful bad doctor. Did you see that pretty little girl with the light brown hair leave the surgery crying?' Pour us all a cup of tea, Bridget, my love."

So they all had cups of tea and ate ginger biscuits.

"Good gracious, look at the time. Mrs. Briggs will be waiting, and complaining. 'I haven't got all day, Doctor dear,' she'll say." Dr. O'Malley tweaked Bridget's curls, smiled at Marianne, and was gone.

"Sorry, Bridget," Marianne mumbled, ashamed.

"It's that loudmouthed Hitler who should be sorry, messing up people's lives. I heard Pa say that the world hasn't got a chance till we get rid of the fascist swine."

"Bridget O'Malley, don't let your mother hear you use words like that," said Marianne.

"I'm only quoting what my father said. Listen, Mary Anne, can I tell you something?"

"You're going to anyway," said Marianne.

"I think your mum is right to try and talk to your father. I mean, she can't just disappear. My mother doesn't even buy a hat without asking Pa's advice," Bridget said.

"But she doesn't know where he is. And with the Nazis in Prague, how can she talk to him?" Marianne tried to keep her voice steady.

"They're bound to have friends who can smuggle messages. Well, it's only polite to discuss something big like going to England. And then there's your grandparents. I expect she needs a bit of time to prepare them, or something. You know what old people are like," said Bridget.

"I never even got a chance to say good-bye to Opa and Oma," said Marianne.

Bridget replied, "That's the way it is. We're children. No one asks us what we want to do. Don't you feel proud that your idea worked? You're eleven years old and you got your mother a job! Cheer up—let's have a game of cards. What about Old Maid?"

"Better not. I can't be late for tea. I never thought I'd be at Aunt Vera's this long. I really thought Mutti would come over in a couple of weeks."

"Stay a bit longer," coaxed Bridget.

"I can't. I've got to copy out my composition for the headmistress. Wonder why she wants to see it?"

"Probably wants to show off the brilliance of her star German pupil to the school inspector," said Bridget.

"One, I'm the only so-called German pupil in the school, and two, don't call me that. I don't call you Irish."

Bridget opened the front door for Marianne, and suddenly hugged her. "Now it's only because I'm Irish I'm doing that. Those cold fishes, the English, would shake hands and they're not too keen on doing that, either. Good-bye, Miss Marianne Kohn," Bridget said, pronouncing her name the German way. "I'll see you tomorrow."

"Sure you will," said Marianne in her best imitation of an Irish brogue.

On the way home, every time she avoided stepping on a line on the pavement, she said, "Mother's coming." By the time she reached her corner, it had turned into a refrain: "Mother's coming, Mother's coming, Mother's coming."

13

After tea, Marianne copied out her composition, careful to correct every word that she'd misspelt. There weren't many red sp. signs in the margin. "Silence" was a tricky one; she'd always thought it was spelled with two s's. That was the trouble with English—there were so many rules and just when you thought you'd learnt them all, there'd be an exception. Like receive—i before e except after c. It'd be so much easier to write "recieve."

Miss Martin hadn't given them a choice of topic as she usually did. She'd said, "Sometimes people have to write about a subject, even if it's difficult." But everyone liked doing this one.

When Miss Martin handed Marianne's composition back to her, she'd given her an A-, and told her to copy it neatly, and hand it in to the office next day.

It was late before she'd finished. She read it over carefully one more time:

18 March, 1939

HOME
by Marianne Kohn

The dictionary says home is the place where you live. I disagree. Home is the place where your parents are.

England is a nice country, but it is not my home.

My name, my face, my clothes, my speech are all from somewhere else. They make me different.

For three and one-half months, I've lived in this house. I eat good food, sleep in a bed in a room only for me.

Still I do not fit. I am a stranger.

Everything is cold. Winter is cold, I know—this cold is the cold I feel without my parents..

A home is where people want you to stay, not from duty. Where they like you, also if you make mistakes.

In a home someone tells you, "Goodnight, sleep well."

Here no one sees when I am sad. I am not family, not a poor relation.

I am "our little refugee."

I will never forget the first days. The words I cannot understand. The long silence when no one speaks to me.

I think it is a bad dream. Tomorrow I will wake up in my own bed.

I remember I feel hungry, and when food comes, I cannot eat because the pain in my heart is so big.

Home is where people love you, and where you love them too.

The end.

Marianne's last thought before going to sleep was of her parents. Ten minutes was all the time Mutti had given her to decide whether she'd go to England. Even then she'd known she'd have to leave. It wasn't a real choice. She hoped Mutti would remember that and realize that *she* didn't have one either.

Next morning, before Assembly, Marianne handed in her composition. Two days later, a prefect knocked at the classroom door, and said, "The headmistress says will you please excuse Mary Anne Kohn. She wants to see her right away in her study."

"Thank you, Millie. Run along, Mary Anne."

Marianne walked down the corridor, smoothing her hair before she knocked on the door marked HEADMISTRESS.

"Come in, Mary Anne, and pull up that chair. That's right."

Opposite the headmistress, sitting in the visitor's chair, was Aunt Vera.

Whatever have I done? Am I in trouble? She couldn't think of anything serious enough for Aunt Vera to be summoned to see the headmistress. *Has something happened to my parents?*

"Don't look so worried, dear," said Miss Barton.

Easy to say. She knew Aunt Vera. She looked her least approachable, and her face was flushed as though she was angry.

"I expect you are surprised to see Mrs. Abercrombie Jones here in the middle of the day."

"Yes, Miss Barton. Good morning, Aunt Vera."

"An opportunity has come Mary Anne's way, Mrs. Abercrombie Jones, which requires a guardian's consent." Miss Barton smiled at Aunt Vera, who sort of smiled back. "If Mary Anne had arrived earlier in this country, she would have sat the scholarship exam with her class. As it is, she has caught up remarkably well and has been offered a free place at St. John's Grammar School for Girls. Well done, my dear. Miss Lacey, the headmistress there, suggests that Mary Anne start school after the Easter holidays. The scholarship includes books, fees, and an allowance toward school uniforms. It would be a pity to deny her such an opportunity. So many more avenues will open up—even university will be within her reach from grammar school. I do hope, Mrs. Abercrombie Jones, you will permit Mary Anne to accept the award."

Marianne held her breath. *Surely Aunt Vera won't say no?* It would be something for Aunt Vera to boast about to her friends: "Look how our little refugee has progressed."

Marianne looked down at the Indian carpet, studying the red and brown design as if her life depended on her memorizing the pattern. She would not let Aunt Vera see how much this meant to her.

Aunt Vera cleared her throat. "I shall of course discuss the matter with my husband. I cannot possibly give you an immediate answer, Miss Barton. It is a very kind gesture; however, I feel . . . *we* feel that Mary Anne must begin to learn something that will enable her to earn her living as soon as possible. Most girls leave school at fourteen. Mary Anne should not be pampered because she is a refugee."

Miss Barton said, "Mary Anne's achievement does you and your husband great credit. That will be all, Mary Anne. You may return to class."

Marianne carefully replaced her chair against the wall. "Thank you, Miss Barton. Good-bye, Aunt Vera."

There, I've managed to say the name correctly for once. Surely that will count for something?

Outside the headmistress' study, the secretary smiled at her, and asked, "Everything alright, dear?"

"Yes, thank you."

Marianne didn't know how she could sit through history class, or the next five minutes, without telling Bridget her news. If only Aunt Vera could be persuaded to let her go to St. John's. She wouldn't be fourteen for over two years, and not even twelve till May. Lots could happen in that time. She didn't want to have to live and work in other people's houses like Miriam and her friend. She wanted to have a choice.

Class had begun. Marianne apologized for being late and sat down. Bridget passed her a note. "What did you do? Are you in trouble?"

Marianne wrote: "I got a skolership to your grammar school." She dropped the note between their desks.

"Stand up, Mary Anne Kohn," thundered Mr. Stevens. "Bring me that note."

"Pardon?" Marianne tried to push it under her desk with the toe of her shoe. Beside her, Bridget was trying to smother her laughter.

"I am sure you are perfectly able to understand a simple request. Bring me that note."

"Yes, Sir." Marianne picked up the piece of paper and gave it to Mr. Stevens. He read it without comment.

"Return to your desk. I trust, Bridget, that you have recovered from your fit of apoplexy. You will both stay after school and write five hundred times: 'I must pay attention in class.' Congratulations, Mary Anne. Oh, and write the word 'scholarship' correctly twenty-five times."

Marianne smiled at Mr. Stevens, thinking him the nicest teacher in the whole school. She decided to send Mutti a copy of the composition—it might help persuade her to come to England.

14

Nothing more had been said to Marianne about St. John's Grammar School for Girls, except one Sunday after church, when the vicar said, "I hear our little protégée has won a scholarship, Mrs. Abercrombie Jones."

Aunt Vera smiled, but said nothing.

"Must be doing something right, wouldn't you say, Vicar?" said Uncle Geoffrey, and laughed, but Marianne had not known she was going for certain until she was measured for her uniform. It was like having an early birthday present—the only one this year, except for the box of chocolates Bridget had given her.

By June the weather had turned hot, and Marianne and Bridget were sprawled on the grass at the edge of the playing field.

"We're bound to be at war soon. It's exciting in a way, isn't it?" said Bridget. "I don't mean the killing, but being evacuated on our own, not knowing where we're going to end up. We'll have fun, Mary Anne. Let's tell everyone we refuse to be separated, that my mother says we have to stay together." Bridget rolled over on her back, shielding her eyes with her straw hat.

Marianne shivered in spite of the heat. The very thought of another railway station and a train journey made her feel sick and afraid.

Everyone seemed to be almost looking forward to the war. *Funny how quickly people get used to something terrible.*

They watched the sausage-shaped silver barrage balloons overhead. They'd been told that the balloons would confuse the German planes when they came, so they'd just turn back. Marianne was afraid that Marshall Goering, shaped like a balloon himself in his gold-braided uniform, would find a way to get the planes through and bomb them all. *If there's nothing to worry about, why are shelters being built, ditches dug, and sandbags filled? And why are we going to be sent away?*

The whistle blew. Lunch hour was over. Bridget and Marianne ran so as not to be late for geography. Marianne liked this class. It was soothing coloring maps of Europe, and outlining the different countries in black ink. She placed a red dot for the capital of each country, and printed the name beside it.

When she came to Czechoslovakia, a tear fell on Prague, so that it looked as if tiny rivers branched out of the city. She dried the smudge with a piece of blotting paper. It didn't look too bad. She was always crying lately. She hated being such a baby.

Whenever she dusted the dining room, she took a long time with the glass decanter set that Uncle Geoffrey had said came from Prague. Liking the idea of touching something from the country which harbored her father, her eyes filled with tears every time.

Aunt Vera noticed last week. "What's the matter, Mary Anne? Big girls of twelve don't cry for no reason," she said.

"I'm getting a cold, Aunt Vera. My eyes are watering, that's all."

Marianne didn't feel like confiding that she hadn't seen her father since last November, and then for only a short time. She was beginning to confuse him with Leslie Howard, the film star. She'd seen him in her first English film, *The Scarlet Pimpernel*. It was all about saving the aristocracy from the guillotine in the French Revolution. Leslie Howard had escaped his pursuers over and over again. She'd watched in agony, fearing each time would be his last. Perhaps her father would manage to escape, too.

Miss Beasley rapped on the table. "Put your work on my desk, girls, and line up in single file to go to the gymnasium. Bring your gas masks. No talking, please."

Gas mask drill was worse than eating porridge on mornings when Gladys had quarreled with her fiancé. On those days the porridge was always lumpy or scorched.

Marianne didn't know anyone who liked wearing a gas mask, even though the drill meant they sometimes got out of classes like math.

"Hold you breath, girls, jut out your chin, hold the straps, and now put them back over your head," said the gym teacher.

What they didn't warn you about was the way your ears roared, as though you were on the deck of a ship in a howling gale when you let out your breath, or about the stench of new rubber. You had to keep the mask on for at least ten minutes. Marianne had found a way to keep the procedure bearable. She recited the last two lines of Walter de la Mare's poem "Five Eyes." Her English teacher said it would help her pronunciation:

> *Out come his cats all grey with meal—*
> *Jekkel, and Jessup, and one-eyed Jill.*

By the time she'd remembered to make the hard *J* sound three times in a row, it'd be time to pull off the gas mask. All the girls looked the same when they emerged from the masks—red and perspiring—and some had tears in their eyes because they hated wearing the masks so much.

Talk of war was everywhere. Uncle Geoffrey's office was going to be evacuated to Torquay any day, right away from London. Aunt Vera had been up to the little seaside town to speak to real estate agents.

Every morning Marianne would rush downstairs to see if there was a letter for her. There was a slot at the front door for the postman to put the letters through. But Gladys had usually picked the post up before she could get to it, and put it beside Uncle Geoffrey's plate, and then she'd have to wait till he gave it to her after he'd finished his breakfast.

At last one morning a letter arrived. Marianne was almost afraid to open it.

June 25, 1939

Dear Marianne,

I'm all packed up and just waiting for one more signature on my exit visa. I can't think what the holdup is. I hope it won't take very much longer. Someone must be playing a game of cat and mouse with us. Opa and Oma send their love to you and are happy that you and I will be together again soon.

Oma has baked gingersnaps for you, and I will bring a loaf of dark rye bread. All that white flour can't be good for you.

Your glass animals are safely stored in the attic, and Opa says he will guard them with his life. How I've missed you, Marianne.

Lots of love from us all,

Mutti

The summer holidays would be starting in July, and she and her mother would have till the middle of September before school began again. *Will Mutti recognize me?* She'd grown a lot, nearly two inches. She wasn't a little girl anymore. She'd help her mother, look after her. It would be lovely to sit down together, the way they used to, both of them drinking coffee, and filling in all the gaps of their time apart. Letters were never enough.

The days passed—still there was no news of her mother's arrival.

The summer holidays began, and a letter was sent to each girl's home outlining instructions to follow if war was declared before the start of the new term.

Still no news from Mutti. *Something must have happened. Supposing Mutti has been arrested?*

The nightmare began again. It was always the same one. She was back in Germany. She watched her mother coming down the street, walking arm in arm with her grandmother towards her grandparents' house. A car stopped beside them. Soldiers pulled them into the car. Marianne called out. They didn't see or hear her. The car roared away. She was left alone in the empty street.

That was the moment Marianne woke up, and only the reality of holding her bear and humming their familiar lullaby gave her enough courage to go back to sleep.

15

The sun shone every day. It should have been a perfect summer, but it wasn't. Marianne waited for news of her mother's arrival, and the country waited for war. In Parliament, Mr. Chamberlain, the prime minister of England, said that England would stand by Poland, if she was attacked by Hitler.

Marianne helped Gladys hem blackout curtains for all the windows. Not even a sliver of light was allowed to show through.

Uncle Geoffrey stored cans of petrol in the garage. "That's the first thing that will be rationed when war comes," he said.

Aunt Vera, Gladys, and Marianne were putting away vast amounts of tinned food in the pantry. "I have no intention of running short of food if there is a siege. How many tins of fruit do we have now, Gladys?" Aunt Vera said.

"One dozen tins of peaches, six large tins of pears, and one dozen tins of fruit salad, Madam." Gladys spoke from the top of the stepladder in the pantry. Marianne had scrubbed all the shelves earlier.

"Mary Anne, I want you to run down to Brown's, and ask for six tins of pineapple chunks—large tins. Have him charge my account. Oh, and ask him to deliver another six tins of corned beef. Is there anything else, Gladys?"

"It wouldn't hurt to have some jars of jam and marmalade, Madam. It might be hard to get sugar later on to make jam."

"Very well. Mary Anne, add six jars of marmalade and four jars of strawberry jam. Can you remember all that?"

"Yes, Aunt Vera."

How long do they think the war is going to last? And "siege," doesn't that mean holding out against the invader? If the invader is Hitler, can they hold out? Marianne ran all the way to the greengrocer at the corner of the High Street.

It was quite embarrassing asking for so much food. Mr. Brown raised an eyebrow. He probably thought that Aunt Vera was being greedy. On the way back, Marianne saw that someone had chalked a slogan on the side of the store: YESTERDAY VIENNA AND PRAGUE, TOMORROW WARSAW AND LONDON.

It was true. Marianne tried to think of logical explanations for her mother's silence. The only bearable one was that her mother was trying to surprise her.

Uncle Geoffrey kept the government pamphlets, which arrived almost daily, in a folder on the sideboard: WHAT TO DO IN AN AIR RAID and IF THE INVADER COMES, along with warnings about always carrying your gas mask.

One day a man came to school, and talked about what happened in the 1914–1918 war, and showed them gruesome pictures about the effects of mustard gas. Some of the girls had looked at Marianne as if she were personally responsible. She remembered the day she had blurted out, "My father fought in the last war." Hilary, who was always making catty remarks, said in that snobbish voice of hers, "On whose side, my dear?" Only the bell at the end of recess had saved her having to answer.

There'd been notices about schoolchildren being evacuated to the countryside, and lists of things to bring. They practiced and practiced how to behave on "the day."

Perfect sunshine continued right through the summer holidays.

"Ma says she thinks my last year's bathing suit will fit you. You do know how to swim, don't you?" Bridget handed Marianne a bright blue shirred elastic suit.

Marianne remembered the last time she'd gone to the swimming baths in Berlin. There was a large notice beside the booth where you paid for your entrance fee. It said: JEWS AND DOGS NOT ADMITTED.

Her mother had taken her hand and they'd walked past. She'd said, "Another time, perhaps, darling." Now here she was doing all those things that she'd missed so much. The knowledge that her mother couldn't share this golden summer nagged at her, making her feel guilty at having fun. The thought kept returning like a wasp that came back even after you'd swatted it away.

"I don't believe there's going to be a war. It's much too hot, who'd want to fight?" Bridget said, fanning herself with the copy of *Film Fun* she'd been reading.

The girls finished their sandwiches. They ate in Bridget's garden, or in the park, most afternoons.

"Your Anderson shelter looks pretty. I like the flowerpots your mother arranged at the side. Kind of like a rockery, with all that greenery on top. Uncle Geoffrey told us, 'I refuse to ruin my lawn or disturb my roses for that tin contraption. We will use the cupboard under the stairs if there is any danger from bombs.' Gladys and I had to clear out the cupboard. I don't know how I'm going to sit in that cubbyhole breathing in smoke from Uncle Geoffrey's pipe and listening to Aunt Vera complaining about everything."

"The Anderson smells damp already, and there's slugs. Think of stepping on them in the dark—ugh! Let's hope there'll never be an air raid," said Bridget, sharing her Milky Way bar with Marianne.

On August 29, the school recalled the girls for a final evacuation dress rehearsal. The headmistress told them to keep their rucksacks and bags packed, as they might have to leave at any moment. They were told to bring a stamped addressed card so they could write their parents as soon as they knew their new addresses. Even the teachers had no idea where they were going.

Bridget smiled at Marianne, who deliberately pretended not to see. She hated being pitied because she had no parents to send information to. The moment war broke out, she'd be cut off from her family forever. She really would be an orphan.

On the way home from school, Bridget and Marianne stopped

to watch the swans in Regent's Park. "What will happen to them in an air raid, do you think?" Marianne asked.

"They'll hide under the little bridge, or in the rushes, I expect. They'll be alright. Stop worrying so much, Mary Anne."

"Can't help it. Bridget, I've had the same dream two nights in a row."

"You mean a nightmare?"

"No, this time it's a good dream. I'm standing on the platform at the station—a train's just come in. The guard opens the carriage door and my mother comes down the steps, and she's holding out her arms to me. It means she's coming, doesn't it?"

"Or that the letter's on its way saying when she's going to arrive. Or, listen, Mary Anne, it may mean that you want it to happen so much. . . ."

"You mean wishful thinking, don't you? It isn't only that, I won't believe that. I'm going to the station every single day to wait for her."

"Every day?"

"I have to go. I'll tell you something I haven't told anyone. I went to Liverpool Street Station once before. I mean, I never actually got there. I turned back. It was after I arrived. I was so lonely. Then I got scared."

"Of what? What did you think could happen?"

"I don't know exactly. I couldn't speak much English, and it reminded me of leaving Berlin. There was no point in going anyway. I wouldn't have known anyone. I'm going to try again. I know that if I do this, she'll be there."

Bridget said, "I'll call for you in the morning. Wait for me. We'll go together the first time. You don't have to go alone."

Next morning the household was in a small uproar. Marianne could tell Gladys was upset by the way she put down the plates. She'd learnt to watch for danger signals even before she could speak English properly. It was important to do that when you lived in someone else's home.

Aunt Vera was speaking in her highest voice and her cheeks were flushed as though she'd put on too much rouge. "I'm afraid you'll have to manage, Gladys. I'm sorry about your afternoon off, but it can't be helped. We're almost at war. I shall catch the 9:10 A.M. to Torquay. Mr. Abercrombie Jones thinks he has found a flat that might do for us while his office is relocated. Please keep the wireless on, in case of any announcements."

"Do you mean about trains to Torquay, Aunt Vera?" Marianne asked.

"Are you being impertinent, or is this another example of your German sense of humor?"

Marianne met Aunt Vera's eyes. It was hard not to answer back. There was no point in aggravating Aunt Vera when she was in this mood. "I'm sorry, Aunt Vera, I did not understand what you meant," Marianne said politely.

Mrs. Abercrombie Jones turned to Gladys, who was wiping the table. "There may be a government announcement concerning the evacuation, or a declaration of war at any moment. Mary Anne, give your room a thorough cleaning and polish the floor, please. Everything must be ready." Aunt Vera swept out of the room.

Ready for what? Do invaders care if the floors are shiny?

There was a knock on the scullery door.

"My hands are soapy," said Gladys.

Marianne opened the door.

"Bridget, I was waiting for you. I'll get my blazer and tell Gladys we'll be gone the rest of the day."

"No, don't. I can't stay. I have to go straight back home, but first I've got to tell you something. Come out a minute." Bridget looked pale. Her eyes were red, as though she'd been crying.

Marianne shut the door behind them, and they crossed the street and walked down Wellington Road towards the park. "What happened?" Marianne asked. "Aren't you allowed to come to the station?"

"Much worse than that." Bridget blew her nose. "I'm leaving for Canada. Uncle John sent a telegram from Montreal. It said: SEND BRIDGET IMMEDIATELY. Then Pa telephoned and it's all arranged—I'm going."

"It's awfully far away," said Marianne.

"I begged Pa," said Bridget. "I told him I wanted to go with the school, that we wanted to stay together. I said, 'I'm not a baby—I'm entitled to my opinion,' and Pa slammed his fist on the table and said, 'The subject is not up for discussion. John is my elder brother. You will be safe with him.' Then he stormed out."

"Didn't your mother say anything?" Marianne asked, hoping that somehow it would end happily, that somehow they wouldn't be parted.

"Naturally, she took Pa's side. She said it's important to be with your own flesh and blood, and how Canada was a wonderful country, and about the food and fresh air, and how it wouldn't be for long. You know the kind of things parents say."

"When are you leaving?" Marianne asked very quietly, trying not to show how upset she was.

"The boat sails tomorrow," said Bridget. "I have to break my promise. Sorry."

"It's not your fault. I understand," said Marianne.

They walked back without talking anymore. When they reached the corner of Circus Road, Bridget handed her a note. "Here is my address in Canada. I wrote it out for you. Tell me everything that happens to you and your parents, and oh, Mary Anne, I wish you were coming with me and let's always stay friends."

They hugged good-bye.

When Marianne got back, she went up to her bedroom and closed the door quietly. Then she threw herself on her bed and cried and cried.

It was late before she finished cleaning her room, too late to go to the station.

16

Marianne got up very early next morning. She scribbled a note to Gladys: "I'll be back tonight, something I must do."

Luckily Gladys was still talking to the milkman on the front steps, so she didn't need to explain. She grabbed a couple of apples and put them in her blazer pocket. Closing the door carefully behind her, she ran to catch the bus that would take her to her mother.

The number eleven stopped at the end of the High Street. Marianne held tightly to the wooden railings so as not to lose her balance as she climbed to the top of the bus. The penny half-penny ride took her through the heart of London. Marianne knew that the moment war was declared, the lights of all the neon signs in Piccadilly Circus, advertising BOVRIL, SCHWEPPES, the latest films, would be blacked out. She couldn't imagine the whole city in darkness.

The statue of the little boy Eros had sandbags around the base. They were piled up around Nelson's Column in Trafalgar Square, too.

The bus went down Threadneedle Street. Marianne visualized all the tailors and seamstresses who had worked and lived here over the centuries, for whom the street had been named. She was sure there were immigrants like her among them. Now they were passing St. Paul's Cathedral—the spires seemed to touch the sky.

The conductor rang the bell. "Liverpool Street Station, next stop."

Marianne hurried down the steps of the bus. The station was just as she remembered it: the tall wrought-iron gates next to the taxi ramp, the newsboys brandishing their papers, the shining glass roof. Today the sun glared through. It was too hot to wear a blazer. Marianne suddenly realized she could understand all the announcements. She did not even have to translate the words first.

She asked a porter, "Which platform for the boat train from Harwich, please?"

"Platform five, ducks, due in three minutes," he said.

A boy shouted a news headline: HITLER SEEKS ENGLISH GERMAN FRIENDSHIP.

A soldier leaning against a pillar said, "Not bloody likely." And stubbed out his cigarette, grinding it into the floor.

Marianne followed a large woman, her husband, and two children onto platform five. The train was just coming in. The ticket collector must have thought she belonged to the family—he didn't ask to see her platform ticket. She hadn't bought one. She was trying to save money for when her mother arrived.

The platform was packed with friends, families, and officials to greet the new arrivals. They surged forward as the compartments emptied. Snatches of Polish, French, German, and Czech floated in the air.

Marianne searched the faces of the passengers. There were students with bulging rucksacks, businessmen wearing Homburg hats and carrying briefcases, tired-looking men and women, some wearing fur coats in spite of the heat. They looked pale and lost standing among their luggage, as though waiting to be rescued.

A woman in a navy coat and hat stood by an open carriage door, her back to Marianne.

She is here. "Mutti!" Marianne ran forward.

The woman turned round slowly, and looked straight at Marianne. Then she raised her hand and waved and smiled, and a man moved out of the crowd towards her. He put out his arms and lifted a little girl from the steps of the carriage. The woman clung to his arm and they walked very close together towards the exit.

Marianne felt dizzy for a moment, as though she were going to faint.

A group of about forty children, labels round their necks, filed neatly past Marianne—not talking, trying to be brave.

Is that what I looked like when I came? Marianne wanted to call out "Don't be afraid," but her mouth felt too dry to speak and she didn't know whether to say it in English or German. She pulled out one of her apples and gave it to a small boy, trailing at the end of the line. He reminded her of Bernard.

Marianne waited until four o'clock. Many other trains arrived during that long hot day.

A train guard holding a green flag asked, "Are you waiting for someone?"

"I'm meeting my mother; she's coming from Harwich."

"That was the last boat train for today," the official said.

"Thank you, Sir." Numbly, Marianne walked away and out of the station.

On the way home on the bus, all Marianne could think was, *She isn't coming. Not today, not ever.*

When she got in, Gladys said, "Where've you *been*? The announcement came." Then she looked at Marianne and said, "You look in a daze. Did you hear what I said? It was on the wireless. You're being evacuated tomorrow. You have to be at school at 6:30 A.M. sharp. Hurry up now and eat your tea, then put your things together. I'll make you cheese and tomato sandwiches for the journey, shall I?"

"Thank you, Gladys," said Marianne. She slumped down on the kitchen chair.

"Don't slump, Marianne. You're such a pretty girl." Marianne looked up. Her mother's voice was as clear as if she were sitting beside her. There was the voice again. "You mean you haven't eaten all day? Drink your milk at once, please. You need your strength for the journey." Marianne drank her milk to the last drop without stopping. She ate three slices of bread and goose-berry jam, and a piece of sultana cake.

Gladys said, "Mrs. Abercrombie Jones rang up. She can't get back till after you leave. She said to give you half a crown from the housekeeping." She slid a coin across the table. "They're closing up the house and staying in Torquay till all this is over."

"But war hasn't started yet. There's got to be time," Marianne said agonizingly, hoping her mother could still reach her.

"Time for what? You've been out too long in the sun. I give it three days at most. Friday, tomorrow, first of September. You'll see."

Marianne stood and hung up her blazer. Her fingers touched the gold school crest on the pocket. IN GOD WE TRUST. There was nothing she could do to stop the war coming. Lots of people would be separated from one another; she wasn't the only one—Bridget and her family, Mutti and Vati, thousands of children and their parents. She'd better start acting her age, be stronger, and not feel sorry for herself all the time. She'd begin right this minute. *I'll be someone my parents can be proud of, so I'll have nothing to be ashamed of after the war's over. Wars don't last forever. Mutti could still get here.*

"What's going to happen to you, Gladys? Are you getting married now?" Marianne asked.

"Not till it's all over. I'll look for war work. There'll be plenty of jobs going. Even the milkman's joining the army. He told me this morning. I always fancied working on the buses. A clippie, you know. Clipping tickets. Now you go up to bed. You look done in," Gladys said kindly.

"Thank you, Gladys, and for all the good meals and everything. Goodnight."

Marianne didn't have much to pack; she'd done most of it. Only last-minute things were left. She washed out her underclothes and hung them out of the window, so that they'd be dry by morning. She checked the room to make sure she hadn't forgotten anything. She wasn't glad or sorry to leave. It was just a room she'd been lent. It had never really felt like her own.

Before she went to bed, she wrote a note to Mr. and Mrs. Abercrombie Jones to leave on the hall table in the morning:

> August 31, 1939
>
> Dear Aunt Vera and Uncle Geoffrey,
>
> Thank you for taking me into your home, and for the half crown. I have learnt a lot here. I am grateful.
>
> Yours sincerely,
> Marianne Kohn

She read it over. Aunt Vera and Uncle Geoffrey had done the best they could. They didn't know about children, and they thought being foreign was something to be got over, like measles. They probably wouldn't see each other again.

In the morning, she shook hands with Gladys. "Thank you, Gladys. One day I might ride on your bus. I hope so."

"Good luck, Mary Anne." Gladys patted Marianne's shoulder awkwardly, and handed her a big lunch bag.

On the way to school the postman stopped her. "Off to the

country, are you? My lad's going too. You've got a card today. Glad I didn't miss you." He rummaged in his bag and handed Marianne a plain white card. It was written in pencil, which had faded a bit. It said:

Dear Marianne,
    I love you. Remember me.

                                        Vati

Marianne put the card in her shoulder bag. Her father seemed very close to her at that moment. It felt almost as if he were walking beside her, reminding her to be brave.

"Postie," Marianne called. "Thank you *very* much. Good-bye."

Her suitcase felt much lighter. She wished she could tell Bridget she'd heard from her father.

17

t was strange being in the school's assembly hall so early. Every girl's eyes were riveted on the headmistress. Miss Lacey led the school in prayers for a safe journey, then she said: "The next time we talk to one another as a school, we will be in a strange hall, in someone else's building. None of us know when we will be back here in St. John's, or even if our school will still be standing after the war. We are setting off on the biggest adventure of our lives, and like our brave soldiers, sailors, and airmen, we do not know where we are going or what awaits us. We do know that homes will be provided for us in places of safety.

"I am proud that our school is part of the greatest exodus from the city that has ever happened. Be good ambassadors wherever you go, so that the generous people who are opening their homes to us will be glad that they have done so."

The girls filed back to their classrooms in total silence to the strains of the organ playing "Land of Hope and Glory." The music had never sounded more eloquent.

When Miss Barry handed out luggage labels, Marianne's hand shook. It was only nine months since she had worn one of those. Everyone in class had to print their names, and that of their school on one. Then they tied the labels round their necks with bits of string. A girl put up her hand and said, "We're not likely to forget our names. Do we have to wear these?"

"Yes. In the event of an accident, that label may be an important means of identification," said Miss Barry.

No one spoke another word after that.

Miss Barry smiled and said, "Time to read one more chapter." She opened *The Railway Children* and continued reading to the class. They'd reached the part where the rock falls on the railway line, and Peter, Bobbie, and Phyllis have to find a way to stop the 11:29 A.M. train from hurtling off the track.

The bell rang.

"That means the buses are here," said Miss Barry. "I'll take the book with me and once school recommences after the holidays and we are settled in our new classroom, I shall finish the story. You may line up and walk to the gates, and remember Miss Lacey's words: 'Be good ambassadors wherever you go' . . . and don't forget to bring your gas masks!"

Outside the gates of the playground, a line of buses was waiting. Marianne saw that someone had written GOOD-BYE HITLER in chalk, on the side of one.

Now that Bridget was on her way to Canada, Marianne didn't have anyone to sit with. The only empty seat was beside Hilary, whose regular partner had been sent to relatives in the country. Hilary edged as far away from Marianne as she could.

When they got to Paddington Station, the foreground was packed with single and double-decker buses. Inside, there were thousands of schoolchildren from all over London, mothers with toddlers, also going to the country, and volunteers, who handed out slabs of chocolate, cups of tea, and kind words for everyone.

The hardest part for Marianne was seeing all the mothers, and even some fathers, shouting advice, tying hair ribbons, and giving last-minute hugs.

Miss Barry had counted their class twice, making sure no one was missing, and at last it was time to board. They were allocated compartments in alphabetical order, so even if Bridget had been here, she and Marianne might not have sat together.

Once the girls were settled, Miss Barry came round and gave them each a packet of barley sugar. "The best cure for travel sickness I know," she said, and left them to say their good-byes. Marianne sat in her seat trying not to mind, or look as if she minded, that she had no one to wave to. She must be the only girl on the train without a relative on the platform. She was glad when the guard blew the whistle at last and the engine began to move.

Miss Barry came in again. "Now I'm just three compartments away, and I'll be in every half hour to check if you're alright," she said.

Celia was crying quietly in her corner seat. "I wish I hadn't come," she sobbed.

Miss Barry said briskly, "We've scarcely left the station, and remember, ambassadors don't cry."

"When will we get to wherever we're going, Miss Barry?" Jane asked.

"I have no idea, Jane, but I suspect we have a long journey ahead, so make yourself comfortable and enjoy the scenery."

The train was smartly painted in blue with gold lettering and inside, it was comfortable. The seats were padded; there were even armrests.

Miss Barry had told them that today all the railways were reserved for the great evacuation, and no one else could travel. It made it seem like a real adventure.

The girls sang: "Ten green bottles hanging on the wall/ There were ten in the bed and the little one said, 'Roll over.'" They sang the First World War song "It's a Long Way to Tipperary," and "Daisy, Daisy, give me your answer do!" They waved to people standing at railway crossings, and to children sitting on stiles. They played "I Spy," and saw towns change to villages and farms. All the stations they passed through had the names covered up, so that any enemy spies wouldn't know where the children were being taken. Then they divided themselves up into teams and kept count of animals. Marianne's team won by one sheep.

The train stopped often. The girls grew restless. Miss Barry let them go in two's to the guards' van, where there was a supply of drinking water in a big churn.

Lucy came back and said, "We're in Wales."

"How do you know?" Jane asked.

"Because the guard said, 'We're coming into Aberdare,' and then he said, 'Not a word, mind.' I happen to know Aberdare is in Wales because we had a holiday there once."

Celia said, "Wales is a foreign country. The Welsh don't even speak English, or not much." And she started crying again.

Marianne wondered if Welsh was harder to learn than English.

Jane said, "What fun if they can't understand what we're saying."

Marianne could have told them it wasn't any fun at all, but decided it wasn't the right moment.

The landscape, which had been a mixture of green hills and little stone cottages, began to change. Now the train plunged into a valley scarred with huge black coal tips, like mountains.

Eight hours after they'd left London, the train drew up into a small station and the girls overflowed onto the narrow gray platform. Buses were waiting for them. The bus driver said, "A friendly little town this is—everything you could want—church, chapel, cinemas, a Rugby team, Woolworth's."

The girls cheered.

"We're going to Old Road School. Everyone's there, getting ready for you. Bit of a rugby scrum. Lovely," he said.

It was a gray little town. The streets looked narrow and old-fashioned after busy London. You could smell the soot and something else, sharp and unpleasant. "Tinworks," the bus driver told them.

When they got to the school, they filed into the gymnasium, where tables and chairs had been set up, and they were offered tea and biscuits.

"We are most pleased to welcome you to Wales, and we hope your stay is a pleasant one," said a gentleman, who spoke almost as if he were singing, his voice gentle and melodious.

At that moment the doors opened and a stream of people came in and surged round the girls, looking them over, reading the names on the labels, and often talking to each other in a strange language.

"Must be Welsh," said Lucy, who'd been in the same compartment as Marianne.

Miss Lacey said something to the gentleman and he announced, "Please tell one of the teachers or helpers which child you are taking and give an address. Can't have anyone getting lost, can we now?" Hardly anyone paid attention to him. The youngest and prettiest girls were quickly signed out. The man spoke in Welsh to the people.

"Oh, David, look—twins. There's alike they are."

"And how old are you, dear? Twelve—well now, that's good. Nice and tidy, are you?"

A lady asked Marianne, "What's your name?"

"I'm Marianne Kohn."

Miss Barry was quickly at Marianne's side. "Mary Anne is a Jewish refugee from Germany."

The lady took a step back. "Oh, I see. No thanks, then. Jewish and German? I don't think so. Wouldn't be proper, would it?" she said to Miss Barry, as if turning down some strange exotic fruit. She moved on.

Slowly the hall emptied. At last only Lucy, two older girls who Marianne didn't know, and Marianne were left.

"I know what's wrong with me," said Marianne, "but why haven't *you* been chosen?"

Before they could answer, Miss Barry said, "There's absolutely nothing wrong with any of you. The billeting officer, Mr. Evans, hadn't expected quite so many of us. Now he's made arrangements for you for the next couple of nights, till more permanent billets can be found. Doreen and Jeannie, you're going to sleep in the nurses' hostel. Some of the probationers are only a little older than you are. Lucy and Mary Anne, you go to a Methodist home for girls. Get a good night's sleep, and don't worry."

"Excuse me, Miss Barry," said Lucy, "I've broken my glasses. I sat on them on the bus and cracked the lenses. I can't see properly."

"We'll sort everything out tomorrow," said Miss Barry. "Doreen and Jeannie, come with me. Goodnight, girls." She left Marianne and Lucy with a distracted billeting officer.

The girls picked up their luggage.

"Follow me, then. We don't have far to go," said Mr. Evans.

18

It was almost dark. A few dim streetlights came on. It began to drizzle. They walked up a hill, lined on both sides with small terraced houses. The houses were a uniform gray, the front windows hung with muslin curtains and the front steps level with the cobbled pavement.

Mr. Evans hurried them past a pub—the smell of beer, the sounds of laughter and foreign words spilled over onto the street. A group of men came out, beer mugs in hand, their mufflers shining white under the lamps. They were singing. One of them raised his hand in greeting to Mr. Evans.

"Friday night, see?" said Mr. Evans, as if to apologize to the small visitors for this sign of life. "Members of the Rugby team, the Scarlets, always meet here on Friday nights. Famous we are for Rugby. Beat the Australian Wallabies in 1908. I grew up going to the games in Stradey Park. My father was on the team there. He's passed away now." He hummed sadly, then he said, "'*Sospan Fach*—Little Saucepan.' I marched to it in the last war. '*Sospan fach yn berwiar y tân*,'" he sang softly.

"What does it mean?" asked Lucy.

"It sounds like 'saucepan,'" said Marianne.

"Quite right, *bach*. Clever girl, you are. It's the theme song of the Scarlets. A silly little ditty about a small saucepan on the stove, and a little cat who knocks it over. But there's nothing silly about our team. Rugby gives us our pride. Wars come and go; the mines shut down; nothing stops us so long as our little red saucepans are on top of the goalposts. Not far now. Getting tired, are you?"

The men's voices grew fainter. "*Dai bach y sowidiwr, Dai bach y sowidiwr . . .*"

Mr. Evans sang along, translating for them: "Young Dai, a soldier, young Dai, a soldier."

They walked along streets that all looked alike. Everywhere the coal tips looked down on them. As they passed a big square building, there came the most beautiful singing Marianne had ever heard. She paused for a moment to listen.

"I can see you like music. That's a good sign, *bach*. Chapel, are you?" Mr. Evans didn't wait for a reply. "Ebenezer Chapel, built in 1891. Fine choir. Well, come along; it's getting late."

They stopped, at last, in front of a row house at the end of a side street. A woman in a shapeless black dress answered the door.

"Ah, Matron, *shwmae heno*—how are you tonight? Here are the two evacuees. Very good of you, I'm sure, to find room for them. This is Lucy and this is Mary Anne."

"Come in, Mr. Evans. Don't stand on the step. A cup of tea before you go?"

"If it's no trouble, Matron."

"I'll just show the girls upstairs." Matron led them up a narrow stairway. "Lucy, you can go in this room, and Mary Anne in here. Unpack, and then come downstairs." She hurried back to Mr. Evans.

Lucy whispered, "I wish we were in the same room. Should we knock?"

Marianne said, "I think so. I'll see you in about ten minutes and we'll go down together."

The rooms were next to each other, the paint peeling off the doors. The girls looked at each other and knocked. They walked in.

Marianne said, "Hello, I'm Marianne Kohn. I'm an evacuee from London."

Two girls sat on the narrow beds farthest from the door. There was a chair beside each bed. The unoccupied bed, made up with a gray blanket, was set against the damp-looking wall. The girls got on with their knitting.

"How far are you gone?" said one to Marianne, not looking up.

"I beg your pardon? I don't understand what you mean," she replied.

"Well, if you don't want to tell us, that's your business, isn't it?"

Marianne put her suitcase on the bed and unlocked it.

"Matron will kill you if you put that on the bed," said the other girl, who was dressed in a loose blue smock. "On the floor—use some common sense, can't you?"

Marianne moved her case, and said, "Please, where is the lavatory?"

The first girl put down her knitting and stood up and walked towards Marianne. Her waist was huge and Marianne realized that she was expecting a baby. Both girls looked a couple of years older than Marianne.

"The lavatory, my dear? Well, now, we don't have those fancy London ways here. The running water comes from the sky." She went to a small window and pointed. "*Tŷ bach*—the lavatory to you—is out there, and in my condition, don't expect me to walk down and show you," the girl said.

Marianne replied, "I'm sorry, we just came off the train. I don't even know where we are."

The girls started to laugh. One of them said, "You're in the Methodist Home for Unmarried Mothers. A disgrace to the community, we are. By the looks of you, you've come to the wrong place."

Marianne didn't know what to say. The girls turned to each other and began to speak quickly in Welsh, staring at her and laughing.

Marianne opened the door and fled downstairs.

"Mary Anne, wait for me." Lucy was behind her. "I can't imagine what Miss Barry would say if she knew we were *here*."

Marianne said, "They're not exactly friendly, are they? It's not for long—only a day or two she said."

Matron appeared at the bottom of the stairs. "There you are. Mr. Evans had to leave. What a busy man he is, and all this extra work." She looked at them accusingly. "Come in the kitchen." She put a bowl of bread and milk in front of each of the girls and waited. Marianne picked up her spoon.

"Before grace?" Matron spoke in a shocked whisper.

Lucy looked at Marianne through her cracked lenses and said, "I'll do it. For what we are about to receive, may the Lord make us truly thankful."

Marianne joined in the amen.

Matron said, "When you've finished, wash your bowls in the scullery. Be quick now, it's late."

When they'd eaten, the girls carried their bowls into a narrow flagstone scullery, and rinsed the dishes in a bowl of water that stood in the sink. The water was cold. There was a greasy towel hanging on a nail by the door, and they used that to dry the dishes.

"The privy is at the end of the path," said Matron. She took a key from the pocket of her dress and unlocked the back door. The yard was dark and smelt of cats.

"Wait for me, Mary Anne. I'm terrified of spiders and I can't see properly," said Lucy.

When they came back to the house, Matron told them to wash at the pump by the back door and handed them a sliver of soap and the same greasy towel they'd used to dry the dishes. As soon as they were back inside, she locked the scullery door behind them.

"Breakfast at seven, and make your beds before you come down." She watched them go up, and then went back into the kitchen.

"Goodnight, Lucy," said Marianne. "Sleep well."

"If Miss Barry doesn't come and get us tomorrow, I'm going to catch the first train back home," said Lucy, and went into her room.

Marianne thought she heard sounds of scuffling behind the door. When she opened it, she saw that one of the girls was hunched over her open suitcase. "What are you doing with my things?" asked Marianne, horrified.

"Did you hear that, Margaret? Did you hear her accuse me? Are you calling me a thief?" The girl got clumsily to her feet.

"You were going through my case," said Marianne.

"You're a dirty spy." The girl held an envelope in her hand.

Marianne tried to stay calm. She said, "Please give me that letter. It's from my mother in Germany."

"Dilys, you were right. She *is* a spy," said Margaret, and got out of bed to stand by her friend.

"I'm too young to be a spy. I'm only twelve years old. My mother sent me here to be safe from the Nazis. I'm Jewish," said Marianne.

Margaret crossed herself, and Dilys gave a scream of horror. "Christ killer," Dilys said. "You did that." And she pushed Marianne forward and forced her to look at the picture on the wall that showed Christ hanging on the cross. Marianne stared at the nails driven through His feet and hands, and the gashes in His side.

The door opened and Matron stood in the doorway. The girls scuttled back to their beds.

"What is the meaning of this? What is going on here?"

Dilys replied, "She's a Jew."

Margaret added, "She gets letters from Germany. She's a spy."

Marianne burst out, "They have no right to touch my things. They went through my suitcase. I want my letter back." And she went up to Dilys and snatched the envelope out of her hand.

"Oh, my poor baby, a Jew," wailed Dilys and put her hands protectively over her stomach. "He'll be marked."

"Come with me. Bring your things," said Matron, "and not one more word. Be quick, now." She pushed Marianne out of the door. "Go down," she said.

They went downstairs.

"You'll wait here till I come back. Don't move."

Matron took the shawl that was hanging on the hook, put it over her head, and opened the front door. Marianne heard her lock the door from the outside. She was too angry to be frightened. After a while, she sat on the bottom stair, her hands over her ears to shut out the words "Christ killer," which Dilys and Margaret called from the upstairs landing.

After a long time, Matron returned. Mr. Evans was with her. He picked up Marianne's suitcase without a word. The door slammed behind them.

"Now then, *bach*," he said, "that was a poor start." They walked in silence for a long time, then they stopped in front of a small row house. It was very dark. Mr. Evans rapped on the door.

19

A very old lady, wearing a lace cap over her wispy gray hair and a shawl over her nightgown, opened the door. She was stooped over, and was only a little taller than Marianne.

"*Y ferch, Mam*," said Mr. Evans.

He turned to Marianne and said, "My mother has very little English. I told her, 'Here's the little girl.' You sleep well now. This is just for one night; I'll find you a billet tomorrow. *Nos da, Mam*. Goodnight, Mary Anne." Mr. Evans disappeared into the dark street.

Mrs. Evans beckoned Marianne inside and made signs to her to follow up the stairs. Mrs. Evans' progress was slow. She hung on to the bannisters, wheezing at every step, threatening to extinguish the candle she held in her other hand. Once upstairs, she maneuvered herself onto the double bed, which took up most of the space in the airless small room.

All Marianne could think of was witches—every witch in every story she'd ever read. She looked at the "witch's" teeth floating in the glass on the narrow mantel. *Do I really have to sleep with this toothless old woman?*

There was a porcelain chamber pot at the foot of the bed. Marianne shivered, though the room was hot and stuffy.

The "witch" made signs for Marianne to get in bed beside her. She kept repeating "*Dech y gwely,*" and patting the pillow beside her. "Come to bed."

Marianne stood at the door, wondering if she dare flee.

After a long time, Mrs. Evans, sounding each word with great difficulty, said again, "Come to bed." She patted the space that was waiting for Marianne, and smiled a very unlike witch's smile, showing clean pink gums. *How hard this poor lady is trying to make herself understood. She's been woken in the middle of the night, and now she is willing to share her bed with me.*

"Thank you," said Marianne. She took a step into the room, undid her suitcase, and pulled out her nightdress. The old lady smiled and nodded at her, blew out the candle, then turned on her side away from Marianne.

Marianne climbed into bed, and lay near the very edge.

"*Nos da*—Goodnight," said Mrs. Evans. They slept.

When Marianne woke up the next morning, the old lady—and the teeth in the glass—were gone. She went downstairs and straight into the kitchen.

"*Bore da*—Good morning," said Mrs. Evans, and pointed Marianne into the tiny scullery. She opened the back door, and

Marianne walked along the path set with flagstones to the lavatory. Someone, perhaps Mr. Evans, had whitewashed the walls. There wasn't a spider in sight.

When she got back, Mrs. Evans was pouring hot water from the kettle into a tin bowl. She put out a clean towel and a piece of soap for Marianne to wash.

When Marianne had finished, she went into the kitchen and Mrs. Evans handed her a plate of brown bread and butter. "*Bara menyn*," she said, pointing to the food.

Marianne repeated the words. *Welsh is quite easy!* Mrs. Evans seemed very pleased. She poured Marianne a cup of tea, and then sat in her rocking chair by the big oven and watched her eat her breakfast. Although the kitchen was small, it was very cosy. As well as the big black oven, there was a tall cupboard full of brightly colored plates and cups. A crocheted rug lay in front of the brass fender. On the mantelpiece were two china figurines and a doll wearing a black hat, red flannel dress, and white apron.

A cat purred under the table. If she had noticed Mrs. Evans' black cat last night, she would truly have been convinced she was in the house of a witch.

Marianne said, "Your house is beautiful."

Mrs. Evans nodded and smiled. "*Diolch*—Thanks," she said. Her teeth moved when she spoke.

There was a knock on the door and Mr. Evans came in. "*Bore da, Mam.* Good morning, Mary Anne. Had a good sleep, did you?" He did not wait for an answer, but started an animated conversation in Welsh with his mother, who nodded and interrupted softly from time to time. Then they'd both stop talking, look at Marianne pityingly, shake their heads, and continue.

At last Mr. Evans sat down and said to Marianne, "Well now, *bach*."

"Please, what does *bach* mean? I thought it was the name of a composer."

Mr. Evans laughed. "I knew last night you were musical, young lady. It's the choir you'll have to be joining. No, no, *bach* just means 'little,' or 'dear.' Now, I'm pleased to say, I have found a very nice home for you, with Mr. and Mrs. Roberts. They are happy to give a home to a little girl. So get your things and we'll be on our way."

When Marianne came down with her suitcase, she said, "Please, will you tell your mother 'thank you very much'? She is so kind."

Mr. Evans said, "Tell her *diolch*."

Marianne went up to Mrs. Evans, said *diolch*, and curtsied. Mrs. Evans pushed herself up from her chair and patted Marianne's cheek with her gnarled fingers.

When they got outside and were walking down the hill, Mr. Evans said, "You must be a very good girl for Mrs. Roberts. A sad time she's had, and her such a pillar of the chapel. Never misses a meeting."

Marianne's stomach gave a warning lurch. "Is this a temporary billet?" she asked.

"Oh no, indeed. Mrs. Roberts is looking forward to having a child in the house again. You'll be settling down there now."

20

The white lace curtains of 66 Queen Victoria Road moved slightly. Marianne straightened her shoulders. The front door opened.

"*Bore da*, Mr. Evans. Come in quick, do. Don't stand outside."

They walked in.

"This is the little girl, Mary Anne Kohn, we were talking about," Mr. Evans said.

Marianne could guess the kinds of things they'd been saying, but he was a very nice man and was doing his best for her. There was no reason to feel so apprehensive. *Why do I feel so uneasy?* she wondered, her stomach lurching again.

"There's skinny, she is. Soon fatten you up, we will. *Diolch*, Mr. Evans, for bringing her. There's a shame you working Saturday. Lots to do with all these 'vacuees, I dare say, and war not started yet. Sometimes I think it's a blessing my Elisabeth isn't here to see it. Very sensitive she was, as you know, Mr. Evans."

Marianne wondered who Elisabeth was. This lady seemed to have a lot to say; perhaps she was lonely. Was there a Mr. Roberts?

"And how's your dear mother, Mr. Evans?"

"*Mam*'s as well as can be expected. Eighty years old last month. Took a great fancy to your little Mary Anne here."

Your? She hadn't been in the house two minutes; she wasn't a parcel to be handed over.

"Well, better be off, Mrs. Roberts. More billets to find. Good-bye, Mary Anne."

"Thank you very much, Mr. Evans. *Diolch*," Marianne said.

"Proper little Welsh girl you're getting to be. Good-bye, both."

Mr. Evans hurried away and Marianne and her new foster mother were alone.

"You can call me Auntie Vi, short for Violet. Later on, I expect you'll be calling me *Mam*," said Mrs. Roberts.

Marianne already knew that· *mam* was Welsh for mother. *Hasn't Mr. Evans told Mrs. Roberts I already have a mother?*

Auntie Vi was small and slim. Her hair was done up in heavy metal curlers, which poked through the scarf round her head. She was very tidy in a dark blue dress and little flowered pinafore. The house smelt of polish.

"Come along, and I'll show you everything. This is the front room—we use it only for special occasions." She straightened the lace curtains in the tiny window. It was a square little room, with a small sofa and two matching armchairs. There was a narrow side table, with a vase of dried flowers on it and a leather-bound bible.

The floor shone. "We had the funeral tea for Elisabeth here. Lovely, it was. That's her picture on the mantelpiece."

A serious-looking child stared down at Marianne from a gilt-framed photograph. She looked like her mother.

"Taken just before she died. There were so many at the tea for her, we had to sit down in shifts. Ten years old, she was." She touched Marianne's hair. "I'd brush her hair every night a hundred times—so silky. Kept all her things. I'll show you."

They went upstairs to a bedroom that was like a shrine to the dead child.

Marianne said, "I'm twelve, not ten."

"Well, never mind. A pity, but never mind." Mrs. Roberts sighed deeply. "Look, there's a picture of Elisabeth when she was four. Like Shirley Temple, she looked. I've kept a lock of her hair."

Marianne hoped Mrs. Roberts wouldn't show it to her.

"Remind me, *bach*, to show it to you. It's in a locket—I wear it on Sundays. . . ." She pulled open a drawer. "Her clothes are still folded just the way they always were. You won't touch the doll, will you?"

Marianne looked at the wax doll sitting on the center of the chest of drawers. The doll's eyes were fixed, so that they remained wide open.

"Ordered it from Cardiff, I did. Elisabeth was lying in that bed, gasping for breath, and we put the doll in her arms. When she died her dadda wanted to bury it with her, but I said no. I look at it when I dust her room. Every day I dust and think about her.

You can dust and keep it nice, can't you, Mary Anne? Dust your little sister's room?" Her singsong voice was like a chant.

Marianne nodded, too mesmerized to speak.

Mrs. Roberts said, "You can hang your clothes in the wardrobe. I've pushed Elisabeth's dresses to one side. And the bottom drawer of the chest is empty. Perfect for two little sisters sharing. Get unpacked now, and then come downstairs."

"Thank you, Auntie Vi."

Marianne tried the window. Thank goodness it opened. It had stopped raining. The coal tips looked black and clear, framing the horizon, walling her in.

She put her things away, and then put her nightdress into the bed. Something soft touched her hand—Marianne screamed.

Mrs. Roberts must have been waiting outside. She rushed in. "What is it? Have you a pain?" She placed her hand on Marianne's forehead.

"I'm fine. I was surprised, that's all. I felt something touch my hand when I put my nightdress under the sheet."

Mrs. Roberts pulled a white satin case from the bedclothes.

"Beautiful, isn't it? See how I've embroidered her name on the cover. Now, if you're very careful, you can keep your nightdress in it too."

Marianne began to perspire. She felt dizzy. The room was very stuffy. "Oh no, thank you. I don't want to spoil it."

"Plenty of room for you both." Her voice was firm. She closed the window. "Don't want you getting chilled. Come on down now. Mr. Roberts will be in for his dinner at one. Saturday's a split shift. Lucky he is working for the railway. All through the Depression, he was in work. Shorter hours, of course, but always something coming in. Not like the colliers—hard times they had. Still, things are bound to pick up now that we're going to war. There's always a silver lining, isn't there? Now you've time to go out to play for a bit." She handed Marianne a ball. "Here's Elisabeth's ball."

Auntie Vi talked nonstop. Her voice was very soft, and her sentences went up at the end as though she were asking a question, but Marianne could tell she was used to having things the way she wanted.

"Thank you, Auntie Vi. May I go for a walk? Not far. I'll leave the ball with you so I won't lose it."

"Don't be long, then. I don't want you catching cold."

"But it's summer," said Marianne.

"Wear your blazer." Auntie Vi's voice was gently insistent.

Marianne didn't argue. "Good-bye, Auntie Vi."

21

Marianne walked down the road, wondering if she was imagining things. There seemed to be something awfully strange about this new "aunt." Now she understood what Mr. Evans had meant when he said, "A sad time she's had." *It must be dreadful to lose an only child. No wonder Auntie Vi seems peculiar.* Marianne wondered what it would be like to sleep in a bed in which someone had died. A good thing she didn't believe in ghosts.

If Bridget were here, she'd say, "Hope she changed the sheets." She had so much to tell Bridget, and it was only four days since they'd said good-bye.

Marianne crossed the street at the end of Victoria Road and was careful to make a note of the buildings, so that she wouldn't lose her way. Not like her first day in England! On the left was a big gray chapel called Zion, and across the street was the library.

She went up the steps and through the glass doors. A lady behind the counter smiled at her.

"You must be one of the London evacuees. Ever so many came in today. There's smart you all look in your blazers."

She handed Marianne a form and said, "Get your auntie to sign and then you can take out a book."

"Thank you," said Marianne.

She was just about to cross the street to go back for dinner, when she heard her name.

"Mary Anne. Wait." It was Lucy. "Oh, Mary Anne, I'm so glad to see you. I'm sorry about last night. How are you? I should have come out and helped you. I was afraid to get into trouble too. Sorry," she said again.

"It doesn't matter. Are you still at that awful place?" asked Marianne.

"No. One of the teachers came and got me quite early. I don't think they knew what was going on yesterday. What a muddle. Can't wait for school to start so we can find out about everyone."

"Me, too," said Marianne. "Wonder how Hilary's getting on in her billet?"

"Can you imagine her face if the lavatory's a wooden hut full of spiders?" said Lucy.

They laughed.

"What's your billet like?" Marianne asked.

"Crowded. It's a little house. I share the back bedroom with the boys—three-year-old twins. Mrs. Taylor's father lives there, too. He sleeps in the kitchen so he can keep warm. Only speaks

Welsh, I think. Uncle Tom's down the mines; haven't seen him yet. When I got there, Auntie Ethel said, 'There's sensible you look. Thank goodness they sent me a girl. I'm all behind this morning. Come in, *bach*.' We had a cup of tea and Welsh cakes. I haven't even unpacked yet. She said, 'I hope you're a good sleeper. Gareth was up all night with toothache, and Peter cries to keep him company.' Then she asked me if I'd mind picking up something at the market. Do you want to come with me? It's not far—I asked at the library."

Marianne said, "I used to like markets once." They walked towards the market hall. "Will you be alright in your billet?"

Lucy replied, "I'm good at getting things done. You know, organizing, and she seemed glad to have me there, not just because she's going to get money for my keep. What about your place?"

Marianne said cautiously, "Auntie Vi seems very nice, a bit strange, but that's because her little girl died. School will start soon, so I won't be there that much, will I?"

Lucy said, "We'll be home before Christmas, I bet. Even if there is a war, it won't last any time."

Marianne wondered where she'd go. She supposed she'd have to go back to Aunt Vera's, if she'd have her.

The heat and smells and noise of the market washed over them like a wave. There were stalls outside on the cobbles, and more inside the big hall. They went in past bake counters piled high with floury buns, Welsh cakes, pies, and tarts oozing with jam and fruit. Vegetables on carts looked as if they'd been picked moments before—drops of rain shone on the wavy cabbage leaves and bits of rich black soil clung to the carrots and sprouts. A butcher in a blood-spattered white apron was arranging feathered chickens in a row. Rabbits hung from metal hooks, their eyes glazed, their necks broken, their fur matted where a drop of blood had trickled down.

Marianne looked away. Lucy asked the woman at the cheese stall if she could tell them where Mrs. Jones had her stall. The beaming huge woman looked at them and laughed. "From London, are you?" She cut them each a corner of crumbly white cheese and said, "Welsh cheese from Carmathen. You won't get that in London."

"*Diolch*," the girls said, and the woman smiled at them even more broadly.

"Jones. Now there's Jones the Fish and Jones Shoes and Jones China—which is it you want, *bach*? A popular name in these parts." She laughed again.

Lucy spelled out the words on her paper: BARA LAWR—LARVER BREAD.

The woman said, "Mrs. Jones is straight down this aisle and then turn left at Sammy's—SAMUEL & SON, TAILOR. Can't miss it, they're right beside each other." She turned to her next customer.

The tailor had bolts of colored fabrics and rows of shirts and dresses on wire hangers, hung on a wooden pole. Sammy was a little old man in a black waistcoat and short leather apron. His chin was stubbly, and he spoke in an accent that wasn't like the Welsh around them. Marianne heard him say, "Only for you, Mrs. Davis, I make a special price, and I throw in a little remnant.

Nu—Well, what do you say?" He held a length of dark blue material.

"Mary Anne, come *on*. Here it is." The sign said JONES—BARA LAWR—LARVER BREAD. Lucy was looking at strands of dark green lengths of some kind of vegetable. "This is what I'm supposed to buy. What is it?"

Marianne said, "It looks like spinach."

The woman said, "Try a piece; tell me how you like it."

Marianne said, "It tastes of fish, a bit like chopped herring."

"Seaweed," said Mrs. Jones. "Very healthy it is too. A pound, is it, you want?" She wrapped the larver bread in newspaper, and Lucy paid her.

"That's the most disgusting thing I've ever tasted," said Lucy. "I don't know how you could say you like it. Come on, let's buy something to take the taste away. There's MYFANWY'S SWEETS over there."

Marianne turned round and saw Sammy the tailor looking after them curiously. He reminded her of the peddlers who'd sometimes come to her grandmother's back door years ago.

"You choose, Mary Anne, and I'll treat, to make up for last night."

There were jars of liquorice wound in coils like snakes, mints, red and yellow pear drops, small white triangular packets of sherbet, black-and-white bull's-eyes, humbugs guaranteed to change color, slabs of chocolate, and brightly wrapped toffees all in tall glass jars.

The big market clock began to strike 12:30. Marianne pointed to the striped aniseed balls, twelve for a penny. Lucy divided them equally.

"Thanks awfully," said Marianne, her cheek bulging. "We'd better go. Don't want to be late on my first day."

"Thanks for coming with me. See you in school. 'Bye. Oh, I forgot to tell you, my foster parents keep a pig in the coal shed." Lucy waved, and they ran back to their billets.

Marianne found her way easily. She saw Mrs. Roberts looking down the road for her.

"There you are, *bach*. Afraid you'd got lost. Come in now and meet your Uncle Dai. Longing to meet his new little girl, he is."

22

Marianne wiped her feet on the little strip of carpet inside the front door. It seemed odd to walk in straight from the street, just over the step and inside. Uncle Dai was sitting at the kitchen table eating soup.

"Here she is," said Auntie Vi proudly. "Sent in answer to our prayers."

Uncle Dai put down his spoon, wiped his hands on his trousers, and said, "Well, well. Let me have a look at you. Come and shake hands. I'm pleased to meet you." Auntie Vi beamed.

Marianne said, "How do you do, Sir?"

"Uncle Dai, Mairi."

"Please, Uncle Dai, my name is Marianne."

"Mary, Mary Anne. Mair in Welsh. A pretty Welsh name for a nice little girl living in a Welsh home. Mairi it is, then. Right, *Mam*?"

"Whatever you say, Dai."

But Marianne had the idea that Auntie Vi had suggested it.

"Mairi it shall be. Mairi Roberts. Got a ring to it."

Marianne wondered if all the other girls in her class were being renamed.

"Sit down, Mairi, and eat your soup. Elisabeth loved my lamb broth. Those last days we had her, it was all she could get down. Do you like it, Mairi?"

"It's very good, thank you." Marianne was beginning to dread every mention of poor little Elisabeth.

"Uncle Dai said, "Church or chapel, Mairi?"

"In London I went to church, but at home in—"

Uncle Dai interrupted her. "Chapel it is. Baptists we are. Wait till you hear the sermon tomorrow. Reverend Thomas guiding us down the paths of righteousness. Your auntie goes to meetings twice a week and sings in the chapel choir; beautiful voice she has."

Marianne offered to do the dishes.

"No, no, you go and play in the garden. I'll just heat up the kettle. Take the ball now," said Auntie Vi, and handed it to her.

Marianne went out into the back. The yard was narrow, with dusty-looking grass. The coal shed took up most of the space. She saw Mrs. Roberts peering at her through the scullery window.

Marianne began to bounce the ball, obediently, doing the accompanying actions.

Charlie Chaplin went to France
To teach the ladies how to dance
And this is what he taught them
Heel toe
Over we go
Don't forget to twist.

Marianne wondered what Elisabeth had died of. Perhaps from breathing in the fine dust that had already turned her white blouse gray.

She didn't feel like playing ball anymore. She was twelve, not a little girl. She leaned against the coal shed, shutting her eyes against the glare of the sun. In London she'd never thought about where coal came from. It was just there, brought in from outside in the brass coal scuttle. Warming cold rooms. Coal so shiny black it sparkled. What must it be like working day after day in all that blackness? Like moles burrowing underground. *Are the miners ever afraid? Don't they miss seeing the sun?*

Marianne went back into the kitchen.

"Excuse me, Auntie Vi, the lady at the library said if you sign this form, I can join the library."

"Library, is it? Dai, you sign it, please, before you go back to work."

"Give me the card. Clever as well as pretty, are you?" He signed it.

They are so nice to me. I couldn't wish for a better billet, so why do I feel so uncomfortable?

When she reached the library, Marianne sat down on the wooden bench in the cool lobby and tried to think things out. How could she explain to anyone that she felt as if she couldn't breathe, that these kind people were smothering her? No one could be part of a family that quickly. She knew Mr. and Mrs. Roberts were looking for someone to fill the gap left by Elisabeth, but they weren't giving her time. How could they love someone they'd only known for five minutes? It was like being sucked down into a whirlpool— no way to escape. It sounded silly to be frightened of people being nice. She looked at the clock. *How many hours till bedtime? Tonight I'll have to go to sleep with that awful doll staring at me. Perhaps I can move it to the floor and put it back in the morning before Auntie Vi notices.*

Marianne handed in her form. She asked the librarian if there were any stories about Wales, and was given a book of Welsh legends. The librarian told her about Merlin the magician, who had been born in South Wales and became advisor to King Arthur and his knights. "He will come and save the land if we need him," the librarian said seriously. "Only sleeping he is, in a cave in the mountains."

That night it took Marianne a long time to go to sleep. She heard Uncle Dai come upstairs and go to bed.

Something woke her. She felt cold lips on her forehead, and then a whispered "*Nos da*, Elisabeth."

She lay very still and, from under almost closed lids, watched

Auntie Vi go to the chest and put the doll back in its usual spot. Then she shut the window and went out.

Marianne waited five minutes, then crept out of bed and opened the window again. There was a moon. *I know you're out there somewhere, Mutti. Please come soon—please come and get me.* Then she took the doll and put her facedown on the chest, and went to sleep holding her bear.

23

After breakfast on Sunday, Auntie Vi tied Marianne's hair with a ribbon she took from Elisabeth's drawer, and they set off for Greenfield Chapel. There was a big sign outside, which said: GREATER LOVE HATH NO MAN THAN HE LAY DOWN HIS LIFE FOR HIS FRIENDS. The roof was almost flat, not like a church spire. But as the sermon was mostly in Welsh, Marianne couldn't tell whether there were any other differences. It was very noisy.

The reverend shouted up to the rafters and to the congregation. *No chance of anyone dozing off here!* The only good part was the singing. Marianne didn't think their school choir could ever produce music that was so magical.

The voices stopped suddenly when the sound of the air-raid siren signaling danger filled the air with a great wailing, floating up and down in a terrifying series of notes.

A man hurried up the aisle and whispered something in the preacher's ear.

"It is war," Reverend Thomas said in English. "God will punish the wicked and bless the meek. Let us pray now for a conclusion to the evil that fills the world."

The prayers in Welsh went on until the long, one-note sound of the all clear.

Their walk home through the streets was slow. Every few minutes they stopped to talk to neighbors, whose comments in both languages ranged from how the Germans would never conquer the French, to the atrocities in Belgium in the last war, and to the dire forecasts of parachutists landing on the beach momentarily.

Marianne stuffed Elisabeth's hair ribbon in her pocket. War meant only one thing to her at this moment—she and her parents were on opposite sides of the English Channel. There would be no more letters. She was alone.

Lucy had said they'd be back in London by Christmas. Would the war be over by then? But what if Lucy was wrong? How many more birthdays and holidays would there be, spent apart from her father and mother?

After dinner, when she had helped Auntie Vi clear up, Marianne excused herself and went to write to Bridget. She'd just written the date—September 3, 1939—when Auntie Vi called her downstairs. "Mairi, come down here, please."

Marianne did as she was told, though she felt like saying, "Please call me by my real name." Her name was all she had left of her life with her parents. Changing her name couldn't turn her into Auntie Vi's daughter.

"Look who's here to say hello, *bach*. It's Mrs. Jenkins from next door. Come and say *shwmae*."

"*Shwmae*, Mair. Now you call me Auntie Blodwen," said their neighbor.

"*Shwmae*, Auntie Blodwen," said Marianne. *Another aunt!* Then she said to Auntie Vi, "I was just going to write a letter to my friend Bridget in Canada."

The two women looked at each other. "No, Mairi. Not on a Sunday. Sinful, that is."

Mrs. Jenkins said, "Terrible to declare war on a Sunday. They should have waited."

"There's glad I am our Elisabeth was spared this day," said Auntie Vi. "I'll just go and make a pot of tea, Blodwen."

"And where are you from, Mair, *bach*? You don't sound like a girl from London. Not that I have much to do with people from there. Swansea's as far as I go. Cardiff once or twice to see my *mam*."

"I've been living in London since last year," said Marianne. "But before that I lived in Germany." The moment she saw Auntie Blodwen's face, she realized her mistake.

"Never! So you speak German, then? Did you ever see Hitler?"

"I don't speak German anymore, and Jews kept away from Hitler."

Auntie Vi came in and poured tea. Mrs. Jenkins drank hers so quickly, it was a wonder her tongue wasn't scalded.

"Have a Welsh cake, Blodwen, do," said Auntie Vi.

"No, no, I must be getting back. Company's coming for supper." She was suddenly in a great hurry.

Perhaps I shouldn't have said anything about coming from Germany. People might not understand that I'm a refugee, that I'm more anti-Hitler than any of them. Or is it because I said I'm Jewish?

Marianne went upstairs to get her book, then remembered she wasn't supposed to do that on Sunday. "Can I go for a walk, Auntie Vi?"

"Don't forget to take your gas mask, and be home in twenty minutes."

As Marianne walked down the street, she saw Mrs. Jenkins on the step of her house. She went inside quickly and shut the door.

Is it all going to start again? Even here?

That night Uncle Dai climbed up and down the stepladder to make sure all the blackout curtains were in place.

Auntie Vi came in with her Sunday face on.

"Don't tell me it's Sunday," said Uncle Dai. "If the German planes bomb the street because they can see our light, that'll be a bigger sin, especially as I've signed on as a warden for A.R.P. duty. Mairi, *bach*, hold the ladder steady, please."

Now seemed a good time to say it. "Excuse me, Uncle Dai," Marianne said. "Would you mind calling me by my real name?"

She'd been wanting to ask him ever since she got here. She had to keep some of her old self. She'd start with her name.

"Now, we don't want to be putting on airs like those stuck-up Londoners, Mairi, *bach*."

"Well, Uncle Dai, I'm not really a Londoner, and . . ." Marianne faltered.

What could she say? She didn't really know who she was anymore.

Uncle Dai got off the stepladder. "Your parents sent you away. We are taking care of you, right?"

Auntie Vi came in. She *must* have been listening.

"Leave my little girl alone, Dai. It's the Lord's will. They took my Elisabeth and sent me Mairi. Her parents sent her away for a purpose. Stands to reason. We'll do what's right and proper. You'll start Sunday school next week."

24

It was a relief when school started. The students were housed in two separate buildings, in different parts of the town, and were always having to run from one class to the other. Marianne ran to be in time when it was English! She didn't want to miss a word of Jane Austen's *Pride and Prejudice*, which Miss Barry had begun to read with them. She dawdled when it was math. Once she and Celia arrived so late, they had to hide in the cloakroom till recess. It was easy to make excuses and fun until Miss Lacey warned the school, in Assembly one morning, that war or no war, there'd be report cards as usual. Marianne knew that one day her mother would want to see those!

Miss Lacey reminded the girls that they were all one family, that their parents had sent them away to be safe from air-raid attacks, and that they should make the most of their new experiences of living in a Welsh mining town. "Write regularly to your parents and try not to worry them."

Marianne dreaded being told to write to her family. *If only I could!*

When Miss Barry called attendance on the second Monday in their temporary classroom, three girls had gone back to London. Miss Barry said, "Don't keep your problems to yourself. Come and tell me after school, so I can try and help."

That day six girls waited to see her. Marianne had so many worries she didn't know where to start, and she didn't think she could explain things to Miss Barry without sounding emotional, something English girls didn't do! She wrote to Bridget instead, waiting till Auntie Vi was shopping, so she could write without her foster mother peering over her shoulder.

September 28, 1939

Dear Bridget,

I got your letter. Thanks for answering me so quickly. I'm glad you like your aunt and uncle and living in Montreal. It must be awfully hard going to a French school. Are you very behind in the classes? I rather like learning bits of Welsh.

Auntie Vi, who's convinced she's my *mother*, has added another routine to her bedtime visits. Now she says a prayer over me as well as saying *nos da*—the Welsh for 'goodnight.' I think of Lady Macbeth driven mad by grief. Miss Barry says Shakespeare wrote about every human emotion. It's all very well on paper, but I'm afraid to go to sleep at night. Did I tell you Auntie

Vi reads tea leaves? She said, "They predicted someone new would be joining the family!"

The school play's going to be A *Midsummer Night's Dream* and I'm Peaseblossom. I've only one word to say: "Ready." Then I have to scratch Bottom's ears. Bottom is the perfect role for Lucy. She's so blind without her spectacles, she bumps into things quite naturally, and is hilarious acting the role of a workman who's been transformed into a donkey. We're performing early in November. Miss Lacey's made a rule that only the sixth formers are allowed out without a grown-up after dark because of the blackout, so rehearsals are mainly during school hours.

The big excitement last week was the visit of the school nurse. Guess who had nits in her hair? Hilary Bartlett Brown. She was in hysterics, you can imagine. We were all sent home with a notice to wash our hair with a special black soap. It reeked. I rinsed my hair in vinegar to take away the smell. Hilary was subdued—for her—for one whole day and then went back to normal.

Mrs. Blodwen Jenkins, next door, heard about the nurse's visit. Nothing's a secret in this town. She said "Dirty *mochyn*" when I passed her door. It means 'dirty pig,' and my hair was clean. You'd think I'd personally brought lice into Wales.

Lucky you, learning to skate. Miss you, Bridget. No, there's no news at all of the family. I wrote to Ruth last week. Hope I get a reply soon—she may know something. Thanks for asking. If ever I hear anything, I'll let you know. It's awful having a German name—people stare at me as if I'm the enemy. Mrs. Jenkins told everyone in the street where I was born. I hear them whisper about me when I go by and I'm *not* exaggerating.

> Love from Marianne, also known as
> Mary Anne, also known as Mairi.

25

Auntie Vi said, "Put down the *Echo*, Dai. I want you to listen to Mairi sing the national anthem."

Uncle Dai folded the newspaper, and Marianne sang, and Uncle Dai joined in the *Gwlad, Gwlad*—Wales, Wales part after the first verse.

> *Mae hen wlad fy nhadau yn annwyl imi,*
> *Gwlad beirdd a chantorion, enwogion o fri.*

Marianne knew it almost by heart—she only had to glance at the words occasionally.

"Getting better, you are," said Uncle Dai, "better than the soloist at the Sunday school concert if you go on like this. Elisabeth had a beautiful voice, didn't she, Vi?"

"Beautiful and good through and through she was."

"I'm supposed to find out what the words mean," said Marianne, thankful to change the subject from Elisabeth. "For school."

"Well, now," said Uncle Dai, "glad it is I am that they're taking an interest. It means—are you writing it down, *bach*?"

"Oh yes, Uncle Dai, I am. It's homework."

> *O land of my fathers'*
> *So precious to me*
> *Proud mother of minstrels*
> *High home of the free.*

"And then, *Gwlad, Gwlad* means 'Wales, Wales,' my heart is in Wales forever. When I was a boy, my father told me stories of our heroes, how they fought and fell in battle, like they do now."

"Thank you very much," said Marianne. "It's very beautiful. Miss Barry, our teacher, has started a rambling club. 'So that we can learn to appreciate the beauty of the countryside,' she said, and the first meeting is on Saturday morning. So will it be alright if I go after I've cleaned up my room?"

Marianne had planned this speech as carefully as though she were asking for some huge favor, not just a walk. Auntie Vi liked to make all Marianne's plans for her.

"Oh, there's disappointed I am, Mairi," she said. "Uncle Dai's managed to get us a railway pass to Swansea. You know how difficult that is in wartime. I wanted to take you to my sister Lilian. She hasn't met her new little niece yet." There was a pause,

"However, as it's educational, you shall go this time. But I don't want to wait till Christmas to introduce you to your relatives."

"Yes, Auntie Vi, thank you."

Relatives! Auntie Vi is getting worse.

Auntie Vi said, "I won't be that late getting back, long before blackout. Isn't that so, Dai? And you'll come straight home after your walk."

"I will, thank you, Auntie Vi," said Marianne with genuine gratitude. She was having to pretend to be someone she was not, more and more lately. Inside, she was still Marianne, and outside, someone called Mairi.

On Saturday, eight girls from Marianne's class were met by Miss Barry in the town hall square. They walked three miles to Pwll, a small village outside the town, named for the pond around which the small houses clustered. They climbed the hill that overlooked the town beach below.

The beach was strictly out-of-bounds now because of the danger of land mines. It was closed off by barbed wire—not that that had stopped some of the local and London children climbing through and looking for any scrap metal washed in by the tide. Everyone knew that one of the evacuees had gone there with her foster brother on a dare, but no one gave her away.

The girls shared their sandwiches and Marianne swapped her jam ones for Celia's larver bread.

"Doesn't seem fair," Celia said. "You don't have to, Mary Anne."

"I love it. Honestly, I'm not being noble."

"It's true," said Lucy. "She likes it."

Hilary said, "Well, keep away from me. I can't stand that fishy smell."

Miss Barry said, "I brought some Welsh cakes. I made them from my landlady's own recipe. I hope they're good; I've kept them warm in the tin." The cakes disappeared rapidly.

"I never thought about teachers being billeted," said Jane.

"I know," said Miss Barry. "We're not supposed to be human. I miss my little flat in London, and my family and friends the same as you do. My brother is in the R.A.F., so I like to listen to the nine o'clock news, but it's not always convenient to have the wireless on at that time. There's only one room for the family, so then I can't listen. And I miss being able to have a cup of tea whenever I feel like it. Small trivial things, so I do understand how hard it is for you all sometimes."

Suddenly all the girl's grievances poured out, released by Miss Barry's openness with them.

"I dread Sundays, nothing but chapel," said Marjorie.

"At home we have a bathroom. Here I have a bath in the scullery once a week in a tin bath, and I have to use the water after my foster sister, and anyone could walk in and see me," Barbara complained.

"I wish I knew for sure my foster mother doesn't read my letters. I don't have any privacy," Celia said.

"Auntie Dilys complains how much I eat. She says ten and sixpence isn't enough to feed me. We had blood pudding yesterday—I couldn't swallow it, and she said, 'There's gratitude for you,' in a mean voice, trying to make me feel guilty," Rebecca said.

Jane agreed, "That's the worst part, always having to be grateful. She should be grateful to me. I get behind in my homework because she gives me so much to do. All she wants is a maid."

"Nothing's like it is at home. I won't stay here for Christmas. I won't. I want my parents and my own room." Hilary's voice was petulant.

Miss Barry said, "I don't think the war will be over by Christmas. You'll have to be patient like everyone else, Hilary. Perhaps your parents might come down and visit you."

"I like my billet, but I do long for a bit of peace and quiet sometimes. There are so many people in our little house." Lucy smiled as she spoke to soften her words.

"My foster father's afraid they're going to bomb the docks. He thinks Swansea will get it too. What will we do if we're invaded?" asked Anne.

Marjorie said, "My foster father said if the enemy lands, he knows a secret way through the mines. The enemy will never find us."

"Girls, you are perfectly safe. This is why you're here," said Miss Barry.

An airplane flew out of the clouds and low over the village.

"Must be one of ours," said Marianne. "We didn't hear an air-raid warning."

No one said anything, and Hilary looked at her and raised her eyebrows. Marianne knew exactly what she was thinking. If Miss Barry hadn't been there, she would have made some remark to remind Marianne she was from the wrong side, the German side.

Lucy said, "Sugar's going to be rationed any minute, like butter and bacon, my foster mother told me; and my foster father says everyone knows we'll have a really cold winter. He was telling me when he was out of work before the war and on the dole, he and the other colliers had to climb up the coal tips in the dark, secretly, and look for bits of coal to take home."

Miss Barry said, "There was terrible unemployment in the valleys in Wales these last years. Real hardship, and yet the people have taken us in. It can't be easy for them, either. Now it looks like rain and we'd better get back. Next week we'll plan a walk along the old colliery line to the reservoir. Even with the coal tips, it's quite beautiful."

After they'd caught the trolley bus from the terminus in Pwll, and got back to town, Lucy asked Marianne, "Do you want to come and see Horace?"

"Who?" asked Marianne.

"You know, the pig," said Lucy.

"Alright, but I can't stay long."

Lucy lived in a small terraced house near the Rugby grounds. She took Marianne round the back. Marianne could hear someone coughing, gasping for breath.

"Who's that? Shouldn't we go and see what's the matter?" Marianne asked Lucy.

"It's Auntie Ethel's father. He's got silicosis. You get it from breathing in coal dust down the mine. He coughs like that all the time. His lungs don't work properly anymore."

She led the way into the small shed that Horace shared with

the coal. Horace lay on his side, fierce-looking and enormously fat. It was hard to see very much in the gloom of the shed, but he seemed to be covered with uneven coarse short hair and his skin was a mottled pink and gray.

"He doesn't have much room, does he?" said Marianne.

"It's not like a dog that needs a run in the park. We're fattening him up. He's a nice pig, he eats everything, and he gets all the scraps. We share him with Mr. and Mrs. Bevan next door. He gets out sometimes, when we clean the shed and Mr. Bevan brings clean straw. He's well looked after."

She tickled Horace behind his ears with a stick. Horace curled his lip, showing yellow pointed teeth. "Look at him smiling. I'm quite fond of him. Not too fond, because we'll be eating him for Christmas. Poor old Horace, you'll be bacon and trotters, and roasts and chops and knuckles and ham and ears."

"Ears? Lucy, you're making it up. You're teasing me, aren't you?" Marianne said.

"Why would I?" said Lucy. "Oh, Mary Anne, you are funny. You've seen meat at the butcher's. Horace will be like that. Mrs. Bevan has a wonderful recipe for ears. You clean them, and singe off the hair, and then you boil them till they're soft, and then cut them into strips and fry them with onions."

Marianne rushed out into the yard and closed her eyes. She tried to breathe deeply, so as not to be sick. The air was sooty and smelled of Horace and coal dust and the fumes from the tinworks. The coughing from the kitchen continued. Horace grunted.

Lucy joined her. "Is there anything wrong?" she asked.

"No, it's getting late. I have to be back before blackout. Thanks for showing me Horace. I've never seen a pig that close up before. I never thought about it. At home, you know with my parents, we don't eat pig." Marianne felt such an enormous burden of guilt and homesickness at that moment that tears threatened. She blinked them away.

Lucy said, "I don't mind it here. It's wartime; you get used to it. Horace is my personal war effort. I collect every scrap of food I can find for him. See you Monday."

When Marianne got back, Auntie Vi was making supper. "There's late you are. Mash the potatoes, Mairi. Uncle Dai's going out to play darts. Auntie Lil sent us some pork chops for supper. She said she can't wait to meet her new little niece." She began to fry onions in the pan and added three bright pink pork chops. "Lucky you are, Mairi, always a good meal on the table. Rissoles and chips is what a lot of the 'vacuees live on."

"I'm not very hungry, Auntie Vi. You gave me a lot of sandwiches, thank you."

Auntie Vi's voice hardened. "You're not going to be difficult about your food I hope, Mairi. Be grateful for what the good Lord provides." She placed a chop, potatoes, and cabbage on a plate in front of Marianne.

Uncle Dai said grace. Marianne looked at the tiny bubbles of blood on her meat, where Auntie Vi had speared the chop with a fork. She put a small piece of potato in her mouth. She was afraid it wouldn't go down.

She wanted her mother, her own bed in her own room. At

home, whenever she had a stomachache, Mutti would bring her a cup of peppermint tea and a hot water bottle. A tear slid down her cheek onto the cabbage. Instead of missing her mother less lately, she was missing her more and more.

Auntie Vi went to put the kettle on. Marianne began to shiver.

Uncle Dai looked at her. "Got a chill staying out in all weathers. No more rambles for you, *bach*." He slid Marianne's pork chop onto his plate.

Auntie Vi came in from the scullery. "After supper we'll listen to the wireless nice and cosy, while you have a good soak in the tub in front of the fire. Uncle Dai's off any minute."

"Thank you, Auntie Vi. You're very kind to me," said Marianne.

"Only Christian, isn't it? You're our little girl. One happy family."

When Marianne finished her bath, she watched Auntie Vi empty the dregs of her teacup onto a saucer, and peer into the cup.

"Look at the shape of the tea leaves, Mairi—a stranger coming to visit from far away. Off to bed, now." She cleared the teacups absentmindedly.

Later, lying in Elisabeth's bed, Marianne thought of all the people she knew who were far away. All the people she loved best in the world. Of course tea leaves were just superstition, but what if the leaves did mean something?

26

One evening a few weeks later, Auntie Vi looked up from the scarf she was knitting for soldiers' Christmas parcels and said, "I want you to call me *Mam*."

Mam? Marianne put down the Latin verbs she was memorizing and stared at Auntie Vi. "But *Mam* means 'Mother,'" Marianne said, shocked.

"Yes. You can be my proper little girl. Like Elisabeth." Mrs. Roberts smiled a blissful smile. Her eyes did not see Marianne at all.

Marianne said, "I have a mother, Auntie Vi. You know that."

"Well, she's not a proper mother, now is she? Sending you to another country. I never heard of a real mother doing that. Not natural, is it? So you'll call me *Mam* if you please, Mairi."

Marianne wanted to scream at her: *She sent me away because she loves me. She's not an unnatural mother. She's not. Stop trying to take her place.* She bit the inside of her cheek hard.

Marianne barely slept that night. After the "*nos da*, Elisabeth" and the bible reading, the ritual of the doll, and the closing of the window followed by Auntie Vi's silent departure, she lay awake for hours, trying to decide what to do.

Next day she was in trouble in school. She'd forgotten to bring her math homework, and there were red crosses against six of the eight problems on Friday's test.

"Mary Anne Kohn," said Miss Joyce in icy tones, "I'm very tired of making allowances for you. You are spoilt and lazy, with disgraceful work habits. There is more to life than dressing up and parading onstage."

The class gasped. Even Hilary didn't smirk.

"You are taking advantage. Your kind always do."

Marianne stood up and said, "Excuse me, Miss Joyce. May I have permission to go home at recess to fetch my homework? And I'm not sure what you mean by 'taking advantage.'"

Every head turned to look at Marianne. Hilary smiled encouragingly at her and Marianne could feel the class shift in their desks, closing ranks around her, almost physically. She might not be one of them exactly, but they were on her side.

"Leave the room and stand in the corridor," thundered Miss Joyce.

Marianne walked out, and closed the door behind her, so softly that it was as much as a statement as if she had slammed it.

Now what? I've really done it. I'll probably be expelled, and then I'll have to stay with Auntie Vi all day. But it did feel good just once to answer back, to stand up and not be silent because she was afraid. Thank goodness the play was over—Miss Joyce might have forbidden her to perform out of spite.

Miss Lacey walked by. "Mary Anne? You are the last student I would have expected to see in the corridor." She entered the classroom and Marianne heard the girls get to their feet and their chorus of "Good morning, Miss Lacey."

After a few minutes the headmistress came out, and said, "I have told Miss Joyce that you and I are going to have a little chat in my office. Come along."

They walked together to the tiny room that was a cupboard compared to the spacious office Miss Lacey used to have in London.

"Sit down, Mary Anne."

Marianne sat on the edge of the chair. She didn't know how she'd explain, even to Miss Lacey, who was always so fair, that she'd answered back because Miss Joyce reminded her of her math teacher in Berlin.

Miss Lacey said, "How are you getting on in your billet, Mary Anne?"

The question was so unexpected that Marianne burst into tears. "She's changed my name. She wants me to call her Mother. I can't. I have a mother, even if I don't know where she is or if she's still alive. She, that is, Mrs. Roberts, said my parents didn't want me. It's not true. She's trying to turn me into her dead child. It's awful being prayed over."

Miss Lacey offered Marianne her own handkerchief and sat in silence until Marianne was calmer.

"Why didn't you tell Miss Barry, or come to me?"

"Because I didn't want to be a nuisance."

"Will you trust me for a few days, Mary Anne? I'm sure between us, Mr. Evans and I can find the right billet for you." Miss Lacey's voice changed. "Now that we've got that out of the way, are you ready to tell me why you were sent out of class? Just the facts, Mary Anne."

"I forgot to bring in my homework, and I did badly on my test. Miss Joyce said I was lazy and that my kind take advantage. I'm sorry. I did answer back."

Miss Lacey was quiet for a moment. Her eyes looked sad. "We don't live in a perfect world, I'm afraid, and wars don't transform ideas overnight. Everyone is under stress. We are away from people we love, and it's not only children who have to adapt to unusual circumstances. You may go home at recess and bring your homework to Miss Joyce." She paused. "And Mary Anne, don't give up hope, will you?"

Miss Lacey stood up and Marianne was dismissed. She'd been really fair and understanding. Marianne knew Miss Lacey was right to tell her to hope. She'd never give up hoping her mother would find her.

Marianne allowed herself to dream for a while. She knew it wasn't possible, not in wartime, but suppose, what if by some miracle, Mutti *had* escaped?

On Friday, three days after her interview with Miss Lacey, Marianne was told she was going to a new billet.

When she got back at lunchtime, her suitcase stood at the bottom of the stairs. Uncle Dai was waiting for her.

"You're being moved," he said. "For the best it is. The neighbors have been talking about us taking in a girl from Germany. Not right, is it, when we're at war? 'Harboring an enemy,' Blodwen Jenkins said." His voice grew cold. "And what have you been telling them in that posh school of yours? Tell me that, Mary Anne."

Auntie Vi came down the stairs. "I've put Elisabeth's room straight. Just the way it was." She looked at Marianne. "And there I was thinking you were like my Elisabeth. You were going to be our own little girl."

Marianne said, "I am very sorry, Auntie Vi, Uncle Dai. But I can't be your little girl because I belong to someone else."

"Not good enough to shine our Elisabeth's shoes, you are. Go on, wait outside, wicked, ungrateful evacuee. I don't want you in my house. Blodwen Jenkins warned me we'd be sorry taking in a foreigner."

Marianne stumbled out, clutching her suitcase. The front door shut.

The curtains on both sides of number sixty-six parted. The neighbors stared at her. If she'd been a bit younger, Marianne might have put out her tongue. She felt sorry for Mr. and Mrs. Roberts, but relieved to be out of that suffocating house. Marianne sat down on her suitcase to wait. *Poor Mr. Evans, he must be tired of trying to find me a permanent billet. I hope he won't be too disappointed with me.*

27

A small car stopped across the street. Mr. Evans got out and called to her: "I'm in a hurry, Mary Anne. Get in quick, in the front seat next to me. That's right. Been waiting long, have you? There's cold it is for November." He hummed "*Sospan Fach.*"

Marianne said, "Please, Mr. Evans, I'm sorry I'm causing you so much trouble." She bit her thumbnail.

"No trouble, *bach*, it's what I'm here for. Better luck next time."

Marianne wondered how many next times there could be.

"Here you are, then. Out you get. Don't forget your case."

"But Mr. Evans, this is the railway station. Where am I going?"

She wondered if her new billet was far away. How would she get to school, then?

"No need to look so worried. Someone's looking forward to meeting you. In the ladies' waiting room, she is. Off you go and get acquainted. I'll be along in a minute. Got to see the station-master." Mr. Evans went off waving cheerfully.

It's all very well for him, he doesn't have to start all over again with another new family.

Marianne had never been inside the ladies' waiting room before. She opened the door cautiously, half hoping her new foster mother hadn't arrived yet. It would be nice to have a few minutes to prepare herself.

A cloud of thick greenish-gray smoke hung in the air. It almost obliterated the tiny fire that someone must have just lit in the small grate. A woman in a dark coat and hat stood warming her hands in front of the orange glow that did not yet offer warmth or heat to brighten the gloomy room.

"Excuse me, please," Marianne said. "Are you the lady who's expecting me? Mr. Evans told me to wait in here. He'll be along in a minute."

The woman turned around slowly, and took a step towards Marianne. For a moment they looked at each other without speaking.

"Mutti, is it you? Are you real?"

"Marianne, you've got so tall."

"I knew you'd come—I always knew you'd find me." Marianne wiped her eyes on her sleeve. "The smoke's making my eyes water," she said.

"Mine, too," said her mother, and then Marianne hugged her as if she'd never let her go.

When Mr. Evans came back, Marianne and her mother were

sitting very close together. They didn't notice the billeting officer until he coughed to get their attention. "Train to London's due in five minutes. Off you go with your mother, *bach*. Take your case. Permanent it is this time, Mary Anne." He smiled at them both.

On the platform Marianne said, "Mr. Evans, how did you manage it?"

"I didn't know anything myself until this morning, *bach*. No one did. Your mother just turned up. A very nice surprise, indeed. Mind you, Mary Anne, Mrs. Evans will be disappointed. Determined she was that I should buy a bed for the parlor so you could stay with her. There's happy she'll be for you both." He smiled.

Mrs. Kohn said, "You are a kind good man. Thank you."

They shook hands.

Mr. Evans helped them onto the train.

"*Diolch yn fawr*—Thank you very much, Mr. Evans," said Marianne.

The train was packed with men and women in uniform. A soldier got up and offered Mrs. Kohn his seat, and went to stand in the corridor beside Marianne. Every few minutes she checked to make sure her mother was still there, that she hadn't imagined the last hour. When the train stopped at Cardiff, several people got out, and at last Marianne could sit with her mother.

"I brought some sandwiches. You must be hungry." Mrs. Kohn unwrapped a small neat package.

"*Mother*, how do you expect me to eat? I'm bursting with questions. I want you to tell me every tiny detail right from the beginning—how you got to England, how you found me, and what took you so long," Marianne said.

"First, eat. We have plenty of time," Mrs. Kohn said affectionately.

That was the moment Marianne knew she hadn't been dreaming. Her mother was really here!

There were government signs in the compartment: CARELESS TALK COSTS LIVES, and HITLER WILL SEND NO WARNING—SO ALWAYS CARRY YOUR GAS MASK.

A sailor in the corner was fast asleep. Three young nurses were laughing and talking to each other. Mrs. Kohn looked around nervously.

"It's alright, Mutti," said Marianne. "Please don't keep me in suspense any longer. It was a delicious sandwich. I'll even eat another one."

"Oma and Opa are well, and send their love. The house was requisitioned. We expected that. They were moved to another part of the city, to a room. I got my visa stamped after I'd almost given up hope. It was on August 31st."

"That was the day I looked for you at the station. I'd dreamt about you coming to England. I was so sure you'd get there." Marianne squeezed her mother's hand.

Mrs. Kohn continued, "I finally arrived in London on Saturday, September 2nd—one day before war was declared. I was so excited knowing I'd see you."

"By then I was already in Wales," Marianne interrupted.

"If I'd only known that," her mother said. "When I got to

12 Circus Road, the house was closed up. There was no one next door to ask what had happened. I found my way to the school. The sign on the gate read: EVACUATED TILL FURTHER NOTICE. Marianne, I can't begin to tell you how I felt." She looked away.

"Go on," said Marianne.

"I could do nothing more that day. Mrs. Davy was expecting me. I had another train to catch."

"Do you like her? What's the house like?" Marianne was eager to know all about her mother's new life.

"Mrs. Davy is a wonderful person. I enjoy working for her. The house has a beautiful garden. It was full of roses when I came. I have two small rooms for myself, a bedroom and a little sitting room. I can't wait to share them with you.

"One day Mrs. Davy came into the kitchen. I was baking an apple cake, and Mrs. Davy said to me, 'How your family must miss your cooking, my dear, and your wonderful coffee.' I couldn't speak for a moment."

"Admit it, you cried, didn't you, Mutti?" said Marianne.

"Yes. She made me tell her everything. How terrible it was not knowing how to find you. She said, 'Mary Anne must have made some friends. Surely their parents would know where the girls are?'

"I ran upstairs to get your letters. I did not have Bridget's address, but you had written her name, and that her father was a doctor. The rest was easy. Dr. O'Malley contacted Bridget in Canada, and Mrs. Davy came with me to the police station to explain to the sergeant why I needed another travel permit."

"I don't understand, Mutti."

"Aliens over sixteen are not allowed to move more than five miles away from their homes without permission. It's a sensible precaution in wartime. Before I left, Mrs. Davy said, 'Be sure to bring Mary Anne back with you. It will be so nice to have a child in the house again.'"

"I'm not a child," said Marianne. "I'll be thirteen next year."

"You haven't changed a bit. You still have an answer for everything," said her mother lovingly.

Why haven't we spoken about Vati? Marianne looked at her mother. There were lines on her face that hadn't been there a year ago.

Marianne took out the card that her father had sent her just before the outbreak of war. She gave it to her mother to read. Mrs. Kohn looked at the brief message and then sat quietly for a moment, just holding the card.

"It's only good-bye until after the war," Marianne said. "It's not forever. We'll see him again, won't we, and Oma and Opa and Ruth?"

The train lurched to a stop.

The all clear sounded, welcoming them to London.

Finding

SOPHIE

Prologue

J ust before the guard reached their compartment door, a woman threw in a rucksack, then lifted a little girl and stood her beside Marianne. "Please look after her! Thank you." She moved away without looking back.

One of the boys put the little girl's rucksack on the rack for her. "Thank you," she said. "I'm Sophie Mandel. I'm seven."

After lunch they practiced English phrases and taught Sophie to say, "The sun is shining."

At the Dutch border, the Gestapo came on board. An officer pointed to the luggage. "Open up," he ordered.

The children put their suitcases on the seat for inspection. The Gestapo officer, with a quick movement, overturned each case and rifled his black-gloved hand through the contents. He pulled out Werner's stamp album and flicked carelessly through the pages, then put the album under his arm.

The officer stepped deliberately on Brigitte's clean white blouse, which had fallen to the floor. Josef's prayer shawl was thrown aside. Sophie's doll was grabbed, its head twisted off. Then the officer turned the doll upside down and shook it. Sophie cried quietly.

After the officer left, Brigitte twisted the doll's head back onto the neck and said, "Good as new," and handed the doll back to Sophie.

LIVERPOOL STREET STATION, LONDON, ENGLAND
DECEMBER 2, 1938

"Come on, Sophie, keep up," said Marianne as they walked along the platform to the waiting room to meet their sponsors. She could see some women talking about them and shaking their heads, the way mothers do when their child has been out in the rain without a coat.

"See them poor little refugees."

"What a shame."

"Look at that little one. Sweet, isn't she?"

"More German refugees, I suppose. Surely they could go somewhere else?"

"We'll have to try to speak English all the time," Marianne told Sophie, taking her hand.

"But I don't know how. I want to go home," Sophie said.
Marianne was too tired to answer.

The woman in charge called: "Sophie Mandel."

"That's you, Sophie. Come on, you've got to wake up."

"Hello, Sophie," said a lady in gray, picking up the rucksack at Sophie's feet. "I am Aunt Margaret, a friend of your mother's. I've come to take you home."

Sophie put her arms around Marianne's neck and hugged her, as if she didn't want to leave her behind.

"Good-bye Sophie. She looks very nice," Marianne whispered and kissed her cheek.

I

Do people know the precise moment when their lives change? All I know is that, for me, it happened just before my fourteenth birthday.

I've had six birthdays in England, five of those in wartime, and now at last everyone says peace is just around the corner. It's hard for anyone my age to remember a time before blackouts and rationing and bombing. I think of peace as being like one long holiday.

Unless you count being evacuated, I've only ever had one real holiday. It was the last summer before the war. I think it must have been August 1939. I was eight. Aunt Em—that's what I call Aunt Margaret—and I went to Brighton and stayed in a brown-and-cream painted boardinghouse near the beach. She bought me a bucket and spade and a red bathing suit. I built elaborate sand castles all day long and Aunt Em rented a striped deck chair and sat with the mothers, who watched the children. I got sunburned and my back peeled, so did Aunt Em's nose.

There was a pier with a puppet show. We ate ice-cream cones and I had a ride on a merry-go-round on a shiny pony with black leather stirrups. Aunt Em taught me a nursery rhyme:

I had a little pony,
His name was Dapple Gray;
I lent him to a lady
To ride a mile away.

At night the pier lit up with thousands of colored lights. We walked along it before I went to bed, and I sang all the way back to the boardinghouse.

I remember the salt water splashing my face when I jumped up and down in the knee-high waves. I remember my first taste of fish-and-chips, sprinkled with brown vinegar, which we ate straight out of the newspaper wrapping and not off plates. The sun shone every day, just like the first English sentence I'd learned, which was, "The sun is shining."

When we got back to London, I drew everything in a sketchbook Aunt Em let me choose in Woolworth's. I've still got some of those drawings.

Funny how everything about that week is so clear. If I go further back, there are lots of gaps. I don't remember much about the journey to England, or about my mother and father who stayed behind in Germany. They seem like photographs you haven't seen for a long time. You can't quite recall where they were taken, or who all the people are—they're like figures in a dream. By the time you wake up, most of the dream's evaporated.

I haven't heard from my parents since before the war—six years. I'm not sure how I know, or who told me, but my father's Jewish and my mother isn't. He used to call her Lottie, which is short for Charlotte. I've almost stopped missing them.

I did wonder at first what happened to Marianne—the girl who took care of me on the train to England. For a while I pretended she was my sister, and that one day she'd come and live with Aunt Em and me. In the beginning I didn't know the words to tell Aunt Em about her, and so Marianne began to fade away.

On the first night, when I arrived in London, Aunt Em tucked my doll into my bed with me. I screamed and screamed.

"Why, Sophie? Tell me what's wrong."

I hurled Käthe across the room. I refused to have her near me. I never wanted to play with or own a doll again. Next day we went to a toy shop and Aunt Em bought me a furry gray monkey, which I loved passionately. He still sits on my desk.

The last time I consciously thought about Marianne was when Aunt Em waved me good-bye at Paddington Station, two days before war broke out, in September 1939. I half expected to see Marianne lining up with all the other school children who were being evacuated to safe places too.

Once we had boarded the train, the guard walked up and down the corridor outside our compartment and I hid under the seat with Monkey, afraid the guard would steal him.

"Did you lose something, Sophie?" my teacher asked. "You don't want to arrive in the country looking all dusty, do you?"

Mandy and Nigel Gibson, red-haired twins my senior by three weeks, promptly joined me under the seat. "She's looking for her pencil, Miss," they said in unison. "We're helping her." We've been best friends ever since.

Evacuation was a miserable experience for all three of us. The twins were separated. Mandy told Nigel she wasn't getting enough to eat, so he stole food for her from his foster mother's larder, got found out, and was beaten.

I was put with an old couple who spoke to me only when necessary, and reminded me daily to be grateful that they were giving me a home. I talked to Monkey a lot.

We lasted six months before Mrs. Gibson and Aunt Em brought us home.

It was still the "phony" war. Air raids hadn't started. When the Blitz proper began, Aunt Em murmured about sending me to a safe place. Instead she ordered a Morrison shelter, which had an iron top, mesh sides, and served as both a dining room table and a comfortable and safe place in which to sleep if air raids continued all night.

Mrs. Gibson had her cupboard under the stairs reinforced, and the twins stayed home too.

The person who's cared for me since I was seven is Aunt Em. Her real name is Margaret Simmonds—Miss Margaret Simmonds. We're not actually related.

She explained it very carefully: "I'm your temporary guardian, Sophie, which means I protect you and take care of you because your parents live in Germany. One day you'll live with them again."

When I started school, the girls asked me, "Is that your gran?" I wanted Aunt Em and me to belong together, so I told them she's my aunt.

"Did you know we have the same initials, Aunt Em?" I asked her. "Only they're in a different order. My first name starts with the same letter as your last—S—and my last name starts the same as your first—M—Sophie Mandel." I sort of hoped she might suggest I change Mandel to Simmonds. Sophie Simmonds sounds a lot more English. I never liked having a German name. Once the war began, I never spoke German again, and now I've forgotten it all.

One night the sirens wailed for the third night in a row, so Aunt Em brought her photograph album for me to look at in the Morrison shelter. "It will keep our minds off the war," she said. But it couldn't shut out the noise of the planes and the ack-ack guns trying to shoot them down, or the thump of the bombs not so very far away, but it helped.

"I was the only girl in the family. Don't I look solemn? I was seven when this was taken," said Aunt Em.

"Well, you're not solemn now," I replied.

Aunt Em has a lovely smile, and her brown hair is only a little bit gray. She wears it twisted into a bun. You can see it's naturally wavy.

"Who are the boys standing beside you, Aunt Em?"

"The tall one is Gerald; you've met him. He's my eldest brother. He lives in a village in Suffolk, in the house where I was born. This little boy is William, my youngest brother. He was my favorite."

We put our hands over our ears as bombs exploded nearby.

"What happened to him?" I asked, when the noise had died away.

"He was a soldier in the First World War. He died on the Somme, in France, in 1915."

"I'm sorry. Poor Aunt Em. Is this a brother, too? He looks very handsome."

"That's Robert, the boy who lived next door. We were all great friends. Sometimes the boys got tired of me tagging along when they went fishing, but I could beat them all at tennis."

"You liked him a lot, didn't you, Aunt Em? What happened next?"

"Robert and I got engaged when I was eighteen. He was killed in France, two years after William. At Passchendaele."

"Please don't be sad, Aunt Em."

"I'm not. It happened a long time ago, Sophie."

A long single note sounded. "There's the all clear. Off to bed, now. School tomorrow, and I have lots of new recipes to test for Lord Woolton."

Aunt Em works for the Ministry of Food. The Ministry rations food, and distributes pamphlets to help people make it go further. Aunt Em tries out all the new recipes on me. Sometimes they're quite disgusting. I think carrot marmalade was the worst. Not even Nigel Gibson would touch that and he devours almost anything.

"Tell me about one more, please, Aunt Em," I said.

"One more." Aunt Em turned the page of the album.

"After Gerald married Winifred, I decided to move to London to train as a secretary. I bought this little house with a small inheritance from my parents, and settled down.

"In 1928, I traveled to France. I wanted to see the country where William and Robert were buried. Then I hired a bicycle and toured Germany. The countryside there was quite lovely.

"At a youth hostel I met your parents and we became good friends. This is a picture of your mother and me standing outside Heidelberg Castle. I'd forgotten how much you resemble her. Your hair is fair, just like hers, but your eyes are brown like your father's."

It was strange to think that laughing girl, her arms linked with Aunt Em's, was my mother.

"Your father took the photograph, Sophie. It was the evening before your parents announced their engagement. They were so happy. He was going to work for a famous firm of architects in Berlin. When Hitler came to power, he wasn't allowed to work there anymore. Your mother wrote me later that he became a landscape gardener.

"After I returned to England, your mother and I corresponded— we became pen friends. She and Jacob invited me to their wedding, but of course I couldn't afford to go to Europe again so soon. Later, much later, after you came along, she loaned you to me to take care of."

Loaned, like a book from the library?

I went to sleep thinking, *you have to take books back to the library, but I never want to be taken back and leave Aunt Em.*

2

Mandy calls for me as usual on Friday—our film-going night. This time next week, I'll be fourteen.

"Don't forget to keep the wireless on, Aunt Em. The war may be over before we get home."

"I hope you won't be that late, girls. Have a good time."

There was a long queue outside the pictures—there always is. The film was *Cover Girl*, with Rita Hayworth and Gene Kelly.

Mandy and I had long ago settled on our favorite male dancers.

"No one is as elegant as Fred Astaire," I insist.

"Can you imagine Fred jitterbugging? Gene Kelly invents a whole new style. By the way, Soph, has Nigel said anything to you yet?"

"About what?"

"About the Youth Club Victory Dance."

"I know there's going to be one—a costume dance as soon as Victory's announced. I'm helping with the decorations."

Mandy's left eyebrow goes up in the mysterious manner she's been practicing. It makes her look a bit like Harpo Marx. I don't comment.

"Swear you won't tell, but the other night when Mum was working the late shift, Nigel asked me to teach him how to waltz, and sort of mumbled that he might ask you to go with him to the dance."

"In that case I will decline any other invitations that might come my way," I say grandly, and we both burst out laughing.

"Do you remember when we were about eight, we swore we'd live in the same house when we were grown up, and I decided you'd have to marry Nigel as I couldn't?"

"You were always a bossy boots, Amanda Gibson. By the way, what did you cook for supper tonight? It was your turn, wasn't it?" I changed the subject deliberately—learned how to do that from Aunt Em.

"I opened a tin of unknown species of fish and we had it on toast. Nigel gave his to next door's cat. What did you have?"

"Aunt Em's Woolton pie, our Friday night special—anything that's left over from the week's meals baked with potato on top. I'm famished. Do we have enough money to buy chips on the way home?"

We pool our resources.

"If we share. We'll have to hurry after the show; they sell out early on Friday nights. When the war's over," Mandy says dreamily, "I'm going to live on bananas. With custard, or ice cream, or mashed with sugar, or sliced on white bread and butter."

The GI standing in front of us in the queue turns round and winks. "Can't have our allies starving," he says, in that wonderful slow American drawl. "Here, have some chocolate." He offers us a bar each.

Riches! Mandy and I look at each other hesitatingly. We're getting a bit too old to accept sweets from strangers.

"Go ahead, my intentions are honorable, right, hon?" The blonde girl with him puts her arm through his possessively.

"Thank you very much, Sergeant."

He turns away with a smile.

The *Pathé Gazette* news comes on after the big picture and before the cartoons. It shows English and U.S. forces liberating concentration camps. Dead bodies in heaps. Living dead. Bones barely covered with bits of striped rags, or huddled under shreds of blankets. Eyes staring from skulls peering through tiers of bunks, or pressed against barbed wire fences. I don't want to look, but can't turn away. *Are they real, or are they waxwork figures like those in the torture chamber at Madame Tussaud's?*

We leave before the cartoons. Mandy won't look at me. We hold hands all the way home, the way we used to when we were little. Neither of us speak.

I let myself in and hang up my mackintosh.

"I'm in the kitchen, Sophie," Aunt Em calls out. "You're home early."

"I'm not feeling very well," I say, and slump down beside her at the kitchen table.

"Shall I get you an aspirin, dear?" Aunt Em measures the sleeve of the cardigan she's knitting.

"Don't fuss, Aunt Em, I'm all right." I sense her looking at me as if she hadn't noticed that I'd snapped at her.

"I'm going to make some cocoa before I go to bed. Would you like a cup?" she asks.

I burst into tears.

Aunt Em rolls up her knitting and puts it away neatly in the old prewar tapestry knitting bag. "Do you want to tell me what's wrong, Sophie?"

I blow my nose. "Mandy and I were larking about in the queue, complaining about our starvation diets, and an American sergeant gave us chocolate. Oh, Aunt Em, it was awful." I put my half-eaten bar on the table.

"The chocolate?"

I'm not in the mood for jokes. "All those people dead, or dying in ways I haven't even heard of. They showed camps. Concentration camps—Belsen and Buchenwald. I'll never forget their names, or what's there."

"Yes. I heard a war reporter on the BBC earlier."

Aunt Em measures the cocoa powder into two mugs, adds a dash of milk and a bit of sugar, stirs, and pours on boiling water.

How can Aunt Em stand there and make cocoa?

She continues quietly: "I remember a broadcast I heard many years ago. It was given by Lord Baldwin in 1938. He was trying to get help for children in danger from the Nazis. Children who were Jewish or half Jewish, or whose parents were politically opposed to Hitler. He wanted English people to give homes to those children."

"Like you did?"

"Yes. I wrote down what he said: 'It's not an earthquake, not a famine, not a flood, but an explosion of man's inhumanity to man.' I wanted to help. It wasn't enough, obviously. How could we let it happen?" She sighs and puts her arm around me for a moment. "War and its atrocities."

I have a feeling she was thinking about that other war—the First World War.

"If you don't mind, I'll take my cocoa upstairs with me, Aunt Em."

Does Aunt Em realize how mixed up I feel? How can she? I can't even explain it to myself.

Every time there's been an air raid, every time someone in school hears of a brother shot down over enemy territory, or a father wounded or missing, I feel sad—guilty, too. Sometimes in Assembly when the headmistress says, with a sorrowful note in her voice, that something's been stolen from the cloakroom, or broken, and she hopes the guilty person will do the honorable thing and own up, I always go red, even though it's nothing to do with me. The trouble is, this *is* to do with me—I was born on the enemy side. Owning up's not going to change that. If only the war would end, if only we could forget all about it. . . .

I wish I'd been born right here in this narrow old house with its tiny back garden, almost too small for our vegetable patch, where we grow carrots and brussels sprouts. Where the apple tree's wormy and the blackberries have to be picked from the bush the minute they are ripe, or birds and hungry little boys eat the lot.

My bedroom's next to Aunt Em's, and there is a tiny spare room next to it, for a visitor or a maid. There isn't a maid, though. There's old Mrs. James, who comes in now and again to give everything a "good turnout."

The visitor's room is full of boxes of pamphlets and Red Cross supplies: blankets and patched sheets and secondhand clothes that Aunt Em collects for people in hospital or for blitzed families. She's been a member of the Women's Voluntary Services since 1939.

I love my room. The ceiling slopes down towards the bed and the window's opposite, set back in an alcove and crisscrossed with tape, in case of splintering glass. Sometimes at night, before I go to sleep, I draw back the blackout curtains. Not for long, though, because I'm afraid I might fall asleep, and wake up in the night and switch on the light and give enemy planes a target to aim for.

The walls are painted yellow to make the room look sunny. We're lucky to have walls. Incendiaries fell at the other end of the street, homes collapsed, people we know were hurt, and there was a lot of fire damage.

Aunt Em gave me her old desk—the one she used when she was my age, at her home in Suffolk. There are a couple of little cubbyholes for anything really private. I don't keep a diary—drawing's easier for me than writing. I'm down to my last decent pencil. It's almost impossible to get good drawing pencils. I use mine to the last stub. Wish I still had one of those shiny ones. Can't get them anymore; everything's utility.

There's a print of Van Gogh's bedroom on one wall. It inspires me. Every line means something—tells me about the artist and the character or object he painted. A simple wooden bed covered with a red quilt, two chairs, bare floors, and shuttered windows. *How does he get that quality of light?* Uncluttered and complete.

My other picture is a watercolor called the *Post Office, Clovelly*. It shows a village painted by English artist Arthur Quinton, who lived in London till he died in 1934. I wonder if Clovelly was his favorite holiday place? The streets are cobbled. Two little girls in long dresses covered by white pinafores and wearing sunbonnets are walking up the hill. Behind them is the sea. There are railings in front of the houses. In London railings were given away long ago for the war effort. There's a striped awning over the post office, which has postcards for sale outside. A man leads a donkey, weighed down by panniers, toward the sea. A fishing boat bobs in the distance. Most nights this picture makes me feel safe and calm.

Aunt Em teases me because I can go to sleep anytime. She says the first time she saw me in Liverpool Street Station, I was asleep.

Tonight I can't stop thinking. *What if I hadn't been one of the children brought to England before the war? Where would I be? Where are my parents? Does my father have to wear a yellow star like some of those people on the news?*

The last and most important "where"—the one I keep

pushing aside and which won't go away—is, *where am I supposed to belong? Where am I going to live when the war's over? Here with Aunt Em in my real life? Or with my parents, who are practically strangers, whom I can hardly remember?*

3

Every time I close my eyes, I imagine I hear my wardrobe doors opening. Inside are rows and rows of dead bodies stacked up—one on top of the other. Skeletons wearing striped jackets, with six-pointed stars sewn over their hearts.

I get out of bed, make sure the blackout's in place. Then I switch on the light. The Van Gogh looks as if it's shifted a bit on the wall. I take it down. The nail's come loose. I'd better not hammer it back tonight. I put the print on the table next to the cocoa—there's skin on top. I drink it anyway. Can't bear to waste something with sugar in it. Actually, cocoa's not bad cold.

I sit cross-legged on my bed and look at the clean square of yellow paint—much brighter than the rest of the wall—where the Van Gogh normally hangs.

A long time ago there was a cream-colored wall in another room. . . .

———

A little girl sits cross-legged on the floor and looks for hours at a picture of a horse standing on the edge of a yellow cornfield, surrounded by emerald green hedges. The horse is red and tosses its blue mane, flicks its blue tail. The girl's papa gave the picture to her mother when they got married. It hangs on the wall of their living room.

At school the teacher says, "Draw something beautiful, so that the Führer will be proud of you." Herr Schmidt always walks up and down between the rows of desks. His breath smells of tobacco. His fingers are stained yellow as though he's been painting. He stands at his table and the pointer makes a singing noise in the air before it hits the edge. When he does that, someone's in trouble.

"Zoffie Mandel, bring your picture to the front. Turn around and face the class; show them your drawing."

The girl curtsies and does as she's told. *Her picture is beautiful. No need to be afraid.*

"What is this a picture of, children?"

"A horse, Sir."

"A horse. What color is this horse, children?"

"Red and blue, Sir," the class responds.

Has she done something bad? The colors aren't smudged. She hasn't gone over the lines.

"Who has seen a red and blue horse before? No one. Good. What color are horses, Magda? Yes. Black. Peter? Brown. Very good. Mathias? White. Excellent."

Her arms are getting tired. She needs to go to the toilet.

"Tell us, Zoffie, what color is *your* horse?"

The children scent trouble. They're glad it's someone else and not them.

"Speak up, I can't hear you."

The girl whispers, "Red and blue, Sir."

The class explodes into laughter. The pointer sings before it hits the wood.

"Silence! Hand me your picture."

The girl watches him tear it in half and throw it into the wastepaper basket. It is not over yet.

"This picture is an insult to the Führer. This is a bad picture. Where did you see this horse?"

"In a frame, Sir, in a room."

"What room, may I enquire?"

Even then, at six, she knows she must not tell the truth.

"I can't remember, Sir, just a room."

"Hold out your hand. Liar!" The pointer sings loudly before it stings her fingers. "Stand in the corner for the rest of the morning. Tomorrow, move your things to the back. Next to Samuel Bermann."

More laughter. Fingers pointing. The girl stands facing the wall. *She can't hold out much longer.*

After the bell rings for the end of school, some children chase after the girl, chanting, "Zoffie Mandel wet the floor. Zoffie Mandel sits with Jews. She's a dirty Jewish . . ."

She doesn't know the last word they call her.

When the girl gets home, she curls up on her bed. Papa built the bunk for her in the living room. He said it was like a bed on a ship. Her own little room inside the big one. She draws the curtains and falls asleep in the half-darkness of her bunk.

After Mama comes home from work, she tells her what the teacher said. Mama takes the picture down from the wall. There is a big clean patch where the horse used to be. When Papa comes home, Mama shouts at him: "Give it away, burn it. Suppose it's on the banned list? I've told you over and over we have to be more careful. The child talks. What is to become of you? Of all of us? We are a target."

"What shall I buy you instead? A picture of the Führer?"

"Are you deaf and blind?" Mama's voice quivers.

The girl covers her ears; she does not want to hear her mother crying. She wishes she could hide in the yellow cornfield.

After supper, Papa goes out. He takes the horse away, wrapped in newspaper, and the photograph of his family, whom she has never met.

Next day, when Mama comes home, she carries a big mirror in a gold frame. Four fat little gold angels decorate each corner. Papa hangs the mirror on the wall. He's tired from cutting the hedges outside the big houses along the Grunewald pine forest. He lies down.

"Doesn't the mirror look beautiful, Zoffielein?"

"Yes, Mama." The little girl misses the red horse.

"Listen carefully. This mirror was a christening present from your Grandmother Weiss."

"Grandmother? I have a grandmother?" the girl asks her mother. "Why doesn't she come to see me?"

Mama says, "You've forgotten. I told you about her. She lives far away in Dresden—she can't come to visit."

The girl wants to ask, may she send her a letter? Perhaps her grandmother will write back. Papa appears in the doorway, puts his finger on his lips. The girl does not ask any more questions.

Later, before she goes to sleep, Mama reminds her, "How long have we had this mirror, Zoffie?"

"A long time."

"Good girl," Mama says. "Do you remember who gave it to us?"

"The grandmother who lives far away."

I reach for my sketchbook. Only two clean pages left. Aunt Em gives me a new one every birthday. As soon as paper began to get scarce, she must have bought a supply of sketchbooks for me.

I draw the horse, color in the red body and blue mane and tail. Then I rough in the hedges. My green isn't quite the right shade, but close enough. The yellow cornfield gleams like the sun. I sign my initials. S.M.

Zoffie doesn't exist anymore. I'm Sophie Mandel. I draw the way I want to.

I switch off the light and go to sleep.

4

Friday, April 27, 1945. My fourteenth birthday. Mandy's right, I do feel more grown-up. Lots of girls our age have left school and gone out to work.

Aunt Em went to the office extra early, so she could finish the new pamphlet on cooking potatoes in twenty-five different ways. They're one of the few foods that aren't rationed.

She made me the most beautiful birthday card. She used tiny scraps of leftover fabric from the quilts she makes for forces' convalescent homes.

I'm supposed to go to the butcher's on my way home from school. Good thing Aunt Em left the ration books out. I would *not* be happy queuing and then not getting anything because I'd forgotten them.

I hate going to Billy's Best Meats. His real name is William Billy. He always makes me think of the *Three Billy Goats Gruff*—not the goats, but the troll. *Who's that going into my shop?* His teeth are very pointed, as if he's been gnawing on bones, sharpening his incisors.

I may declare myself a vegetarian, then I'd get extra cheese, and wouldn't have to go through this. Nigel's scout troop has an allotment, which is one of the best in London. They grow all kinds of vegetables, and even manage strawberries.

I queue for twenty-five minutes. Finally there is only one woman ahead of me.

"Nice bit of rabbit, Mrs. Wilson?"

"Ta very much, Mr. Billy. A bit of liver'd be nice. My son's home on leave this weekend; liver and bacon's his favorite."

"Now that I can't do. There's still a war on, you know. How about a nice bit of tripe? Tripe and onions. Very tasty."

"Tell you the truth, Mr. Billy, I haven't seen an onion in the shops for weeks, and my son isn't a great one for tripe."

A pause. No one dares to offend Mr. Billy. Tripe is actually the stomach of a large bovine animal, like a cow or an ox. I looked it up in the dictionary one day after they served it for school dinners. Thick gray wobbly stuff, with lines on it. No one touched it. *Poor Mrs. Wilson.*

"Seeing it's a special occasion, I'll throw in a soup bone—nice bit of meat on it. One shilling and fourpence, if you please. Next."

"Good afternoon, Mr. Billy. Miss Simmonds was wondering . . ." I hesitate.

"What did she have in mind then, a little steak?" Mr. Billy laughs uproariously.

"I don't think I've ever tasted steak, Mr. Billy, and I'm four-teen today."

"What kind of world are we living in, I *ask* you?" This, to the patient woman behind me. "Girls growing up who don't know what a piece of steak tastes like? What are they going to feed their husbands on?"

I try a smile.

The lady behind me says, "Should be on the Music Hall, Mr. Billy. Good as George Formby, you are, any day."

"Flattery will get you everywhere." He rubs his hands over his fat stomach.

I think, *it's disgusting what we have to go through just to eat.*

"Mr. Billy, my aunt was rather hoping for some lamb. She was telling me how, before the war, you had the best spring lamb any-where in West London."

Mr. Billy preens. "Times change, my dear." He goes into the back, returns, and swiftly wraps up a small parcel. "That'll be one shilling and sixpence, please, luv. Regards to your aunt. Sausages for the birthday girl." He winks at me.

I cycle home, whistling all the way, and get in just as Aunt Em is hanging up her gray tweed coat. She's had that coat ever since I've known her. It's not that she can't afford a new one, it's that I'm growing so fast she has to use most of her clothing coupons for me. Mrs. Gibson once said, "An English tweed lasts a lifetime." Mandy said, "Doesn't it depend how long a lifetime is?" She got told off for being cheeky.

I go into the kitchen and put the kettle on. Aunt Em looks exhausted.

"You okay, Aunt Em?"

"Sophie, I can't tell you how much I dislike that expression." She kisses me absentmindedly. "Happy birthday, darling. How was Mr. Billy?"

"His usual." I remove the string of pinkish gray sausages from the wrapping and swing them round my head like a lasso. "Look what I got. Doesn't it cheer you up?"

"It does, indeed. There is no doubt you know the way to that ogre's heart."

I pour Aunt Em a cup of tea.

"Thank you. I need this. Are you and Mandy on the same shift at the hospital tomorrow?"

"Sister changed her to mornings this week, and I'm on from five till nine in the evening. I rather like those hours, tidying everything up for visitors, and most people in a good mood."

"It's a bit late for you to cycle home by yourself."

"I come straight home, you know that." Mandy and I have been nursing cadets since we were twelve, and it's got us our war service badge in Guides. "Did you have a rotten day, Aunt Em?"

"I did, rather. Jean Mitchell's husband was killed in action. She got the telegram this morning. I wanted to send her home, and she said, 'I'd *prefer* to stay if you don't mind, Miss Simmonds. You see, there's no one there now.' Her son's just volunteered for the Merchant Navy. Sorry I'm so gloomy. Let me finish this lovely cup of tea and I'll be myself again."

"You've got it." I am given a look.

"Sometimes, Sophie Mandel, I think I'm sharing my home

with a member of the American forces. Where do you pick up these expressions? *Mm*, something smells delicious. I'll lay the table."

We have two sausages each and fried tomato and triangles of fried bread.

"You should be working for the Ministry of Food, Sophie, not me. You're a wonderful cook."

Aunt Em had made me an eggless birthday cake with white icing, which was a bit runny because you can't get real icing sugar. We're saving the cake until Mandy and Nigel get here.

"Time for presents," says Aunt Em.

There are two this year, instead of one. I open the big one first.

"Aunt Em, oh, I was hoping for this. Thank you a million times!"

It is a beautiful new sketchbook, a bit bigger than last year's. "I don't know how you do it."

"This is the last one, Sophie. I bought six in 1939, when it looked as if there might be a shortage. Now open your other gift."

"What a beautiful velvet box." I lift the lid. "Aunt Em, is it an identity bracelet? I've always wanted one of those! It looks like real gold. It's got a charm on it." I falter. It isn't a charm, not exactly, nor a bracelet. Aunt Em has given me a gold necklace and on it is a Jewish star, a Star of David.

"Let me fasten it for you, Sophie."

I go into the hall to look in the mirror.

I hate wearing anything round my neck. It's choking me. Why would Aunt Em give me this? Religion isn't part of our lives.

Aunt Em says, "Last week during my lunch-hour walk, I passed by my favorite antique shop—the tiny one almost hidden away in the mews. I bought my little rose-colored carriage lamp there before the war. On an impulse, I went in. The owner remembered me. He was pricing some estate jewelry on the counter. I decided to buy this piece. He told me it was very old—of Persian design. I wondered who it had belonged to."

"Thank you, Aunt Em. It's lovely. I'll keep it for special occasions."

There is a familiar knock at the door.

"That'll be Nigel and Mandy." I'm relieved to get away. I put the necklace back in the box, and into my pocket.

"Happy birthday, Sophie." Mandy hugs me.

Nigel pushes a big tin into my hand. "Many happy returns."

"What is it?"

"Open it. It's from all of us," Mandy says.

"Toffee. I don't believe it! However did you . . . ?"

"We made it, didn't we, Nigel? It's from one of the Ministries' Christmas recipes. It's called honeycomb toffee."

"Carrot-based," Nigel says solemnly.

"Liar. Don't listen to him, Soph. We saved our sugar ration, and Mum gave us the syrup and voilà!"

For the rest of the evening we play Monopoly and eat toffee and almost finish the birthday cake. "You must take the last piece home for your mother. Please thank her for the syrup," I remind Mandy.

After they leave, Aunt Em says, "I'll do the dishes. You've done more than your fair share, getting supper and facing Mr. Billy."

"Good night, Aunt Em. You do spoil me. It's been a wonderful birthday."

5

All evening I'd been conscious of the box in my pocket. I'm not sure why I was in such a hurry to put the necklace out of sight.

I wish I hadn't said I'd been hoping for an identity bracelet. In a way, it is. In Europe Jews wear a star to identify who they are. Like us carrying identity cards to prove we're entitled to a ration book. It's not the same, though. Hitler hates the Jews more than all his other enemies.

I'm sure Mother said once that I'd been christened. She'd have told Aunt Em those kinds of things, seeing they were pen friends. Aunt Em's a Quaker and doesn't believe in organized religion. I go to midnight mass at Christmas with the Gibsons, and Aunt Em stays home and greets us with cocoa after the service.

The little velvet box fits into one of the desk's cubbyholes. I can't think of a special occasion when I'd wear it.

I breathe in the special newness of my sketchbook. At school we use exercise books that have thin yellowish utility paper. Hopeless for real drawing. This paper is thick and made specially for sketching.

Five years ago, I, Sophie Mandel, of 16, Great Tichfield Street, London WC1, made an unbreakable rule: THE OLD SKETCH-BOOK MUST BE COMPLETED BEFORE I AM ALLOWED TO BEGIN DRAW-ING IN THE NEW ONE.

Two pages left. I decide to let my pencil improvise, the way a musician does.

Twenty minutes later, I look at my drawing. It's of a rather grand brick building. I've shaded the bricks gray, but they should be old rose. There's an arched doorway of thick heavy wood, not the kind that would break easily. Above the arch is a stone tablet inscribed with ancient writing. The windows are high and nar-row, like church windows. There's a small courtyard enclosed by a low stone wall. Wrought-iron gates in the center are ornamental. The gates are open. In the middle of each one is a circle and a perfect six-point star. . . .

Papa comes home early. He holds a handkerchief to his face.

"Are you hurt, Papa?" Zoffie asks.

"Your papa was careless; he fell out of a tree. Put your hand in my pocket, Zoffie."

The little girl finds a fir cone. "Mm, it smells the way you do when you come home from work—like pine trees. Thank you, Papa."

"Where is Mama?"

"Mama works late on Fridays, Papa."

Sometimes on Saturday mornings, Zoffie goes to the shop to help her mama. She picks up pins that are scattered on the floor of the workroom, where Mama does alterations for rich ladies. Mama shortens sleeves and lengthens hems and always talks with a pin between her teeth. They play a game—will Mama drop the pin?

Papa says, "Let's go for a little walk. Put your coat and hat on; it's cold for November."

Zoffie thinks it is a very long walk. They stop outside a big stone house and pass through some pretty gates. There is a side door, and they go in. Papa keeps his hat on. They cross a large hall and stand at the back of a high-ceilinged room filled with people.

Zoffie sees many candles flickering. On a small balcony, some little girls sit with their mothers. A man sings a song that makes Zoffie want to cry. The men wear long white scarves embroidered with silver and gold. They sway back and forth and sing words that Zoffie doesn't understand.

Papa bows to a man with a long beard; he stares at them.

Papa holds the girl's hand tight. "Time to go," he whispers. Outside it's dark. "Let's hurry, Mama will have supper waiting."

Footsteps behind them. They come closer. Papa's breath is loud and fast.

"Will it snow, Papa?" He doesn't answer.

"Jacob, wait," a voice calls out behind them.

They stop. Papa turns round slowly, gently nudging Zoffie so she stands in front of him. Papa puts his hands on her shoulders.

"A beautiful child, Jacob. It is good to see you once more. We must leave for Poland next week."

Papa puts out a hand. The old man covers it with both of his own. Then he touches Zoffie's cheek with one finger, turns, and goes back toward the stone house.

"Papa, is that St. Nicholas?"

"Can you keep a secret?" he asks.

Zoffie nods.

"That is your grandfather. My father. He is going away. I wanted him to see you. A long time ago, we had a disagreement."

"Were you angry with him, Papa?"

"We were angry with each other."

"What is the palace called, Papa?"

"It is not a palace, Zoffie. It is a place where Jews go to pray. It is called a synagogue. Now hurry, and remember it's a secret."

Mother is waiting for us. "Zoffie, your cheeks are cold like little winter apples." She puts the back of her hand against my cheek, where Grandfather's finger had touched it. "Quickly wash your hands for supper."

Zoffie hears Mama say, "Jacob, your face is bruised."

"I got in the way of a small demonstration. It is nothing for you to worry about."

"Where were you tonight? I asked you not to go out late. It's too dangerous."

Zoffie sees Papa put his arms round Mama. "A little walk, that's all, Liebchen. Even a Jew must have exercise."

"Only a crazy Jew goes out on a Friday night. Promise me to

be more careful. Go to work, come home. Stay home with us."

"I promise."

For supper there are sausages and fried potatoes. Zoffie eats two sausages.

6

Victory in Europe. V-E Day. Thursday, May 8, 1945. At last it's official: Victory in Europe.

"We want the king. We want the king."

Jammed amongst the crowd of thousands, we wait outside a floodlit Buckingham Palace for the Royal Family to appear. Every time the palace curtains move, the chants get louder. Mandy digs her fingers into my arm with excitement.

At last the French windows open. The moment we've been waiting for. The king in naval uniform, Her Majesty Queen Elizabeth smiling radiantly, and the princesses standing beside their parents.

"They're waving at us," Mandy screams. "Doesn't Princess Margaret look beautiful? She's exactly my age. Oh, I love that little blue hat."

"Don't you wish we'd been old enough to join up, Mandy? I could have been a war artist."

"Can't hear you!" Mandy shouts in my ear.

"Good old Winnie," yells the crowd as Prime Minister Winston Churchill comes out on the balcony. He raises his arm and holds up his fingers in the Victory sign, puffing away at his fat cigar.

We must have stood and cheered for hours, and then, when finally the balcony's empty again, we follow the crowd into the gardens of Buckingham Palace, where the lake shimmers with the reflection of a thousand lights, and a bonfire sparks into the warm May night.

Later, carried along by the crowd surging down the wide avenue of Pall Mall and into Trafalgar Square, we're hugged and kissed, jostled and squeezed.

"This is the most exciting night of our whole lives. Hang on to me, Sophie, so we don't get separated." Mandy's voice is beginning to sound hoarse.

We push our way up the steps of the Portrait Gallery. All you can see for miles are people. It's as if the whole of London is standing at the feet of Nelson's Column.

Words can't begin to describe it. *I need to draw it.*

Buildings dark for so long, now bathed in light. Colored streamers, bunting, and flags everywhere. The splash of fountains, and girls pulling up their skirts and wading into the water. A sailor climbs up a lamppost waving his cap at a bobby, who wants him to get down. Couples sit entwined on the massive dark stone lions. Men and women in uniform from around the world: Poles, Americans, Czechs, Canadians, and the forces of the Free French. Our own Tommies and two Highlanders in kilts blowing bagpipes.

I clutch the pencil stub in my pocket, willing myself not to forget a single thing.

A snaking line of dancers follows a makeshift band and struggles to keep in time to the conga beat. We run down to join in, matching our steps and voices with the conga line: "I came, I saw, I conga." On the Thames behind us, ships hoot and blow Victory whistles, drowning us out. The line makes it to Piccadilly Circus before it disperses into smaller groups.

We collapse out of breath. "I've got to take my shoes off," Mandy gasps. We find a small space on the crowded steps below the statue of the little winged archer. Eros is still partly boarded up, but his wings gleam.

"This morning, church bells woke me up. I jumped out of bed in a panic, thinking we'd been invaded, and then I remembered it's v-e Day," I say. "Can you remember the sound of church bells?"

Mandy shakes her head. "I'll miss it, you know," she confesses.

"Miss what?"

"The war. I don't mean the killing and the bombs or my dad going to war, but the good part."

"Amanda Gibson, there is no good part. I know what you mean, though. The excitement and us being part of something so huge, and the danger."

Mandy says, "I don't know how to live in peacetime. None of us knows."

"Well, the grown-ups will have to work it out." Then I look up and see a group of nurses, quite young—first year's. One of them wears her cap rakishly over one ear. She looks straight at me. Pauses, stares, and looks back after her group has moved on.

People say if you sit in Piccadilly Circus long enough, you're bound to see someone you know. *I know the face, but from where?*

"Sophie, you're as white as a sheet. What's the matter?"

"Nothing. Ghosts."

"What?"

"I saw someone I thought I knew."

"For a minute you looked as if you were going to faint. Are you hungry?" Mandy's worried.

"How could I possibly be hungry after all the food at the celebration tea? I'm going to dream about that trifle. Sponge fingers and jelly and fruit and custard and cream. Where on earth did they get it all? I must have eaten four salmon sandwiches."

"I thought Nigel was going to finish the sausage rolls by himself. I felt quite proud of Mum's Victory cake. Real icing and eggs," Mandy says. "The whole idea of street parties is amazing. It's as if every mother in the land had put something special away just for today. I can't think where your Aunt Em's been hiding that tin of pineapple. Under the bed, where you wouldn't find it." Mandy laughs. "Mum said it was for us, the children, because we've had to go without for so long. There was plenty for everyone in the street. Old Mrs. Benson ate more than anyone, did you notice?"

"Aunt Em thinks rationing will go on and on. She said, 'We'll have to feed Europe now.' Let's go home." We both yawn.

"Pull me up, Sophie."

"Come on, then. Bus or tube?"

"Buses aren't running, luv," a soldier volunteers cheerfully.

"Tube's quicker anyway." I link arms with Mandy.

The queue goes all the way down the steps. The woman in front of us says to her husband, "Reminds me of the Blitz, waiting for a place to sleep on the platform. All those strangers camped out between white chalk marks, huddled together hoping there wouldn't be a direct hit. People coming off the trains and stepping over us to get home. Thank God it's over."

When we reach Baker Street, Mandy leans against a lamp-post. "Lovely lovely light," she says. "Do you think we can find our street? I only know the way in the dark." She smiles blissfully up at the brightness.

"Time to go home, Mandy. Good night."

"Night, Sophie."

7

When I get in, Aunt Em is sitting by the open window. She'd made tea. "You're wearing your pearls, and your best blouse. You do look nice," I say.

"Thank you, dear. Did you have a lovely time?"

"I don't think I'll ever forget it. Is peace always going to be like this? Like Brighton Pier? It never got dark tonight. Bonfires and searchlights and floodlights and lamplight. I think every lightbulb in London must be on."

"Goodness, I hope not. What a waste of energy."

"How was your party, Aunt Em? Did you have a splendid celebration?"

"It was very festive. We all toasted the king after his speech with prewar sherry, and then the six of us did full justice to Mrs. Mallory's dinner. Corned beef carved in very thin slices, and a lovely salad with cucumber and radishes and tomatoes and new potatoes. Mr. Mallory is a wonderful gardener. After *all* that, we had rhubarb pie with cream from the top of the milk. How I could eat so much after our lovely Victory tea, I don't know."

"It sounds very sumptuous. Aunt Em, do you believe in ghosts?" I ask.

"I don't think so," she says thoughtfully. "I do think there are times when something makes us remember the past very strongly, and we may think we see or sense someone from that time. Tonight there were ghosts with us in the dining room. We talked about that other war, and Armistice Day in 1918. We thought then that peace would last forever."

"It will this time, Aunt Em, you'll see." I want to comfort her.

"I can't help thinking of all the men and women who will never come home. One of the guests tonight has a son in a prison camp in the Far East. He was captured in Malaya in 1941. We've still got that war to finish," Aunt Em says.

The phone rings. "Whoever can be calling at this hour? It's past eleven." Aunt Em picks up the receiver.

"If it's work, say no. Tomorrow's an official holiday," I whisper.

"Gerald, what a nice surprise. Good. Yes, we're fine. It *is* an exciting night. . . . Thank you. We'll try to come down soon. Love to Winifred. Yes. Good-bye, Gerald."

I say, "*Love* to Aunt Winifred? We're going to *see* them?" I pull a face and get one of Aunt Em's looks. Then she gives in and smiles.

"I'll concede, Sophie, that Aunt Winifred is not the easiest person to get along with. I've never quite forgiven her for her attitude when I told her you were coming to stay with me—that air of superiority she had as she said, 'Well, really, Margaret. I find that rather eccentric. You know nothing about bringing up children. People will think it very odd—a single woman with a child.'"

"I think you managed beautifully, Aunt Em."

"Thank you. Oh dear, the first time you met Aunt Winifred, you were so naughty. It was early 1939. You'd been here about two months. I think you must have taken an instant dislike to Winifred."

"Good instincts?" I ask.

"Sophie!"

"Well, Aunt Em, she was looking me over as though I were a dog she was going to buy."

"You can't possibly remember that. You weren't even eight years old."

"I do."

"Winifred was upset because she'd heard that if there was going to be a war, she'd have to take in evacuees. It was actually quite funny. She said, 'I really don't think it's fair. They could send me *anyone*. Slum children, with *things* in their hair. Gerald, you're a solicitor. Do something.'

"Gerald said, 'I don't think that argument will carry any weight with the authorities who are trying to protect the nation's children.'

"She was very put out that Gerald disagreed with her."

"Then Aunt Winifred asked me if I liked dolls," I say.

"Quite right. She announced: 'I've got the perfect solution. I mean, Sophie looks like a dear clean little girl. I can tell the authorities that my sister-in-law and her ward will be using the guest room. After all, Margaret, it would be merely a temporary arrangement, wouldn't it? Should danger arise.'

"It was then that you surprised me. I didn't even know you had such an extensive vocabulary, or could understand so much English!

"'I do not like dolls,' you said. 'I have the tummy ache very often. I cannot sleep. I cry all the time.' Such fibs. You never, well hardly ever, cried. You slept ten hours at least every night, and to the best of my knowledge, had a cast-iron stomach."

"Well, mostly I do," I say.

"I was both proud and ashamed of you. Uncle Gerald, who is surprisingly perceptive, said, 'Sophie seems to have settled the question. We'd better get along, my dear. Two and a half hours' drive, at least. Thanks for tea, Margaret.'"

"Uncle Gerald gave me a shilling when they left."

"More than you deserved, young lady."

"You would have been bored with a perfect child, Aunt Em."

"No danger of that. Good night, darling. Don't stay up drawing too late."

"How did you know I was going to?"

"Like my brother, I'm quite perceptive. I'll come and tuck you up soon."

"Good. I don't think Aunt Winifred has tucked anyone up in her entire life."

"Sophie, Gerald is my only brother. Let's make an effort." I kiss the top of her head and say okay and run!

One of the things I can't bear about Aunt Winifred is that she's always reminding me that I don't belong here. She makes me feel "temporary." I'm not, I *do* belong here. It's my home.

Upstairs I rough in some of the sights: the statue of Eros, the crowds, the face of the girl who had stared at me. No good, I can't do anything justice—I'm too tired. My hair on the pillow smells of smoke from the bonfire in the palace gardens. I close my eyes. . . .

Mama lets Zoffie carry the string bag with apples home from the evening market. It's cold. Zoffie wears her new red hat and mittens. The street lamps are lit; people hurry home.

Mama rolls pastry and slices apples. "*Apfel kuchen für Papa.*" Very carefully Zoffie layers the apple slices, then Mama gives her a handful of raisins to sprinkle over them.

"When is Papa coming home?" Zoffie asks.

"Soon."

The apple pie is ready; it had cooled. Mama and Zoffie wait. Then they eat supper.

A soft tap and a voice at the door. "Frau Mandel, let me in." It is Frau Wiege from upstairs. "There is burning, looting in the streets." She whispers something, and goes out hurriedly. Mama locks the door.

"What is burning, Mama?"

"Leaves, grass."

"The leaves are finished, Mama, it's winter."

"And some are left. It's your bedtime."

"Mama, when is . . . ?"

"No more questions, Zoffie."

There are noises in the night: breaking glass, shouting and laughing, tires screeching in the street outside their apartment. The air is full of smoke.

In the morning, Mama says, "No school today. You can come to work with me."

Mama's shop is beautiful, not like next door. The glass is smashed there. Herr Eckstein is scrubbing the pavement. He does not look at them.

Mama hurries Zoffie into the back room. She begins her search for pins. When the lady who owns the shop comes in, Zoffie hides under the table.

"Good morning, Frau Mandel. I am sorry to bring you bad news. You are a good worker, but there have been changes. I am sure you understand. You need not finish out the week. Here. . . ." She gives Zoffie's mama an envelope.

Papa does not come home again that night.

Next day, very early, they hear Papa's key in the door.

"The Gestapo let me go—this time. I am a Jew with an Aryan wife. My employer says the work I do is 'essential'; it can be done only by someone like me."

"For how long is gardening essential?" Mama asks, and pours Papa his coffee. She does not smile.

"I have not eaten since the ninth."

"Two days?" Mama cuts more bread. "Later we'll talk. Not now."

"Zoffie," Papa says, when he finishes breakfast. "What shall I draw for you?"

"A garden. Papa, we baked you an apple pie. Where were you?"

"In a garden like the one I'm drawing for you. It's called a maze—a labyrinth."

"Where are the flowers? Why are the paths going round and round in circles?"

"It is a crazy garden—a kind of puzzle. People go into the labyrinth. Some stay and go round and round forever. Some are lucky and find the way out."

"Let me draw, too." Zoffie draws labyrinths for the rest of the day.

That night I dream of Nazi soldiers chasing a girl round and round a garden. They follow her into a labyrinth. Someone starts a fire.

I wake up and call out a name—*Marianne*.

I hardly ever remember my dreams, and I haven't seen Marianne in almost seven years.

8

We'd eaten our sandwiches and lay in the long, sweet-smelling grass on top of Parliament Hill. The three of us had cycled all the way to Hampstead Heath, and I was almost asleep.

Mandy, who's incapable of staying still for more than one minute, tickles my neck with a blade of grass. "Let's do something."

Nigel mumbles, "Too hot."

"You know what she's like. We may as well give in graciously. I'll agree to anything as long as I don't have to move," I say.

"How about best thing/worst thing?" Mandy says.

"No point doing best thing because we're bound to say it's V-E Day."

"Worst thing's more fun," says Nigel.

"It's got to be the worst thing we've ever done that we've not told each other before," I say. "One minute thinking time. Go."

"I'll start," Nigel says. "I was very young, you understand . . ."

"Oh, get on with it, twin . . ."

"I'd got a new penknife for cubs and Mike Rivers—"

"Mike—the worst boy in the street—the one Dad said you weren't supposed to play with?" Mandy exclaims.

"I'm not sure that this story's going to be suitable for our delicate sensibilities," I add.

"Do you want me to tell you or not?" Nigel says severely.

"Mike got hold of a piece of alder wood, which is easy to carve. I said, 'Let's make a pipe.' I carved the bowl, scooping out the wood to make a little cup. Then we cut down a piece of garden cane, made a notch in the side of the bowl, and twisted the cane into it. We found some oak leaves and stuffed the pipe and lit it. We had a really good smoke, except for the coughing."

"That's it?" I say. "Every little boy in the country smokes at some time, and that's the worst thing you ever did? Pathetic!"

"I expected something awful. It's not good enough. I hoped for better from my twin," Mandy says.

"Put it this way," says Nigel, trying to reestablish his authority, "that's all I'm prepared to confess at this time."

Mandy sticks her tongue out at Nigel and says, "I'll go next. When we were evacuated and I was at Mrs. Kingsley's in Kent, she sent me out one Saturday morning for a loaf of bread. She gave me two shillings and told me not to lose the change. It was early; the loaf was still warm—it had just come out of the oven. I was starving, as usual. The bread smelled so good, I thought, 'If I pick off a tiny bit of the crust, no one will notice.' I broke off a tiny piece, and it tasted wonderful. I still don't know how it happened, but next time I looked, I'd eaten half the loaf.

"I started to cry. I didn't know what to do. I wanted to go and tell Nigel. Then I had an inspiration: 'If I finish all the bread, I can tell her I lost the money. Anyone can fall down and lose two shillings.' I convinced myself that I'd fallen on the path down to the village, scraped my knee, and seen the coin roll away before I could catch it. I even rubbed dirt on my knee. So I went back and said, 'I'm very very sorry Mrs. Kingsley, I lost the money. I'll write Mummy and she'll send you some more.'

"She gave me a spanking and sent me up to bed for the rest of the day. She didn't give me anything, not even a drink. I could smell her cooking tea, something with fried onions."

"Old witch," Nigel mutters. I have a feeling if he'd been with Mike Rivers, he'd have said something a lot worse.

"What's the verdict?" Mandy asks.

"She was an awful woman and she ill-treated you, so the lie was out of fear," I comment.

"Still, it was a lie and stealing. In fact, a premeditated act," Nigel says.

We consult. "The punishment is, you have to write a letter to her, explaining what you did, and enclose a postal order for the amount you stole, and tell her how she drove you to it," I say.

"By the way, what *did* you do with the change?" Nigel asks.

"I threw it away, so the lie would only be a little fib. I love the punishment. It'll get rid of my guilt."

"Mandy," I say, "you can't mean that. I mean, about feeling

guilty. She stole. The government and your mother paid her to take care of you and she starved you. Actually, for a child of eight, I think it was rather a brilliant way out of the situation.

"Now I'll tell you my evil deed. It happened about three years ago. Miss Merton was teaching us gym. She was at least sixty even then because all the young teachers had been called up for the war effort. I hated going to class and that morning I'd forgotten to bring my gym blouse. She told me I'd have to participate in my vest and knickers. So I told her I hadn't brought my blouse because I had an awful headache and a stomachache and I was hoping she'd excuse me. She said I'd better go home and bring her a note next day.

"I couldn't believe my luck, and decided I'd do some sketching. There'd been a raid the night before and I thought, 'If London keeps getting bombed, there'll be no record of any of the great buildings left.'

"I started close to the school. First I drew Nash Crescent, that lovely curve of houses near Albany Street. Then I cycled to the Royal Academy of Music. I thought I'd have time to draw the BBC before lunch too. I'd just got the outline right when I felt a tap on my shoulder. A policeman was looking down at me. 'I'll take care of that, Miss,' he said, and removed my sketchbook and began to leaf through it.

"'It's all right,' I explained, 'I've got permission to be absent from school.' I thought Miss Merton had changed her mind and sent a policeman to find me, and I'd be punished for missing school.

"'Fond of drawing important landmarks, are you?' he said. 'I think you'd better come along to the station, young lady, and tell the sergeant about what you've been up to.'

"I had to wheel my bike while he walked beside me. I couldn't think what all the fuss was about. It's not as if I'd been stealing, or anything like that. He took me into the sergeant's office. I was allowed to sit down while they conferred. I thought I'd better apologize, so I did and said I'd never do it again.

"The sergeant looked at my sketches and asked, 'Who put you up to this?'

"I got confused at the question, so I told him the truth—that I'd forgotten to bring my gym blouse to change into, and that I hated gym anyway, had pleaded a headache, and was sent home.

"He demanded my name and wrote it down. Then he wanted to know my age and place of birth. The looks on their faces when I said Berlin, Germany made me feel like a criminal. He wanted to know if I lived with my parents. I was a bit frightened by then, so I said I was an orphan, and I lived with my guardian, who worked at the Ministry of Food.

"'Who told you to tell this story if you're caught?' he asked, and he and the constable kept giving each other meaningful looks. Honestly, I didn't know what he was talking about. I mean it's not as though I'd deliberately planned to forget my gym blouse.

"Then he said they'd check my statements, and my drawings were confiscated. I was just going to ask him not to do that because they were important, when he pointed his finger at me— you know the way they always show on the posters when they issue a warning to the public about something. He said that the enemy was everywhere, and I wouldn't be the first child who'd been recruited as a spy. He said any drawing or photograph that might give information to the enemy was a major offence. 'I want the truth,' he said. He was really stern and I had visions of being locked up for years. I wondered when they were going to take my fingerprints.

"I said, 'Please, Sir, I am telling you the truth: I'm not a spy. I'm a refugee from the Nazis. Drawing's my hobby.' I promised him I'd never miss gym again, even if I had to take it in my vest and knickers. I prayed they'd believe me."

Nigel's shoulder's shook with laughter and Mandy was rolling on the grass and howling. A woman walking her dog made a wide berth round us. "Hooligans," we heard her say.

"I think it was the vest part that convinced them. The sergeant told the constable to escort me back to school. 'If you were a few years older, young lady, you would be interned as an enemy alien. As it is, you may well be taken into protective custody. I hope I have made myself clear?'

"I didn't dare speak after that, and just nodded.

"The constable took me right inside the school and made sure I went into the office. I told the secretary that I hadn't felt well and had permission to go home, but that I now felt very much better, and please would she tell Miss Merton that I was back for my lessons. Can you imagine if I had to ask Aunt Em for a note?"

"Old Miss Merton, who's almost senile?" Mandy says, wobbling her chin in imitation of the gym teacher.

"This is definitely the worst thing I've ever heard you do, Sophie," Nigel says. "I can see the sergeant's point. You *could* have been passing on information."

Nigel and Mandy whisper for a few minutes. "We think a suitable punishment would be to give up your sweet ration for a month, then buy some chocolate for Miss Merton, and write a note telling her how much you appreciate all she's done for the school, and how you've always loved her lessons."

"That would be another lie, and awfully cruel," I say.

"No appeals, not even on the grounds of being a foreigner who didn't know any better."

The game is almost turning into something unpleasant. For a moment, Nigel has seen me not as his best friend, but as an alien—a foreigner. *Is this what peace is going to be like?*

Mrs. Gibson is cooking spam fritters for supper, with mashed potatoes and runner beans from their garden. There is a lovely smell of baked apples.

"Nigel's doing dishes tonight, Mum," Mandy says, looking meaningfully at her brother. "He offered, didn't you, twin?"

Mrs. Gibson is just pouring the last of the custard over Mandy's helping of baked apple, when a voice booms from the hall: "Anyone home?"

"Dad!" The three of them fly out of the kitchen and I just manage to save the jug from tipping over. I'm mopping up a few drops of custard that have dripped onto the table when Mr. Gibson, or rather Corporal Gibson of His Majesty's Transit Corps, puts his kit bag down in the corner.

"Hello, young Sophie, you've grown again. How's your aunt?"

"Fine, Sir. Thank you. It's awfully good to see you."

"Sit down, Dan. I'll make you some bacon and eggs, all right?" asks Mrs. Gibson.

"Perfect, luv. Good to stretch my legs under my own kitchen table. Seven days' leave. Surprised you, didn't I?"

Mandy stands behind his chair and twines her arms round his neck. Mrs. Gibson is putting what looks like a month's ration of bacon into the pan.

"Thank you very much for the delicious supper, Mrs. Gibson. I'd better get on home. Good night, Mr. Gibson."

Nigel follows me into the hall. "It was a great day, Soph. See you at the dance on Friday."

Everything's all right again.

It takes me only five minutes to cycle home from the Gibsons'. Their happiness at being together again reminds me how few relatives I've got. For years there's been only Aunt Em. Her parents died in the influenza epidemic of 1919, or I'd have "adopted" grandparents the way Aunt Em's my "adopted" aunt.

How did she get through such an awful time—losing her parents, her brother, and her fiancé? She must have loved him an awful lot to have never got married.

Supposing it wasn't a lie that time I told the police I was an orphan? If it *was* true, would Aunt Em adopt me? Not that I *want* to be an orphan. I'm not wishing away my parents, or anything. They're safe. Parents don't die without their children finding out. I'd *know* something like that.

At birthdays and Christmas, Aunt Em always says she's certain my parents are thinking of me, that once the war's over letters will start arriving.

At breakfast this morning, Aunt Em reminded me again that it won't be long before we hear from Mama and Papa. She said if there's too much of a delay, she'd get in touch with the Red Cross. I was hoping we could talk about what would happen when letters do start arriving. *Will Aunt Em and I go on as before?* When you've lived in a place more than half your life, it's pretty devastating to think about changing.

Aunt Em seems to avoid talking about the subject, and I don't want to make an issue of it. *I'm a coward.*

9

"Wasn't it heaven getting two days off in the middle of the week, Sophie? Tomorrow's the Victory dance. Have you got your costume ready?"

Mandy and I are in the school cafeteria, at lunchtime on Thursday.

"Mum's helping me finish off a witch's cloak from the upstairs blackout curtains. She says she's only too pleased to get rid of them! I still need a hat, though."

"I requisitioned a piece of cardboard from the salvage box. Thought the war effort could spare it. I'll make it into a coned hat for you, and we can paste stars and symbols on it."

"Thanks, Sophie. How about your costume?"

"Mine's easy. I'll go as an Impressionist artist—you know, wearing a beret. Aunt Em found a sort of Russian-looking smock in amongst the Red Cross things in the spare room. It's got very wide sleeves. I'll wear her spotted scarf tied in a floppy bow round my neck. That should do. I've got a pair of black woolen stockings too. I may die of heatstroke, though. Which reminds me, what are you wearing under your cloak?"

"Mum's come to the rescue again. She got a blue full-length slip; if I knot the shoulder straps it'll fit me. Bother, there's the bell. Biology, next. If Miss Carter asks me to dissect an earthworm, I shall refuse on the grounds of animal rights," Mandy declares.

"I think she looks a bit wormy herself," I add.

On Friday night, we get to the dance at 7:30 and the room is already packed.

"Great decorations, Sophie," Mandy says.

"I can only take half the credit—Nigel did a lot of ladder-climbing too."

The kitchen committee has put colored cotton strips of red, white, and blue bunting to cover the tables, and there are jugs of homemade lemonade, as well as an urn of tea and platters of sand-wiches, with little flags stuck into the bread: meat paste, fish paste, and Marmite. There are several plates of biscuits too.

We'd painted the lightbulbs in different colors—green, red, and blue—so the old rec room would be romantically transformed.

Nigel looks very dashing as a pirate with a patch over his eye. I am a bit concerned about his feet, stuck in huge Wellington boots. Mandy says other than the waltz, not too much progress has been made with the dancing lessons.

We all wear numbers pinned to our backs so that the prize committee can judge our costumes more easily as we dance.

The M.C. (who is Reverend Peter's curate) announces a general "Excuse Me" dance. Vera Lynn's voice drifts enticingly through the loudspeaker.

Mandy is dancing with Reverend Peter at the far end of the room, and Simon and I circle slowly under the blue lights.

Nigel is talking to Stanley, a newcomer. I don't like him— he's already made some nasty comments about people and then laughed them off as a joke. I notice that Stanley's wearing jodhpurs and riding boots, and carrying a crop.

Nigel comes over and takes my hand. Simon shrugs his shoulders in exaggerated disappointment. Everyone is having fun.

Stanley says loudly, over the music, "Bit soon to be fraternizing with the enemy, isn't it? Time to go home, Fräulein."

Nigel's face is so white, every one of his freckles stands out. He lets go of my hand, walks over to Stanley, grabs his arm, and pushes him out of the back door. "Wait for me," he says over his shoulder.

Someone cranks up the gramophone. Simon comes over to me, and we finish the dance. Luckily it's almost over.

When I get outside, Mandy is already there. The twins have a sort of built-in radar about each other. Mandy is staunching a stream of blood from Nigel's nose. Stanley is on his hands and knees, shaking his head. He stands up, and I see he has a black eye.

Mandy is furious. "You're a fine pair," she says. "Look at you. This is supposed to be a dance celebrating Victory, not the start of a new war."

Reverend Peter comes out to join us. "I have no idea what this is about, however, I suggest you shake hands and then come into the kitchen for repairs. There should be some ice there," he says.

Stanley mumbles something and walks off.

I pick up the riding crop. I feel like hurling it after him. Instead I hand it to Reverend Peter.

"Thank you, Sophie. You know where I am if you need me."

Nigel speaks for the first time. "Thanks, Mandy. I think the bleeding's stopped." He shoves the bloody handkerchief in his pocket.

"I'll go back in, then. Hurry up or you'll be too late for the judging." Mandy goes back in to the dance.

"Sorry, Nigel." I say.

"For what?"

"You know." *Does he expect me to say that I am the cause of the fight because of where I've been born?*

Nigel leans against the wall of the alley.

A thin black kitten twines its body round my legs and begins to scratch my stockings. "Ow." I pick up the kitten and stroke its fur. "Are you hungry?" The kitten begins to purr. "Nigel, you don't have to fight my battles. I've been called names before."

Nigel says, "Remember when you and Mandy were being bullied by that gang in the village? Didn't I sort it out? No one's going to get away with calling you names while I'm around. If that Stanley what's-his-name so much as looks your way again, you let me know."

"I told you. I don't want anyone to fight about me. People like Stanley aren't worth it." I smile at him. I don't want him to think he's not appreciated. "Now, let's take this poor starving animal inside and feed it."

"Okay." Nigel leans forward and strokes the cat's ears. His head is very close to mine; his hair brushes my cheek.

I smile. This is almost as romantic as the shipboard scene when Paul Henreid and Bette Davis share a cigarette in *Now Voyager*.

"What's the joke about?" Nigel asks, as we go back inside.

"I was actually thinking about smoking."

"Smoking! I didn't know you smoked, Sophie."

"I don't."

Mandy wins first prize for her witch costume, and Nigel walks me home.

If I was asked to say the best thing about this evening, it would have to be the touch of Nigel's hair on my face. The worst thing—that horrible Stanley. How dare he? *Time to go home, Fräulein.*

I am home. This is my home and no one's going to say or do anything to change that.

10

’m always early for my volunteering at the hospital—partly because of what Sister would say if I weren’t punctual, but mostly because I enjoy it more than anything I do for the war effort. Peace effort, I suppose I should say now, even though the war in the Far East is still on.

A hospital’s a world of its own, quite different from what goes on outside. I should think working here is a bit like being in the forces. I’m on the lowest rung, like a recruit—someone who’s just joined up—but I feel useful.

The porter recognizes me now. “Nice day, Miss,” or “Looks like rain.” Most of the nurses seem pleased to have an extra pair of hands, and even talk about the patients in front of me as if I belong.

I know that the bandages I’ve rolled will be used for wounds almost at once. When I arrange a vase of flowers, or plump a pillow, or make up beds with the corners tucked in tightly, I'm doing something useful. Last week I was allowed to sterilize the thermometers. I admit polishing bedpans is not what I enjoy doing most, but Sister-in-charge actually said, "Well done, dear."

For the next five Saturdays, I'm on women's surgical. My favorite is the children's ward. I love the babies; they're not afraid to tell you if something hurts—they scream. Adult patients think they're a nuisance.

I've barely put on my apron when I'm told to wipe all the wheels on the screens that are put round the beds for privacy. When I've done that, it is time to bring in the supper trays. There are twenty-four women on this ward. Poor things, they're having boiled fish tonight—white fish, with lumpy white gravy. You can smell it all the way down the corridor.

I'd changed the water in the flower vases when a voice, with the trace of a foreign accent, says, "Please make sure beds thirteen and seventeen get the first two trays. The women are on salt-free diets."

I look up and say, "Yes, Nurse." Pick up the trays and put them down again, very slowly and carefully. I need to be sure. I say, "Excuse me, Nurse, didn't we see each other on V-E night . . . ?"

"The nurse pauses a moment, then says, "Sophie? You can't be Sophie, *my* Sophie."

We hug each other. "Marianne, I've been thinking about you all week."

"You've grown up. I can't believe it. Do you still sleep all the time?" Marianne takes my hands in both of hers and beams.

"Your hair's different and you're not taller than me anymore," I say.

We laugh and hug again. I can feel tears threatening to well up.

The Ward Sister appears. Her snowy cap sits on her gray hair at a precisely correct angle. As I look down, I can almost see my face reflected in her polished black shoes. She crackles starch with each breath.

"What is the meaning of this unseemly display? I would have thought you knew better, Nurse Kohn. This is a surgical ward, not Piccadilly Circus."

We freeze as though posing for a family portrait.

"Your cap is crooked. Straighten it. Pull down your cuffs."

Marianne adjusts her uniform.

"The supper trays are late. I will see you at the end of your shift, Nurse Kohn."

"Yes, Sister. I'm sorry, Sister," Marianne says. I pick up the trays again and overhear Marianne explain: "Sophie is a great friend. I haven't seen her for over seven years. I'd lost her."

And then Sister's reply: "That will do, Nurse. There will be no further emotional outbursts on my ward."

When supper is over, I wipe the trays down before stacking them neatly on the trolleys to take them down to the kitchen. Marianne whisks in to refill a water jug. She whispers urgently, "My half-day's on Wednesday, let's meet. Are you still at school?"

I nod. "We finish at four. I can meet you anywhere."

"Outside Goodge Street tube station—four thirty. I'd better go."

She glides out. No one ever runs in a hospital; it's the first rule they teach us.

I cycle home in a daze. I can't wait to tell Aunt Em that I've found my ghost. There is a car parked outside number sixteen. A Ford. Which of Aunt Em's friends owns a Ford? I know it's not Uncle Gerald's. Unless he's changed his car, and that's pretty unlikely in wartime. I've got to stop thinking "wartime." It isn't anymore, even though we're being told everything's going to be in shorter supply because of the people in Europe, who have a lot less than we do.

"Aunt Em?" I call, as I enter the house.

"I'm in the sitting room, dear."

We don't usually use that room, except for visitors. We're "kitchen people." Aunt Em is sitting in the armchair. A strange man, at least one I haven't seen before, is holding her wrist.

"This is Sophie, Dr. O'Malley."

"How do you do, Sir?"

The doctor drops Aunt Em's wrist, smiles at me, and says, "Good. We'll soon have you back to normal. Hello, Sophie."

"Aunt Em, what happened—did you fall?"

"Your aunt had a little dizzy spell and called the surgery. Very sensible thing to do."

The man in the tweed jacket, with leather patches at the elbows and the lilt in his speech, isn't our lovely Dr. Baines, who'd taken out my tonsils, painfully, a couple of years ago and nursed me through measles and mumps.

"No need to look so worried, young lady. Dr. Baines is taking his first holiday since 1938, and I'm covering for him. Why don't you help your aunt to her room? Meanwhile, if I might use your telephone, Miss Simmonds, I'll phone a prescription through to Boots Chemist. There's one open late on Baker Street."

When we get upstairs Aunt Em says, "I'm all right now, Sophie. Put a clean towel out for Dr. O'Malley. I'll be tucked up in bed before you know it."

I run down as Dr. O'Malley is replacing the receiver. "Now I'll just wash my hands and be off. I've two more calls to make tonight."

"Will Aunt Em be all right?" I force myself to ask. *I have to know.*

The doctor puts his hand on my shoulder for a moment. "Yes," he says. "Now that the war is over, the strain is showing, that's all. People are tired. They haven't had enough to eat, enough rest, or any holidays for six years of war. Worries about family, getting through air raids. Making do month after month. I call it war fatigue.

"All your aunt needs is some 'peace' and a bit of spoiling. I've told her not to go back to work for a few days. Dr. Baines will be back by then. Good night, Sophie."

I put a white cloth on a tray, and two digestive biscuits on a plate beside the cup and saucer. A jug of milk and the small glazed brown teapot for one, which Aunt Em has had for years and years.

Tomorrow I'll pick some lilies of the valley. There's a clump behind the apple tree. I'll put it on her breakfast tray.

I knock on Aunt Em's door. She's lying against her pillows, her eyes closed. I start to tiptoe out again. . . .

"I'm not asleep, Sophie, just resting."

I plump up the pillows, put another one behind her back, and pour her tea.

"How lovely. It's nice to have my own resident nurse. Sit down and tell me about your day." Aunt Em nibbles a biscuit.

"Tomorrow. I have to cycle down to Boots' now for the prescription. Back in a jiffy."

When I get back, Aunt Em is asleep. I put the medicine, a spoon, and a glass of water beside her. On a note I write: WAKE ME IF YOU NEED ME. Underneath I draw a picture of a lady stranded on a mountain calling help.

I leave both doors open. It is almost eleven before I am in bed. I don't feel the least bit sleepy.

I want to think some more about finding Marianne again, to get used to the idea. Keep her to myself a bit longer before telling Aunt Em about a girl I knew for only two days when I was seven— a girl who's so important to me because she took care of me as if she were my older sister.

I open my new sketchbook and begin to draw.

It is the first time I'd been to a station. I draw the train and the smoke belching up into the roof, which is as high as the sky. I draw a woman wearing a scarf over her head, tied like a kerchief.

I draw hands waving handkerchiefs and mouths shouting good-bye.

I draw the little girl looking at steps too big for her to manage.

I draw the inside of the compartment. There are seven children—four girls and three boys. The seats are hard. Wood. *How do I remember that?*

It's as if I'm sitting there again, instead of on my own soft mattress. Sometimes that happens when I draw. It's as if I'm right inside the picture.

I am squeezed in the middle of the row, between Marianne and a girl with long braids. A boy puts my rucksack overhead. . . .

Papa says, "Take Zoffie to your mother. It's our best chance."

Chance. Chance of what? Is she going to her grandmother's?

"What about you?" asks Mama.

"What about me? I'll trust to luck. Go to work, dig my ditches, come home. Wait for what the next day brings."

What luck is Papa waiting for?

"For how long, Jacob? Face the situation. You are safe only if I stay here with you. I want to stay. I will never leave you."

"Take the child to Dresden. Disappear with her."

Disappear?

"Zoffie is half yours. Mother will close the door in our faces."

Zoffie says, "I want to go to Grandpa with the long beard. I don't want to disappear."

Mama is angry. "Now see what you've done."

Papa says, "Bed, Zoffie."

The girl overhears him telling Mama: "He is an old man, by now over the border in Poland, who knows where. We must get the child away somehow."

Zoffie sits up in her bunk and opens her storybook. She shows the pictures of Hansel and Gretel to Käthe. "This is Hansel and this is Gretel. Their cruel stepmother left them alone in the forest. They could not find their way home. The birds ate the breadcrumbs that Hansel dropped on the path to help the children find their way back. Hansel and Gretel walked and walked. They came to a house made of gingerbread and icing sugar. They ate a piece of the door. It was a knob made of chocolate, and it grew right back again.

"A cruel witch lived in the house. She put Hansel in a cage, to fatten him up for a pie. Each day she said, 'Let me feel your finger,' but Gretel had given her brother a twig to push through the bars to trick the old woman. The witch got tired of waiting for Hansel to get fat, and lit a big fire in the black stove. She opened the door to put on more wood, and Gretel pushed her inside. The witch went up in smoke.

"Then Gretel freed her brother and a little bird showed them the way home and they lived happily ever after."

That must be the night her parents decided to send her away to be safe with Aunt Em.

11

Wednesday's my favorite day of the week because we get a double period of art. Miss Potter, the art teacher, has brought three objects for our still-life project. When she cuts the orange into quarters, we gasp longingly; it's ages since most of us have even seen an orange. Miss Potter says she'll draw lots after class, so four lucky people will each get a piece.

She arranges the orange quarters on a thick blue platter, and places a plain glass tumbler beside it. The light from the window bounces off them so that the glass catches the colors, like a prism.

After a while Miss Potter comes and stands beside me. She doesn't say anything, she doesn't have to. We both know I'm not concentrating today.

The sight and smell of the orange brings back so many memories that I connect with Marianne. My mother had put an orange in the pocket of my dress before we left Berlin. We were given more oranges on the boat, by the sailors, and again when we arrived in England. Marianne had said she couldn't bear the smell of oranges and offered me hers. I remember being too sleepy to keep awake long enough to answer her.

It's a relief when the bell rings.

Mandy and I hurry so as not to be late for library duty, which is supposed to be a privilege. We've been revising all the catalog cards, making sure that every book on the shelves has a matching card and that all the cards are in alphabetical order.

"You're miles away, Sophie," Mandy says. "Is it because of meeting your friend?"

"That's just it. I don't know if she's a friend or some stranger I spent two days of my life with, and I've built it up out of all proportion."

"What does it matter? Either way, you'll have lots to talk about. It sounds rather like being evacuated," Mandy whispers, but not quietly enough. The librarian materializes.

"Girls, you are not here to gossip. Get on with your work, please." She glares at us.

Rather like being evacuated. I suppose it was—not knowing where we were going, or who'd take us in, and saying good-bye to our parents, except that I'd never actually said good-bye.

The difference I hadn't talked about to Mandy was, the Nazis on the train stole or spoiled our things and twisted Käthe's head off.

Mandy mutters, "Stop biting your nails, Sophie. They're just beginning to look decent."

———

Four o'clock comes at last. Washing my hands in the cloakroom, I look in the mirror and see my face. I have two bright red blotches on my cheeks. Nerves.

Mandy says, "Put your hat on, take three deep breaths, and calm down. This isn't an exam."

"Suppose she doesn't turn up?"

"Then you'll go home and listen to the radio, or draw, or go for a bike ride, or talk to Aunt Em, or read. Come on, Sophie, pull yourself together, as our 'revered' headmistress would say. Tell you what—why don't I walk to the tube with you? Let's hurry, though. Dad went back to his unit today, so Mum will want cheering up."

On the way to meet Marianne, I try to explain to Mandy. "You see, she's the only person in England who remembers me from before. I'm not complaining or anything—I know I'm lucky—but you've got Nigel and your parents, and two grand-mothers and a grandfather, and goodness knows how many uncles and aunts and cousins."

"You've got Aunt Em," Mandy says.

"You know perfectly well she's not really my aunt. Even her name's not real. I started calling her Aunt Em after the aunt in *The Wizard of Oz*."

"Okay, I forgot. You have my permission to be as nervous as you like. Look, is that her? The nurse by the telephone kiosk. She's waving."

"That's her." I wave back. "Come and be introduced."

"Next time. I'll see you tomorrow."

I cross the road to where Marianne's waiting.

I 2

"'m a bit early. I couldn't wait to see you again," Marianne
says, smiling broadly.

"Me, too." We shake hands rather formally, and that
makes us laugh, breaking the ice. "I hope you didn't get into too
much trouble with Sister."

"She went on a bit about decorum, and setting an example.
She's actually quite decent under all that starch. Sophie, I cannot get over how tall you are. What happened to you?"

"I grew. I was fourteen on April 27."

"I was eighteen on May 3. Let's have some tea. There's a
Lyon's restaurant round the corner. It's self-serve. Would you like
a sticky bun? I'm always starved. The food at the nursing residence is even worse than the patients get."

Marianne insists on paying.

"Before I forget, Aunt Em said please come for tea or supper when you're free. She's longing to meet you."

"Aunt Em?" Marianne looks puzzled. "Who is Aunt Em?"

"My guardian, alias Miss Margaret Simmonds."

"In that case, of course, I'd love to. Is she the lady who fetched you from Liverpool Street Station—the one in the gray coat?"

"That's her. Still wearing that coat."

"She looked very kind. I watched her face when she spoke to you, and the way she held your hand when you left."

"She *is* kind. She and my mother were pen friends for years before the war, and when things got difficult, she wrote and asked Aunt Em to take care of me. The day we left, Mother said I was going on holiday to England."

The men at the table beside ours are smoking. The gray-blue haze swirls behind Marianne's head. I remember the first time I saw her. . . .

Mama says, "Today is a special day, Zoffie. It's the day you are going on holiday to England. Look, you have a new dress to wear, and so has Käthe. Two pretty girls. There is something in the pocket for you."

"Is the orange for me?"

"Yes, to eat on the journey. Stop jumping up and down. You don't want to be late, do you? Let me brush your hair."

"Are you coming on holiday to England too, Mama?"

"No, how could I? Who would look after Papa? You are such a big girl, you can manage on your own. . . ."

"Is that the holiday train, Mama? It's so big. Why are we waiting? I want to go through the gate."

Mama is talking to a woman holding a list. She is blocking our way.

"Please check again. Her name is Zoffie Mandel. She was promised a place."

"Mama, they are closing the little doors on the train. The guard is blowing the whistle. The train will leave without me!"

"No. It won't. Come quickly." Mama pushes me onto the platform. So many children waving. All going away like me. Mama pulls me along. I hold Käthe away from the soldiers and the fierce dogs.

"Run, Zoffie. See, the door is still open. Good girl. Stay with the children." She lifts me up into the compartment.

"Mama?"

Marianne says, "Your mother kissed your hand before she left and asked me to take care of you. You wore a blue dress."

"With white stripes. Mother sewed it for me."

"I thought so. You wore it over a little white blouse with a Peter Pan collar. By the time we got to England, it was gray. Do you remember how we all stood in a line on the platform at Liverpool Street Station? I was trying to scrub your face clean because photographers were taking pictures of us. We were that day's news: the first refugee children to arrive in England on a

Kindertransport out of Nazi Germany. I wanted us to make a good impression," Marianne says.

"Later, when we were evacuated from Paddington Station, I was sure you'd be on the train, taking care of me like you did before," I say. "For a long time, in the beginning, I waited for you to come and live with Aunt Em and me."

Marianne bites her thumbnail, then puts her hand back in her lap as if someone had slapped it down. "After you left, Sophie, I really missed you. I waited and waited for my name to be called. Finally, when I was the only girl left in the waiting room, Mrs. Abercrombie Jones agreed to take me."

"Was she kind to you, Marianne?"

"I'll be charitable and say she did her best. Aunt Vera had hoped for an older girl, someone the same age you are now, Sophie, whom she could train as a maid. She hadn't the least idea of how homesick I was, or what we'd been through in Germany.

"It wasn't all bad, of course. I wasn't hungry or beaten, and I made a wonderful friend. It was Bridget who got me through those first awful weeks. She helped me make up job applications to find employment for my parents. Imagine two eleven-year-olds going door-to-door with our little bits of paper, soliciting work."

"What happened?"

"My mother did get a job offer. My father was trapped in Czechoslovakia when Hitler marched in, so there wasn't much hope of him getting out.

"I waited for Mutti's letter, which never arrived, to say when she was coming. We missed each other by hours. She actually arrived in London the day after I was evacuated to Wales. The school was closed, Mrs. Abercrombie Jones had shut the house and moved away, so there was no forwarding address for me. I'd just been thrown out of my third billet when she found me, and by Christmas we were living together. That reminds me, Sophie—write down your address; I don't want to lose you again."

I scribble my address for her. Marianne gasps, "I can't believe it. When I lived with Mrs. Abercrombie Jones, I was less than half an hour's walk away from you. We lived in St. John's Wood, on Circus Road. Destiny meant us to meet again."

"Absolutely," I say. "Tell me about Bridget—what happened to her?"

"Bridget's parents sent her to Canada at the beginning of the war, to live with an uncle in Montreal. She's sailing home as soon as she can get a berth on a ship. She's done her probationary year of nursing in Canada. Her father, Dr. O'Malley, is pulling strings like mad so she gets accepted at the Middlesex. Bridget and I really want to finish our training together."

"Marianne, does Dr. O'Malley look anything like this?"

I do a quick sketch on the back of the paper Marianne gives me, roughing in the doctor's shaggy eyebrows and the lines under his eyes.

"Sophie, are you clairvoyant or something? That's him."

"Your Dr. O'Malley came to our house last week because our regular doctor is on holiday."

"It's amazing. Not just that you know him, but the way you draw."

I try to shrug modestly. "Marianne, where is your mother?"

"She's still working for Mrs. Davy. Now that the war's over, we're hoping to hear news about my father. Waiting's awful, isn't it?"

"Yes. Do you have any other relatives over there?"

Normally I wouldn't ask anything so personal, but this isn't an ordinary conversation. Or an ordinary meeting.

"My Aunt Grethe is safe in Holland. She and Uncle Frank were in Westerbork Concentration Camp. He died there. She's back at home in Amsterdam now. My cousin Ruth, her daughter, lives in Palestine. She's two years older than me. She sailed there on a rickety old boat just before the Nazis overran Holland in 1940. Ruth lives on a kibbutz called Degania. She and her group are making orchards out of the desert."

"Kibb. . . . I've never heard that word before."

"A kibbutz is a farm that belongs to all the people who live and work there. Uncle Frank was always against her going. He thought the work would be too hard for her. He did relent at the last moment, so Ruth was able to leave with his blessing." Marianne stirs her tea.

I remember the pictures of the camps I've seen. Somehow I can't imagine my father being in such a place. *They'll be all right. After all, my mother isn't Jewish.*

Marianne looks up at me. "My grandparents, my mother's father and mother, were deported to Poland. Early on, I think in 1941. Mutti had a card from a neighbor in Düsseldorf. They'd arranged that before she left for England, in case anything happened to her parents. The card arrived from Switzerland; all it said was YOUR PARENTS HAVE RELOCATED TO LODZ. Jews from all over Germany were sent there. When the Russians liberated the camp in January, only a few hundred people were still alive."

"My father's Jewish and my mother's Aryan. I never knew my mother's parents. I met my grandfather, my father's father, only once. He said he was being sent to Poland too."

"I'm sure you'll have some news soon, Sophie. It's probably a great help to have one parent who's not Jewish, a protection."

How did the conversation turn so serious? I change the subject.

"What made you decide to be a nurse, Marianne? Is it fun living in the nurses' residence?"

"I always wanted to be a nurse. We do have fun, but the girls who join because they think uniforms are glamorous and they'll find a rich doctor to marry don't last long. Well, you know how hard the work is, Sophie. I don't know what's worse: never having enough hot water for a bath, or having to eat last night's supper when we come off night duty!

"Now, on that cheerful note, I'd better go or I'll be late for supper. See you on the ward on Saturday."

We hug each other good-bye.

13

Aunt Em is waiting for me, wanting to hear all about Marianne. When I come to the part about Dr. O'Malley, she says, "What an extraordinary week. Dr. O'Malley suggested I get out of London for a few days. I've decided to go. It's the first holiday weekend since the war. It'll be quite an adventure. I might meet a mysterious person from the past too!"

"Aunt Em, you know everyone's always buried behind the newspaper. People only talk in air-raid shelters and thank goodness we don't need those anymore. Where will you go?"

"I thought I'd accept Uncle Gerald's invitation. It will give me the opportunity to settle dull business matters." She doesn't look at me.

Perhaps Aunt Em wants to discuss my adoption? After all, I have been sort of stranded with her for seven years.

"I'll take the 7:30 train on Friday morning. My friend Louisa lives fairly near, so I'll probably spend Saturday with her. That will ease the 'burden' for Winifred. Uncle Gerald will drive me back on Sunday night."

"Aunt Em, you surely won't leave a poor defenseless fourteen-year-old alone for the whole weekend? May Mandy come over, and would it be all right if she came early, to settle in before you leave?"

"I was going to ask Mrs. Gibson if you could go there."

"Please, Aunt Em, do let us stay here. We're not children anymore."

"I don't see why not. I'll walk over to Mrs. Gibson's now. It's a lovely evening. If Mandy's going to sleep in the spare room tomorrow, there's work to be done. You'll need to push all those Red Cross boxes I've been storing to the far wall. They'll have to be labeled too. The bed's made up, but the room should be aired and dusted."

I fling my arms around Aunt Em's neck. "Lovely, lovely Aunt Em."

"I recognize 'cupboard love,' Sophie Mandel. You don't fool me. Up you go then—get started."

Opening, labeling, and securing the boxes takes longer than I expect. There is one that must have got mixed in with the others by mistake. It is marked SOPHIE. I open it, thinking it might be outgrown clothes. Usually Aunt Em cuts them up for other things, or gives them to needy families. But the box only holds letters and drawings and a folder with my early report cards. I put it in my room to sort later.

———

Aunt Em comes in carrying a little vase of wildflowers from the garden. "Mrs. Gibson said Mandy could visit. So that's taken care of." She hands me a one pound note.

"That's an awful lot, Aunt Em. What's it for?"

"Call it a combination of emergency and fun money. I wouldn't want you to be destitute, without a penny in your pocket."

"Thank you very much, Aunt Em."

"Go to bed, dear. You've been having too many late nights. I'm surprised you haven't fallen asleep in class."

"It is a strain to keep awake sometimes, I admit."

Aunt Em laughs and kisses me good night. "I *am* pleased you found your friend again, Sophie."

On Thursday, when we go to pick up Mandy's things, Mrs. Gibson gives us homemade scones and Mandy's egg and bacon ration to take home for breakfast next day. Then we hear lecture number one about being responsible, and does Mandy have enough money, etc.

"Mother," Mandy says, "you'll see us Saturday, remember? I'm coming home right after my hospital shift to have tea with you before we go to the pictures. Sophie will pick me up when she's finished at nine o'clock so you can check us both over before we cycle home." She raises her left eyebrow at me.

Mandy loves the spare room. "Is this the wall next to your bed?"

"I think so."

We experiment for a while sending Morse code messages to each other. Over supper, we get lecture number two from Aunt Em about not coming in too late, and locking up and putting our bikes away, and then we have to write down a list of emergency numbers. We nod yes to everything, and stay up half the night gossiping.

On Friday morning, the taxi arrives for Aunt Em at 6:30. We wave her off and collapse in the kitchen.

"Alone at last," I say.

"Extra half hour in bed, or breakfast?" Mandy asks, yawning.

"I'll make us dried egg omelette, and we'll save the real eggs for tomorrow. You make the tea. The secret of making dried eggs slightly less revolting, Mandy, is to stir in the water very slowly so all the powder is dissolved. Not a lump in sight," I say, and pour the mixture into the hot pan. I grate a bit of cheese on top.

"Delicious," Mandy says, with her mouth full. "A bit like pancakes. Actually, I think keeping house is easy. I can't think why mothers make such a fuss about it."

It is fun coming home together to our "own" house. We have tea in the garden, and Mandy admits that Simon hopes to see her at the Youth Club tonight.

"He's so nice, Sophie. Let's go. It's mixed table tennis on Friday nights. Can I borrow your blue blouse?"

"Yes, and I want to borrow your black leather belt," I say.

"Done."

We get to the semifinals. Simon and Nigel are our partners and invite us to go to Fred's Fish Bar for chips. Later they walk us home.

"Night, Sophie. Don't get up in the morning. No point in us both losing our beauty sleep. See you after work tomorrow."

"Sleep well, Mandy."

I double-check the front door and the windows.

When I come down at nine next morning, there are two letters lying on the front mat. A bill for Aunt Em and a letter addressed to me c/o Miss Simmonds.

My letter is from someplace in Germany—not from Berlin, where my parents live. The return address on the back is marked U.S. ARMY HOSPITAL, MUNICH, GERMANY.

My mouth goes dry. This must be the letter I've been half expecting since the end of the war.

I can hear Mandy's voice in my head: "Why don't you open it, idiot?"

I can't. The minute I touch the envelope, I feel exactly the way I did on V-E night when I saw Marianne again.

Who else is going to appear from the past? Isn't that what Aunt Em said?

I sense the letter staring at me, urging me to open it.

The phone rings. It's Aunt Em.

"Oh, yes, everything's fine. No, there's nothing wrong. My voice doesn't sound funny. It must be a bad connection. . . . Tuesday . . . you're staying over for Whit Monday?"

I'm repeating everything Aunt Em says. She must wonder what's the matter with me.

"Honestly, Aunt Em, I don't mind a bit. We're having fun. See you Tuesday, then."

An envelope is a piece of paper, that's all. I draw two eyes and a smiling mouth on the back. I slit open the envelope and pull out a thin sheet of writing paper. It's dated May 21, 1945.

My Dearest Daughter,

Yes, I am alive. I have been in hospital since the U.S. Army liberated Dachau Concentration Camp. An army nurse is helping me write to you. I am making a good recovery from typhus and feel a little stronger each day.

I hope this letter will reach you and that you and dear Fräulein Margaret still live at the same address. I was so worried that I would not remember it. Each night, before I slept, I repeated the words and numbers.

I have sad news for you, Sophie. Your mother died on January 12, 1943. The factory where she worked received a direct hit in an air raid.

In February, in the last sweep to make Berlin *Judenrein*—Jew free, I was picked up by the Gestapo. I was no longer a "privileged" Jew, married to an Aryan.

Dear child, your mother and I spoke of you every day. She was a loving and courageous woman.

I hope to leave the hospital before long and will look for work. There will have to be much rebuilding. I long to see you again. I pray it will be soon.

Write soon to your loving father,

Jacob Mandel

By the time I get to the end, I can't remember what I've read. My heart is pounding so hard, I can hear it thumping away. *Papa wants me back!*

I read the letter again slowly. Mama, Mama is dead. *It's my fault. I didn't wish hard enough for her to be safe.*

14

For a long time I sit reading and rereading every word. The signature at the bottom of the page looks as if the person who'd formed the letters is just learning to write. Jacob Mandel.

I don't know what I'm supposed to feel—should I be crying with joy that Papa's alive, or heartbroken that Mama's dead? It's hard being happy and sad at the same time. The feelings cancel each other out. It's as if I'm reading a letter meant for someone else. I can imagine telling Mandy, "Think how awful—she heard her mother died on the same day she found out that her father was still alive."

Last year I had to have a second tooth out. My left cheek was numb all day where the dentist froze it. That's how I feel inside, numb.

I read the letter once more, then fold it back along its original creases and replace it in the envelope. I put it in my pocket.

Mother died on January 12, 1943. That's two years and four months ago. *What was I doing that day? Why didn't I know? Shouldn't a person feel something when their mother dies? Have some kind of premonition at least?*

I always thought people got telegrams in one of those special buff-colored envelopes from the post office when someone dies. You couldn't send one, of course, not in the middle of the war, not from Germany.

I go into the sitting room and take Aunt Em's photograph album off the bookshelf. I turn the pages till I come to the "laughing girls."

If only you could speak to me. You're laughing, Mama. I can't remember the sound of your laugh. I wish I had more memories of you. Did you sing to me? Did you read me stories? What was your life really like? You should have explained to me why you sent me to be brought up by Aunt Em. Why did you say it was a holiday? Why didn't you tell me that we might never meet again?

I wish you'd known how happy I've been here. Would you understand and let me stay? Papa took that photo of you, when you were both so young, before you turned into my parents. One of you dead, the other a Jew from a concentration camp, ill with typhus.

At four fifteen, I leave for the hospital. All the way there I try to decide what to do if the worst happens: if Father wants me to go back to live with him in Germany and Aunt Em agrees because she thinks it's the "fair thing to do." If I run away, I could easily earn my living selling sketches and portraits. I could be a pavement artist. It wouldn't be any harder than painting white lines along curbs and lampposts in the blackout. I'd only agree to leave my garret and go back to school if Aunt Em promises to let me live with her forever. Yes, I know, it's blackmail. . . . It'd be worth it.

The porter greets me as if he's been waiting just for my arrival. "Don't look so glum, Miss. It's keeping so cheerful as keeps me going, as Mrs. Mop says." I manage a smile. Our porter's a Tommy Handley fan, always quoting from everyone's favorite radio show: "It's that man again—ITMA." Aunt Em and I try never to miss a program.

"Thank goodness for an extra pair of hands." Staff Nurse rattles off instructions as if afraid an emergency might arrive in the ward before she's finished telling me what to do.

After I've made up the beds, and my "hospital corners" won a smile of approval from Staff Nurse, I mop the bathroom, arrange all the screens for visitors, and am sent down to the kitchen to remind them about sending up the special trays for the diabetics. Then I refill the water jugs and am in the middle of dusting the radiators, when I am told I can go for a ten minute break.

Marianne passes me on the stairs. "Can't stop, Sophie, I'm being moved to 'maternity.' Bridget's home. I'll call you soon. The three of us must meet." She squeezes my arm.

At nine o'clock, when my shift ends, I'm just thankful I've made it through. My legs feel as if they've run a five minute mile. I think I forgot to eat today.

———

At the Gibsons' house, Nigel opens the door. "Hello, Sophie. Mother and Mandy aren't home from the pictures yet. What's new?"

"My mother's dead."

He stares, horrified. "I'm sorry, Sophie." He puts his arms round me and pats my back as though I'm a baby.

I want to go on standing there in the half-light of the hallway, to put my head on his shoulder and cry. Of course, I don't. "I had a letter from my father."

"When?"

The front door opens. Nigel and I turn away from each other.

"Hello, sorry we're late. You should have come, Nigel. Mum was petrified."

"Don't exaggerate, Mandy. Now, shall we all have some cocoa before you girls cycle home?"

"Please. Any biscuits, Mother?" Mandy follows her into the kitchen.

"Nigel, don't tell them yet. I'll tell Mandy myself."

"All right."

"Come on, you two, stop whispering. I thought I was going to scream when Charles Boyer was creeping around the attic looking for Ingrid Bergman's jewelry. I shan't sleep a wink tonight." Mandy chatters on and on, so I don't need to talk much.

"Thanks awfully for the cocoa, Mrs. Gibson," I say.

"Nigel, it's late. Cycle home with the girls, please. You look so tired, Sophie. Is there anything wrong?"

"It was a bit frantic on the ward tonight, Mrs. Gibson."

"Come on, twin, let's be on our way." Nigel hurries Mandy out.

The moment Nigel leaves us and I close the front door, Mandy bursts out: "What's going on? All of a sudden I'm shut out. First it's your friend Marianne and now Nigel."

"Mandy, what are you talking about?"

"Don't pretend, Sophie. I could tell as soon as Mum and I came into the house. Do you think I'm blind and deaf? Since when do we keep secrets from each other?"

I hang up my blazer and walk into the kitchen. I need to sit down.

"Don't walk away from me when I'm talking to you, Sophie Mandel!"

"I'm not. Stop bullying me, Mandy."

"Did something happen to upset you? Was there a death on the ward?"

"Not on the ward. Somewhere else." I pull the letter out of my pocket and push it over to her. "Read it. I'm going to bed. Good night."

I brush my teeth, get into pajamas, and sit on my bed and hold Monkey.

Mandy knocks on the door and comes in before I have a chance to answer. She throws herself at me. "Sophie, dearest Soph, I'm a selfish jealous pig. I'm so very sorry. Why didn't you tell me? Please please forgive me." She gives me the letter back.

I almost laugh. She's so tragic. "Don't be humble, Mandy, you didn't know. The letter only came after you left this morning. I told Nigel because he was the one to open the door. If you'd opened it, I would have told you first. . . . You know what upsets me, Mandy? Not just that she's been dead for so long without my knowing, though that's bad enough, but the awful waste. She had me and sent me away before I was old enough to really know her. She cut herself off from her family, well they both did, so I never knew my relatives."

"She saved your father, didn't she? You're alive. That's two lives. How can you call that a waste?"

I don't answer. I can't think logically.

Mandy tiptoes out as if I'm ill.

One part of me is mourning and the other part is terrified of losing the person who became my "foster mother" all these years. My brain's going in a million directions.

I'm fourteen years old—I think I have the right to decide about my life. . . . I'll write to the Home Office. They decide about naturalization, visas, passports, and things like that. How do I convince the Minister I'm the right "material" to become a loyal British subject? What I need is a letter of reference from someone in a position of authority—a person who is willing to say I'm doing a job of national importance and deserve British citizenship. Once I've got that, no one can send me anywhere I don't want to go.

There's the headmistress, but I hardly think helping in the library would be considered crucial. It's got to be an essential service, like coal mining or driving an ambulance. . . . Why didn't I think of that before? *The hospital.* I'll ask Matron. She's very imposing. Everyone's in awe of her. The nurses say she's aware of everything that goes on anywhere in the building. The Middlesex has a terrific reputation.

I even spoke to Matron once. She was walking down the corridor, with a chart in her hand, doctors in tow. I flattened myself against the wall and said, "Good morning, Madam," and she sort of nodded in my direction. A letter from her saying I'm indispensable would be nearly as good as a recommendation from the king.

It is almost four in the morning before I'm satisfied with my efforts:

Dear Matron,

I am one of the Junior Red Cross cadets in your hospital. At present I work a Saturday afternoon and evening shift. I look forward to being there each week and hope that, in a small way, I can help to make the hospital run even more smoothly than it does already. A *bit of flattery never hurts*. I am in the process of applying for British citizenship and would greatly appreciate a note from you supporting my application.

It is vital for me to be allowed to remain in this country and not be returned to Germany, my place of birth. After seven years in England, my complete loyalty is to the country that has given me refuge.

Thank you very much for your time and consideration,
Yours truly,
Sophie Mandel

Then I draw a cartoon of a cadet making beds, taking temperatures, and scrubbing bedpans, and a nurse looking on, smiling approvingly. I add a balloon shape with the words: "How could we ever manage without you?"

15

After Mandy leaves, I cycle to the hospital to ask the porter to deliver my letter to Matron personally. That way she'll get it almost immediately. He says he'll take it on his tea break.

The house seems eerily quiet when I get back. You can tell there's been a death. Even though it happened in a foreign country two years ago, somehow the news of it lingers in the air.

Poor Mama, not even to have a funeral. I know that happens a lot in wartime, but when it's my own mother who is buried under piles of rubble, it's so horrible I want to scream; do anything to stop thinking about her like that.

I close my eyes, trying to remember something about her when she was alive. She used to hum when she worked. Even when she was sewing, she'd hum through a mouthful of pins. Once I asked her, "What's the song about, Mama?" She'd said, "I don't know all the words, but once upon a time there was a boy and he saw a little rose standing in the meadow."

Sah ein Knab' ein Röslein steh'n
Röslein auf der Heiden . . .

Until this moment, I'd totally forgotten that. *Was the rose a flower or a girl?* It doesn't matter.

It's going to rain, the sun's gone in. My window's wide-open. I rush upstairs to shut it. While I'm making my bed, I stub my toe on the box marked SOPHIE. I drag it out and undo the lid. It looks as if Aunt Em has kept most of my early report cards: "Sophie is settling down well." "Her drawing shows promise." "Sophie's spelling needs attention."

The usual. Everything neatly tied up in a cardboard folder, a thick gray one. A rubber band to keep the contents in place. There's a copy of my school registration form. All it says is the day I started school—January 9, 1939. Aunt Em must have kept me home those first few weeks in England, to give me a chance to learn some English, I expect. In the box where it says NAME OF PARENT OR GUARDIAN, there's Aunt Em's name. That should help my chances with the Home Office—having a solid British citizen as my guardian all these years.

There are some of my early drawings too. One is of a gruesome-looking old woman glaring at two little girls. Underneath I'd printed: PLEAS CAN WE CUM HOME? That must have been when I was still an evacuee.

There are two letters in German, one dated 3 *Januar* 1939, and the other one a month later—1 *Februar* 1939. Those are the only words I can still read, other than the greeting and the signature and a row of O's instead of X's, the way we write them over here.

I remember how angry the letters made me feel then. There was the day Aunt Em handed me the envelope and I'd torn off the stamp for Nigel's stamp collection. I'd burst out rudely: "I don't know how to read this letter and I don't want to. It's too hard. We don't write like that in school."

Aunt Em must have written to my parents and explained because there's one more letter addressed to me in the file. This time it's printed in English, and says:

Dear Sophie,

Thank you for your letter. You write very good English. Papa and I are well. Today I went for a walk in the Grunewald, our green forest. I waved to Papa, and watched him cut a hedge into the shape of a little bird. He says he would like to be a bird and fly to England to visit you.

Love from your mama and papa OOOOO

There's a drawing of a bird-shaped hedge at the bottom of the page. The date on the letter is August 15, 1939, two weeks before the outbreak of World War Two. That day Aunt Em explained to me that we'd have to wait until the end of the war before there would be any more letters from my parents.

Another letter, addressed to Aunt Em, is from a Quaker group in Berlin. It's postmarked November 14, 1938—that's when I still lived in Berlin. Aunt Em had clipped a column from a January 2, 1939 *Times* to the envelope. She'd circled NEW ANTI-JEWISH MEA-SURES IN GERMANY, and then a quote from a Quaker group: JEWS DESPERATE TO LEAVE.

Snooping's horrible. But if this is something really private, why would Aunt Em leave it in a box marked SOPHIE? *I have to read it.*

Berlin
November 14, 1938

Dear Margaret,

I think our days are numbered here. I don't know how much longer the Nazi government will tolerate our presence. I'm sure they'll close down the office.

The world reports on the "action" taken against the Jewish people on November 9 and 10 are not exaggerated. In fact, they cannot accurately describe the viciousness of the attacks against men, women, and children, under the benign eye of officialdom. Burning, looting, and imprison-ment of Jews. We are able to help so few to get out of Germany. Desperate men and women, some with babies in arms, sit helplessly in the corridors waiting to be placed on some kind of list that will get them to safety.

I'll talk more to you in the new year, when I hope to be back at home.

> Affectionately and in haste,
> Louisa

Mama wasn't in that kind of danger—she wasn't Jewish. I wonder if she guessed what it might be like marrying Papa. She was very brave to stand by him.

Tucked down inside the flap of the cardboard is a luggage label on a string. I remember wearing that on the *Kindertransport*. We all wore them. My number was two hundred and seventeen. What's that bit of old blanket doing in there . . . ? *Käthe?*

Sophie Mandel, you're too old to cry over a doll. . . .

We're going to have a party. Mama, Papa, and me. It's my birthday. I run all the way home from school and Mama is waiting at the door.

She ties a scarf round my eyes. Papa's voice asks: "How many fingers can you see?"

I shout: "None." In the living room, I tear off the blindfold. Papa throws me in the air seven times, *himmelhoch*—sky-high, because I'm seven today.

The cake is on the table; it is chocolate and white, in the shape of a ring. Mama has sprinkled powdered sugar over the top. It looks like snow crystals. I have a present too—a box tied with blue ribbon. I lift the lid. It is the doll from the window of the big toy shop near Mama's work. She has light brown hair. It is parted in the middle. Her hair is braided. She wears a skirt and a pull-over. There are real white socks and leather shoes on her feet.

"What will you call her?" Papa asks me.

"Her name is Käthe," I answer, and hug her to my chest.

Next day is Saturday, and we go for a picnic in the woods. Papa knows the names of all the trees. I do too. Pine and spruce and beech.

Mama pours coffee from a thermos. There's milk for me. We sit on the blanket and finish the birthday cake. Then we play hide-and-seek. It is Papa's turn to hide. I count to a hundred, hiding my eyes on Mama's lap. When I open them, there are two shadows on the blanket, tall like trees. They are not trees. They are men wearing black boots and uniforms with silver buttons. They smile at Mama. "*Ganz allein, Gnädige Frau*—All alone, dear lady?" I move closer to Mama. She holds my hand so tight she squishes my fingers. I want to go and find Papa. He will think I've forgotten him. *Poor Papa*, waiting to be found.

"It is the little one's birthday. Tell the gentlemen how old you are, Liebchen." I pull my hand away from Mama's and hold up seven fingers.

"Three cups and plates, and who else is in this party?" They stare at Mama—they are not smiling now.

"It is Käthe, my new doll." I hold her up—close to me, so they can't touch her.

"Happy birthday. *Heil Hitler*." The boots click and move away. When they are gone, I help Mama fold the blanket.

Papa comes over to us from behind the tree, where he was hiding. We go home. When I put Käthe to bed, I tell her not to be frightened of the soldiers. "I will always take care of you, my little Käthe."

16

For years I've been afraid to look at Käthe. It was all right at first, when that nice girl, whose name I've forgotten, twisted Käthe's head back after the Gestapo left the train. It was all right when Marianne was with me, but after that I was afraid to look at Käthe, convinced there'd be a jagged scar where the officer's hands had touched her neck—that somehow it had grown there.

Käthe, my Käthe. You look perfect. There isn't a mark on you.

I hold the doll for a while and then wrap the blanket snugly round her and put her back in her box bed.

That's how I'll think of you, Mama—perfect, without a blemish. I won't think about the damage bombs and broken glass can do. I'll remember you rolling out pastry, or letting me come to the shop to help you, or hugging Papa when he came home from work or upset because you were worried the Nazis might hurt him.

When I give Käthe to my daughter, I'll tell her it was you who sewed the dress. I'll say, "This is a present from your grandmother, the one who lived in Germany long ago."

I go downstairs and settle down to write to my father. Someone's at the back door. *Mandy?* She'll wonder why Aunt Em isn't here. It's stupid of me not to have told her the truth. I could have said I need time to be alone for a bit.

"Nigel, I wasn't expecting you. I mean, come in."

"Thanks, I can only stay a minute. Swotting for my science exam. Mother sent me over with a loaf for your tea. She's been baking. Is your aunt back yet?"

"Not yet. Thanks, awfully. I was just going to write to my father. Hard to know what to say."

"Rotten luck to hear like that, but it's great news about your dad."

"Somehow I'd never thought about one of my parents dying. To be honest, I didn't think very much about them at all. Do you think I'll be allowed to choose who I live with? *There, I've finally said it out loud—the thing I'm most afraid of. If I can't go on living with Aunt Em, it means I'll lose friends, country, everything I know. How many times in a lifetime am I supposed to do that?* Got time for a cup of tea?" I put the kettle on.

Nigel perches on the corner of the kitchen table. "You know how we always had these huge family gatherings at Christmas? On Boxing Day, the last one before the war, Uncle Bert asked me in front of everyone: 'Tell me, son, who's your favorite—your mum or your dad?' There'd been lots of talking and laughing, and suddenly all those hot red faces looked at me, waiting for an answer. Asking me to choose. Whatever I'd say, I'd hurt someone's feelings. I was afraid I was going to cry. Mandy saved me. She jumped on Dad's lap and said, 'Well, I love my daddy to bits.' They all laughed and I ran upstairs and wouldn't come down again.

"Dad came to my room later and brought me a slice of Christmas cake and the last cracker. I gave it to Mandy. It had a thimble and a paper crown in it. People think kids don't matter, that they don't have feelings. It'll be all right, Soph. I'll see you soon, science calls."

I return to my letter.

> 16, Great Tichfield Street
> London WC1

> May 23, 1945

Dear Father:

I am glad you are feeling stronger. The nurses seem to be taking good care of you. It was a shock to hear about Mother. I'm sorry.

Aunt Em told me about the holiday she had in Germany when she first met you. We have a photograph of Mother that you took the day before you got engaged. It's beautiful. I'm sorry, so sorry, that things didn't turn out the way they were supposed to.

This is a holiday weekend. Aunt Em is visiting her brother in the country. I will tell her when she comes back. She will be glad about you and sad about Mama, as of course am I.

I'm fourteen now. Aunt Em thinks I look a bit like both of you. Get well soon.

Your affectionate daughter,
Sophie Mandel

After I finish the letter, I get out my sketchbook and begin a family portrait. First I draw Grandpa Mandel, with his silver and white prayer shawl, the fringes hanging below his waist. *Papa must have told me it's a prayer shawl.* I draw his face in shadow, the way it looked that time in the synagogue. I draw candles flickering round the walls. Papa, his hand on my shoulder, and myself as a little girl, looking up at him. I sketch Mama in her best dress, the one with the big lace collar, and her hair in wispy curls round her forehead. I have no idea what Mama's parents looked like. She never mentioned her father.

When I was small, I wondered what happened to the baby in the cradle in the photo of the Mandels, the photo that Papa had to hide from the Nazis. He told me once, "That's my baby sister in the crib. My mother—your grandmother—died when the baby was only a few months old." I expect my aunt kept house for Grandpa Mandel when she grew up.

I draw Aunt Em on the next page, with her kind eyes and the little wrinkles round them. She's never tried to take Mother's place, but she's the most perfect aunt anyone could ask for.

17

On Tuesday morning I arrive at school just as orchestra practice ends. Mandy must have spread the word because Sally Jones, who I usually try to avoid, simpers up to me and says, "Sorry to hear about your mother. When are you going back to live in Germany with your father?"

I mumble something noncommittal.

Is the whole world waiting for me to be sent back there?

I sit down on the bench in the cloakroom. For a minute I can't think where I'm supposed to be heading.

"Sophie, come on, we'll be late for prayers." Mandy pulls me to my feet and drags me down the corridor to Assembly.

"What did Aunt Em say?"

"Nothing."

"Well, what did you tell her?"

"I haven't."

"Why haven't you?"

"If you must know, because she's not coming home till this afternoon."

We sit.

"You mean, you stayed by yourself for two whole nights?" Mandy hisses in my ear.

"Yes."

"Weren't you frightened?"

"Of what? Charles Boyer looking for my jewelry?"

We stand in silence as the staff file in and take their places on the platform.

Later, as we go into class, I remember I'd left my history notes in the cloakroom.

"Hurry up, we'll be late. You know how Miss Jasper hates that," Mandy says.

"I didn't ask you to wait, and please stop telling me what to do."

I walk away from her. Miss Jasper doesn't hear me enter the class. She's writing on the blackboard. I copy the question into my notebook: HOW DID THE INDUSTRIAL REVOLUTION AFFECT THE WORKING CLASSES IN THE NINETEENTH CENTURY? *Words. They don't mean anything to me.*

When the bell rings at the end of the first period, Mandy sweeps past me, talking to Sally. Instead of going to English, I walk into the cloakroom, fetch my hat, and saunter out of school.

I wish I'd stayed home. Joanne Fisher did when her brother's ship was torpedoed, with all hands lost at sea. Anthea Warren was away a whole week when her father died in a Japanese prisoner of war camp.

Aunt Em will be home soon. What am I going to tell her? How shall I do it?

The moment I get back, I dial the nurses' residence. I badly want to talk to Marianne. A soft Scot's burr informs me that Nurse Kohn left that morning on a leave of absence.

Voices in the hall.

"Aunt Em, you're early. I'm so glad you're back. Hello, Uncle Gerald, Aunt Winifred."

Aunt Em hugs me, obviously pleased to be home—worn-out with listening to Aunt Winifred, I should think. "Sophie, everything looks beautifully tidy. Did you and Mandy have a nice time?"

Aunt Winifred interrupts before I have a chance to reply. "You must be getting quite excited about going home, Sophie."

What on earth is she talking about?

"Going home, Aunt Winifred? I *am* home."

Aunt Em sits down. Uncle Gerald takes his pipe from his breast pocket, turns to me and says, "Would you find me a match, my dear? I must have left mine in the car."

I hand him the box on the mantelpiece above the fireplace. *Surely he can see it there?*

"No, dear, I mean your real home—in Germany with your parents. I expect all you children will be on your way soon. Isn't that so, Gerald?"

I look at Aunt Winifred's carefully marcelled hair, the silly little hat she wears, her slightly caked bright lipstick.

I hate her! I really truly hate her and I think I'm going to tell her so.

"Why are you staring at me in that way, child?"

"Because it's none of your business."

Aunt Em's shocked "Sophie, apologize to Aunt Winifred at once" is exactly what I don't need to hear at this moment.

"I will not and she's not my aunt any more than you are."

I manage to get myself out of the room without crying or slamming the door. I hear Uncle Gerald saying, "Must be getting along, Margaret," as I go upstairs, then Aunt Em's response, which I can't hear, and their footsteps going into the kitchen. I suppose they'll all have a "nice" cup of tea while they discuss how fast they can get rid of me.

And I haven't even had a chance to tell Aunt Em about Mama.

It's ages before the front door opens and closes. Moments later, Aunt Em calls me to come downstairs. She's putting away the tea things. "Would you mind telling me exactly what that exhibition was about?"

"Mine, or Aunt Winifred's?" I feel the teapot; it's still warm. I pour myself a cup of tea.

"I want an explanation, and you will give it to me in a civilized manner."

"Perhaps you'd better read this first." I hand Aunt Em Papa's letter, and turn away to drink my tea. When I hear her blow her nose, I wait a few minutes before turning round. She is almost composed again.

"Sophie, my dear. Why didn't you tell me? I would have come home at once." Her hands, holding the letter, tremble a little. She puts the page on the table between us and clasps her fingers together tightly.

"You've got so tall, Sophie. I wish Charlotte. . . . Jacob won't recognize you."

"Aunt Em, please *please* don't send me back to Germany. I'm afraid to live there. I won't know anyone. I can't speak the language. Of course I love my father, but I hardly remember him and he doesn't know anything about me. I thought I belonged here with you."

"Sophie, Aunt Winifred's words were out of place and premature. No one is going to send you anywhere immediately."

"Never—I won't go."

"Listen to me. Don't interrupt, please. I always knew I only had you on loan until it was safe for you to rejoin your parents. I thought you understood that. Didn't I make it clear to you?"

"No. You didn't, Aunt Em. All you ever said was, after the war there'd be letters. Every time I wanted to talk about what was going to happen then, you changed the subject. I'm not a thing to be shuffled back and forth. Doesn't what *I* want matter at all? Don't you want me to stay?"

"What you or I want isn't the point, Sophie. You have a father who loves you and who has lost everything except you. Your parents trusted me and I will never break that trust."

I'm fighting for my life.

"It's not fair," I blurt out.

Aunt Em doesn't reply.

Oh, Aunt Em, why can't you try to keep me with you? Why can't you admit that I'm the daughter you didn't have? It's hopeless. You never will. I understand. You can't. I'll just have to go on with my plans without your help.

"Sophie, your mother was my dear friend. I shall miss her very much. I know how hard losing her must be for you. Remember, you have a father who longs to see you and get to know you again. This is what is important. Now let's make plans. It will take time to get a visitor's permit for your father, but I'm sure, in view of the circumstances, the Home Office will cooperate. He won't have recovered sufficiently from his illness to travel yet, but I'll start setting things in motion tomorrow.

"Time for me to unpack. Later on we might start on a list of things to send to Jacob in hospital."

End of discussion. As usual.

"Aunt Em, I wrote to Father earlier. I'll go and post the letter now, if you don't mind."

"Do. I'll speak to Uncle Gerald and Aunt Winifred later. Under the circumstances, I shall apologize on your behalf."

"Thanks, Aunt Em." I hug her.

"Sophie, you do understand, don't you?"

I pour away the tea—it's stone-cold now. I run the tap so I don't have to answer.

After I post my letter, I wait outside Mandy's gate till she comes home from school. She walks straight past me as if I'm invisible.

"Mandy, I've got something to say to you."

"Again? I thought you'd finished."

"I'm sorry. I was awfully rude and I didn't mean it."

"Yes, you did. You're right. I am bossy. Mum's always telling me."

"I had a fight with Aunt Winifred."

"Metaphorically, I hope."

"It nearly wasn't and then I started on Aunt Em."

"Do you want to come in and tell me all the gory details?"

"I will, but not today. Aunt Em's a bit upset. I'd better get home."

"My *Girl's Crystal* just came—you can read it first." Mandy hands me her magazine.

"Thanks, awfully."

"I've come to the conclusion that Sally is a stuck-up, big-mouthed snob."

When I get back, Aunt Em says, "I phoned the headmistress. She agrees with me that you should stay home this week, but she wants you to continue revising for the June exams."

"Does she know I walked out of school?"

"It was not discussed, so I think you may forget about it."

18

On Wednesday, when Aunt Em comes home from the office, she says, "I've been making some enquiries through the Red Cross. Things in Europe are pretty chaotic. I'm told, much worse than the London Blitz. Thousands and thousands of homeless people, soldiers returning from war, cities reduced to rubble, and hardly any food. If the war had lasted any longer, many people would have died of starvation. I know you'll keep this confidential, Sophie, but it's almost certain that our own rations will be cut again in the next few months. Rationing may go on for years."

"I always thought the moment war was over, food would miraculously reappear in the shops. I've begun making a list for Father's parcel, Aunt Em. Shall I read it to you? I tried to think what the patients in our hospital seem to want most: instant coffee, tea, biscuits, condensed milk, tinned fruit, soap, socks. I've still got that bar of Yardley's soap Aunt Winifred gave me for Christmas—we could send that."

"Add cigarettes. Even if your father doesn't smoke, cigarettes can be exchanged for almost anything. I hadn't thought of socks, but I can knit a pair quite quickly. There's some of that gray wool left from your last winter's cardigan. Shirts. We must assume that Jacob has no clothes except what the hospital may provide."

"There's a whole boxful of men's shirts in the boxes I labeled last week."

"Why don't you see if you can find one or two shirts in a plain color, dear? Your father is exactly the kind of recipient those shirts are meant for."

I rush upstairs. I know why Aunt Em said shirts in a plain color. We've both seen too many pictures of prisoners in striped jackets lately. I find a blue one and a white one, both in good condition.

"I tried some on, Aunt Em. These reach to my knees and the sleeves are miles too long, so they should be all right. I expect Father's pretty thin."

"Excellent. Bring the shopping basket, Sophie, and we'll see what we can do."

On our way to the grocer's, we pass Mr. Billy's. There's a notice in the window: NO LAMB, BEEF, OR OFFAL. Mr. Billy is standing in the shop doorway.

"Good day, Miss Simmonds. Haven't seen you in a while." He leers at me.

Aunt Em nods politely. "Good afternoon, Mr. Billy. I wonder if you might have any tins of meat today? We're putting together a care package for a friend in Europe. People are having a bad time over there."

"Tins of meat, Miss Simmonds? That's a joke. Haven't you heard? There's a peace on. If I did come across such a thing, and I say *if* . . . well, charity begins at home, Madam. Meat for the enemy—that's a good one. Good day, Madam, Miss."

"I think, Sophie," Aunt Em says, "we must try to find another butcher to register with. I really don't want to have any more dealings with Mr. Billy. In future we shall shop elsewhere."

"What did you expect, Aunt Em?"

"Decency. He really is a most odious man."

We walk in silence to the grocer's.

I give our list to Mrs. Logan, and she looks at us as if we've gone mad. Her eyebrows shoot up to her hair net. Aunt Em puts our ration books on the counter.

"No need to look so astonished, Mrs. Logan. We're putting together a parcel for a friend in hospital, in Germany. He's recovering from typhus. Is this list too unrealistic?"

I realize suddenly that Aunt Em intentionally does not mention who the parcel is for. I hope she doesn't think I'd be embarrassed.

"It's for my father, actually," I say.

"In that case, we'll have to see what we can do, won't we?"

Mrs. Logan reappears five minutes later. "Digestive biscuits—you don't want anything too rich. I can let you have some Bovril cubes too—very strengthening. There's a tin of peaches. I'm sorry about the sugar, but you can have a tin of golden syrup."

"We're truly grateful, Mrs. Logan."

"We must all be that, Miss Simmonds. This time let's hope the peace lasts."

After she takes our points, she puts a tin of corned beef in the basket. "No charge. That's from me to your father, Sophie. My dad didn't come back from the war in 1918. You send that with my good wishes. That'll be nineteen shillings and eight pence, please."

I put a pound note—the one that Aunt Em had given me to spend—on the counter.

"Thank you, Mrs. Logan. It's very kind of you."

When we get back from our shopping expedition, the afternoon post has arrived. There is a letter for me from Middlesex Hospital.

May 24, 1945

Dear Miss Mandel,

I am pleased to hear that you find your time with us so rewarding. The dedicated work of Junior Red Cross cadets is invaluable in nursing homes and hospitals across the British Isles.

With your permission, I will ask Sister Tutor to include your drawing in our next staff newsletter. Wishing you every success.

Yours truly and on behalf of Matron,
L.A. Ransome

I enclose the letter with my application to the Home Office, and send it off next morning.

On Friday Mandy and Nigel call on their way to the Youth Club, and ask if I want them to put my name forward for next year's planning committee. I tell them to go ahead.

I'll be here. Matron's letter will work, I know it will.

Aunt Em's rule is that if I don't go to school, I can't go out socially either. She does agree to let me do my hospital shift as usual on Saturday.

Marianne telephones from the nurses' residence just before I leave for work.

"I'm back, Sophie. I don't go on the ward till Monday. Bridget wants to meet you. Are you free Sunday? I could call for you around two and we can go for a walk first."

"Who is it?" Aunt Em comes into the hall.

"Marianne. She's invited me to tea on Sunday. Is it all right if I go?"

"It'll do you good."

Marianne arrives early. The first thing she says to me is, "You're looking awfully tired, Sophie. Are you getting enough sleep?"

"We had some bad news—at least . . ."

I still haven't worked out how to say it's both good and bad.

"Let's go and sit in Regent's Park—we've got time," she says.

We sit watching the swans swimming in elegant circles, ignoring the chattering ducks.

19

"While you were away, Marianne . . . ," I begin.

"Do you know why I had to go home?" She starts speaking at the same time. "You first, Sophie. Is it something to do with Aunt Em?"

"In a way it is because she and my mother were friends. A letter arrived from my father –"

"Then he's safe . . . ," Marianne interrupts. "That's wonderful news."

"Yes. He's recuperating from typhus in a hospital in Munich."

"I thought you said your parents lived in Berlin?"

"My mother died there in an air raid. The factory where she worked got a direct hit. That was in 1943. My father wrote he was picked up and sent to a camp called Dachau. The Americans liberated him three weeks ago."

Marianne takes my hand. "Sorry is such a little word. People use it all the time, don't they? When they make a mistake, or drop something, or bump into you in the blackout. I wish I knew how to . . ." She seems to be having trouble keeping her voice steady.

"Marianne, do you think Mama knew she wouldn't see me again? Is that why she didn't make any promises, or say I'll see you in a little while, or when your holiday's over? I mean, she just handed me over, like a puppy you can't keep any longer."

"I think my father had a feeling that he wouldn't see us again too." Marianne's voice is low.

When I look at her, tears are rolling down her cheeks. After a few minutes, she wipes her face with the back of her hand. By this time I'm crying too.

"Mother heard from the Red Cross," Marianne says. "That's why I got leave. In 1942, Father was sent to Terezin, a concentration camp near Prague. It was liberated by the Russians on V-E Day. The letter said he died of malnutrition—a kind way of saying of hunger—at the end of April."

Marianne turns to me. She'd kept her head averted till then, as if she couldn't finish what she had to say if she looked at me. "It's not fair. Another week and the war would have been over. He'd never hurt anyone. He loved his books and he loved us. Hunted down and starved to death. . . ."

"Because he was a Jew." I finish the sentence for her.

I touch my neck, feeling the choking sensation I felt the first time I'd tried on my Star of David that I keep hidden away in a cubbyhole in my desk. *Had Mama been trying to save me from being punished, the way she'd been for marrying a Jew? From suffering like my father, or being starved to death like Mr. Kohn?*

People pass by on their Sunday outings. No one takes any notice of us.

"I hope you'll see your father soon, Sophie."

I was going to tell Marianne how hard I was trying not to leave England and go and live with Papa in Germany. *How can I tell her now?*

"Aunt Em's hoping to bring him over for a visit."

"I'm glad." Marianne opens her handbag, takes out a powder compact, and dabs at her cheeks. "Look at me, Sophie. Awful. You're supposed to make a good impression on Bridget and her parents." She pats my face with the powder puff.

"You're always telling me to make a good impression." I sneeze. Actually I enjoy her "big sister" act.

"Gesundheit."

"I think I'll have to disgrace you with my shiny nose." I sneeze again. "Anything with perfume always makes me sneeze."

"You're hopeless." She smiles at me. "Come on, or we'll be late." We run for the bus.

At Circus Road, Marianne points out Bridget's house, "That big one on the corner of St. Anne's Terrace. Number twenty-two."

"Mary Anne. It *is* Mary Anne, isn't it?" A thin-lipped woman wearing a black straw hat comes toward us.

"Good afternoon, Mrs. Abercrombie Jones."

"What a surprise to see you after all these years. And is this your sister?"

"No, this is my friend, Sophie Mandel. You'll have to excuse us—we're on our way to visit Bridget O'Malley."

"You kept in touch, did you? My husband will be so interested to hear I've met you again. You've quite grown up."

"Is Gladys still with you?"

"She left. Joined the forces. It's impossible to find good help these days. Are your parents well?"

"Actually, my father died recently in a concentration camp in Czechoslovakia. Do you remember once you said to me that he must wait his turn like other refugees? 'It is not a question of saving, but of good manners.'"

"My dear Mary Anne, we had no possible way of knowing."

"I suppose not. Good-bye, Mrs. Abercrombie Jones."

Marianne links her arm through mine. "That felt good. I used to call her Aunt Wera, instead of Vera, before I could speak English properly. It used to drive her mad."

A slim girl with short dark curly hair runs down the steps to greet us. She kisses Marianne on both cheeks, then shakes hands with me.

"I'm so pleased to see you both. Do come in. We're going to have tea in the garden."

"How nice to see you again, Sophie." Dr. O'Malley emerges from his study to greet us. His arms go round Marianne and he murmurs: "My dear child, we are all deeply grieved for you and your mother. We have written to her."

Bridget and Marianne begin to cry, and then Mrs. O'Malley hugs us both and says, "Come along with me now. Dry your eyes and let's have tea." She plies us with bread and honey that her sister sent from Galway in Ireland, chocolate biscuits Bridget brought back from Canada, and homemade Irish soda bread.

Bridget is what Aunt Em would call a character. She talks nonstop, about Canada.

"I've learned to curl and ski and skate and speak French, but there's nowhere like home." She kisses her mother's cheek, and I think, *I'll never be able to do that.*

The three of us do the dishes and then go upstairs to Bridget's room.

"Presents." Bridget tosses a beautifully wrapped parcel into Marianne's arms.

"Bridget!" Marianne shrieks.

Bridget says quickly, "Don't you dare say you'll never wear them."

"Thank you a million times. I've never in my whole life owned a pair of nylon stockings."

"Well, now you've got two pairs. They won't ladder if you roll them on very carefully—I'll show you how."

"I'm not going to wear them. I'll just look at them."

"I knew it was a waste to give them to you. I'll just have to take them back, I suppose."

"I *will* wear them. But it will have to be a very special occasion. Thank you, dear Bridget."

"This is for you, Sophie. I'm afraid it's only a small box of chocolates. I didn't know we were going to meet, you see."

"It's very kind of you, Bridget. Thank you."

I undo the blue ribbon, the tissue paper, and the little gold seal and offer the chocolates around.

"Heaven! It melts in your mouth," Marianne mumbles. "Six months of chocolate rations in there, Sophie."

Bridget refuses to take one. "I've been spoiled long enough. These are for you, Sophie. Now if you two can stop eating for a minute, I'm ready for a proper talk."

"Isn't that what we've been having?" I ask innocently.

Marianne and Bridget look at each other.

"All right, Bridget, confession time. Is it fit for Sophie to hear?"

"Of course it is. I've been bursting to tell you. I've met someone."

"You've only been home a few days," Marianne says.

"Don't interrupt, I'm going to tell you everything. On Tuesday, I had my appointment with Matron. I can't tell you how nervous I was, but she was perfectly charming. Glanced at my Canadian hospital records and said, 'It all seems very satisfactory.' I'm to begin on Monday week. I was so relieved that I ran down the front steps of the hospital, and went flying."

"Into the arms of a handsome stranger?" Marianne says.

"Almost. Everything in my purse scattered all over the sidewalk."

"It's hard to believe, Bridget O'Malley, that you once lectured me on speaking English. What is your 'purse' and could you please translate 'sidewalk' for us poor English girls?"

"A purse is a handbag and the sidewalk is the pavement. Now for the exciting part. A young man in an air force uniform helped me up and asked me if I was hurt. The Royal Canadian Air Force, can you imagine? By the time we'd gathered my things, we'd introduced ourselves. His name is Dominic St. Pierre. He's from Longueuil, which is on the outskirts of Montreal. He's twenty-two, and he wants me to go out with him again."

"Again? Bridget O'Malley, I'm shocked. He's a perfect stranger."

I know Marianne is only pretending to be horrified.

"We went to have a cup of coffee in Fullers. He asked for my phone number, and whether he could take me out. Marianne, don't look so scandalized! He's a most respectable Canadian boy, I can tell. I'll ask him to come to the house first to meet Mother."

"Just so long as you don't fall in love with him and go and live in Canada and leave us again," Marianne says.

When it is time to go home, Dr. O'Malley insists on driving us both.

Mrs. O'Malley says, "I hope Marianne will bring you again, Sophie. We've missed young voices around the place."

After we drop Marianne off at the nurses' residence, I tell Dr. O'Malley about my parents.

"You're a very brave girl," he says. He takes me to the front door and Aunt Em asks him in.

"Thank you for bringing me home," I say. "Night, Aunt Em."

Upstairs I divide the tissue paper from the box of chocolates into three squares. There are fourteen chocolates left. Four for Mandy, four for Nigel, four for Aunt Em, and two for me. I cut up the ribbon and tie up each of the little parcels. I put Aunt Em's on her bedside table, and Mandy's in my satchel to give to her in school tomorrow. I'll see Nigel after his cricket match.

Dr. O'Malley and Aunt Em talk for a long time before I hear her come upstairs.

20

Uncle Gerald came down to London. He and Aunt Em and Dr. O'Malley consult endlessly about how to reunite me with my father. Uncle Gerald thumps the table and says, "Red tape. Stupid bureaucrats who do nothing but shuffle pieces of paper."

"Gerald, dear, you are not in a court of law. You don't have to convince us," Aunt Em says.

One afternoon three weeks later, Bridget, Marianne, and I are sitting in Bridget's garden. We've made lemonade from the first lemons to reach the shops in over a year. It would taste better with more sugar.

"Father's on a crusade. If he can help to bring Mr. Mandel over, he feels it would make up for . . ." She looks at Marianne. "You know, some of the people he couldn't help."

I keep telling myself how grateful and happy I am—I mean, I'd be a monster if I wasn't—but deep down I'm dreading telling Father I want to stay with Aunt Em.

Father and I write regularly to each other. More than anything else, it was the socks that pleased him.

> The wool is so soft and new. I look at the beautiful gifts that you and Fräulein Margaret packed for me. I wonder sometimes if I am dreaming.
> I have left the hospital now and am back in Berlin. The birds have not returned to the Grunewald. Trees are gone, cut down for firewood. Cities throughout Germany are flattened. Armies of woman—*Trümmer Frauen*—rubble women—work twelve hour days to clear the debris. I long for fields and trees and birdsong.

Father writes of people I've never heard of whom he's trying to locate. Each letter ends with the same words—that he's impatient to see me again.

I find it hard to know what to write about. It's usually a variation of the weather report and comments about his health. Aunt Em's not much help. She says I should write about my life, ordinary things. It feels dishonest somehow not to tell him about my plans to stay in England forever. I take Aunt Em's advice.

Mandy and I play tennis. Our Girl Guide troop is planning its first overnight camp since the war. We're going to Windsor Great Park. Nigel and I are helping to plan the Guy Fawkes party. The first since 1939. November 5 is the anniversary of the Great Gunpowder Plot of 1605. There'll be fireworks this year and we'll be burning a huge guy—an effigy of the traitor who tried to blow up the king and the House of Lords.

I write we're still short of food, queues for almost anything are endless, and that large parts of London are bombed and laid waste too. It's like writing to a stranger and the thought of meeting him unnerves me. I can't talk about that to anyone, least of all to Marianne, who is still mourning her father.

One Friday afternoon in late July, a few days before the end of term, I find Aunt Em waiting for me outside school. She hasn't done that in years.

"Is something wrong, Aunt Em?"

"On the contrary. Your father has been granted a temporary visitor's permit. He'll be here in a few days. It's exciting news, isn't it, Sophie?"

I wonder what Aunt Em really feels.

"Yes, it is." I do my best to sound enthusiastic.

Marianne and I manage to get a ten minute break together in the cafeteria during my Saturday shift at the hospital.

"I'll be thinking of you next Saturday," Marianne says, when I tell her the news.

"I'm frightened, Marianne."

"Don't be. I'm sure he's nervous about meeting you again too. Have you sent him a picture of yourself? Bother, times up. I've got to get back. We're horribly busy. Talk to you soon, Sophie."

I know I can't live up to being the only person Father's got left in the world. Being sorry for all he's been through is not enough to make me want to live in Germany again.

On Monday morning a letter arrives from the Home Office. They apologize for the delay, due to the many enquiries they receive of a similar nature, etc.

In order to be considered for British citizenship, the present law requires a person to have lived in the United Kingdom for a minimum of five years and to have reached the age of twenty-one.

However, we anticipate modifications to this law in 1946. The changes under consideration will permit young people who were forced to leave their homes and have lived in Britain for five years to apply for naturalization if they meet the following criteria:

1. They must be fifteen years or older and under the age of twenty-one.

2. Neither mother nor father are living.

They returned Matron's letter to me. *I'll just have to find enough courage to tell my father how I feel.*

21

He's arriving today! I didn't sleep at all last night.

Neither Aunt Em nor I manage to eat lunch. Tea is ready to be wheeled in on the little trolley in the kitchen. "Perhaps he'd prefer coffee. I'll make some," Aunt Em says and leaves me alone in the sitting room, staring through the window, so I can open the front door the minute he arrives.

Dr. O'Malley's gone to the airport to fetch Father. It was decided he'd stay with the O'Malleys because his health is not up to managing stairs yet, and Dr. O'Malley thinks it'd be a good idea if he was nearby. Father will spend most of the day with us.

A car draws up outside. A frail-looking stooped man with white hair, wearing a suit that seems much too big for him, gets out of the car hesitantly. Dr. O'Malley offers his arm. I suddenly think of my grandfather.

"Aunt Em, they're here."

I rush upstairs, and fasten the Star of David necklace around my neck. Voices drift up the stairs. "No, thank you. I can't stay for tea, Margaret. I'll be back for you in an hour or two, Jacob, and then you can settle in."

I don't know how I get back down. In the hall we stare at each other, the old man and I. He moves toward me, and touches my hair.

"*Wie deine Mutter*. Like your mother."

Aunt Em disappears and we're alone in the sitting room. I've been practicing what to say.

"Papa. I've been waiting for you. Did you have a good journey? You must be tired. Please sit down." We sit beside each other. "I'm sorry, Papa, I've forgotten how to speak German."

"Don't be sorry. I am happy to speak English. Zoffie, you are a grown-up young lady. What a long time it has been."

"Yes. In English my name is pronounced Sophie. Sorry."

Now I have to apologize again. I shouldn't have corrected him.

He smiles at me, showing broken teeth. *Gaunt.* Now I know what *gaunt* looks like—it's this—those dark sad eyes watching me. I look away, afraid I'm going to cry.

I don't remember you at all. My real father is young and handsome and smells of pine trees.

I try not to stare at the bent fingers and thick knuckles.

Are you truly my father? Where is Aunt Em? Why isn't she here?

Father takes a grubby piece of paper from his pocket. It's been folded many times. He offers it to me. I'd prefer not to touch it. I do, of course. The paper is almost transparent. I look at the way his bony wrist protrudes below his shirtsleeve. He's wearing the white shirt I sent him from the Red Cross. I remember Mama ironing a clean shirt for him every day.

"Allow me, Sophie." Father unfolds the creases very carefully, as if afraid the precious paper might tear.

It's a drawing of a house. Two windows decorated with window boxes. Red dots for geraniums. A crayoned yellow sun shines in a bright blue sky. Smoke billows from the chimney in perfect circles. The house is surrounded by a neat fence. Stick figures walk along the path. A man and a little girl with a bow in her hair. The girl holds a red balloon.

The letters in the bottom right-hand corner are faded. I can just make them out: FÜR PAPA. SOPHIE 5.

He takes the drawing back, folds it again. Puts it away in his pocket.

"I kept it hidden—*immer*—always."

The days pass quickly. Papa and I gradually get to know each other again. There are so many things we can't talk about. When he looks at me, I can see him wondering where his "Zoffie" has gone, just as I puzzle about the half of my life he and Mama spent without me.

I show him my favorite places, though Papa can't walk very far yet. He loves the penguin pool in Regent's Park. "I knew him."

"Who, Papa?"

"Lubetkin—the man who designed the zoo. That was before he was famous." I'm suitably impressed.

Aunt Em drives us down to meet Uncle Gerald and Aunt Winifred. She gives me a long lecture about what she expects of me. I'm on my best behavior.

Papa is an instant success. He bows over Aunt Winifred's hand. For a horrible moment, I think he is going to kiss it.

"Let me show you my garden, Mr. Mandel." Aunt Winifred takes his arm!

Before we go home, Papa designs a rose arbor for Aunt Winifred, down by the place where the Anderson shelter used to be.

In the car on the way home, Aunt Em says, "How did you do that, Jacob?"

"Yes, Papa. I've never seen Aunt Winifred all fluttery like that."

Papa says, "She seems a charming lady."

I don't know my father well enough yet to know when he is serious or joking, so I keep quiet. Perhaps after the Nazis, everyone seems charming to him.

One afternoon we're in the garden. I'm weeding the border under the kitchen window, and Papa's resting, watching me from Aunt Em's old basket chair.

"How happy you must be here, Sophie," he says.

"I am, Papa." I sit on the grass beside him, scraping damp soil from my fingers.

"Have you always been happy with Miss Em?"

"Mm."

He's leading up to it. He's going to say it—tell me we'll be happy in Germany too.

"Mama and I hoped for this so much. Your happiness, until we could have you back home with us."

I jump to my feet.

I'm not brave enough to tell you, Papa. Not brave enough to say you left me too long. I can't go back with you! I love you, but I can't go back.

"My hands are filthy, Papa. I'll wash and then I'll bring down some of my sketches to show you, if you're not too tired."

"I have a better idea. Help your old papa up the stairs. I want so much to see your room, your studio."

Papa sits at my desk, catches his breath. "This is a beautiful room, Sophie. When I was a student in Heidelberg, I lived in a little attic room—up four flights of stairs. It was much smaller than this one. From my window I could see the walls of Heidelberg Castle. Germany was beautiful once. A good place to be an artist."

Papa looks at all my drawings carefully. Once or twice he makes a comment about perspective, or the shading on a face. "This one, Sophie, this one is my favorite. I like all your work, but this one is special."

"It's Parliament Hill on Hampstead Heath. I'll ask Nigel to frame it—he's really good at carpentry. I want you to have it, a present to remember me by."

The minute I say it, I know I shouldn't have. I didn't mean to blurt it out like that. It's as good as telling him I'm not leaving.

Papa looks at me. He smiles. *Does he understand?* We make our way downstairs, one step at a time.

I don't see how there can be a happy ending. Papa knows it too, that's why he hasn't said anything yet. We're all trying not to upset each other. No one seems to want to start talking about what comes next. Not Papa, not me, and certainly not Aunt Em. I'm under twenty-one. . . . I may not have a choice. According to the Home Office letter, I don't.

22

This is Papa's last week with us. Aunt Em and I are having breakfast. Papa's coming at ten and we're going to the National Portrait Gallery.

Aunt Em cuts her toast into neat triangles. "When we started out together, Sophie, I tried never to think about this moment and how hard it was going to be to part with you."

"Please talk to Papa! Tell him you need me. Why can't he stay in England? Why has no one thought of that?. . . . Someone's at the door. Much too early for Papa."

"I suggest you go and see who it is, Sophie."

"Papa, you're early. Come in. We were just talking about you."

"Jacob, how nice. Would you like a cup of tea?"

Papa sits down. "Nothing, thank you. I have something important to tell you. It cannot wait. I cannot wait."

"Papa, I have something to say too. . . ."

I mustn't put off telling him any longer.

"You will let me finish, please, Zoffie?"

That old German name. I can't listen to this.

Aunt Em puts her hand over mine.

"Before I left Germany, when I was still in Munich, in the hospital, a nurse helped me to write a letter to the British Home Office. I told them about you, Zoffie—how it is important that we find each other, that we must be together because we are the only ones left, you and I."

Papa takes out a letter. "This arrived with the early post today. It is from the Home Office." He reads

> We are pleased to inform you that the Ministry has agreed to extend your permit to remain in the United Kingdom indefinitely. After five years, you may apply for naturalization.

"Oh, Papa, it's wonderful." I throw my arms around his neck.

"Sophie, stop. You are choking me."

"I am very happy for you both," Aunt Em says, "for all of us."

"I am a lucky man. Do you know, Miss Em, your brother and Dr. O'Malley wrote on my behalf? They sponsored me. So now, I can begin again. A small studio, no stairs, I promise. I shall plan gardens, teach drawing. What do you think, Sophie?"

"Let's put up a sign: JACOB MANDEL—LANDSCAPE GARDENER."

"There is one more thing I want to say. Miss Em, dear Miss Em, Charlotte and I had Sophie with us for seven years, and then she came to you for another seven years. The question is, what shall we do with her now?"

This time I don't hesitate. "I think you should share me. I would like that very much," I say.

"I agree one hundred percent," Papa says. There is a pause.

"Thank you, Jacob." Aunt Em's eyes are bright. "That sounds like a perfect solution."

I live with Aunt Em and see Papa most days. He rents a little flat close to Hampstead Heath. We walk, and go sketching together. On Fridays I cook supper for him and I've learned to say the Hebrew prayer for lighting the Sabbath candles. Marianne joins us whenever she can.

It's hard for Papa to talk about the war, about the past.

"I want to ask you something, Papa. You don't need to answer me if you don't want to."

"What is the question?"

"How did you go on when . . . after Mama . . . in the camp, how do I say it?"

"*Aushalten*—Endure? Each day, in my head I drew a garden and I tell myself, one day I will find my Sophie. One day we will draw gardens together."

The End